Praise for *Our Story Begins*

'He is a short-story writer whose work can rival that of John Cheever and Raymond Carver. His stories, at their best, are unique hybrids that manage to be both wildly anarchic and highly moral, that merge the wondrously strange with the highly familiar ... The dramatic space opened up by these brief, faulty encounters is often filled with exquisite sadness and scalding truths ... A fascinating new direction for one of America's best short-story writers. By navigating around the collisions that comprise so much drama, Wolff allows the reader to penetrate deeper, into the quiet, obscure realm where submerged lives are lived'

Sunday Times

'The great short story burns its presence into your memory. It catches the moment, alludes to a reality and leaves the reader complicit and involved as well as awestruck, grateful, moved and alive. Several of those elusive moments are contained within the covers of Tobias Wolff's volume'

Eileen Battersby, *Irish Times*

'The reader is drawn in by an intriguing set-up and bundled along an energetic, ballsy narrative rich in detail and event ...[Wolff is] as good at conveying downtown LA in a fresh light as he is at rural New York, which is a grand skill and makes this collection worth the read'

Evening Standard

'The aspirant short story writer will learn much from Wolff's technical expertise: his deployment of descriptive detail, the judicious economy of his digressions, his deft handling of suspense and timing ... a collection that seeks fresh formal departures, slyly coaxing out the possibilities of the genre'

Times Literary Supplement

'His stories [are] tightly knotted flower buds which unfurl before your eyes. You never know what wonders might be revealed ... Wolff has that rare ability to communicate a mood or emotion with the flick of his pen. He also has great empathy with his characters and senses their deprivations and limitations ... Wolff's stories are admirably short, and seldom did I want them to end sooner than they did'

Literary Review

'Wolff's characters may vary in class and culture and setting, but they all exist in a zone of moral heaviness, in the presence of an almost apprehended truth. *Our Story Begins* confirms the American writer's impressive talent'

Financial Times

'Wolff reminds us again and again why we still return to fiction for what we need to know about how people live their lives'

Esquire

'At his best, Wolff conjures stories that etch your memory – which is to say, they become a part of you ... This is a volume that belongs on everybody's shelf along with Hemingway's *In Our Time*, Salinger's *Nine Stories* and the collected works of Flannery O'Connor, Raymond Carver, Gabriel García Márquez, William Trevor and Alice Munro'

LA Times

'We now have absolute confirmation that, aside from perhaps Alice Munro, there's no one else practicing the form with as much warm devotion and cool mastery. The men and women who populate Wolff's universe are weary and nervous, saddled with one or another kind of emotional debt, though often unable to articulate the exact terms of that debt ... Every one of the stories before and after it is good enough to merit reading again, immediately after finishing'

Washington Post

'Restrained, droll and nearly flawless in structure, Wolff's keen-edged stories often concern confused folks who want to do the right thing, or at least find a way to allow themselves to believe that they're doing the right thing'

Entertainment Weekly

'Tender, dazzling, heart-stopping fiction from a master of deep truths and unexpected turns ... This collection provides a clean, swift tour through Wolff's famous earlier stories and ends with ten new ones, each a more polished gem than the last ... Intensely pleasurable'

O, the Oprah magazine

'This collection is a masterclass in how to create small but acutely observed human dramas that live and breathe on the page'

Psychologies

Our Story Begins

TOBIAS WOLFF is the author of seven previous books and the editor of *The Vintage Book of American Short Stories* and other anthologies. Among his honors are the PEN/Malamud Award and the Rea Award, both for excellence in the short story, the *Los Angeles Times* Book Prize and the PEN/Faulkner Award. He lives in Northern California and teaches at Stanford University.

Our Story Begins

Tobias Wolff

BLOOMSBURY

LONDON · BERLIN · NEW YORK · SYDNEY

for my dear friends
George Crile (1945–2006)
and
Bill Spohn (1944–2005)

First published in Great Britain 2008
This paperback edition published 2009

Grateful acknowledgment is made to HarperCollins Publishers for
permission to reprint the stories "Hunters in the Snow," "In the
Garden of the North American Martyrs," "The Liar," and "Next
Door" from In the Garden of the North American Martyrs by
Tobias Wolff, copyright © 1981 by Tobias Wolff.
Reprinted by permission of HarperCollins Publishers.

Bloomsbury Publishing Plc,
50 Bedford Square,
London WC1B 3DP

Bloomsbury Publishing, London, New York, Berlin and Sydney

www.bloomsbury.com

A CIP catalogue record for this book
is available from the British Library

ISBN 978 0 7475 9743 8
10 9 8 7 6 5

Printed in Great Britain by Clays Ltd, St Ives plc

FSC
www.fsc.org
MIX
Paper from
responsible sources
FSC® C018072

Once again, and always, my deepest thanks to Catherine Wolff and Gary Fisketjon for the gift of their attention to these stories over many readings, and many years. And, as ever, my thanks to Amanda Urban for her friendship and support.

CONTENTS

Contents

NEW STORIES

A NOTE FROM THE AUTHOR

The first of these stories was written some three decades ago, the most recent just last year. In preparing such a selection, I had to confront this question: Should I present my stories, of whatever vintage, in their original form? Or should I allow myself the liberty of revisiting them here and there?

You could make a good argument for the first approach. It might be said that I am no longer the man who wrote a story published twenty-five, or ten, or even two years ago, and that I should be a respectful executor and do the actual, now-vanished writer the honor of keeping my mitts off his work. But there's a problem here. What would the "original form" of a story be? The very first draft of what may have been as many as twenty drafts? Surely not—nobody would want to read that. Do we mean the story as it made its debut in a periodical? Or as published in the first edition of the collection it belonged to? Bear in mind that before the magazine brought it out, an editor had read it with pencil in hand, and that at least some of her suggestions survived our negotiations, not because I was bullied but because I thought they improved the story. Then another editor looked it over before signing off on the collection, and no doubt he had something helpful to say. And if the story was chosen for an anthology, as many if not most of these were, I would have given it yet another going-over on my own, and done so again before the collection went into paperback.

The truth is that I have never regarded my stories as sacred texts.

To the extent that they are still alive to me I take a continuing interest in giving that life its best expression. This satisfies a certain aesthetic restlessness, but I also consider it a form of courtesy. If I see a clumsy or superfluous passage, so will you, and why should I throw you out of the story with an irritation I could have prevented? Where I have felt the need for something better I have answered the need as best I can, for now.

Tobias Wolff

August 2007

Selected Stories

In the Garden of the
North American Martyrs

When she was young, Mary saw a brilliant and original man lose his job because he had expressed ideas that were offensive to the trustees of the college where they both taught. She shared his views but did not sign the protest petition. She was, after all, on trial herself—as a teacher, as a woman, as an interpreter of history.

Mary watched herself. Before giving a lecture she wrote it out in full, using the arguments and often the words of other, approved writers so she would not by chance say something scandalous. Her own thoughts she kept to herself, and the words for them grew faint as time went on; without quite disappearing they shrank to remote, nervous points, like birds flying away.

When the department turned into a hive of cliques, Mary went about her business and pretended not to know that people hated one another. To avoid seeming bland she let herself become eccentric in harmless ways. She took up bowling, which she learned to love, and founded the Brandon College chapter of a society dedicated to restoring the good name of Richard III. She memorized comedy routines from records and jokes from books; people groaned when she rattled them off, but she didn't let that stop her, and after a time the groans became the point of the jokes. They were a kind of tribute to Mary's willingness to expose herself.

In fact no one at the college was safer than Mary, for she was making herself into something institutional, like a custom or a mascot—part of the college's idea of itself.

Now and then she wondered whether she had been too careful. The things she said and wrote seemed flat to her, pulpy, as though someone else had squeezed the juice out of them. And once, while talking with a senior professor, Mary saw herself reflected in a window: she was leaning toward him and had her head turned so that her ear was right in front of his moving mouth. The sight disgusted her. Years later, when she had to get a hearing aid, Mary suspected that her deafness was a result of always trying to catch everything anyone said.

In the second half of Mary's fifteenth year at Brandon the president called a meeting of all faculty and students to announce that the college was bankrupt and would not open its gates again. He was every bit as much surprised as they were; the report from the trustees had reached his desk only that morning. It seemed that Brandon's financial manager had speculated in some kind of futures and lost everything. The president wanted to deliver the news in person before it reached the papers. He wept openly and so did the students and teachers, with only a few exceptions—some cynical upperclassmen who claimed to despise the education they'd received.

Mary could not rid her mind of the word "speculate." It meant "to guess," in terms of money "to gamble." How could a man gamble a college? Why would he want to do that, and how could it be that no one stopped him? It seemed to belong to another time; Mary thought of a drunken plantation owner gaming away his slaves.

She applied for jobs and got an offer from a new experimental college in Oregon. It was her only offer, so she took it. The college was in one building. Bells rang all the time, lockers lined the hallways, and at every corner stood a buzzing water fountain. The student newspaper came out twice a month on mimeograph paper that felt wet. The library, which was next to the band room, had no librarian and few books. "We are a work in progress," the provost was fond of saying, cheerfully.

The countryside was beautiful, though, and Mary might have enjoyed it if the rain hadn't caused her so much trouble. There was something wrong with her lungs that the doctors could neither agree upon nor cure; whatever it was, the dampness made it worse. On

4

rainy days, condensation formed in Mary's hearing aid and shorted it out. She began to dread talking with people, never knowing when she'd have to take out her control box and slap it against her leg.

It rained nearly every day. When it wasn't raining it was getting ready to rain, or clearing. The ground glinted under the grass, and the light had a yellow undertone that flared up during storms.

There was water in Mary's basement. Her walls sweated, and she found toadstools growing behind the refrigerator. She felt as though she were rusting out, like one of those old cars people thereabouts kept in their front yards, propped up on pieces of wood. Mary knew that everyone was dying, but it did seem to her that she was dying faster than most.

She continued to look for another job, without success. Then, in the fall of her third year in Oregon, she got a letter from a woman named Louise who'd once taught at Brandon. Louise had scored a great success with a book on Benedict Arnold and was now on the faculty of a famous college in upstate New York. She said that one of her colleagues would be retiring at the end of the year and asked if Mary might be interested in the position.

The letter surprised Mary. Louise thought of herself as a great historian and of almost everyone else as useless; Mary had not known that she felt differently about her. Moreover, enthusiasm for other people's causes did not come easily to Louise, who had a way of sucking in her breath when familiar names were mentioned, as though she knew things that friendship kept her from disclosing.

Mary expected nothing but sent a résumé and a copy of her book. Shortly afterward Louise called to say that the search committee, of which she was chair, had decided to grant Mary an interview in early November. "Now don't get your hopes *too* high," Louise said.

"Oh, no," Mary said, but thought: *Why shouldn't I hope?* They wouldn't go to the bother and expense of bringing her to the college if they weren't serious. And she was certain the interview would go well. She would make them like her, or at least give them no cause to dislike her.

She read about the area with a strange sense of familiarity, as if the land and its history were already known to her. And when her plane left Portland and climbed easterly into the clouds, Mary felt like she was going home. The feeling stayed with her, growing stronger when they landed. She tried to describe it to Louise as they left the airport at Syracuse and drove toward the college, an hour or so away. "It's like déjà vu," she said.

"Déjà vu is a hoax," Louise said. "It's just a chemical imbalance of some kind."

"Maybe so," Mary said, "but I still have this sensation."

"Don't get serious on me," Louise said. "That's not your long suit. Just be your funny, wisecracking old self. Now tell me—honestly—how do I look?"

It was night, too dark to see Louise's face well, but in the airport she had seemed gaunt and pale and intense. She reminded Mary of a description in the book she'd been reading, of how Iroquois warriors gave themselves visions by fasting. She had that kind of look about her. But she wouldn't want to hear that. "You look wonderful," Mary said.

"There's a reason," Louise said. "I've taken a lover. My concentration has improved, my energy level is up, and I've lost ten pounds. I'm also getting some color in my cheeks, though that could be the weather. I recommend the experience highly. But you probably disapprove."

Mary didn't know what to say. She said that she was sure Louise knew best, but that didn't seem to be enough. "Marriage is a great institution," she added, "but who wants to live in an institution?"

Louise groaned. "I know you," she said, "and I know that right now you're thinking *But what about Ted? What about the children?* The fact is, Mary, they aren't taking it well at all. Ted has become a nag." She handed Mary her purse. "Be a good girl and light me a cigarette, will you? I know I told you I quit, but this whole thing has been very hard on me, very hard, and I'm afraid I've started again."

They were in the hills now, heading north on a narrow road. Tall trees arched above them. As they topped a rise Mary saw the forest all around, deep black under the plum-colored sky. There were a few lights and these only made the darkness seem greater.

"Ted has succeeded in completely alienating the children from me," Louise was saying. "There is no reasoning with any of them. In fact, they refuse to discuss the matter at all, which is very ironic because over the years I have tried to instill in them a willingness to see things from the other person's point of view. If they could just *meet* Jonathan I know they'd feel differently. But they won't hear of it. Jonathan," she said, "is my lover."

"I see," Mary said.

Coming around a curve they caught two deer in the headlights. Mary could see them tense as the car went by. "Deer," she said.

"I don't know," Louise said, "I just don't know. I do my best, and it never seems to be enough. But that's enough about me—let's talk about you. What did you think of my latest book?" She squawked and beat her palms on the steering wheel. "Seriously, though, what about you? It must have been a real shockeroo when good old Brandon folded."

"It was hard. Things haven't been good, but they'll be a lot better if I get this job."

"At least you have work," Louise said. "You should look at it from the bright side."

"I try."

"You seem so gloomy. I hope you're not worrying about the interview, or the class. Worrying won't do you a bit of good. Look on this as a vacation."

"Class? What class?"

"The class you're supposed to give tomorrow, after the interview. Didn't I tell you? Mea culpa, hon, *mea maxima culpa*. I've been uncharacteristically forgetful lately."

"But what will I do?"

"Relax," Louise said. "Just pick a subject and wing it."

"Wing it?"

"You know, open your mouth and see what comes out. Extemporize."

"But I always work from a prepared lecture."

"All right. I'll tell you what. Last year I wrote an article on the Marshall Plan that I got bored with and never published. You can read that."

Parroting what Louise had written seemed wrong to Mary, at first; then it occurred to her that she'd been doing the same kind of thing for many years, and that this was no time to get scruples.

"Here we are," Louise said, and pulled into a circular drive with several cabins grouped around it. In two of the cabins lights were on; smoke drifted straight up from the chimneys. "The college is another two miles thataway." Louise pointed down the road. "I'd invite you to stay at my house, but I'm spending the night with Jonathan and Ted is not good company these days. You would hardly recognize him."

She took Mary's bags from the trunk and carried them up the steps of a darkened cabin. "Look," she said, "they've laid a fire for you. All you have to do is light it." She stood in the middle of the room with her arms crossed and watched as Mary held a match under the kindling. "There," she said. "You'll be snugaroo in no time. I'd love to stay and chew the fat but I really must run. You just get a good night's sleep, and I'll see you in the morning."

Mary stood in the doorway and waved as Louise, spraying gravel, pulled out of the drive. She filled her lungs, to taste the air: it was tart and clear. She could see the stars in their figurations, and the vague streams of light that ran among the stars.

She still felt uneasy about reading Louise's work as her own. It would be her first complete act of plagiarism. It would surely change her. It would make her less—how much less, she didn't know. But what else could she do? She certainly couldn't "wing it." Words might fail her, and then what? Mary had a dread of silence. When she thought of silence she thought of drowning, as if it were a kind of water she could not swim in.

"I want this job," she said, and settled deep into her coat. It was cashmere and Mary hadn't worn it since moving to Oregon, because people there thought you were pretentious if you had on anything but a Pendleton shirt or, of course, rain gear. She rubbed her cheek against the upturned collar and thought of a silver moon shining through bare black branches, a white house with green shutters, red leaves falling in a hard blue sky.

Louise woke her a few hours later. She was sitting on the edge of the bed, pushing at Mary's shoulder and snuffling loudly. When Mary asked her what was wrong she said, "I want your opinion on something. It's very important. Do you think I'm womanly?"

Mary sat up. "Louise, can this wait?"

"No."

"Womanly?"

Louise nodded.

"You are very beautiful," Mary said, "and you know how to present yourself."

Louise stood and paced the room. "That son of a bitch," she said. She came back and stood over Mary. "Let's suppose someone said I have no sense of humor. Would you agree or disagree?"

"In some things you do. I mean, yes, you have a good sense of humor."

"What do you mean, 'in some things'? What kind of things?"

"Well, if you heard that someone had been killed in an unusual way, like by an exploding cigar, you'd think that was funny."

Louise laughed.

"That's what I mean," Mary said.

Louise went on laughing. "Oh, Lordy," she said. "Now it's my turn to say something about you." She sat down beside Mary.

"Please," Mary said.

"Just one thing," Louise said.

Mary waited.

"You're trembling," Louise said. "I was just going to say—oh, forget it. Listen, do you mind if I sleep on the couch? I'm all in."

"Go ahead."

"Sure it's okay? You've got a big day tomorrow." She fell back on the sofa and kicked off her shoes. "I was just going to say, you should use some liner on those eyebrows of yours. They sort of disappear and the effect is disconcerting."

Neither of them slept. Louise chain-smoked cigarettes and Mary watched the coals burn down. When it was light enough that they could see each other, Louise got up. "I'll send a student for you," she said. "Good luck."

The college looked just like colleges are supposed to look. Roger, the student assigned to show Mary around, explained that it was an exact copy of a college in England, right down to the gargoyles and stained-glass windows. It looked so much like a college that moviemakers sometimes used it as a set. *Andy Hardy Goes to College* had been filmed there, and every fall they had an Andy Hardy Goes to College Day, with raccoon coats and goldfish-swallowing contests.

Above the door of the Founder's Building was a Latin motto that, roughly translated, meant "God helps those who help themselves." As Roger recited the names of illustrious graduates Mary was struck by the extent to which they had taken this precept to heart. They had helped themselves to railroads, mines, armies, and states, to empires of finance with outposts all over the world.

Roger took Mary to the chapel and showed her a plaque bearing the names of all the alumni who had been killed in battle, going back to the Civil War. There weren't many names. Here too, apparently, the graduates had helped themselves. "Oh yes," Roger said as they were leaving, "I forgot to tell you. The communion rail comes from some church in Europe where Charlemagne used to go."

They went to the gymnasium, and the two hockey rinks, and the library, where Mary inspected the card catalog as if she'd turn down this job if they didn't have the right books. "We have a little more time," Roger said as they went outside. "Would you like to see the power plant?"

Mary wanted to keep busy until the last minute, so she agreed.

Roger led her into the depths of the service building, explaining things about the machine they were about to see, evidently the most advanced in the country. "People think the college is really old-fashioned," he said, "but it isn't. They let girls come here now, and some of the teachers are women. In fact, there's a statute that says they have to interview at least one woman for each opening. There it is."

They were standing on an iron catwalk above the biggest machine Mary had ever beheld. Roger, who was majoring in earth sciences, said it had been built from a design pioneered by a professor in his department. Where before he had been gabby, Roger now became reverent. It was clear that for him this machine was the soul of the college, that indeed the purpose of the college was to provide outlets for the machine. Together they leaned against the railing and watched it hum.

Mary arrived at the committee room exactly on time for her interview, but the room was empty. Her book was on the table, along with a water pitcher and some glasses. She sat down and picked up the book. The binding cracked as she opened it. The pages were smooth, clean, unread. Mary turned to the first chapter, which began, "It is generally believed that . . ." *How dull,* she thought.

Nearly twenty minutes later Louise came in with several men. "Sorry we're late," she said. "We don't have much time so we'd better get started." She introduced Mary to the committee, but with one exception the names and faces did not stay together. The exception was Dr. Howells, the department chairman, who had a porous blue nose and terrible teeth.

A shiny-faced man to Dr. Howells's right spoke first. "So," he said, "I understand you once taught at Brandon College."

"It was a shame that Brandon had to close," said a young man with a pipe in his mouth. "There is a place for schools like Brandon." As he talked the pipe wagged up and down.

"Now you're in Oregon," Dr. Howells said. "I've never been there. How do you like it?"

"Not very much," Mary said.

"Is that right?" Dr. Howells leaned toward her. "I thought everyone liked Oregon. I hear it's very green."

"That's true," Mary said.

"I suppose it rains a lot," he said.

"Nearly every day."

"I wouldn't like that," he said, shaking his head. "I like it dry. Of course it snows here, and you have your rain now and then, but it's a *dry* rain. Have you ever been to Utah? There's a state for you. Bryce Canyon. The Mormon Tabernacle Choir."

"Dr. Howells was brought up in Utah," said the young man with the pipe.

"It was a different place altogether in those days," Dr. Howells said. "Mrs. Howells and I have always talked about going back when I retire, but now I'm not so sure."

"We're a little short on time," Louise said.

"And here I've been going on and on," Dr. Howells said. "Before we wind things up, is there anything you want to tell us?"

"Yes. I think you should give me the job." Mary laughed when she said this, but no one laughed back, or even looked at her. They all looked away. Mary understood then that they were not really considering her for the position. She'd been brought here to satisfy a rule. She had no hope.

The men gathered their papers and shook hands with Mary and told her how much they were looking forward to her class. "I can't get enough of the Marshall Plan," Dr. Howells said.

"Sorry about that," Louise said when they were alone. "I didn't think it would be so bad. That was a real bitcheroo."

"Tell me something," Mary said. "You already know who you're going to hire, don't you?"

Louise nodded.

"Then why did you bring me here?"

When Louise began to explain about the statute, Mary interrupted. "I know all that. But why me? Why did you pick *me*?"

Louise walked to the window and spoke with her back to Mary. "Things haven't been going very well for old Louise," she said. "I've been unhappy, and I thought you might cheer me up. You used to be so funny, and I was sure you'd enjoy the trip—it didn't cost you anything, and it's pretty this time of year with the leaves and everything. Mary, you don't know the things my parents did to me. And Ted is no barrel of laughs either. Or Jonathan, the son of a bitch. I deserve some love and friendship but I don't get any at all." She turned and looked at her watch. "It's almost time for your class. We'd better go."

"I would rather not give it. After all, there's not much point, is there?"

"But you *have* to give it. That's part of the interview." Louise handed her a folder. "All you have to do is read this. It isn't much, considering all the money we've laid out to get you here."

Mary followed Louise down the hall to the lecture room. The professors were sitting in the front row with their legs crossed. They smiled and nodded at Mary. Behind them the room was full of students, some of whom had spilled over into the aisles. One of the professors adjusted the microphone to Mary's height, crouching down as he went to the podium and back as though he'd prefer not to be seen.

Louise called the room to order, then introduced Mary and gave the subject of the lecture. But Mary had decided to wing it after all. She came to the podium unsure of what she would say; sure only that she would rather die than read Louise's article. The sun poured through the stained glass onto the people around her, painting their faces. Thick streams of smoke from the young professor's pipe drifted through a circle of red light at Mary's feet, turning crimson and twisting like flames.

"I wonder how many of you know," she began, "that we are in the Long House, the ancient domain of the Five Nations of the Iroquois."

Two professors looked at each other.

"The Iroquois were without pity," Mary said. "They hunted people down with clubs and arrows and spears and nets, and blowguns made from elder stalks. They tortured their captives, sparing no one, not even the little children. They took scalps and practiced cannibalism and slavery. Because they had no pity they became powerful, so powerful that no other tribe dared to oppose them. They made the other tribes pay tribute, and when they had nothing more to pay the Iroquois attacked them."

Several of the professors began to whisper. Dr. Howells was saying something to Louise, who was shaking her head.

"In one of their raids," Mary said, "they captured two Jesuit priests, Jean de Brébeuf and Gabriel Lalement. They covered Lalement with pitch and set him on fire in front of Brébeuf. When Brébeuf rebuked them they cut off his lips and put a burning iron down his throat. They hung a collar of red-hot hatchets around his neck and poured boiling water over his head. When he continued to preach to them they cut strips of flesh from his body and ate them before his eyes. While he was still alive they scalped him and cut open his breast and drank his blood. Later, their chief tore out Brébeuf's heart and ate it, but just before he did this Brébeuf spoke to them one last time. He said—"

"That's enough!" yelled Dr. Howells, jumping to his feet. Louise stopped shaking her head. Her eyes were perfectly round.

Mary had come to the end of her facts. She did not know what Brébeuf had said. Silence rose up around her; just when she thought she would go under and be lost in it she heard someone whistling in the hallway outside, trilling the notes like a bird, like many birds.

"Mend your lives," she said. "You have deceived yourselves in the pride of your hearts and the strength of your arms. Though you soar aloft like the eagle, though your nest is set among the stars, thence I will bring you down, says the Lord. Turn from power to love. Be kind. Do justice. Walk humbly."

Louise was waving her arms. "Mary!" she shouted.

But Mary had more to say, much more. She waved back at Louise, then turned off her hearing aid so that she would not be distracted again.

Next Door

I wake up afraid. My wife is sitting on the edge of my bed, shaking me. "They're at it again," she says.

I go to the window. All their lights are on, upstairs and down, as if they have money to burn. He yells, she screams something back, the dog barks. There is a short silence, then the baby cries, poor thing.

"Better not stand there," says my wife. "They might see you."

I say, "I'm going to call the police," knowing she won't let me.

"Don't," she says.

She's afraid they'll poison our cat if we complain.

Next door the man is still yelling, but I can't make out what he's saying over the dog and the baby. The woman laughs, not really meaning it—"*Ha! Ha! Ha!*"—and suddenly gives a sharp little cry. Everything goes quiet.

"He struck her," my wife says. "I felt it just the same as if he struck me."

Next door the baby gives a long wail and the dog starts up again. The man walks out into his driveway and slams the door.

"Be careful," my wife says. She gets back into her bed and pulls the cover up to her neck.

The man mumbles to himself and jerks at his fly. Finally he gets it open and walks over to our fence. It's a white picket fence, ornamental more than anything else. It couldn't keep anyone out. I put it in myself and planted honeysuckle and bougainvillea all along it.

My wife says, "What's he doing?"

"Shh," I say.

He leans against the fence with one hand and with the other he goes to the bathroom on the flowers. He walks the length of the fence like that, not missing any of them. When he's through he gives Florida a shake, then zips up and heads back across the driveway. He almost slips on the gravel but he catches himself and curses and goes into the house, slamming the door again.

When I turn around my wife is leaning forward, watching me. She raises her eyebrows. "Not again," she says.

I nod.

"Between him and the dog it's a wonder you can get anything to grow out there."

I would rather talk about something else. It depresses me, thinking about the flowers. Next door the woman is shouting. "Listen to that," I say.

"I used to feel sorry for her," my wife says. "Not anymore. Not after last month."

"Ditto," I say, trying to remember what happened last month. I don't feel sorry for her either, but then I never have. She yells at the baby, and pardon me, but I'm not about to get all weepy over someone who treats a child like that. She screams things like "I thought I told you to stay in your bedroom!" and here the baby can't even talk yet.

As far as her looks, I guess you would have to say she's pretty. But it won't last. She doesn't have good bone structure. She has a soft look to her, like she's never eaten anything but doughnuts and milk shakes. Her skin is white. The baby takes after her, not that you'd expect it to take after *him*, dark and hairy. Even with his shirt on you can tell that he has hair all over his back and on his shoulders, thick and springy like an Airedale's.

Now they're all going at once over there, plus they've got the stereo turned on full blast. One of those bands. "It's the baby I feel sorry for," I say.

My wife puts her hands over her ears. "I can't stand another minute of it," she says. She takes her hands away. "Maybe there's something on TV." She sits up. "See who's on Johnny Carson."

I turn on the television. It used to be down in the den but I brought it up here a few years ago when my wife got sick. I took care of her myself—made the meals and everything. I got to where I could change the sheets with her still in the bed. I always meant to take the television back down when my wife recovered from her illness, but I never got around to it. It sits between our beds on a little table I made. Johnny is saying something to Sammy Davis Jr., and Ed McMahon is bent over laughing. He's always so cheerful. If you were going to take a really long voyage you could do worse than bring Ed McMahon along.

My wife wants to know what else is on. "*'El Dorado,'*" I read. "'Brisk adventure yarn about a group of citizens in search of the legendary city of gold.' It's got two and a half stars beside it."

"Citizens of what?" my wife asks.

"It doesn't say."

Finally we watch the movie. A blind man comes into a small town. He says that he has been to El Dorado and that he will lead an expedition there for a share of the proceeds. He can't see, but he'll call out the landmarks one by one as they ride. At first people make fun of him, though eventually all the leading citizens get together and decide to give it a try. Right away they get attacked by Apaches and some of them want to turn back, but every time they get ready the blind man gives them another landmark, so they keep riding.

Next door the woman is going crazy. She is saying things to him that no person should ever say to another person. It makes my wife restless. She looks at me. "Can I come over?" she says. "Just for a visit?"

I pull down the blankets and she gets in. The bed is just fine for one, but with two of us it's a tight fit. We are lying on our sides with me in back. I don't mean for it to happen but before long old Florida begins to stiffen up on me. I put my arms around my wife. I move my hands up onto the Rockies, then on down across the plains, heading south.

"Hey," she says. "No geography. Not tonight."

"I'm sorry," I say.

"Can't I just visit?"

"Forget it. I said I was sorry."

The citizens are crossing a desert. They've just about run out of water, and their lips are cracked. Though the blind man has delivered a warning, someone drinks from a poisoned well and dies horribly. That night, around the campfire, the others begin to quarrel. Most of them want to go home. "This is no country for a white man," one says, "and if you ask me nobody has ever been here before." But the blind man describes a piece of gold so big and pure that it will burn your eyes out if you look directly at it. "I ought to know," he says. When he's finished the citizens are silent; one by one they move away and lie down on their bedrolls. They put their hands behind their heads and look up at the stars. A coyote howls.

Hearing the coyote, I remember why my wife stopped feeling sorry for the woman next door. It was a Monday evening, about a month ago, right after I got home from work. The man next door started to beat the dog, and I don't mean just smacking him once or twice. He was beating him, and he kept at it until the dog couldn't even cry anymore; you could hear the poor creature's voice breaking. Finally it stopped. Then, a few minutes later, I heard my wife say "Oh!" and I went into the kitchen to find out what was wrong. She was standing by the window, which looks into the kitchen next door. The man had his wife backed up against the fridge. He had his knee between her legs and she had her knee between his legs and they were kissing really hard. My wife could hardly speak for a couple of hours afterward. Later she said that she would never waste her sympathy on that woman again.

It's quiet over there. My wife has gone to sleep and so has my arm, which is under her head. I slide it out and open and close my fingers, considering whether to wake her up. I like sleeping in my own bed, and there isn't enough room for the both of us. Finally I decide that it won't hurt anything to change places for one night.

I get up and fuss with the plants for a while, watering them and moving some to the window and some back. I trim the coleus, which is starting to get leggy, and put the cuttings in a glass of water on the sill. All the lights are off next door except the one in their bedroom window. I think about the life they have, and how it goes on and on, until it seems like the life they were meant to live. Everybody always says how great it is that human beings are so adaptable, but I don't know. In Istanbul, a friend of mine saw a man walking down the street with a grand piano on his back. Everyone just moved around him and kept going. It's awful, what we get used to.

I turn off the television and get into my wife's bed. Her smell, sweet and heavy, rises off the sheets. It makes me a little dizzy but I like it. It reminds me of gardenias.

The reason I don't watch the rest of the movie is that I can already see how it will end. The citizens will kill each other off, probably about ten feet from the legendary city of gold, and the blind man will stumble in by himself, not knowing that he has made it back to El Dorado.

I could write a better movie than that. My movie would be about a group of explorers, men and women, who leave behind their homes and their jobs and their families—everything they've ever known. They cross the sea and are shipwrecked on the coast of a country that isn't on their maps. One of them drowns. Another gets attacked by a wild animal and eaten. But the others want to push on. They ford rivers and cross an enormous glacier by dogsled. It takes months. On the glacier they run out of food and for a while there it looks like they might turn on each other, but they don't. Finally they solve their problem by eating the dogs. That's the sad part of the movie.

At the end we see the explorers sleeping in a meadow filled with white flowers. The blossoms are wet with dew and stick to their bodies, petals of columbine, clematis, blazing star, baby's breath, larkspur, iris, rue—covering them completely, turning them white so you cannot tell one from another, man from woman, woman from man. The sun comes up. They stand and raise their arms, like white trees in a land where no one has ever been.

Hunters in the Snow

Tub had been waiting for an hour in the falling snow. He paced the sidewalk to keep warm and stuck his head out over the curb whenever he saw lights approaching. The fall of snow thickened. Tub stood below the overhang of a building. Across the road the clouds whitened just above the rooftops, and the whiteness seeped up through the sky. He shifted the rifle strap to his other shoulder.

A truck slid around the corner, horn blaring, rear end sashaying. Tub moved to the sidewalk and held up his hand. The truck jumped the curb and kept coming, half on the street and half on the sidewalk. It wasn't slowing down at all. Tub stood for a moment, still holding up his hand, then jumped back. His rifle slipped off his shoulder, clattering on the ice, and a sandwich fell out of his pocket. The truck went careening past him and stopped at the end of the block.

Tub picked up his sandwich and slung the rifle and walked down to the truck. The driver was bent against the steering wheel, slapping his knees and drumming his feet on the floorboards. He looked like a cartoon of a person laughing. "Tub, you ought to see yourself," he said. "You look just like a beach ball with a hat on. Doesn't he, Frank?"

The man beside him smiled and looked off.

"You almost ran me down," Tub said. "You could've killed me."

"Come on, Tub," said the man beside the driver. "Be mellow. Kenny was just messing around." He opened the door and slid over to the middle of the seat.

Tub took the bolt out of his rifle and climbed in beside him. "My feet are frozen," he said. "If you meant ten o'clock, why didn't you *say* ten o'clock?"

"Tub, you haven't done anything but complain since we got here," said the man in the middle. "If you want to piss and moan all day you might as well go home and bitch at your kids. Take your pick." When Tub didn't say anything, he turned to the driver. "Okay, Kenny, let's hit the road."

Some juvenile delinquents had heaved a brick through the windshield on the driver's side, so the cold and snow funneled right into the cab. The heater didn't work. They covered themselves with a couple of blankets Kenny had brought along and pulled down the flaps on their caps. Tub tried to keep his hands warm by rubbing them under the blanket, but Frank made him stop.

They left Spokane and drove deep into the country, running along black lines of fences. The snow let up, but still there was no edge to the land where it met the sky. Nothing moved in the chalky fields. The cold bleached their faces and made the stubble stand out on their cheeks and along their upper lips. They stopped twice for coffee before they got to the woods where Kenny wanted to hunt.

Tub was for trying someplace different; two years in a row they'd been up and down this land and hadn't seen a thing. Frank didn't care one way or the other, he just wanted to get out of the goddamned truck. "Feel that," he said, slamming the door. He spread his feet and closed his eyes and leaned his head back and breathed deeply. "Tune in on that energy."

"Another thing," Kenny said. "This is open land. Most of the land around here is posted."

"I'm cold," Tub said.

Frank breathed out. "Stop bitching, Tub. Get centered."

"I wasn't bitching."

"Centered," Kenny said. "Next thing you'll be wearing a nightgown, Frank. Selling flowers out at the airport."

"Kenny," Frank said, "you talk too much."

"Okay," Kenny said. "I won't say a word. Like I won't say anything about a certain babysitter."

"What babysitter?" Tub asked.

"That's between us," Frank said, looking at Kenny.

Kenny laughed.

"You're asking for it," Frank said.

"Asking for what?"

"Hey," Tub said, "are we hunting or what?"

They started off across the field. Tub had trouble getting through the fences. Frank and Kenny could have helped him; they could've lifted up the top wire and stepped on the bottom wire, but they didn't. They stood and watched him. There were a lot of fences, and Tub was puffing when they reached the woods.

They hunted for two hours and saw no deer, no tracks, no sign. Finally they stopped by the creek to eat. Kenny had several slices of pizza and a couple of candy bars; Frank had a sandwich, an apple, two carrots, and a square of chocolate; Tub ate one hard-boiled egg and a stick of celery.

"You ask me how I want to die today," Kenny said, "I'll tell you burn me at the stake." He turned to Tub. "You still on that diet?" He winked at Frank.

"What do you think? You think I like hard-boiled eggs?"

"All I can say is, it's the first diet I ever heard of where you gained weight from it."

"Who said I gained weight?"

"Oh, pardon me. I take it back. You're just wasting away before my very eyes. Isn't he, Frank?"

Frank had his fingers fanned out on the stump where he'd laid his food. His knuckles were hairy. He wore a heavy wedding band and on his right pinkie another gold ring with a flat face and an "F" in what looked like diamonds. "Tub," he said, "you haven't seen your own balls in ten years."

Kenny doubled over laughing. He took off his hat and slapped his leg with it.

"What am I supposed to do?" Tub said. "It's my glands."

They left the woods and hunted along the creek. Frank and Kenny worked one bank and Tub worked the other, moving upstream. The snow was light but the drifts were deep and hard to move through. Wherever Tub looked the surface was smooth, undisturbed, and after a time he lost interest. He stopped looking for tracks and just tried to keep up with Frank and Kenny on the other side. A moment came when he realized he hadn't seen them in a long time. The breeze was moving from him to them; when it stilled he could sometimes hear Kenny laughing—nothing more. He quickened his pace, breasting the drifts, fighting away the snow. He heard his heart and felt the flush on his face but never once stopped.

Tub caught up with Frank and Kenny at a bend of the creek. They were standing on a log that stretched from their bank to his. Ice had backed up behind the log. Frozen reeds stuck out.

"See anything?" Frank asked.

Tub shook his head.

There wasn't much daylight left and they decided to head back toward the road. Frank and Kenny crossed the log and they all started downstream, using the trail Tub had broken. Before they'd gone very far Kenny stopped. "Look at that," he said, and pointed to some tracks going from the creek back into the woods. Tub's footprints crossed right over them. There on the bank, plain as day, were several mounds of deer shit. "What do you think that is, Tub?" Kenny kicked at it. "Walnuts on vanilla icing?"

"I guess I didn't notice."

Kenny looked at Frank.

"I was lost."

"You were lost. Big deal."

They followed the tracks into the woods. The deer had gone over a fence half buried in drifting snow. A no-hunting sign was nailed to the top of one of the posts. Kenny wanted to go after him but Frank said no way, the people out here didn't mess around. He thought maybe the farmer who owned the land would let them use it if they asked. Kenny wasn't so sure. Anyway, he figured that by the time they walked to the truck and drove up the road and doubled back it would be almost dark.

"Relax," Frank said. "You can't hurry nature. If we're meant to get that deer, we'll get it. If we're not, we won't."

They started back toward the truck. This part of the woods was mainly pine. The snow was shaded and had a glaze on it. It held up Kenny and Frank but Tub kept falling through. As he kicked forward, the edge of the crust bruised his shins. Kenny and Frank pulled ahead of him, to where he couldn't even hear their voices anymore. He sat down on a stump and wiped his face. He ate both his sandwiches and half the cookies, taking his own sweet time. It was dead quiet.

When Tub crossed the last fence into the road the truck started moving. He had to run for it and just managed to grab hold of the tailgate and hoist himself into the bed. He lay there, panting. Kenny looked out the rear window and grinned. Tub crawled into the lee of the cab to get out of the freezing wind. He pulled his earflaps low and pushed his chin into the collar of his coat. Someone rapped on the window but Tub wouldn't turn around.

He and Frank waited outside while Kenny went into the farmhouse to ask permission. The house was old and paint was curling off the sides. The smoke streamed westward off the top of the chimney, fanning away into a thin gray plume. Above the ridge of the hills another ridge of blue clouds was rising.

"You've got a short memory," Tub said.

"What?" Frank said. He had been staring off.

"I used to stick up for you."

"Okay, so you used to stick up for me. What's eating you?"

"You shouldn't have just left me back there like that."

"You're a grown-up, Tub. You can take care of yourself. Anyway, if you think you're the only person with problems I can tell you that you're not."

"Is something bothering you, Frank?"

Frank kicked at a branch poking out of the snow. "Never mind," he said.

"What did Kenny mean about the babysitter?"

"Kenny talks too much," Frank said.

Kenny came out of the farmhouse and gave the thumbs-up and they began walking back toward the woods. As they passed the barn a large black hound with a grizzled snout ran out and barked at them. Every time he barked he slid backward a bit, like a cannon recoiling. Kenny got down on all fours and snarled and barked back at him, and the dog slunk away into the barn, looking over his shoulder and peeing a little as he went.

"That's an old-timer," Frank said. "A real graybeard. Fifteen years if he's a day."

"Too old," Kenny said.

Past the barn they cut off through the fields. The land was unfenced and the crust was freezing up thick, so they made good time. They kept to the edge of the field until they picked up the tracks again and followed them into the woods, farther and farther back toward the hills. The trees started to blur with the shadows, and the wind rose and needled their faces with the crystals it swept off the glaze. Finally they lost the tracks.

Kenny swore and threw down his hat. "This is the worst day of hunting I ever had, bar none." He picked up his hat and brushed off the snow. "This will be the first season since I was fifteen I haven't got my deer."

"It isn't the deer," Frank said. "It's the hunting. There are all these forces out here and you just have to go with them."

"You go with them," Kenny said. "I came out here to get me a deer, not listen to a bunch of hippie bullshit. And if it hadn't been for Dimples here I would have too."

"That's enough," Frank said.

"And you—you're so busy thinking about that little jailbait of yours you wouldn't know a deer if you saw one."

"Drop dead," Frank said, and turned away.

Kenny and Tub followed him back across the fields. When they were coming up to the barn Kenny stopped and pointed. "I hate that post," he said. He raised his rifle and fired. It sounded like a dry branch cracking. The post splintered along its right side, up toward the top. "There," Kenny said. "It's dead."

"Knock it off," Frank said, walking ahead.

Kenny looked at Tub. He smiled. "I hate that tree," he said, and fired again. Tub hurried to catch up with Frank. He started to speak but just then the dog ran out of the barn and barked at them. "Easy, boy," Frank said.

"I hate that dog." Kenny was behind them.

"That's enough," Frank said. "You put that gun down."

Kenny fired. The bullet went in between the dog's eyes. He sank right down into the snow, his legs splayed out on each side, his yellow eyes open and staring. Except for the blood he looked like a small bearskin rug. The blood ran down the dog's muzzle into the snow.

They all looked at the dog lying there.

"What did he ever do to you?" Tub asked. "He was just barking."

Kenny turned to Tub. "I hate you."

Tub shot from the waist. Kenny jerked backward against the fence and buckled to his knees. He knelt there with his hands pressed across his stomach. "Look," he said. His hands were covered with blood. In the dusk his blood was more blue than red. It seemed to belong to the shadows. It didn't seem out of place. Kenny eased himself onto his back. He sighed several times, deeply. "You shot me," he said.

"I had to," Tub said. He knelt beside Kenny. "Oh God," he said. "Frank. Frank."

Frank hadn't moved since Kenny killed the dog.

"Frank!" Tub shouted.

"I was just kidding around," Kenny said. "It was a joke. Oh!" he said, and arched his back suddenly. "Oh!" he said again, and dug his heels into the snow and pushed himself along on his head. Then he stopped and lay there, rocking back and forth on his heels and head like a wrestler doing warm-up exercises.

"Kenny," Frank said. He bent down and put his gloved hand on Kenny's brow. "You shot him," he said to Tub.

"He made me," Tub said.

"No, no, no," Kenny said.

Tub was weeping from the eyes and nostrils. His whole face was wet. Frank closed his eyes, then looked down at Kenny again. "Where does it hurt?"

"Everywhere," Kenny said, "just everywhere."

"Oh God," Tub said.

"I mean, where did it go in?" Frank said.

"Here." Kenny pointed at the wound in his stomach. It was welling slowly with blood.

"You're lucky," Frank said. "It's on the left side. It missed your appendix. If it had hit your appendix you'd really be in the soup." He turned and threw up onto the snow, holding his sides as if to keep warm.

"Are you all right?" Tub said.

"There's some aspirin in the truck," Kenny said.

"I'm all right," Frank said.

"For me," Kenny said.

"We'd better call an ambulance," Tub said.

"Jesus," Frank said. "What are we going to say?"

"Exactly what happened," Tub said. "He was going to shoot me but I shot him first."

"No sir!" Kenny said. "I wasn't either!"

Frank patted Kenny on the arm. "Easy does it, partner." He stood. "Let's go."

Tub picked up Kenny's rifle as they walked down toward the farm-house. "No sense leaving this around," he said. "Kenny might get ideas."

"I can tell you one thing," Frank said. "You've really done it this time. This definitely takes the cake."

They had to knock on the door twice before it was opened by a thin man with lank hair. The room behind him was filled with smoke. He squinted at them. "You get anything?" he asked.

"No," Frank said.

"I knew you wouldn't. That's what I told the other fellow."

"We've had an accident."

The man looked past Frank and Tub into the gloom. "Shoot your friend, did you?"

Frank nodded.

"I did," Tub said.

"I suppose you want to use the phone."

"If it's okay."

The man in the doorway looked behind him, then stepped back. Frank and Tub followed him into the house. There was a woman sitting by the stove in the middle of the room. The stove was smoking badly. She looked up and then down again at the child asleep in her lap. Her face was white and damp; strands of hair were pasted across her forehead. Tub warmed his hands over the stove while Frank went into the kitchen to call. The man who'd let them in stood at the window, his hands in his pockets.

"My friend shot your dog," Tub said.

The man nodded without turning around. "I should have done it myself. I just couldn't."

"He loved that dog so much," the woman said. The child squirmed and she rocked it.

"You asked him to?" Tub said. "You asked him to shoot your dog?"

"He was old and sick. Couldn't chew his food anymore. I should have done it myself."

"You couldn't have," the woman said. "Never in a million years."

The man shrugged.

Frank came out of the kitchen. "We'll have to take him ourselves. The nearest hospital is fifty miles from here and all their ambulances are out already."

The woman knew a shortcut but the directions were complicated and Tub had to write them down. The man told them where they could find some boards to carry Kenny on. He didn't have a flashlight but said he'd turn the porch light on.

It was dark outside. The clouds were low and heavy and the wind blew in shrill gusts. There was a screen loose on the house and it banged slowly and then quickly as the wind rose again. Frank went for the boards while Tub looked for Kenny, who was not where they had left him. Tub found him farther up the drive, lying on his stomach. "You okay?" Tub said.

"It hurts."

"Frank says it missed your appendix."

"I already had my appendix out."

"All right," Frank said, coming up to them. "We'll have you in a nice warm bed before you can say Jack Robinson." He put the two boards on Kenny's right side.

"Just as long as I don't have one of those male nurses," Kenny said.

"Ha ha," Frank said. "That's the spirit. Ready, set, *over you go,*" and he rolled Kenny onto the boards. Kenny screamed and kicked his legs in the air. When he quieted down Frank and Tub lifted the boards and carried him down the drive. Tub had the back end, and with the snow blowing into his face he had trouble with his footing. Also he was tired and the man inside had forgotten to turn the porch light on. Just past the house Tub slipped and threw out his hands to catch himself. The boards fell and Kenny tumbled out and rolled to the bottom of the drive, yelling the whole way down. He came to rest against the right front wheel of the truck.

"You fat moron," Frank said. "You aren't good for diddly."

Tub grabbed Frank by the collar and backed him hard up against the fence. Frank tried to pull his hands away but Tub shook him and snapped his head back and forth and finally Frank gave up.

"What do you know about fat," Tub said. "What do you know about glands." As he spoke he kept shaking Frank. "What do you know about me."

"All right," Frank said.

"No more," Tub said.

"All right."

"No more talking to me like that. No more watching. No more laughing."

"Okay, Tub. I promise."

Tub let go of Frank and turned away. His arms hung straight at his sides.

"I'm sorry, Tub." Frank touched him on the shoulder. "I'll be down at the truck."

Tub stood by the fence for a while and then got the rifles off the porch. Frank had rolled Kenny back onto the boards and they lifted him into the bed of the truck. Frank spread the seat blankets over him. "Warm enough?" he asked.

Kenny nodded.

"Okay. Now how does reverse work on this thing?"

"All the way to the left and up." Kenny sat up as Frank started forward to the cab. "Frank!"

"What?"

"If it sticks don't force it."

The truck started right away. "One thing," Frank said, "you've got to hand it to the Japanese. A very ancient, very spiritual culture and they can still make a hell of a truck." He glanced over at Tub. "Look, I'm sorry. I didn't know you felt like that, honest to God I didn't. You should've said something."

"I did."

"When? Name one time."

"A couple hours ago."

"I guess I wasn't paying attention."

"That's true, Frank," Tub said. "You don't pay attention very much."

"Tub," Frank said, "what happened back there, I should've been more sympathetic. I realize that. You were going through a lot. I just want you to know it wasn't your fault. He was asking for it."

"You think so?"

"Absolutely. It was him or you. I would've done the same thing in your shoes, no question."

The wind was blowing into their faces. The snow was a moving white wall in front of their lights; it swirled into the cab through the hole in the windshield and settled on them. Tub clapped his hands and shifted around to stay warm, but it didn't work.

"I'm going to have to stop," Frank said. "I can't feel my fingers."

Up ahead they saw some lights off the road. It was a tavern. In the parking lot there were several jeeps and trucks. A couple of them had deer strapped across their hoods. Frank parked and they went back to Kenny. "How you doing, partner?" Frank said.

"I'm cold."

"Well, don't feel like the Lone Ranger. It's worse inside, take my word for it. You should get that windshield fixed."

"Look," Tub said, "he threw the blankets off." They were lying in a heap against the tailgate.

"Now look, Kenny," Frank said, "it's no use whining about being cold if you're not going to try and keep warm. You've got to do your share." He spread the blankets over Kenny and tucked them in at the corners.

"They blew off."

"Hold on to 'em, then."

"Why are we stopping, Frank?"

"Because if me and Tub don't get warmed up we're going to freeze solid and then where will you be?" He punched Kenny lightly in the arm. "So just hold your horses."

The bar was full of men in colored jackets, mostly orange. The waitress brought coffee. "Just what the doctor ordered," Frank said, cradling the steaming cup in his hand. "Tub, I've been thinking. What you said about me not paying attention, that's true."

"It's okay."

"No. I really had that coming. I guess I've just been a little too interested in old number one. I've had a lot on my mind. Not that that's any excuse."

"Forget it, Frank. I sort of lost my temper back there. I guess we're both a little on edge."

Frank shook his head. "It isn't just that."

"You want to talk about it?"

"Just between us, Tub?"

"Sure, Frank. Just between us."

"Tub, I think I'm going to be leaving Nancy."

"Oh, Frank. Oh, Frank." Tub sat back and shook his head.

Frank reached out and laid his hand on Tub's arm. "Tub, have you ever been really in love?"

"Well—"

"I mean *really* in love." He squeezed Tub's wrist. "With your whole being."

"I don't know. When you put it like that, I don't know."

"Then you haven't. Nothing against you, but you'd know it if you had." Frank let go of Tub's arm. "This isn't just some bit of fluff I'm talking about."

"Who is she, Frank?"

Frank paused. He looked into his empty cup. "Roxanne Brewer."

"Cliff Brewer's kid? The babysitter?"

"You can't just put people into categories like that, Tub. That's why the whole system is wrong. And that's why this country's going to hell in a rowboat."

Tub shook his head. "But she can't be more than—"

"Sixteen. She'll be seventeen in May." Frank smiled. "May fourth, three twenty-seven p.m. Hell, Tub, a hundred years ago she'd have been an old maid by that age. Juliet was only thirteen."

"Juliet? Juliet Miller? Jesus, Frank, she doesn't even have breasts. She's still collecting frogs."

"Not Juliet Miller. The *real* Juliet. Tub, don't you see how you're dividing people up into categories? He's an executive, she's a secretary, he's a truck driver, she's sixteen years old. Tub, this so-called babysitter, this so-called sixteen-year-old, has more in her little finger than most of us have in our entire bodies. I can tell you this little lady is something special."

"I know the kids like her."

"She's opened up whole worlds to me that I never knew were there."

"What does Nancy think about all this?"

"She doesn't know."

"You haven't told her?"

"Not yet. It's not so easy. She's been damned good to me all these years. Then there's the kids to consider." The brightness in Frank's eyes trembled and he wiped quickly at them with the back of his hand. "I guess you think I'm a complete bastard."

"No, Frank. I don't think that."

"Well, you *ought* to."

"Frank, when you've got a friend it means you've always got someone on your side, no matter what. That's how I feel about it, anyway."

"You mean that, Tub?"

"Sure I do."

"You don't know how good it feels to hear you say that."

Kenny had tried to get out of the truck. He was jackknifed over the tailgate, his head hanging above the bumper. They lifted him back into the bed and covered him again. He was sweating and his teeth chattered. "It hurts, Frank."

"It wouldn't hurt so much if you just stayed put. Now we're going to the hospital. Got that? Say it—'I'm going to the hospital.'"

"I'm going to the hospital."

"Again."

"I'm going to the hospital."

"Now just keep saying that to yourself and before you know it we'll be there."

After they had gone a few miles Tub turned to Frank. "I just pulled a real boner," he said.

"What's that?"

"I left the directions on the table back there."

"That's okay. I remember them pretty well."

The snowfall lightened and the clouds began to roll back off the fields, but it was no warmer, and after a time both Frank and Tub were bitten through and shaking. Frank almost didn't make it around a curve, and they decided to stop at the next roadhouse.

There was an automatic hand dryer in the bathroom and they took turns standing in front of it, opening their jackets and shirts and letting the jet of hot air blow across their faces and chests.

"You know," Tub said, "what you told me back there, I appreciate it. Trusting me."

Frank opened and closed his fingers in front of the nozzle. "The way I look at it, Tub, no man is an island. You've got to trust someone."

"Frank?"

Frank waited.

"When I said that about my glands, that wasn't true. The truth is I just shovel it in. Day and night. In the shower. On the freeway." He turned and let the air play over his back. "I've even got stuff in the paper-towel machine at work."

"There's nothing wrong with your glands at all?" Frank had taken his boots and socks off. He held first his right foot, then his left, up to the nozzle.

"No. There never was."

"Does Alice know?" The machine went off and Frank started lacing up his boots.

"Nobody knows. That's the worst of it, Frank. Not the being fat—I never got any big kick out of being thin—but the lying. Having to lead a double life like a spy or a hit man. I understand those guys, I know what they go through. Always having to think about what you say and do. Always feeling like people are watching you, trying to catch you at something. Never able to just be yourself. Like when I make a big deal about only having an orange for breakfast and then scarf all the way to work. Oreos, Mars bars, Twinkies. Sugar Babies. Snickers." Tub glanced at Frank and looked quickly away. "Pretty disgusting, isn't it?"

"Tub. Tub." Frank shook his head. "Come on." He took Tub's arm and led him into the restaurant half of the bar. "My friend is hungry," he told the waitress. "Bring four orders of pancakes, plenty of butter and syrup."

"Frank—"

"Sit down."

When the dishes came Frank carved out slabs of butter and just laid them on the pancakes. Then he emptied the bottle of syrup, moving it back and forth over the plates. He leaned forward on his elbows and rested his chin in one hand. "Go on, Tub."

Tub ate several mouthfuls, then started to wipe his lips. Frank took the napkin away from him. "No wiping," he said. Tub kept at it. The syrup covered his chin; it dripped to a point like a goatee. "Weigh in, Tub," Frank said, pushing another fork across the table. "Get down to business." Tub took the fork in his left hand and lowered his head and started really chowing down. "Clean your plate," Frank said when the pancakes were gone, and Tub lifted each of the four plates and licked it clean. He sat back, trying to catch his breath.

"Beautiful," Frank said. "Are you full?"

"I'm full," Tub said. "I've never been so full."

Kenny's blankets were bunched up against the tailgate again.

"They must've blown off," Tub said.

"They're not doing him any good," Frank said. "We might as well get some use out of them."

Kenny mumbled. Tub bent over him. "What? Speak up."

"I'm going to the hospital," Kenny said.

"Attaboy," Frank said.

The blankets helped. The wind still got their faces and Frank's hands, but it was much better. The fresh snow on the road and the trees sparkled under the beam of the headlight. Squares of light from farmhouse windows fell onto the blue snow in the fields.

"Frank," Tub said after a time, "you know that farmer? He told Kenny to kill his dog."

"You're kidding!" Frank leaned forward, considering. "That Kenny. What a card." He laughed, and so did Tub.

Tub smiled out the back window. Kenny lay with his arms folded over his stomach, moving his lips at the stars. Right overhead was the Big Dipper, and behind, hanging between Kenny's feet in the direction of the hospital, was the North Star, polestar, Help to Sailors. As the truck twisted through the gentle hills the star went back and forth between Kenny's boots, staying always in his sight. "I'm going to the hospital," Kenny said. But he was wrong. They had taken a different turn a long way back.

35

The Liar

My mother read everything except books. Advertisements on buses, entire menus as we ate, billboards; if it had no cover it interested her. So when she found a letter in my drawer that wasn't addressed to her, she read it. *What difference does it make if James has nothing to hide?*— that was her thought. She stuffed the letter in the drawer when she finished it and walked from room to room in the big empty house, talking to herself. She took the letter out and read it again. Then, without putting on her coat or locking the door, she went down the steps and headed for the church at the end of the street. No matter how angry and confused she might be, she always went to four o'clock Mass.

It was a fine day, blue and cold and still, but Mother walked as though into a strong wind, bent forward at the waist with her feet hurrying behind in short, busy steps. My brother and sisters and I considered this walk of hers funny, and we smirked at one another when she crossed in front of us to stir the fire or water a plant. We didn't let her catch us at it. It would have puzzled her to think that anything about her might be amusing. Her one concession to the fact of humor was an insincere, startling laugh. Strangers sometimes stared at her.

While Mother waited for the priest, who was late, she prayed. She prayed in a familiar, orderly, firm way: first for her late husband, my father, then for her parents—also dead. She said a quick prayer for my father's parents—just touching base; she had disliked them—and finally for her children in order of their ages, ending with me. Mother did not consider originality a virtue and until my name came up her prayers were exactly the same as on any other day.

But when she came to me she spoke up boldly. "I thought he wasn't going to do it anymore. Murphy said he was cured. What am I supposed to do now?" There was reproach in her tone. Mother put great hope in her notion that I was cured, which she regarded as an answer to her prayers. In thanksgiving she had sent a lot of money to the Thomasite Indian Mission, money she'd been saving for a trip to Rome. Now she felt cheated and she let her feelings be known. When the priest came in, Mother slid back on the seat and followed the Mass. After communion she began to worry again and went straight home without stopping to talk to Dorothea, the woman who always cornered Mother after Mass to talk about the plots hatched against her by Communists, devil worshippers, and Rosicrucians. Dorothea watched her go with narrowed eyes.

Once in the house, Mother took the letter from my drawer and brought it into the kitchen. She held it over the stove with her fingernails, looking away so she wouldn't be drawn into it again, and set it on fire. When it began to burn her fingers she dropped it in the sink and watched it blacken and flutter and close upon itself like a fist. Then she washed it down the drain and called Dr. Murphy.

The letter was to my friend Ralphy in Arizona. He used to live across the street from us but he had moved. Most of the letter was about a tour we, the junior class, had taken of Alcatraz. That was all right. What got Mother was the last paragraph where I said that she had been coughing up blood, and the doctors weren't sure what was wrong with her, though we were hoping for the best.

This wasn't true. Mother took pride in her physical condition, considered herself a horse: "I'm a regular horse," she would reply when people asked about her health. For several years now I'd been saying unpleasant things that weren't true, and this irked Mother greatly, enough to persuade her to send me to Dr. Murphy, in whose office I was sitting when she burned the letter. Dr. Murphy was our family physician and had no training in psychoanalysis, but he took an interest in "things of the mind," as he put it. He had treated me for appendicitis and tonsillitis, and Mother thought he could put the truth into me as easily as he took things out of me, a hope Dr. Murphy did not share. He was basically interested in getting me to understand what I did, and lately he'd been moving toward the conclusion that I understood what I did as well as I ever would.

Dr. Murphy listened to Mother's account of the letter. He was curious about the wording I had used and became irritated when Mother told him she had burned it. "The point is," she said, "he was supposed to be cured and he's not."

"Margaret, I never said he was cured."

"You certainly did. Why else would I have sent over a thousand dollars to the Thomasite mission?"

"I said that he was responsible. That means that James knows what he's doing, not that he's going to stop doing it."

"I'm sure you said he was cured."

"Never. What do you mean by curing James?"

"You know."

"Tell me anyway."

"Getting him back to reality, what else?"

"Whose reality? Mine or yours?"

"Murphy, what are you talking about? James isn't crazy, he's a liar."

"Well, you have a point there."

"What am I going to do with him?"

"I don't think there's much you can do. Be patient."

"I've been patient."

"If I were you, Margaret, I wouldn't make too much of this. James doesn't steal, does he?"

"Of course not."

"Or beat people up or talk back?"

"No."

"Then you have a lot to be thankful for."

"I don't think I can take any more of it. That business about leukemia last summer. And now this."

"Eventually he'll outgrow it, I think."

"Murphy, he's sixteen years old. What if he doesn't outgrow it? What if he just gets better at it?"

Finally Mother saw that she would get no satisfaction from Dr. Murphy, who kept reminding her of her blessings. She said something cutting to him and he said something pompous back and she hung up. Dr. Murphy stared at the receiver. "Hello," he said, then replaced it on the cradle. He ran his hand over his head, a habit remaining from the days when he had hair. To show he was a good sport he often joked about his baldness, but I had the feeling that he regretted it deeply. Looking at me across the desk, he must have wished that he hadn't taken me on. Treating a friend's child was like investing a friend's money.

"I don't have to tell you who that was."

I nodded.

Dr. Murphy pushed his chair back and swiveled it around so he could look out the window behind him, which took up most of the wall. There were still a few sailboats out on the bay, and they were all making for shore. A woolly gray fog had covered the bridge and was moving in fast. The water seemed calm from this far up, but when I looked closely I could see white flecks everywhere, so it must've been pretty choppy.

"I'm surprised at you," he said. "Leaving something like that lying around for her to find. If you really have to do these things, you could at least be kind enough to do them discreetly. It's not easy for your mother, what with your father dead and all the others somewhere else."

"I know. I didn't mean for her to find it."

"Really." He tapped his pencil against his teeth. He was not convinced professionally, but personally he may have been. "I think you ought to go home now and straighten things out."

"I guess I'd better."

"Tell your mother I might stop by, either tonight or tomorrow. And James—don't underestimate her."

While my father was alive we usually went to Yosemite for three or four days during the summer. My mother would drive and he would point out places of interest, meadows where boomtowns once stood, hanging trees, rivers that were said to flow upstream at certain times. Or he read to us; he had that grown-ups' idea that children love Dickens and Sir Walter Scott. The four of us sat in the backseat with our faces composed, attentive, while our hands and feet pushed, pinched, stomped, goosed, prodded, dug, and kicked.

One night a bear came into our camp just after dinner. Mother had made a tuna casserole and it must have smelled to him like something worth dying for. He wandered in while we were sitting around the fire and stood swaying back and forth. My brother Michael saw him first and elbowed me, then my sisters saw him and screamed. Mother and Father had their backs turned, but she must have guessed what it was because she immediately said, "Don't scream like that. If you frighten him there's no telling what he'll do. We'll just sing and he'll go away."

We sang "Row Row Row Your Boat," but the bear stayed. He circled us several times, rearing up now and then on his hind legs to stick his nose into the air. By the light of the fire I could see his doglike face and watch the muscles rolling under his loose skin like rocks in a sack. We sang harder as he circled us, coming closer and closer. "All right," Mother said, "enough's enough." She stood abruptly. The bear stopped moving and watched her. "Beat it," Mother said. The bear sat down and looked from side to side. "Beat it," she said again, and picked up a rock.

"Margaret, don't," my father said.

She threw the rock hard and hit the bear in the stomach. Even in the dim light I could see the dust rising from his fur. He grunted and stood to his full height. "See that?" Mother shouted. "He's filthy. Filthy!" One of my sisters giggled. Mother picked up another rock.

"Please, Margaret," my father said. Just then the bear turned and shambled away. Mother pitched the rock after him. For the rest of the night he loitered around the camp until he found the tree where we'd hung our food. He ate it all. The next day we drove back to the city. We could have bought more supplies in the valley, but my father wanted to go home and would not give in to any argument. Though he tried to jolly everyone up by making jokes, Michael and my sisters ignored him and looked stonily out the windows.

Things were never easy between my mother and me, but I never underestimated her. She underestimated me. When I was little she suspected me of delicacy, because I didn't like being thrown into the air, and because when I saw her and the others working themselves up for a roughhouse I found somewhere else to be. When they did drag me in I got hurt, a knee in the lip, a bent finger, a bloody nose, and this too Mother seemed to hold against me, as if I arranged my little hurts to get out of playing.

Even things I did well got on her nerves. We all loved puns except Mother, who didn't get them, and next to my father I was the best in the family. My forte was the Swifty: " 'You can bring the prisoner down,' said Tom condescendingly." Father encouraged me to perform at dinner, which must have been a trial for outsiders. Mother wasn't sure what was going on, but she didn't like it.

She suspected me in other ways. I couldn't go to the movies without her examining my pockets to make sure I had enough money to pay for the ticket. When I went away to camp she tore my pack apart in front of all the boys who were waiting in the bus outside the house. I would rather have gone without my sleeping bag and a few changes of underwear, which I'd forgotten, than be made such a fool of.

And she thought I was coldhearted because of what happened the day my father died and afterward. I didn't cry at his funeral and showed signs of boredom during the eulogy, fiddling around with the hymnals. Mother put my hands into my lap and I just let them lie there like something I was holding for someone else; the effect was ironic, and she resented it. We had a sort of reconciliation a few days later after I closed my eyes at school and refused to open them. When several teachers and then the principal failed to persuade me to look at them, or at some reward they claimed to be offering, I was handed over to the school nurse, who tried to pry the lids open and scratched one of them. My eye swelled up and I went rigid. The principal panicked and called Mother, who fetched me home. I wouldn't talk to her, or open my eyes, and when we reached the house Mother had to guide me up the steps one at a time. Then she put me on the couch and played the piano to me all afternoon. Finally I opened my eyes, we hugged each other, and I wept. Mother didn't really believe my tears but was willing to accept them, if only because I'd staged them for her benefit.

My lying separated us, too, and the fact that my promises not to lie anymore seemed to mean nothing to me. Often my lies came back to her, people stopping her in the street and saying how sorry they were to hear this or that. No one in the neighborhood enjoyed embarrassing Mother, and these situations stopped occurring once everybody got wise to me. There was no saving her from strangers, though. The summer after my father died I visited my uncle in Redding, and at the depot coming back I tried slipping away from the gentleman who'd sat next to me, but I couldn't shake him. When he saw Mother embrace me he came up and presented her with a card and told her to get in touch if things got any worse. She handed his card back and told him to mind his own business.

It wasn't only the lies that disturbed Mother; it was their morbidity. This was the real issue between us, as it had been between her and my father. She did volunteer work at Children's Hospital and St. Anthony's Dining Hall, collected things for the St. Vincent de Paul Society. She was a lighter of candles, and in this my brother and sisters took after her. My father was a curser of the dark. And he loved to curse the dark. He was never more alive than when he was indignant about something. For this reason, the most important act of his day was the reading of the evening paper.

Ours was a terrible paper, indifferent to the city that bought it, indifferent to politics and art. Its business was outrage, horror, gruesome coincidence. When my father sat down in the living room with the paper, my mother stayed in the kitchen and kept the children busy, all except me, because I was quiet and could be trusted to amuse myself. I amused myself by watching my father.

He sat with his knees spread, leaning forward, his eyes only inches from the print, nodding as he read to himself. Sometimes he threw the paper down and paced the room, then picked it up and began again. Now and then he read a choice passage aloud. He always started with the society section, which he called the parasite page. This column began to take on the character of a comic strip or a serial, with the same people showing up from one day to the next, blinking in chiffon, awkwardly holding their drinks for the sake of foreign orphans, grinning behind sunglasses on the deck of a ski hut in the Sierras. The skiers really got his goat, probably because he couldn't understand them. The activity itself was inconceivable to him. When my sisters came back from Lake Tahoe one winter weekend in raptures over the beauty of the place, Father calmed them right down. "Snow," he said, "is overrated."

Then the news, or what passed in the paper for news: bodies unearthed in Scotland; former Nazis winning elections; rare animals slaughtered; misers expiring naked in freezing houses on mattresses stuffed with thousands, millions; marrying priests; divorcing actresses; high-rolling oilmen building fantastic mausoleums in honor of a favorite horse; cannibalism. Through all this my father waded with a fixed and weary smile.

Mother encouraged him to take up causes, to join groups, but he would not. He was uncomfortable with people outside the family. My parents rarely went out, and rarely had people in, except on feast days and national holidays. Their guests were always the same, Dr. Murphy and his wife and several others whom they'd known since childhood. Most of these people never saw one another outside our house and didn't have much fun together. Father discharged his obligations as host by teasing everyone about stupid things they'd said or done in the past, forcing them to laugh at themselves.

Though my father did not drink, he insisted on mixing cocktails for the guests. He wouldn't serve straight drinks like rum-and-Coke or even Scotch-on-the-rocks, only drinks of his own devising. He gave them lawyerly names like the Hanging Judge, the Ambulance Chaser, the Mouthpiece, and described their concoction in detail. He told long, complicated stories in a near whisper, making everyone lean in his direction, and repeated important lines; he also repeated the important lines in the stories my mother told, and corrected her when she got something wrong. When guests came to the ends of their own stories he would point out the morals for them.

Dr. Murphy had several theories about my father, which he used to test on me in the course of our meetings. Dr. Murphy had by this time given up his glasses for contact lenses and lost weight in the course of fasts that he undertook regularly. Even with his baldness he looked years younger than when he'd come to the parties at our house. Certainly he did not look like my father's contemporary, which he was.

One of Dr. Murphy's theories was that my father had exhibited a classic trait of people who had been gifted children by taking an undemanding position in an uninteresting firm. "He was afraid of finding his limits," Dr. Murphy told me. "As long as he kept stamping papers and making out wills he could go on believing that he didn't *have* limits." Dr. Murphy's fascination with my father made me uneasy, and I felt traitorous listening to him. While he lived, my father would never have submitted himself for analysis; it seemed a betrayal to put him on the couch now that he was dead.

I did enjoy Dr. Murphy's recollections of my father as a child. He told me about something that happened when they were in the Boy Scouts. Their troop had been on a long hike and Father had fallen behind. Dr. Murphy and the others decided to ambush him as he came down the trail. They hid in the woods on each side and waited. But when my father walked into the trap none of them moved or made a sound, and he strolled on without even knowing they were there. "He had the sweetest look on his face," Dr. Murphy said, "listening to the birds, smelling the flowers, just like Ferdinand the Bull." He also told me that my father's drinks tasted like medicine.

While I rode my bicycle home from Dr. Murphy's office, Mother fretted. She felt lonely in her confusion but didn't call anyone because she also felt like a failure. My lying had that effect on her. She took it personally. At such times she didn't think of my sisters, one happily married, the other doing brilliantly at Fordham. She didn't think of my brother, Michael, who had given up college to work with runaway children in Los Angeles. She thought of me. She thought that she had made a mess of her family.

Actually she managed the family very well. When my father lay dying upstairs she pulled us together. She made lists of chores and gave each of us a fair allowance. Bedtimes were adjusted and she stuck by them. She set regular hours for homework. Each child was made responsible for the next eldest, and I was given a dog. She told us frequently, predictably, that she loved us. At dinner we were each expected to contribute something, and after dinner she played the piano and tried to teach us to sing in harmony, which I couldn't do. Mother, an admirer of the von Trapp family, considered this a character defect.

Our life together was more orderly, healthy, while my father was dying than it had been before. He had set us rules to follow, not really much different from the ones Mother gave us after he got sick, but he had administered them arbitrarily. Though we were supposed to get an allowance we always had to ask him for it and then he'd give us too much because he enjoyed seeming magnanimous. Sometimes he punished us for no reason, because he was in a bad mood. He was apt to decide, as one of my sisters was going out to a dance, that she had better stay home and do something to improve herself. Or he'd sweep us all up on a Wednesday night and take us ice-skating.

He changed as the cancer did its work. He was quieter, less emphatic and faultfinding. He relaxed his coolly teasing way with us. For the first time in my life I began seeking out his company, at my mother's urging to begin with, then because I found I liked him. He taught me to play poker and chess and sometimes helped me with my schoolwork. Mostly we just sat and read. I was working my way through Sherlock Holmes; he had given up the newspaper and begun rereading the Norse sagas he'd fallen in love with in college, to the point that he'd considered devoting himself to them as a scholar. The sagas made him boyish. Now and then he'd stop and read aloud a particularly brutal passage: "Hard men!" he'd say, happily. "Men you would not care to meet outside the pages of a book."

One afternoon he looked up and saw me watching him. "What?" he asked.

"Nothing."

"Now then, what is it?"

"Are you afraid?"

"Of course not." He looked down at his book, then back at me. "Yes."

"Me too."

"Ah, son. I'm sorry. But don't ask me that again, please."

Toward the end he slept most of the time. From below, sometimes, faintly, I heard Mother playing the piano. Occasionally he nodded off in his chair while I was reading to him; his bathrobe would fall open then, and I would see the long scar on his stomach. His ribs all showed and his legs were like cables.

I once read in a biography of a great man that he "died well." I assume the writer meant that he kept his pain to himself, did not set off false alarms, and didn't grossly inconvenience those who were to stay behind. My father died well, even serenely. It was as though the irritability and solitude of his life had been a kind of stage fright. He managed his audience—us—with an old trouper's sense of when to clown and when to stand on his dignity. We were all moved, and admired his courage, as he intended we should. He died downstairs in his favorite chair while I was writing an essay for school. I was alone in the house and didn't know what to do. His body didn't frighten me, but immediately and sharply I missed my father. It seemed wrong to leave him sitting up and I tried to carry him upstairs to the bedroom but it was too hard, alone. So I called my friend Ralphy across the street. When he came over and saw what I wanted him for he started crying. I made him help me anyway. Mother got home not long afterward, and when I told her that Father was dead she ran upstairs, calling his name. A few minutes later she came back down. "Thank God," she said, "at least he died in bed." This seemed important to her and I didn't tell her otherwise. But that night Ralphy's parents called. They were, they said, shocked at what I'd done, and so was my mother when she heard the story, shocked and furious. Why? Because I hadn't told her the truth? Or because, having learned the truth, she could not go on believing that my father had died in bed?

When I came home my mother was arranging wood in the fireplace and did not look at me or speak for a moment. Finally she finished and straightened up and brushed her hands. She stepped back and looked at the fire she'd laid. "That's all right," she said. "Not bad for a consumptive."

"I'm sorry about the letter."

"Sorry? Sorry you wrote it or sorry I found it?"

"I wasn't going to mail it. It was a sort of joke."

"Ha ha." She took up the whisk broom and swept bits of bark into the fireplace, then closed the drapes and settled on the couch. "Sit down," she said. She crossed her legs. "Listen, do I give you advice all the time?"

"Yes."

"I do?"

I nodded.

"Well, I'm supposed to. I'm your mother. I'm going to give you some more advice, for your own good. You don't have to make all these things up, James. They'll happen anyway." She picked at the hem of her skirt. "Do you understand?"

"I think so."

"You're cheating yourself, that's what I'm trying to tell you. When you get to be my age you won't know anything at all about life. All you'll know is what you've made up."

I thought about that. It seemed logical.

She went on. "I think maybe you need to get out of yourself more. Think more about other people."

The doorbell rang.

"Go see who it is," Mother said. "We'll talk about this later."

It was Dr. Murphy. He and my mother made their apologies and she insisted that he stay for dinner. I went to the kitchen to fetch ice for their drinks, and when I returned they were talking about me. I sat on the sofa and listened. Dr. Murphy was telling her not to worry. "James is a good boy," he said. "I've been thinking about my oldest, Terry. He's not really dishonest, you know, but he's not really honest either. I can't seem to reach him. At least James isn't furtive."

"No," Mother said, "he's never been furtive."

Dr. Murphy clasped his hands between his knees and stared at them. "Well, that's Terry. Furtive."

Before we sat down to dinner Mother said grace. Dr. Murphy bowed his head and closed his eyes and crossed himself at the end, though he had lost his faith in college. When he told me that, during one of our meetings, in just those words, I had the picture of a rain-coat hanging by itself outside a dining hall. He drank a good deal of wine and persistently turned the conversation to the subject of his relationship with Terry. He admitted that he had come to dislike the boy. He used the word "dislike" with relish, like someone on a diet permitting himself a single potato chip. "I don't know what I've done wrong," he said abruptly, and with reference to nothing in particular. "Then again maybe I haven't done anything wrong. I don't know what to think anymore. Nobody does."

"I know what to think," my mother said.

"So does the solipsist. How can you prove to a solipsist that he's not creating the rest of us?"

This was one of Dr. Murphy's favorite riddles, and almost any pre-text was sufficient for him to trot it out. He was a child with a card trick.

"Send him to bed without dinner," Mother said. "Let him create that."

Dr. Murphy turned to me. "Why do you do it?" he asked. It was a

pure question, it had no object beyond the satisfaction of his curiosity. Mother looked at me and there was the same curiosity in her face.

"I don't know," I said, and that was the truth.

Dr. Murphy nodded, not because he'd anticipated my answer but
because he accepted it. "Is it fun?"

"No, it's not fun. I can't explain."

"Why is it all so sad?" Mother asked. "Why all the diseases?"

"Maybe," Dr. Murphy said, "sad things are more interesting."

"Not to me," Mother said.

"Not to me either," I said. "It just comes out that way."

After dinner Dr. Murphy asked Mother to play the piano. He particularly wanted to sing "I'll Take You Home Again, Kathleen."

"That old thing," Mother said. She stood and folded her napkin
deliberately, and we followed her into the living room. Dr. Murphy
stood behind her as she warmed up. Then they sang "I'll Take You
Home Again, Kathleen," and I watched him stare down at my mother,
as if he were trying to remember something. Her own eyes were
closed. After that they sang "O Magnum Mysterium." They sang it in
parts and I regretted I had no voice, it sounded so good.

"Come on, James," Dr. Murphy said as Mother played the last
chords. "These old tunes not good enough for you?"

"He just can't sing," Mother said.

When Dr. Murphy left, Mother lit the fire and made more coffee. She
slouched down in the big chair, sticking her legs straight out and
moving her feet back and forth. "That was fun," she said.

"Did you and Father ever do things like that?"

"A few times, when we were first going out. I don't think he really
enjoyed it. He was like you."

I wondered if they'd had a good marriage. He admired her and
liked to look at her; every night at dinner he had us move the candle-
sticks slightly to right or left of center so he could see her down the
length of the table. And every evening when she set the table she put
them in the center again. She didn't seem to miss him very much. But

I wouldn't really have known if she did, and I didn't miss him all that much myself anymore. Most of the time I thought about other things.

"James?"

I waited.

"I've been thinking that you might like to go down and stay with Michael for a week or two."

"What about school?"

"I'll talk to Father McSorley. He won't mind. Maybe this problem will take care of itself if you start thinking about other people— helping them, like Michael does. You don't have to go if you don't want to."

"It's okay with me. I'd like to see Michael."

"I'm not trying to get rid of you."

"I know."

Mother stretched, then tucked her feet under her. She sipped at her coffee. "What did that word mean that Murphy used? You know the one?"

"Paranoid? That's where somebody thinks everyone is out to get him. Like that woman who always grabs you after Mass—Dorothea."

"Not paranoid. Everyone knows what that means. Solipsist."

"Oh. A solipsist is someone who thinks he creates everything around him."

Mother nodded and blew on her coffee, then put it down without drinking. "I'd rather be paranoid. Do you really think Dorothea is?"

"Sure. No question about it."

"I mean really *sick*?"

"That's what paranoid is, is being sick. What do you think, Mother?"

"What are you so angry about?"

"I'm not angry." I lowered my voice. "I'm not angry."

"I don't think she knows what she's saying, she just wants some-one to listen. She probably lives all by herself in some little room. We should pray for her. Will you remember to do that?"

I thought of Mother singing "O Magnum Mysterium," saying grace, praying with easy confidence. She could imagine things as coming together, not falling apart. She looked at me and I shrank; I knew exactly what she was going to say.

"Son," she said, "do you know how much I love you?"

The next afternoon I took the bus to Los Angeles. I looked forward to the trip, to the monotony of the road and the empty fields by the roadside. Mother walked with me down the long concourse. The station was crowded and oppressive. "Are you sure this is the right bus?" she asked at the loading platform.

"Yes."

"It looks so old."

"Mother—"

"All right." She pulled me against her and kissed me, then held me an extra second to show that her embrace was sincere, not just like everyone else's, never having realized that everyone else does the same thing. I boarded the bus and we waved at each other until it became awkward. Then she began checking through her handbag for something. When she finished I stood and adjusted the luggage over my seat. I sat and we smiled at each other, waved when the driver gunned the engine, shrugged when he got up suddenly to count the passengers, waved again when he resumed his seat. As the bus pulled out my mother and I were looking at each other with plain relief.

I had boarded the wrong bus. This one was bound for Los Angeles but not by the express route. We stopped in San Mateo, Palo Alto, San Jose, Castroville. When we left Castroville it began to rain, hard; my window wouldn't close all the way, and a thin stream of water ran down the panel onto my seat. To keep dry I had to lean forward and away from the window. The rain fell harder. The engine of the bus sounded as though it were coming apart.

In Salinas the man sleeping beside me jumped up but before I had a chance to change seats his place was taken by an enormous woman in a print dress, carrying a shopping bag. She took possession of her seat and spilled over onto half of mine. "That's a storm," she said loudly, then turned and looked at me. "Hungry?" Without waiting for an answer she dipped into her bag and pulled out a piece of chicken and thrust it at me. "Hey, by God," she hooted, "look at him go to town on that drumstick!" A few people turned and smiled. I smiled back around the bone and kept at it. I finished that piece and she handed me another. Then she started handing out chicken to the people in the seats near us.

Outside of San Luis Obispo the noise from the engine grew louder and just as suddenly there was no noise at all. The driver pulled off to the side of the road and got out, then got on again dripping wet. A few moments later he announced that the bus had broken down and they were sending another one to pick us up. Someone asked how long that might take and the driver said he had no idea. "Keep your pants on!" shouted the woman next to me. "Anybody in a hurry to get to LA ought to have his head examined."

The wind was blowing hard, driving sheets of rain against the windows on both sides. The bus swayed gently. Outside the light was brown and thick. The woman next to me pumped all the people around us for their itineraries and said whether or not she'd ever been where they were from or where they were going. "How about you?" She slapped my knee. "Parents own a chicken ranch? I hope so!" She laughed. I told her I was from San Francisco. "San Francisco, that's where my husband was stationed." She asked me what I did there and I told her I worked with refugees from Tibet.

"Is that right? What do you do with a bunch of Tibetans?"

"Seems like there's plenty of other places they could've gone," said a man in front of us. "We don't go there."

"What do you do with a bunch of Tibetans?" the woman repeated.

"Try to find them jobs, locate housing, listen to their problems."

"You understand that kind of talk?"

"Yes."

"Speak it?"

"Pretty well. I was born and raised in Tibet. My parents were missionaries over there."

"Missionaries!"

"They were killed when the Communists took over."

The big woman patted my arm.

"It's all right," I said.

"Why don't you say some of that Tibetan?"

"What would you like to hear?"

"Say 'The cow jumped over the moon.'" She watched me, smiling, and when I finished she looked at the others and shook her head. "That was pretty. Like music. Say some more."

"What?"

"Anything."

They bent toward me. The windows went blind with rain. The driver had fallen asleep and was snoring gently to the swaying of the bus. Outside the muddy light flickered to pale yellow, and far off there was thunder. The woman next to me leaned back and closed her eyes and then so did all the others as I sang to them in what was surely an ancient and holy tongue.

Soldier's Joy

On Friday Hooper was named driver of the guard for the third night that week. He'd recently been broken in rank again, this time from corporal to PFC, and the first sergeant had decided to keep Hooper's evenings busy so he wouldn't have leisure to brood. That was what the first sergeant told him when Hooper came to the orderly room to complain.

"It's for your own good," the first sergeant said. "Not that I expect you to thank me." He moved the book he'd been reading to one side of his desk and leaned back. "Hooper, I have a theory about you," he said. "Want to hear it?"

"I'm all ears, Top," Hooper said.

The first sergeant put his boots up on the desk and stared out the window to his left. It was getting on toward five o'clock. Work details had begun to return from the rifle range and the post laundry and the day-care center, where Hooper and several other men were excavating a wading pool without aid of machinery. As the trucks let them out they gathered on the barracks steps and under the dead elm beside the mess hall, their voices a steady murmur in the orderly room where Hooper stood waiting to hear himself analyzed.

"You resent me," the first sergeant said. "You think you should be sitting here. You don't know that's what you think because you've totally sublimated your resentment, but that's what it is, all right, and that's why you and me are developing a definite conflict profile. It's like you have to keep fucking up to prove to yourself that you don't really care. That's my theory. You follow me?"

"Top, I'm way ahead of you," Hooper said. "That's night school talking."

The first sergeant continued to look out the window. "I don't know," he said. "I don't know what you're doing in my army. You've put your twenty years in. You could retire to Mexico and live like a dictator. So what are you doing in my army, Hooper?"

Hooper looked down at the desk. He cleared his throat but said nothing.

"Give it some thought," the first sergeant said. He stood and walked Hooper to the door. "I'm not hostile," he said. "I'm prepared to be supportive. Just think nice thoughts about Mexico, okay? Okay, Hooper?"

Hooper called Mickey and told her he wouldn't be coming by that night after all. She reminded him that this was the third time in one week, and said that she wasn't getting any younger.

"What am I supposed to do?" Hooper asked. "Go AWOL?"

"I cried three times today," Mickey said. "I just broke down and cried, and you know what? I don't even know why."

"What did you do last night?" Hooper asked. When Mickey didn't answer he said, "Did Briggs come over?"

"I've been inside all day," Mickey said. "Just sitting here. I'm going out of my tree." Then, in the same weary voice, she said, "Touch it, Hoop."

"I have to get going," Hooper said.

"Not yet. Wait. I'm going into the bedroom. I'm going to pick up the phone in there. Hang on, Hoop. Think of the bedroom. Think of me lying on the bed. Wait, baby."

There were men passing by the phone booth. Hooper watched them and tried not to think of Mickey's bedroom but now he could think of nothing else. Mickey's husband was a supply sergeant. The walls of the bedroom were knotty pine he'd derailed en route to some colonel's office. The brass lamps beside the bed were made from howitzer casings. The sheets were parachute silk. Sometimes, lying on those sheets, Hooper thought of the men who'd drifted to earth below them. He was no great lover, as the women he went with usually got around to telling him, but in Mickey's bedroom Hooper had turned in his saddest performances and always when he was most aware that everything around him was stolen. He wasn't exactly sure why he kept going back. It was just something he did, again and again.

"Okay," Mickey said. "I'm here."

"There's a guy waiting to use the phone," Hooper told her.

"Hoop, I'm on the bed. I'm taking off my shoes."

Hooper could see her perfectly. He lit a cigarette and opened the door of the booth to let the smoke out.

"Hoop?" she said.

"I told you, there's a guy waiting."

"Turn around, then."

"You don't need me," Hooper said. "All you need is the telephone. Why don't you call Briggs? That's what you're going to do after I hang up."

"I probably will," she said. "Listen, Hoop, I'm not really on the bed. I was just pulling your chain."

"I knew it," Hooper said. "You're watching the tube, right?"

"Somebody just won a saw," Mickey said.

"A saw?"

"Yeah, they drove up to this man's house and dumped a truckload of logs in his yard and gave him a chain saw. This was his fantasy."

"Maybe I can swing by later tonight," Hooper said. "Just for a minute."

"I don't know," Mickey said. "Better give me a ring first."

After Mickey hung up Hooper tried to call his wife but there was no answer. He stood there and listened to the phone ringing. At last he put the receiver down and stepped outside the booth, just as they began to sound retreat over the company loudspeaker. With the men around him Hooper came to attention and saluted. The record was scratchy, but the music, as always, caused Hooper's mind to go abruptly and perfectly still. He held his salute until the last note died away, then broke off smartly and walked down the street toward the mess hall.

The Officer of the Day was Captain King from Headquarters Company. He had also been Officer of the Day on Monday and Tuesday nights, and Hooper was glad to see him again because Captain King was too lazy to do his own job or to make sure that the guards were doing theirs. He stayed in the guardhouse and left everything up to Hooper.

Captain King had gray hair and a long, grayish face. He was a West Point graduate. His classmates were majors or even lieutenant colonels but he himself had been held back for good reasons, many of which he admitted to Hooper their first night together. It puzzled Hooper at first, this officer telling him about his failures to perform, his nervous breakdowns and Valium habit, but finally he understood: Captain King regarded him, a PFC with twenty-one years' service, as a comrade in dereliction, a disaster like himself with no room left for judgment against anyone.

The evening was hot and muggy. Captain King proceeded along the rank of men drawn up before the guardhouse steps. He objected to the alignment of someone's belt buckle. He asked questions about the chain of command but gave no sign as to whether the answers he received were right or wrong. He inspected a couple of rifles and pretended to find something amiss with each of them, and when he reached the last man in line he began to deliver a speech. He said he'd never seen such sorry troops in his life. He asked how they expected to stand up to a determined enemy. On and on he went. Hooper lit another cigarette and sat down on the running board of the truck he'd been leaning against.

The sky was turning a weird purple. It had a damp, heavy look and it felt heavy too, hanging close overhead, nervous with rumblings and small flashes in the distance. Just sitting there made Hooper sweat. Beyond the guardhouse a stream of cars rushed along the road to Tacoma. From the officers' club farther up the road came the muffled beat of rock music, which was almost lost, like every other sound of the evening, in the purr of crickets that rose up everywhere and thickened the air like heat.

When Captain King finished talking he turned the men over to Hooper for transportation to their posts. Two of them, both privates, were from Hooper's company, and these he allowed to ride with him in the cab of the truck while everybody else slid around in back. One was a cook named Porchoff, known as Porkchop. The other was a radio operator named Trac who'd supposedly managed to airlift himself out of Saigon during the fall of the city by hanging on to the skids of a helicopter. That was the story, anyway. Hooper didn't believe it. When he tried to picture his son Woody at the same age, eight or nine, doing that, dangling over a burning city by his fingertips, he had to smile.

Trac didn't talk about it. Nothing about him suggested a hard past except perhaps the deep, sickle-shaped scar above his right eye. To Hooper there was something familiar about this scar. One night, watching Trac play the pinball machine in the company rec room, he was overcome with the certainty that he'd seen him before somewhere—astride a water buffalo in some reeking paddy or running alongside Hooper's APC with a bunch of other kids begging money, holding up melons or a bag full of weed or a starving monkey on a stick.

Though Hooper had the windows open, the cab of the truck smelled strongly of aftershave. Hooper noticed that Trac was wearing orange Walkman earphones under his helmet liner. They were against regulations but Hooper said nothing. As long as Trac had his ears plugged he wouldn't be listening for trespassers and end up blasting away at some squirrel cracking open an acorn. Of all the guards only Porchoff and Trac would be carrying ammunition, because they'd been assigned to the battalion communications center, which was tied into the division mainframe computer. The theory was that an intruder who knew his stuff could get his hands on highly classified material. That was how it had been explained to Hooper, who thought it was a load of crap. The Russians knew everything anyway.

Hooper let out the first two men at the PX and the next two at the parking lot outside the main officers' club, where lately there'd been several cars vandalized. As they pulled away, Porchoff leaned past Trac and grabbed Hooper's sleeve. "You used to be a corporal," he said.

Hooper shook his hand loose and said, "I'm driving a truck, in case you didn't notice."

"How come you got busted?"

"None of your business."

"I'm just asking," Porchoff said. "So what happened, anyway?"

"Cool it, Porkchop," said Trac. "The man doesn't want to talk about it, okay?"

"Cool it yourself, fuckface." Porchoff looked at Trac. "Was I addressing you?"

Trac said, "Man, you must've been eating some of your own food."

"I don't believe I was addressing you," Porchoff said. "In fact, I don't believe you and me have been properly introduced. That's another thing I don't like about the army, the way people you haven't been introduced to feel perfectly free to get right in your face and unload whatever shit they've got in their brains. It happens all the time. But I never heard anyone say 'cool it' before. You're a real phrasemaker, fuckface."

"That's enough," Hooper said.

Porchoff leaned back and said, "That's enough," in a falsetto voice. A few moments later he started humming to himself.

Hooper dropped off the rest of the guards and turned up the hill toward the communications center. There were chokeberry bushes along the gravel drive, with white blossoms going gray in the dusky light. Gravel sprayed up under the tires and rattled against the floorboards. Porchoff stopped humming. "I've got a cramp," he said.

Hooper pulled up next to the gate and turned off the engine, then looked over at Porchoff. "Now what's your problem?" he said.

"I've got a cramp," Porchoff repeated.

"For Christ's sake," Hooper said. "Why didn't you say something before?"

"I did. I went on sick call but the doctor couldn't find it. It keeps moving around. It's here now." Porchoff touched his neck. "I swear to God."

"Keep track of it," Hooper told him. "You can go on sick call again in the morning."

"You don't believe me," Porchoff said.

The three of them got out of the truck. Hooper counted out the ammunition to Porchoff and Trac and watched as they loaded their clips. "That ammo's strictly for show," he said. "Forget I even gave it to you. If you run into a problem, which you won't, use the phone in the guard shack. You can work out your own shifts." Hooper opened the gate and locked the two men inside. They stood watching him, faces in shadow, black rifle barrels poking over their shoulders. "Listen," Hooper said, "nobody's going to break in here, understand?"

Trac nodded. Porchoff just looked at him.

"Okay," Hooper said. "I'll drop by later. Me and the captain." Captain King wasn't about to go anywhere, but Trac and Porchoff didn't know that. Hooper behaved better when he thought he was being watched and he supposed the same was true of everyone else.

He climbed back inside the truck, started the engine, and gave the V sign to the men at the gate. Trac gave the sign back and turned away. Porchoff didn't move. He stayed where he was, fingers laced through the wire. He looked about ready to cry. "Damn," Hooper said, and hit the gas. Gravel clattered in the wheel wells. When Hooper reached the main road a light rain began to fall, but it stopped before he'd even turned the wipers on.

Hooper and Captain King sat on adjacent bunks in the guardhouse, which was empty except for them and a bat that was flitting back and forth among the dim rafters. As on Monday and Tuesday nights, Captain King had brought along an ice chest filled with little bottles of Perrier water. From time to time he tried pressing one on Hooper, whose refusals made Captain King apologetic. "It's not a class thing," he said, looking at the bottle in his hand. "I don't drink this fancy stuff because I went to the Point or anything like that." He leaned down and put the bottle between his bare feet. "I'm allergic to alcohol," he said. "Otherwise I'd probably be an alcoholic. Why not? I'm everything else." He smiled at Hooper.

Hooper lay back and clasped his hands behind his head and stared up at the mattress above him. "I'm not much of a drinker myself," he said. He knew that Captain King wanted him to explain why he refused the Perrier, but there was really no reason in particular.

"I drank eggnog one Christmas when I was a kid and it almost killed me," Captain King said. "My arms and legs swelled up to twice their normal size. The doctors couldn't get my glasses off because my skin was all puffed up around them. You know how a tree will grow around a rock? It was like that. A few months later I tried beer at some kid's graduation party and the same thing happened. Pretty strange, eh?"

"Yes sir," Hooper said.

"I used to think it was all for the best. I have an addictive personality and you can bet your bottom dollar I would've been a problem drinker. No question about it. But now I wonder. If I'd had one big weakness like that maybe I wouldn't have had all these little pissant weaknesses instead. I know that sounds like bull-pucky, but look at Alexander the Great. Alexander the Great was a boozer. Did you know that?"

"No sir," Hooper said.

"Well, he was. Read your history. So was Churchill. Churchill drank a bottle of cognac a day. And of course Grant. You know what Lincoln said when someone complained about Grant's drinking?"

"Yes sir. I've heard the story."

"He said, 'Find out what brand he uses so I can ship a case to the rest of my generals.' Is that the way you heard it?"

"Yes sir."

Captain King nodded. "I'm beat," he said. He stretched out and assumed exactly the position Hooper was in. It made Hooper uncomfortable. He sat up and put his feet on the floor.

"Married?" Captain King asked.

"Yes sir."

"Kids?"

"Yes sir. One. Woodrow."

"Oh my God, a boy," Captain King said. "They're nothing but trouble, take my word for it. They're programmed to hate you. It has to be like that, otherwise they'd spend their whole lives moping around the house. Just the same, it's no fun when it starts. I have two, and neither one can stand me. Breaks my heart. Of course I was a worse father than most. How old is your boy?"

"Sixteen or seventeen," Hooper said. He put his hands on his knees and looked at the floor. "Seventeen. He lives with my wife's sister in Spokane."

Captain King turned his head and looked at him. "Sounds like you're not much of a dad yourself."

Hooper began to lace his boots up.

"I'm not criticizing," Captain King said. "At least you were smart enough to get someone else to do the job." He yawned. "You need me for anything? You want me to make the rounds with you?"

"I'll take care of things, sir."

"Fair enough." Captain King closed his eyes. "If you need me just shout."

Hooper went outside and lit a cigarette. It was almost midnight, well past the time appointed for inspecting the guards. As he walked toward the truck mosquitoes droned around his head. A breeze was rustling the treetops, but on the ground the air was hot and still.

Hooper took his time making the rounds. He visited all the guards except Porchoff and Trac and found everything in order. There were no problems. He started down the road toward the communications center but when he reached the turnoff he drove past. Warm, fragrant air rushed into his face from the open window. The road ahead was empty. Hooper leaned back and mashed the accelerator. The engine roared. He was moving now, really moving, past darkened barracks and bare flagpoles and bushes whose flowers blazed up in the glare of the headlights. Hooper grinned. He felt no pleasure but he grinned and pushed the truck as hard as it would go.

Hooper slowed down when he left the post. He was AWOL now. Even if he couldn't find it in him to care much about that, he saw no point in calling attention to himself.

Drunk drivers were jerking their cars back and forth between lanes. It seemed like every half mile or so a police car with flashing lights had someone stopped by the roadside. Other cruisers sat idling behind billboards. Hooper stayed in the right lane and drove slowly until he reached his turn, then he gunned the engine again and raced down the pitted street that led to Mickey's house. He passed a bunch of kids sitting on the hood of a car with cans of beer in their hands. The car door was open and Hooper had to swerve to miss it. As he went by he heard a blast of music.

When he reached Mickey's block Hooper turned off the engine. The truck coasted silently down the street, and again Hooper became aware of the sound of crickets. He stopped on the shoulder across from Mickey's house and sat listening. The thick, pulsing sound seemed to grow louder every moment. Hooper drifted into memory, his cigarette dangling unsmoked, burning down toward his fingers. At the same instant he felt the heat of the ember against his skin Hooper was startled by another pain, the pain of finding himself where he was. He roused himself and got out of the truck.

The windows were dark. Mickey's Buick was parked in the driveway beside a car Hooper didn't recognize. It didn't belong to her husband and it didn't belong to Briggs. Hooper glanced around at the other houses, then walked across the street and ducked under the hanging leaves of the willow tree in Mickey's front yard. He knelt there, holding his breath to hear better, but there was no sound but the song of the crickets and the rushing of the air conditioner. Hooper got up and walked over to the house. He looked around again, then went into a crouch and moved along the wall. He rounded the corner of the house and was starting up the side toward Mickey's bedroom when a circle of light burst around his head and a woman's voice said, "Thou shalt not commit adultery."

Hooper closed his eyes. There was a long silence. Then the woman said, "Come here."

She was standing in the driveway of the house next door. When Hooper came up to her she stuck a pistol in his face and told him to raise his hands. "A soldier," she said, moving the beam of light up and down his uniform. "All right, put your hands down." She snapped the light off and stood watching Hooper in the flickering blue glow that came from the open door behind her. Hooper heard a dog bark twice and a man say, "Remember—nothing is too good for your dog. It's *ruff-ruff* at the sign of the double R." The dog barked twice again.

"I want to know what you think you're doing," the woman said.

Hooper said, "I'm not exactly sure." He saw her more clearly now. She was thin and tall. She wore glasses with black frames, and she had on a blue bathrobe cinched at the waist with a leather belt. Shadows darkened the hollows of her cheeks. Under the hem of the bathrobe her feet were big and bare.

"I know what you're doing," she said. She pointed the pistol, a small silver automatic, at Mickey's house. "You're sniffing around that whore over there."

Someone came to the door behind the woman. A deep voice called out, "Is it him?"

"Stay inside, Dads," the woman answered. "It's nobody."

"It's him!" the man shouted. "Don't let him talk you out of it again!"

"What do you want with that whore?" the woman asked Hooper. Before he could answer, she said, "I could shoot you and nobody would say boo. You're on my property now. I could say I thought you were my husband. I've got a restraining order."

Hooper nodded.

"I don't see the attraction," she said. "But then I'm not a man." She made a laughing sound. "You know something? I almost did it. I almost shot you. I was that close, but then I saw the uniform." She shook her head. "Shame on you. Where is your pride?"

"Don't let him talk," said the man in the doorway. He came down the steps, a tall white-haired man in striped pajamas. "There you are, you sonofabitch," he said. "I'll dance on your grave."

"It isn't him, Dads," the woman said sadly. "It's someone else."

"So he says," the man snapped. He started down the driveway, hopping from foot to foot over the gravel. The woman handed him the flashlight and he turned it on in Hooper's face, then moved the beam slowly down to his boots. "Sweetie pie, it's a soldier," he said.

"I told you it wasn't him," the woman said.

"But this is a terrible mistake," the man said. "Sir, I'm at a loss for words."

"Forget it," Hooper told him. "No hard feelings."

"You are too kind," the man said. He reached out and shook Hooper's hand, then nodded toward the house. "Come have a drink."

"He has to go," the woman said.

"That's right," Hooper told him. "I was just on my way back to base."

The man gave a slight bow with his head. "To base with you, then. Good night, sir."

Captain King was still asleep when Hooper returned to the guardhouse. His thumb was in his mouth. Hooper lay in the next bunk with his eyes open. He was still awake at four in the morning when the telephone rang.

It was Trac calling from the communications center. He said that Porchoff was threatening to shoot himself—and him, if he tried to interfere. "This dude is mental," Trac said. "You get me out of here, and I mean now."

"We'll be right there," Hooper said. "Just give him lots of room. Don't try to grab his rifle or anything."

"Fat fucking chance," Trac said. "Man, you know what he called me? He called me a gook. I hope he wastes himself. I don't need no assholes with loaded guns declaring war on me, man."

"Just hold on," Hooper told him. He hung up and went to wake Captain King, because this was a mess and he wanted it to be Captain King's mess and Captain King's balls that got busted if anything went wrong. He walked over to Captain King and stood looking down at him. Captain King's thumb had slipped out of his mouth. Hooper decided not to wake him after all. Captain King would probably refuse to come anyway, but if he did come he'd screw things up for sure.

A light rain had begun to fall. The road was empty except for one jeep coming toward him. Hooper waved at the two men in front as they went past, and they both waved back. He followed their lights in his mirror until they vanished behind him.

Hooper parked the truck halfway up the drive and walked the rest of the distance. The rain was falling harder now, tapping steadily on the shoulders of his poncho. Sweet, thick, almost unbreathable smells rose from the earth. He walked slowly, gravel crunching under his boots. When he reached the gate a voice to his left said, "Shit, man, you took your time." Trac stepped out of the shadows and waited as Hooper tried to get the key into the lock. "Come on, man," he said, and knelt with his back to the fence and swung the barrel of his rifle from side to side.

"Got it," Hooper said. He took the lock off, and Trac pushed the gate open. "The truck's down there," Hooper told him. "Just past the turn."

Trac's face was dark under the hood of his glistening poncho. "You want this?" he asked, holding out his rifle.

Hooper looked at it. He shook his head. "Where's Porchoff?"

"Around back," Trac said. "There's some picnic benches out there."

"All right," Hooper said. "I'll take care of it. Wait in the truck."

"Shit, man, I feel like shit," Trac said. "I'll back you up, man."

"It's okay," Hooper told him. "I can handle it."

"I don't cut out on anybody." Trac shifted back and forth.

"You aren't cutting out," Hooper said. "Nothing's going to happen."

Trac started down the drive. When he disappeared around the turn Hooper kept watching to make sure he didn't double back. A stiff breeze began to blow, shaking the trees, sending raindrops rattling down through the leaves.

Hooper turned and walked through the gate into the compound. The forms of shrubs and pines were dark and indefinite in the slanting rain. He followed the fence to the right, squinting into the shadows, and saw Porchoff hunched over a picnic table. He stopped and called out, "Hey, Porchoff! It's me—Hooper."

Porchoff raised his head.

"It's just me," Hooper said, showing his empty hands. The rifle was lying on the table in front of Porchoff. "It's just me," he repeated, as monotonously as he could. He stopped beside another picnic table about ten feet away and lowered himself onto the bench. He looked over at Porchoff. Neither of them spoke for a while. Then Hooper said, "Okay, let's talk about it. Trac tells me you've got some kind of attitude problem."

Porchoff didn't answer. Raindrops streamed down his helmet onto his shoulders and dripped steadily past his face. His uniform was soggy and dark, plastered to his skin. He stared at Hooper and said nothing. Now and then his shoulders jerked.

"Are you gay?" Hooper asked.

Porchoff shook his head.

"Well then, what? You on acid or something? You can tell me, Porchoff. It doesn't matter."

"I don't do drugs." It was the first time Porchoff had spoken. His voice was calm.

"Good," Hooper said. "I mean, at least I know I'm talking to you and not to some fucking chemical. Now listen up, Porchoff—I don't want you turning that rifle on me. Understand?"

Porchoff looked down at the rifle, then back at Hooper. "You leave me alone and I'll leave you alone."

"I already had someone throw down on me once tonight," Hooper said. "I'd just as soon leave it at that." He reached under his poncho and took out his cigarette case. He held it up for Porchoff to see.

"I don't use tobacco," Porchoff said.

"Well I do." Hooper shook out a cigarette and bent to light it. "Hey, all right," he said. "One match." He put the case back in his pocket and cupped the cigarette under the picnic table to keep it dry. The rain was falling lightly now in fine, fitful gusts like spray. Misty gray light was spreading through the sky. Porchoff's shoulders kept twitching, and his lips were blue and trembling. "Put your poncho on," Hooper told him.

Porchoff shook his head.

"You trying to catch pneumonia?" Hooper nodded at Porchoff. "Go ahead, boy. Put your poncho on."

Porchoff bent over and covered his face with his hands. Hooper realized that he was crying. He smoked and waited for it to stop, but Porchoff kept crying and Hooper grew impatient. He said, "What's all this about you shooting yourself?"

Porchoff rubbed at his eyes with the heels of his hands. "Why shouldn't I?"

"Why shouldn't you? What do you mean, why shouldn't you?"

"Why shouldn't I shoot myself? Give me a reason."

"No. But I'll give you some advice," Hooper said. "You don't run around asking why you shouldn't shoot yourself. That's decadent, Porchoff. Now do me a favor and put your poncho on."

Porchoff sat shivering for a moment. Then he took his poncho off his belt, unrolled it, and began pulling it over his head. Hooper considered making a grab for the rifle but held back. There was no need, he was home free now. People who were going to kill themselves didn't come in out of the rain.

"You know what they call me?" Porchoff said.

"Who's 'they,' Porchoff?"

"Everyone."

"No. What does everyone call you?"

"Porkchop. *Porkchop.*"

"Come on," Hooper said. "What's the harm in that? Everyone gets called something."

"But that's my *name*," Porchoff said. "That's *me*. It's got so even when people use my real name I hear 'Porkchop.' All I can think of is this big piece of meat. And that's what they're seeing too. You can say they aren't, but I know they are."

Hooper recognized some truth in this, a lot of truth, in fact, because when he himself said Porkchop that was what he saw: a porkchop.

"I've got this cramp all the time," Porchoff said, "but no one believes me. Not even the doctors. You don't believe me either."

"I believe you," Hooper told him.

Porchoff blinked. "Sure," he said.

"I believe you," Hooper said, keeping his eyes on the rifle. He was about to ask Porchoff to give it to him but decided to wait a little while. The moment was wrong, somehow. Hooper pushed back the hood of his poncho and took off his fatigue cap. He glanced up at the pale clouds.

"I don't have any buddies," Porchoff said.

"No wonder," Hooper said. "Calling people gooks, making threats. Let's face it, Porchoff, your personality needs some upgrading."

"But they won't give me a chance," Porchoff said. "All I ever do is cook food. I put it on their plates and they make some crack and walk on by."

Hooper was still gazing up at the clouds, feeling the soft rain on his face. Birds were starting to sing in the woods beyond the fence. "I don't know. It's just part of this rut we're all in." He lowered his head and looked over at Porchoff, sitting there hunched inside his poncho, shaking as little tremors passed through him. "Any day now," Hooper said, "everything's going to change."

"My dad was in the National Guard back in Ohio," Porchoff said. "He's always talking about the great experiences he and his buddies used to have. Nothing like that ever happens to me." He looked down at the table, then looked up and said, "How about you? What was your best time?"

"My best time," Hooper said. He thought of telling some sort of lie, but the effort of making things up was beyond him, and the memory Porchoff wanted was close at hand. For Hooper it was closer than the memory of home. In truth it was a kind of home. It was where he went to be back with his friends again, and his old self. "Vietnam," he said.

Porchoff just looked at him.

"We didn't know it then," Hooper said. "We used to talk about how when we got back in the world we were going to do this and we were going to do that. Back in the world we were going to have it made. But ever since then it's been nothing but confusion." Hooper took the cigarette case from his pocket but didn't open it. He leaned forward on the table.

"Everything was clear," he said. "You learned what you had to know and forgot the rest. All this chickenshit. You didn't spend every minute of the day thinking about your own sorry-ass little self. Am I getting laid enough? What's wrong with my kid? Should I insulate the fucking house? That's what does it to you, Porchoff. Thinking about yourself. That's what kills you in the end."

Porchoff hadn't moved. In the gray light Hooper could see Porchoff's fingers spread out before him on the tabletop, white and still as if they'd been drawn there in chalk. His face was the same color.

"You think you've got problems, Porchoff, but they wouldn't last five minutes in the field. There's nothing wrong with you that a little search-and-destroy wouldn't cure." Hooper paused, smiling to himself, already deep in the memory. He wanted to bring it back for Porchoff, put it into words so that Porchoff could see it too, the beauty of that life, the faith so deep that in time you were not separate men anymore, but part of one another.

But the words came hard. Hooper saw that Porchoff did not understand, and that he could not make him understand. He said, "You'll see, Porchoff. You'll get your chance."

Porchoff stared at him. "You're crazy," he said.

"We're all going to get another chance," Hooper said. "I can feel it coming. Otherwise I'd take my walking papers and hat up. You'll see. All you need is a little contact. The rest of us too. Get us out of this rut."

Porchoff shook his head. "You're really crazy."

"Let's call it a day," Hooper said. He stood and held out his hand. "Give me the rifle."

"No," Porchoff pulled the rifle closer. "Not to you."

"There's no one here but me," Hooper said.

"Go get Captain King."

"Captain King's asleep."

"Then wake him up."

"No," Hooper said. "I'm not going to tell you again, Porchoff, give me the rifle." He walked toward him but stopped when Porchoff picked the weapon up and pointed it at his chest.

"Leave me alone," Porchoff said.

"Relax," Hooper told him. "I'm not going to hurt you."

Porchoff licked his lips. "No," he said. "Not you."

Behind Hooper a voice called out, "Hey! Porkchop! Drop it!"

Porchoff sat bolt upright. "Jesus," he said.

"It's Trac," Hooper said. "Put the rifle down, Porchoff—now!"

"Drop it!" Trac shouted.

"Oh, Jesus," Porchoff said, and stumbled to his feet with the rifle still in his hands. Then his head flapped and his helmet flew off and he toppled backward over the bench. Hooper's heart leaped as the shock of the blast hit him. Then the sound went through him and beyond him and into the trees and the sky, echoing on in the distance like thunder. Afterward there was silence. Hooper took a step forward, then sank to his knees and lowered his forehead to the wet grass. The rain fell around him with a soft whispering sound. A blue jay squawked.

Hooper heard the swish of boots through the grass behind him. He sat back on his heels and drew a long breath.

"You okay?" Trac said.

Hooper nodded.

Trac walked on to where Porchoff lay. He said something in Vietnamese, then looked back at Hooper and shook his head.

Hooper tried to stand but went to his knees again.

"You need a hand?" Trac asked.

"I guess so," Hooper said.

Trac came over to Hooper. He slung his rifle and bent down and the two men gripped each other's wrists. Trac's skin was dry and smooth, his bones as small as a child's. "Go for it," he said, tensing as Hooper pulled himself to his feet, and for a moment they stood face-to-face, swaying slightly, hands still locked. "All right," Hooper said. Each of them slowly loosened his grip.

In a soft voice, almost a whisper, Trac said, "They gonna put me away?"

"No," Hooper said. He walked over to Porchoff and looked down at him. He immediately turned away and saw that Trac was still swaying, his eyes glassy. "Better get off those legs," Hooper said. Trac looked at him dreamily, then unslung his rifle and leaned it against the picnic table farthest from Porchoff. He sat down and took his helmet off and rested his head on his crossed forearms.

The wind had picked up again, carrying with it the whine of distant engines. Hooper fumbled a cigarette out of his case and smoked it down, staring toward the woods, feeling the rain stream down his face and neck. When the cigarette went out Hooper dropped it, then picked it up again and crumbled the tobacco around his feet so that no trace of it remained. He put his cap back on and raised the hood of his poncho. "How's it going?" he said to Trac.

Trac looked up. He began to rub his forehead, pushing his fingers in little circles above his eyes.

Hooper sat down across from him. "We don't have a whole lot of time," he said.

Trac nodded. He put his helmet on and looked at Hooper.

"All right, son," Hooper said. "Let's get our story together."

The Rich Brother

There were two brothers, Pete and Donald.

Pete, the older brother, was in real estate. He and his wife had a Century 21 franchise in Santa Cruz. Pete worked hard and made a lot of money, but not any more than he thought he deserved. He had two daughters, a sailboat, a house from which he could see a thin slice of the ocean, and friends doing well enough in their own lives not to wish bad luck on him. Donald, the younger brother, was still single. He lived alone, painted houses when he found the work, and got deeper in debt to Pete when he didn't.

No one would have taken them for brothers. Where Pete was stout and hearty and at home in the world, Donald was bony, grave, and obsessed with the fate of his soul. Over the years Donald had worn the images of two different Perfect Masters around his neck. Out of devotion to the second of these he entered an ashram in Berkeley, where he nearly died of undiagnosed hepatitis. By the time Pete finished paying the medical bills Donald had become a Christian. He drifted from church to church, then joined a Pentecostal community that met somewhere in the Mission District to sing in tongues and swap prophecies.

Pete couldn't make sense of it. Their parents were both dead, but while they were alive neither of them had found it necessary to believe that gods and devils were personally interested in securing their company for all eternity. They managed to be decent people without making fools of themselves, and Pete had the same ambition.

He thought the whole thing was an excuse for Donald to take himself seriously.

The trouble was that Donald couldn't content himself with worrying about his own soul. He had to worry about everyone else's, and especially Pete's. He handed down his judgments in ways he thought subtle: through significant silence, innuendo, looks of mild despair that said, *Brother, what have you come to?* What Pete had come to, as far as he could tell, was prosperity. That was the real issue between them. Pete prospered and Donald did not prosper.

At the age of forty Pete took up skydiving. He made his first jump with two friends who'd started only a few months earlier and were already doing stunts. Pete would never use the word "mystical," but that was how he felt about the experience. Later he made the mistake of describing it to Donald, who kept asking how much it cost and then acted appalled when Pete told him.

"At least I'm trying something new," Pete said. "At least I'm breaking the pattern."

Not long after that conversation Donald also broke the pattern, by moving to a farm outside Paso Robles. The farm was owned by several members of Donald's community, who'd bought it with the idea of forming a family of faith. That was how Donald explained it in the first letter he sent. Every week Pete heard how happy Donald was, how "in the Lord." He told Pete they were all praying for him, he and the rest of Pete's brothers and sisters on the farm.

I only have one brother, Pete wanted to answer, *and that's enough.* But he kept this thought to himself.

In November the letters stopped. Pete didn't worry about this at first, but when he called at Thanksgiving Donald was grim. He tried to sound upbeat, but didn't try hard enough to make it convincing. "Now listen," Pete said, "you don't have to stay in that place if you don't want to."

"I'll be all right," Donald answered.

"That's not the point. Being all right is not the point. If you don't like what's going on up there, then get out."

"I'm all right," Donald said again, more firmly. "I'm doing fine."

But he called Pete a week later and said that he was quitting the farm. When Pete asked him where he intended to go, Donald admitted that he had no plan. His car had been repossessed just before he left the city, and he was flat broke.

"I guess you'll have to stay with us," Pete said.

Donald put up a show of resistance. Then he gave in. "Just until I get my feet on the ground."

"Right," Pete said. "Check out your options." He told Donald he'd send him money for a bus ticket, but as they were about to hang up Pete changed his mind. He knew that Donald would try hitchhiking to save the fare, and he didn't want him out on the road all alone where some creep could pick him up, where anything could happen. "Better yet," he said, "I'll come and get you."

"You don't have to do that. I didn't expect you to do that," Donald said. "It's a pretty long drive."

"Just tell me how to get there."

But Donald wouldn't give him directions. He said the farm was too depressing, that Pete wouldn't like it. Instead, he insisted on meeting him at a service station called Jonathan's Mechanical Emporium.

"You must be kidding," Pete said.

"It's close to the highway," Donald told him. "I didn't name it."

"That's one for the collection," Pete said.

The day before he left to bring Donald home, Pete received a letter from a man who described himself as "head of household" at the farm where Donald had been living. He told Pete that Donald had not quit the farm but had been asked to leave. The letter was written on the back of a mimeographed survey form asking people to record their response to a ceremony of some kind. The last question read:

What did you feel during the liturgy?
a) Being
b) Becoming
c) Being and Becoming
d) None of the Above
e) All of the Above

Pete tried to forget the letter, but of course he couldn't. Each time he thought of it he felt crowded and breathless, the same feeling that came over him when he drove into the service station and saw his brother sitting against a wall with his head on his knees. It was late afternoon. A paper cup tumbled slowly past his feet, pushed by the damp wind.

Pete honked and Donald raised his head. He smiled at Pete, then stood and stretched. His arms were long and thin and white. He wore a red bandanna across his forehead and a T-shirt with a logo on the front that Pete couldn't read because the letters were inverted.

"Grow up," Pete yelled. "Get a Mercedes."

Donald came up to the window. He bent down and said, "Thanks for coming. You must be totally whipped."

"I'll make it." Pete pointed at the T-shirt. "What's that supposed to say?"

Donald looked down at his shirt front. "TRY GOD. I guess I put it on backwards. Pete, could I borrow a couple dollars? I owe these people for coffee and sandwiches."

Pete took five twenties from his wallet and held them out the window.

Donald stepped back as if horrified. "I don't need that much."

"I can't keep track of all these nickels and dimes," Pete said. "Just pay me back when your ship comes in." He waved the bills impatiently. "Go on—take it."

"Only for now." Donald took the money and went into the service station. He came out carrying two orange sodas, one of which he handed to Pete as he got into the car. "My treat," he said.

"No bags?"

"Wow, thanks for reminding me." Donald balanced his drink on the dashboard, but the slight rocking of the car as he got out tipped it onto the passenger's seat, where half its contents foamed over before Pete could snatch it up again. Donald looked on while Pete held the bottle out the window, soda running down his fingers.

"Wipe it up," Pete told him. "Quick!"

"With what?"

Pete stared at him. "That shirt. Use the shirt."

Donald pulled a long face but did as he was told, his pale skin puckering against the wind.

"Great, just great," Pete said. "We haven't even left the gas station yet."

Afterward, on the highway, Donald said, "This is a new car, isn't it?"

"Yes. This is a new car."

"Is that why you're so upset about the seat?"

"Forget it, okay? Let's just forget about it."

"I said I was sorry."

"I just wish you'd be more careful," Pete said. "These seats are made of leather. That stain won't come out, not to mention the smell. I don't see why I can't have leather seats that smell like leather instead of orange pop."

"What was wrong with the other car?"

Pete glanced over and saw that Donald had raised the hood of the blue sweatshirt he'd put on. The peaked hood above his gaunt, watchful face gave him the look of an inquisitor.

"There wasn't anything wrong with it," Pete said. "I just happened to like this one better."

Donald nodded.

There was a long silence between them as Pete drove on and the day darkened. On either side of the road lay stubble-covered fields. Low hills ran along the horizon, topped here and there with trees black against the evening sky. In the approaching line of cars a driver turned on his headlights. Pete did the same.

"So what happened?" he asked. "Farm life not your bag?"

Donald took some time to answer, and at last he said, simply, "It was my fault."

"What was your fault?"

"The whole thing. Don't play dumb, Pete. I know they wrote to you." He looked at Pete, then stared out the windshield again.

"I'm not playing dumb."

Donald shrugged.

"All I really know is they asked you to leave," Pete went on. "I don't know any of the particulars."

"I blew it," Donald said. "Believe me, you don't want to hear the gory details."

"Sure I do," Pete said. He added, "Everybody likes the gory details."

"You mean everybody likes to hear how someone else messed up."

"Right," Pete said. "That's how it is here on Spaceship Earth."

Donald bent one knee onto the front seat and leaned against the door. Pete was aware of his scrutiny. He waited. Night was coming on in a rush, filling the hollows of the land. Donald's long cheeks and deep-set eyes were dark with shadow. His brow was white. "Do you ever dream about me?" he asked.

"Do I ever dream about you? What kind of a question is that? Of course I don't dream about you," Pete said, untruthfully.

"What do you dream about?"

"Sex and money. Mostly money. A nightmare is when I dream I don't have any."

"You're just making that up," Donald said.

Pete smiled.

"Sometimes I wake up at night," Donald went on, "and I can tell you're dreaming about me."

"We were talking about the farm," Pete said. "Let's finish that conversation and then we can talk about our various out-of-body experiences and the interesting things we did during previous incarnations."

For a moment Donald looked like a grinning skull; then he turned serious again. "There's not that much to tell," he said. "I just didn't do anything right."

"That's a little vague," Pete said.

"Well, like the groceries. Whenever it was my turn to get the groceries I'd blow it somehow. I'd bring the groceries home and half of them would be missing, or I'd have all the wrong things, the wrong kind of flour or the wrong kind of chocolate or whatever. One time I gave them away. It's not funny, Pete."

Pete said, "Who'd you give the groceries to?"

"Just some people I picked up driving home. Some field-workers. They had about eight kids with them and didn't even speak English— just nodded their heads. Still, I shouldn't have given away the groceries. Not all of them, anyway. I really learned my lesson about that. You have to be practical. You have to be fair to yourself." Donald leaned forward, and Pete could sense his excitement. "There's nothing actually wrong with being in business," he said. "As long as you're fair to other people you can still be fair to yourself. I'm thinking of going into business, Pete."

"We'll talk about it," Pete said. "So, that's the story? There isn't any more to it than that?"

"What did they tell you?" Donald asked.

"Nothing."

"They must've told you something."

Pete shook his head.

"They didn't tell you about the fire?" When Pete shook his head again Donald regarded him for a time, then folded his arms across his chest and slumped back into the corner. "Everybody had to take turns cooking dinner. I usually did tuna casserole or spaghetti with garlic bread. But this one night I thought I'd do something different, something really interesting." He looked sharply at Pete. "It's all a big laugh to you, isn't it?"

"I'm sorry," Pete said.

"You don't know when to quit. You just keep hitting away."

"Tell me about the fire, Donald."

Donald kept watching him. "You have this compulsion to make me look foolish."

"Come off it, Donald. Don't make a big thing out of this."

"I know why you do it. It's because you don't have any purpose in life. You're afraid to relate to people who do, so you make fun of them."

"Relate," Pete said.

"You're basically a very frightened individual," Donald said. "Very threatened. You've always been like that. Do you remember when you used to try to kill me?"

"I don't have any compulsion to make you look foolish, Donald— you do it yourself. You're doing it right now."

"You can't tell me you don't remember," Donald said. "It was after my operation. You remember that."

"Sort of." Pete shrugged. "Not really."

"Oh yes," Donald said. "Do you want to see the scar?"

"I remember you had an operation. I don't remember the specifics, that's all. And I sure as hell don't remember trying to kill you."

"Oh yes," Donald repeated, maddeningly. "You bet your life you did. All the time. The thing was, I couldn't have anything happen to me where they sewed me up because then my intestines would come apart again and poison me. That was a big issue, Pete. Mom was always in a state about me climbing trees and so on. And you used to hit me there every chance you got."

"Mom was in a state every time you burped," Pete said. "I don't know. Maybe I bumped into you accidentally once or twice. I never did it deliberately."

"Every chance you got," Donald said. "Like when the folks went out at night and left you to babysit. I'd hear them say good night, and then I'd hear the car start up, and when they were gone I'd lie there and listen. After a while I could hear you coming down the hall, and I'd close my eyes and pretend to be asleep. There were nights when you'd stand outside the door, just stand there, and then go away again.

But most nights you'd open the door and I'd hear you in the room with me, breathing. You'd come over and sit next to me on the bed—you remember, Pete, you have to—you'd sit next to me on the bed and pull the sheets back. If I was on my stomach you'd roll me over. Then you would lift up my pajama top and start hitting me on my stitches. As hard as you could, over and over. I was afraid you'd get mad if you knew I was awake. Is that strange or what? I was afraid you'd get mad if you found out that I knew you were trying to kill me." Donald laughed. "Come on, you can't tell me you don't remember that."

"It might have happened once or twice. Kids do those things. I can't get all excited about something I maybe did twenty-five years ago."

"No maybe about it. You did it."

Pete said, "You're wearing me out with this stuff. We've got a long drive ahead of us, and if you don't back off pretty soon we aren't going to make it. You aren't, anyway."

Donald turned away.

"I'm doing my best," Pete said. The self-pity in his voice made this sound like a lie. But it wasn't a lie! He *was* doing his best.

The car topped a rise. In the distance Pete saw a cluster of lights that blinked out when he started downhill. There was no moon. The sky was low and black.

"Come to think of it," Pete said, "I did have a dream about you the other night. Quite a few nights ago, actually. Are you hungry?"

"What kind of dream?"

"It was strange. You were taking care of me. Just the two of us. I don't know where everyone else was supposed to be."

Pete left it at that. He didn't tell Donald that in this dream he was blind.

"I wonder if that was when I woke up," Donald said. "Look, I'm sorry I got into that thing about my scar. I keep trying to forget it but I guess I never will. Not really. It was pretty strange, having someone around all the time who wanted to get rid of me."

"Kid stuff," Pete said. "Ancient history."

They ate dinner at a Denny's on the other side of King City. As Pete was paying the check he heard a man behind him say, "Excuse me, but I wonder if I might ask which direction you're going in?"

Donald answered, "Santa Cruz."

"Perfect," the man said.

Pete could see him in the fish-eye mirror above the cash register: a red blazer with some kind of crest on the pocket, little black mustache, glossy black hair combed down on his forehead like a Roman emperor's. *A rug,* Pete thought. *Definitely a rug.*

He got his change and turned. "Why is that perfect?" he asked.

The man looked at Pete. He had a soft ruddy face that was doing its best to express pleasant surprise, as if this new wrinkle were all he could have wished for, but the eyes behind the aviator glasses showed signs of regret. His lips were moist and shiny. "I take it you're together," he said.

"You got it," Pete told him.

"All the better, then," the man went on. "It so happens I'm going to Santa Cruz myself. Had a spot of car trouble down the road. The old Caddy let me down."

"What kind of trouble?" Pete asked.

"Engine trouble," the man said. "I'm afraid it's a bit urgent. My daughter is sick. Urgently sick. I've got a telegram here." He patted the breast pocket of his blazer.

Before Pete could say anything Donald got into the act again. "No problem," he said. "We've got tons of room."

"Not that much room," Pete said.

Donald nodded. "I'll put my things in the trunk."

"The trunk's full," Pete told him.

"It so happens I'm traveling light," the man said. "This leg of the trip, anyway. In fact I don't have any luggage at this particular time."

Pete said, "Left it in the old Caddy, did you?"

"Exactly," the man said.

"No problem," Donald repeated. He walked outside, and the man

82

went with him, Pete following at a distance. When they reached Pete's car Donald raised his face to the sky, and the man did the same. They stood there looking up. "Dark night," Donald said.

"Stygian," the man said.

Pete still had it in mind to brush him off, but he didn't. Instead he unlocked the car and opened the back door for him. He wanted to see what would happen. It was an adventure, though not a dangerous adventure. The man might steal Pete's ashtrays but he wouldn't kill him. If anyone killed Pete on the road it would be some spiritual person in a sweat suit, someone with his eyes on the far horizon and a wet TRY GOD T-shirt in his duffel bag.

As soon as they left the parking lot the man lit a cigar. He blew a cloud of smoke over Pete's shoulder and sighed with pleasure.

"Put it out," Pete told him.

"Of course," the man said. Pete looked into the rearview mirror and saw the man take another long puff before dropping the cigar out the window. "Forgive me," he said. "I should have asked. Name's Webster, by the way."

Donald turned and looked back at him. "First name or last?"

The man hesitated. "Last," he said finally.

"I know a Webster," Donald said. "Mick Webster."

"There are many of us," Webster said.

"Big fellow, wooden leg," Pete said.

Donald gave Pete a look.

Webster shook his head. "Doesn't ring a bell. Still, I wouldn't deny the connection. Might be one of the cousinry."

"What's your daughter got?" Pete asked.

"That isn't clear," Webster answered. "It appears to be a female complaint of some nature. Then again it may be tropical." He was quiet for a moment, and added: "If indeed it *is* tropical, I will have to assume some of the blame myself. It was my own vaulting ambition that first led us to the tropics and kept us there all those many years, exposed to every evil. Truly, I have much to answer for. I left my wife there."

"You mean she died?" Donald asked.

"I buried her with these hands. The earth will be repaid, gold for gold."

"Which tropics?" Pete asked.

"The tropics of Peru."

"What part of Peru are they in?"

"The lowlands," Webster said.

"What's it like down there? In the lowlands."

"Another world," Webster said. His tone was sepulchral. "A world better imagined than described."

"Far out," Pete said.

The three men rode in silence for a time. A line of trucks went past in the other direction, trailers festooned with running lights, engines roaring.

"Yes," Webster said at last, "I have much to answer for."

Pete smiled at Donald, but he'd turned in his seat again and was gazing at Webster. "I'm sorry about your wife," Donald said.

"What did she die of?" Pete asked.

"A wasting illness," Webster said. "The doctors have no name for it, but I do." He leaned forward and said, fiercely, "*Greed.* Mine, not hers. She wanted no part of it."

Pete bit his lip. Webster was a find, and Pete didn't want to scare him off by hooting at him. In a voice low and innocent of knowingness, he asked, "What took you there?"

"It's difficult for me to talk about."

"Try," Pete told him.

"A cigar would make it easier."

Donald turned to Pete and said, "It's okay with me."

"All right," Pete said. "Go ahead. Just keep the window rolled down."

"Much obliged." A match flared. There were eager sucking sounds.

"Let's hear it," Pete said.

"I am by training an engineer," Webster began. "My work has exposed me to all but one of the continents, to desert and alp and forest, to every terrain and season of the earth. Some years ago I was hired by the Peruvian government to search for tungsten in the tropics. My wife and daughter accompanied me. We were the only white people for a thousand miles in any direction, and we had no choice but to live as the Indians lived—to share their food and drink and even their culture."

"You knew the lingo, did you?" Pete said.

"We picked it up." The ember of the cigar bobbed up and down. "We were used to learning as necessity decreed. At any rate, it became evident after a couple of years that there was no tungsten to be found. My wife had fallen ill and was pleading to be taken home. But I was deaf to her pleas, because by then I was on the trail of another metal—a metal far more valuable than tungsten."

"Let me guess," Pete said. "Gold?"

Donald looked at Pete, then back at Webster.

"Gold," Webster said. "A vein of gold greater than the Mother Lode itself. After I found the first traces of it nothing could tear me away from my search—not the sickness of my wife nor anything else. I was determined to uncover the vein, and so I did, but not before I laid my wife to rest. As I say, the earth will be repaid."

Webster was quiet. Then he said, "But life must go on. In the years since my wife's death I've been making the necessary arrangements to open the mine. I could have done it immediately, of course, enriching myself beyond measure, but I knew what that would mean—the exploitation of our beloved Indians, the brutal destruction of their environment. I felt I had too much to atone for already." Webster paused, and when he spoke again his voice was dull and rushed, as if he'd used up all the interest he had in his own words. "Instead I drew up a program for returning the bulk of the wealth to the Indians themselves. A kind of trust fund. The interest alone will allow them to secure their ancient lands and rights in perpetuity. At the same time, our investors will be rewarded a thousandfold. Two thousandfold. Everyone will prosper together."

"That's great," Donald said. "That's the way it ought to be."

Pete said, "I'm willing to bet you have a few shares left. Am I right?"

Webster made no reply.

"Well?" Pete knew that Webster was on to him now, but he didn't care. The story had bored him. He'd expected something different, something original, and Webster had let him down. He hadn't even tried. Pete felt sour and stale. His eyes burned from cigar smoke and the high beams of road-hogging truckers. "Douse the stogie," he said to Webster. "I told you to keep the window down."

"Got a little nippy back here."

"Hey, Pete," Donald said. "Lighten up."

"Douse it!"

Webster sighed, then slipped the cigar out the window.

"I'm a wreck," Pete said to Donald. "You want to drive for a while?"

"Too much! I was just about to offer! I mean, the words were right on the tip of my tongue."

Pete pulled over and they changed places.

Webster kept his own counsel in the backseat. Donald hummed while he drove, until Pete told him to stop. Then everything was quiet.

Donald was humming again when Pete woke up. He stared sullenly at the road, at the white lines sliding past the car. After a few moments of this he turned and said, "How long have I been out?"

Donald glanced at him. "Twenty, twenty-five minutes."

Pete looked behind him and saw that Webster was gone. "Where's our friend?"

"You just missed him. He got out in Soledad. He told me to say thanks and good-bye."

"Soledad? What about his sick daughter? How did he explain her away?"

"He has a brother living there. He's going to borrow a car from him and drive the rest of the way in the morning."

"I'll bet his brother's living there," Pete said. "Doing fifty concurrent life sentences. His brother and his sister and his mom and his dad."

"I kind of liked him," Donald said.

"I'm sure you did," Pete said.

"He was interesting. He'd been places."

"His cigars had been places, I'll give you that."

"Come on, Pete."

"Come on yourself. What a phony."

"You don't know that."

"Sure I do."

"How? How do you know?"

Pete stretched. "Brother, there are some things you're just born knowing. What's the gas situation?"

"We're a little low."

"Then why didn't you get some more?"

"I wish you wouldn't snap at me like that," Donald said.

"Then why don't you use your head? What if we run out?"

"We'll make it," Donald said. "I'm pretty sure we've got enough to make it. You didn't have to be so rude to him."

"I don't feel like running out of gas tonight, okay?"

Donald pulled in at the next station they came to and filled the tank while Pete went to the men's room. When Pete came back, Donald was sitting in the passenger's seat. As Pete got in behind the wheel the attendant came up to his window, bent down, and said, "Twenty-one fifty-five."

"You heard the man," Pete said to Donald.

Donald looked straight ahead. He didn't move.

"Cough up," Pete said. "This trip's on you."

"I can't."

"Sure you can. Break out that wad."

"Please," he said. "Pete, I don't have it anymore."

Pete took this in. He nodded, and paid the attendant.

Donald began to speak when they pulled out but Pete cut him off. He said, "I don't want to hear from you right now. You just keep quiet or I swear to God I won't be responsible."

They left the fields and entered a forest of tall pines. The trees went on and on. "Let me get this straight," Pete said at last. "You don't have the money I gave you."

"You treated him like a bug or something," Donald said.

"You don't have the money," Pete said again.

Donald shook his head.

"Since I bought dinner, and since we didn't stop anywhere in between, I assume you gave it to Webster. Is that right? Is that what you did with it?"

"Yes."

Pete looked at Donald. His face was dark under the hood but he still managed to convey a sense of remove, as if none of this had anything to do with him.

"Why?" Pete asked. "Why did you give it to him?" When Donald didn't answer, Pete said, "A hundred dollars, gone. Just like that. I *worked* for that money, Donald."

"I know, I know," Donald said.

"You don't know! How could you? You get money by holding out your hand."

"I work too," Donald said.

"You work too? Don't kid yourself, brother." Donald leaned toward him, about to say something, but Pete cut him off again. "You're not the only person on the payroll, Donald. I don't think you understand that. I have a family."

"Pete, I'll pay you back."

"Like hell you will. A hundred dollars!" Pete hit the steering wheel with the palm of his hand. "Just because you think I hurt some goofball's feelings. Jesus, Donald."

"That's not the reason," Donald said. "And I didn't just *give* him the money."

"What do you call it, then? What do you call what you did?"

"I *invested* it. I wanted a share, Pete." When Pete looked over at him Donald nodded and said again, "I wanted a share."

Pete said, "I take it you're referring to the gold mine in Peru."

"Yes," Donald said.

"You believe that such a gold mine exists?"

Donald looked at him, and Pete could see he was just beginning to catch on. "You'll believe anything, won't you?" Pete said. "You really will believe anything at all."

"I'm sorry," Donald said, and turned away.

Pete drove on between the trees and considered the truth of what he'd just said—that Donald would believe anything at all. And it came to him that it would be just like this unfair life for Donald to come out ahead in the end, by believing in some outrageous promise that turned out to be true and that he, Pete, rejected out of hand because he was too wised up to listen to anybody's pitch anymore, except for laughs. What a joke. What a joke if there really was a blessing to be had, and the blessing didn't come to the one who deserved it, the one who did all the work, but to the other.

And as if this had already happened Pete felt a shadow move upon him, darkening his thoughts. After a time he said, "I can see where all this is going, Donald."

"I'll pay you back," Donald said.

"No," Pete said. "You won't pay me back. You can't. You don't know how. All you've ever done is take. All your life."

Donald shook his head.

"I see exactly where this is going," Pete went on. "You can't work, you can't take care of yourself, you believe anything anyone tells you. I'm stuck with you, aren't I?" He looked over at Donald. "I've got you on my hands for good."

Donald pressed his fingers against the dashboard as if to brace himself. "I'll get out," he said.

Pete kept driving.

"Let me out," Donald said. "I mean it, Pete."

"Do you?"

Donald hesitated. "Yes," he said.

"Be sure," Pete told him. "This is it. This is for keeps."

"I mean it."

"All right. You made the choice." Pete braked the car sharply and swung onto the shoulder. He turned off the engine and got out. Trees loomed on both sides of the road, shutting out the sky. The air was cold and musty. Pete took Donald's duffel bag from the backseat and set it down behind the car. He stood there, facing Donald in the red glow of the taillights. "It's better this way," Pete said.

Donald just looked at him.

"Better for you," Pete said.

Donald hugged himself. He was shaking. "You don't have to say all that," he told Pete. "I don't blame you."

"Blame me? What the hell are you talking about? Blame me for what?"

"For anything," Donald said.

"I want to know what you mean about blaming me."

"Nothing. Nothing, Pete. You'd better get going. God bless you."

"That's it," Pete said, and took a step toward Donald.

Donald touched Pete's shoulder. "You'd better go," he said.

Somewhere in the trees overhead a branch snapped. Pete looked up, and felt the fists he'd made of his hands. He turned his back on Donald and walked to the car and drove away. He drove fast, hunched over the wheel, conscious of how he was hunched and the shallowness of his breathing, refusing to look at the mirror above his head until there was nothing behind him but darkness.

Then he said, "A hundred dollars," as if there were someone to hear.

The trees gave way to fields. Pete drove on between metal fences plastered with windblown scraps of paper. Tule fog hung above the ditches, spilling into the road, dimming the ghostly halogen lights that burned in the yards of the farms he passed. The fog left beads of water rolling up the windshield.

Pete rummaged among his cassettes. He found Pachelbel's Canon and pushed it into the tape deck. When the violins began to play he leaned back and assumed an attentive expression, as if he really were listening to them. He smiled to himself like a man at liberty to enjoy music, a man who has finished his work and settled his debts, done all things meet and due.

And in this way, smiling, nodding to the music, he went another mile or two and pretended that he was not already slowing down, that he wouldn't turn back, that he would be able to drive on like this, alone, and have the right answer when his wife stood before him in the doorway of his home and asked, *Where is he? Where is your brother?*

Leviathan

On her thirtieth birthday Ted threw a surprise party for Helen. A small party—Mitch and Bliss were the only guests. They'd chipped in with Ted and bought Helen three grams of white-out blizzard that lasted the whole night and on into the next morning. When it got light enough everyone went for a swim in the courtyard pool. Then Ted took Mitch up to the sauna on the fifth floor while Helen and Bliss put together a monster omelette.

"So how does it feel," Bliss said, "being thirty?" The ash fell off her cigarette into the eggs. She stared at the ash for a moment, then stirred it in. "Mitch had his fortieth last month and totally freaked. He did so much Maalox he started to taste like chalk. I thought he was going to start freebasing it or something."

"Mitch is *forty*?" Helen said.

Bliss looked over at her. "That's classified information, okay?"

"Incredible. He looks about twenty-five, maybe twenty-seven at the absolute most." Helen watched Bliss crumble bacon into the bowl. "Oh, God," she said, "I don't believe it. He had a face-lift."

Bliss closed her eyes and leaned against the counter. "I shouldn't have told you. Please don't say anything," she murmured hopelessly.

When Mitch and Ted came back from the sauna they all had another toot, and Ted gave Helen the mirror to lick. He said he'd never seen three grams disappear so fast. Afterward Helen served up the omelette while Ted tried to find something on TV. He kept flipping the dial until it drove everyone crazy, looking for Road Runner cartoons, then he gave up and tuned in on the last part of a movie about the Bataan Death March. They didn't watch it for very long, though, because Bliss started to cry and hyperventilate. "Come on, everyone," said Mitch. "Love circle." Ted and Mitch went over to Bliss and put their arms around her while Helen watched them from the sofa, sipping espresso from a cup as blue and dainty as a robin's egg— the last of a set her grandmother had brought from the old country. Helen would have hugged Bliss too but there wasn't really any point; Bliss pulled this stunt almost every time she got herself a noseful, and it just had to run its course.

When Helen finished her espresso she gathered the plates and carried them out to the kitchen. She scattered leftover toast into the courtyard below and watched the squirrels carry it away as she scoured the dishes and listened to the proceedings in the next room. This time it was Ted who talked Bliss down. "You're beautiful," he kept telling her. It was the same thing he always said to Helen when she felt depressed, and she was beginning to feel depressed right now.

She needed more fuel, she decided. She ducked into the bedroom and did a couple of lines from Ted's private stash, which she'd discovered while searching for matches in the closet. Afterward she looked at herself in the mirror. Her eyes were bright. They seemed lit from within and that was how Helen felt, as if there were a column of cool white light pouring from her head to her feet. She put on a pair of sunglasses so nobody would notice and went back to the kitchen.

Mitch was standing at the counter, rolling a bone. "How's the birthday girl?" he asked without looking up.

"Ready for the next one," Helen said. "How about you?"

"Hey, bring it on," Mitch answered.

At that moment Helen came close to letting him know she knew, but she held back. Mitch was good people and so was Bliss. Helen didn't want to make trouble between them. All the same, Helen knew that someday she wasn't going to be able to stop herself from giving Mitch the business. It just had to happen. And Helen knew that Bliss knew. Still, she hadn't done it this morning and felt good about that.

Mitch held up the joint. "Taste?"

Helen shook her head. She glanced over her shoulder toward the living room. "What's the story on Bliss?" she asked. "All bummed out over World War Two? Ted should've known that movie would set her off."

Mitch picked a sliver of weed from his lower lip. "Her ex is threatening to move back to Boston. Which means she won't get to see her kids except during the summer, and that's only if we can put together the scratch to fly them here and back. It's tough. Really tough."

"I guess," Helen said. She dried her hands and hung the towel on the refrigerator door. "Still, Bliss should've thought about that before she took a walk on them, right?"

Mitch turned and started out of the kitchen.

"Sorry," Helen called after him. "I wasn't thinking."

"Yes you were," Mitch said, and left her there.

Oh, hell, she thought. She decided she needed another line but made no move to get it. Helen stood where she was, looking down at the pool through the window above the sink. The manager's Afghan dog was lapping water from the shallow end, legs braced in the trough that ran around the pool. The two British Airways stewardesses from down the hall were bathing their white bodies in the morning sunshine, both wearing blue swimsuits. The redheaded girl from upstairs was floating on an air mattress. Helen could see its long shadow gliding along the bottom of the pool like something stalking her.

Helen heard Ted say, "Jesus, Bliss, I can understand that. Everyone has those feelings. You can't always beat them down." Bliss answered him in a voice so soft that Helen gave up trying to hear; it was hardly more than a sigh. She poured herself a glass of Chablis and joined the others in the living room. They were all sitting cross-legged on the floor. Helen caught Mitch's eye and mouthed the word *Sorry.* He stared at her, then nodded.

"I've done worse things than that," Ted was saying. "I'll bet Mitch has too."

"Plenty worse," Mitch said.

"Worse than what?" Helen asked.

"It's awful." Bliss looked down at her hands. "I'd be embarrassed to tell you." She was all cried out now, Helen could see that. Her eyes were heavy-lidded and serene, her cheeks flushed, and a little smile played over her swollen lips.

"It couldn't be that bad," Helen said.

Ted leaned forward. He still had on the bathrobe he'd worn to the sauna and it fell open almost to his waist, as Helen knew he intended it to. His chest was hard-looking from the Nautilus machine in the basement, and dark from their trip to Mazatlán. Helen had to admit it, he looked great. She didn't understand why he had to be so obvious and crass, but he got what he wanted: she stared at him and so did Bliss.

"Bliss, it *isn't* that bad," Ted went on. "It's just one of those things." He turned to Helen. "Bliss's little girl came down with tonsillitis last month and Bliss never got it together to go see her in the hospital."

"I can't deal with hospitals," Bliss said. "The minute I set foot inside of one my stomach starts doing flips. But still. When I think of her all alone in there."

Mitch took Bliss's hands in his and looked right at her until she met his gaze. "It's over," he said. "The operation's over and Lisa's out of the hospital and she's all right. Say it, Bliss. *She's all right.*"

"She's all right," Bliss said.

"Again."

"She's all right," Bliss repeated.

"Okay. Now believe it." Mitch put her hands together and rubbed them gently between his palms. "We've built up this big myth about kids being helpless and vulnerable and so on because it makes us feel important. We think we're playing some heavy role just because we're parents. We don't give kids any credit at all. Kids are tough little monkeys. Kids are survivors."

Bliss smiled.

"But I don't know," Mitch said. He let go of Bliss's hands and leaned back. "What I said just then is probably complete bullshit. Everything I say these days sounds like bullshit."

"We've all done worse things," Ted told Bliss. He looked over at Helen. When Helen saw that he was waiting for her to agree with him she tried to think of something to say. Ted kept looking at her. "What have you got those things on for?" he asked.

"The light hurts my eyes."

"Then close the curtains." He reached across to Helen and lifted the sunglasses away from her face. "There," he said. He cupped her chin in one hand and with the other brushed her hair back from her forehead. "Isn't she something?"

"She'll do," Mitch said.

Ted stroked Helen's cheek with the back of his hand. "I'd kill for that face."

Bliss was studying Helen. "So lovely," she said in a solemn, wistful voice.

Helen laughed. She got up and drew the curtains shut. Spangles of light glittered in the fabric. She moved across the dim room to the dining nook and brought back a candle from the table there. Ted lit the candle and for a few moments they silently watched the flame. Then, in a thoughtful tone that seemed part of the silence, Mitch began to speak.

"It's true that we've all done things we're ashamed of. I just wish I'd done more of them. I'm serious," he said when Ted laughed. "I wish I'd raised more hell and made more mistakes, real mistakes, where you actually do something wrong instead of just let yourself drift into things you don't like. Sometimes I look around and I think, *Hey—what happened?* No reflection on you," he said to Bliss.

She seemed puzzled.

"Forget it," Mitch told her. "All I'm saying is that looking out for the other fellow and being nice all the time is a bunch of crap."

"But you *are* nice," Bliss said.

Mitch nodded. "I know," he said bitterly. "I'm working on it. It gets you exactly nowhere."

"Amen," said Ted.

"Case in point," Mitch went on. "I used to paralegal with this guy in the city and he decided that he couldn't live without some girl he was seeing. So he told his wife and of course she threw him out. Then the girl changed her mind. She didn't even tell him why. We used to eat lunch together and he would give me the latest installment and I swear to God it was enough to break your heart. He wanted to get back together with his family, but his wife couldn't make up her mind whether to let him. One minute she'd say yes, the next minute she'd say no. Meanwhile he was living in this ratbag on Post Street. All he had in there was lawn furniture. I don't know, I just felt sorry for him. So I told him he could move in with us until things got straightened out."

"I can feel this one coming," Helen said.

Mitch stared at the candle. "His name was Raphael. Like the angel. He was creative and good-looking and there was a nice aura around him. I guess I wanted to be his friend. But he turned out to be completely bad news. In the nine months he stayed with us he never once washed a glass or emptied an ashtray. He ran up hundreds of dollars' worth of calls on our phone bill and didn't pay for them. He wrecked my car. He stole things from me. He even put the moves on my wife."

"Classic," Helen said.

"You know what I did about it?" Mitch asked. "I'll tell you. Nothing. I never said a word to him about any of it. By the time he left, my wife couldn't stand the sight of me. Beginning of the end."

"What a depressing story," Helen said.

"I should've killed him," Mitch said. "I might have regretted it later on, but at least I could say I *did* something."

"You're too sweet," Bliss told him.

"I know," Mitch said. "But I wish I had, anyway. Sometimes it's better to do something really horrendous than just let things slide."

Ted clapped his hands. "Hear, hear. You're on the right track, Mitch. All you need is a few pointers, and old Ted is the very man to give them to you. Because where horrendous is concerned I'm the expert. You might say that I'm the king of horrendous."

Helen held up her empty glass. "Anybody want anything?"

"Put on your crash helmets," Ted went on. "You are about to hear my absolute bottom-line confession. 'The Worst Story Ever Told.'"

"No thanks," said Helen.

He peered at her. "What do you mean 'No thanks.' Who's asking permission?"

"I wouldn't mind hearing it," Mitch said.

"Well I would." Helen stood and looked down at Ted. "It's my birthday party, remember? I just don't feel like sitting around and listening to you talk about what a crud you are. It's a downer."

"That's right," Bliss said. "Helen's the birthday girl. She gets to choose. Right, Ted?"

"I know what," Helen said. "Why don't you tell us something good you did? The thing you're most proud of."

Mitch burst out laughing. Ted grinned and punched him in the arm.

"I mean it," Helen said.

"Helen gets to choose," Bliss repeated. She patted the floor beside her, and Helen sat down again. "All right," Bliss said. "We're listening."

Ted looked from Bliss to Helen. "I'll do it if you will," he said. "But you have to go first."

"That's not fair," Helen said.

"Sounds fair to me," said Mitch. "It was your idea."

Bliss smiled at Helen. "This is fun."

Before Helen began, she sent Ted out to the kitchen for more wine. Mitch did some sit-ups to get his blood moving again. Bliss sat behind Helen and let down Helen's hair. "I could show you something for this dryness," she said. She combed Helen's hair with her fingers, then started to brush it, counting off the strokes in a breathy whisper until Ted came back with the bottle.

They all had a drink.

"Ready and waiting," Ted told Helen. He lay back on the sofa and clasped his hands behind his head.

"One of my mother's friends had a boy with Down syndrome," Helen began. "Actually, three or four of her friends had kids with problems like that. One of my aunts, too. They were all good Catholics and didn't think twice about having babies right into their forties. This was before Vatican Two and the Pill and all that—before everything got watered down.

"Anyway, Tom wasn't really a boy. He was older than me by a couple of years, and a lot bigger. But he seemed like a boy—very sweet, very gentle, very happy."

Bliss stopped the brush in midstroke and said, "You're going to make me cry again."

"I used to take care of Tom sometimes when I was in high school. I was into a serious good-works routine back then. I wanted to be a saint. Honestly, I really did. At night, before I went to sleep, I used to put my fingers under my chin like I was praying and smile in this really holy way that I practiced all the time in front of the mirror. Then if they found me dead in the morning they would think I'd gone straight to heaven—that I was smiling at the angels coming to get me. At one point I even thought of becoming a nun."

Bliss laughed. "I can just see you in a habit—Sister Morphine. You'd have lasted about two hours."

Helen turned and looked at Bliss in a speculative way. "It's not something I expect you to understand," she said, "but if I had gone in I would have stayed in. To me, a vow is a vow." She turned away again. "Like I said, I began taking care of Tom as a kind of beatitude number, but after a while I started looking forward to it. Tom was fun to be with. And he really loved me. He even named one of his hamsters after me. We were both crazy about animals, so we'd usually go to the zoo or I'd take him to this stable out in Marin that had free riding lessons for special kids. That was what they called them, instead of handicapped or retarded—special."

"Beautiful," Mitch said.

"Don't get too choked up," Helen told him. "The story isn't over yet." She took a sip of her wine. "So. After I started college I didn't get home all that much, but whenever I did I'd stop by and get Tom and we'd go somewhere. Over to the Cliff House to look at the sea lions, something like that. Then one day I got this real brainstorm. I thought, *Hey, why not go whale watching?* Tom had whale posters all over his bedroom but he'd never seen a real one, and neither had I. So I called up this outfit in Half Moon Bay and they said it was getting towards the end of the season, but still worth a try. They were pretty sure we'd see something.

"Tom's mother wasn't too hot about the idea. She kept going on about the fact that he couldn't swim. But I brought her around, and the next morning Tom and I drove down and got on the boat. It wasn't all that big. In fact it was a lot smaller than I thought it would be, and that made me a little nervous at first, though after we got under way I figured the hell with it—they must know what they're doing. The boat rocked a little, but not dangerously. Tom loved it.

"We cruised around all morning and didn't see a thing. They would take us to different places and cut the engine and we'd sit there, waiting for a whale to come along. I stopped caring. It was nice out on the water. We were with a good bunch of people and one of them fixed up a sort of fishing line for Tom to hang over the side while we waited. I just leaned back and got some sun. Smelled the good smells. Watched the seagulls. After an hour or so they'd start the engine up again and go somewhere else and do the same thing. This happened three or four times. Everybody was kidding the guide about it, threatening to make him walk the plank and so on. Then, right out of nowhere, this whale came up beside us.

"He was just suddenly *there*. All this water running off his back. This unbelievably rancid smell all around him. Covered with barnacles and shells and long strings of seaweed trailing off him. Big. Maybe half again as long as the boat we were in." Helen shook her head. "You just can't imagine how big he was. He started making passes at the boat, and every time he did it we'd pitch and roll and take on about five hundred gallons of water. We were falling all over each other. At first everyone laughed and whooped it up, but after a while it started to get heavy."

"He was probably playing with you," Mitch said.

"That's what the guide told us the first couple of times it happened. Then he got scared too. I mean, he went white as a sheet. You could tell he didn't know what was happening any better than the rest of us did. We have this idea that whales are supposed to be more civilized than people, smarter and friendlier and more together. Cute, even. But it wasn't like that. It was hostile."

"You probably got a bad one," Mitch said. "It sounds like he was bent out of shape about something. Maybe the Russians harpooned his mate."

"He was a monster," Helen said. "I mean that. He was hostile and huge and he stank. He was hideous too. There were so many shells and barnacles on him that you could hardly see his skin. It looked as if he had armor on. He scraped the boat a couple of times and it made the most terrible sound, like people moaning underwater. He'd swim ahead a ways and go under and you'd think *Please God don't let him come back,* and then the water would start churning alongside the boat and there he'd be again. It was just terrifying. I've never been so afraid in my life. And then Tom started to lose it."

Bliss put the brush on the floor. Helen could feel her stillness and hear the sound of her breathing.

"He started to make these little noises," Helen said. "I'd never heard him do that before. Little mewing noises. The strange thing was, I hadn't even thought of Tom up to then. I'd completely forgotten about him. So it gave me a shock when I realized he was sitting right next to me, scared half to death. At first I thought, Oh no, what if he goes berserk! He was so much bigger than me I wouldn't have been able to control him. Neither would anyone else. He was incredibly strong. If anyone had tried to hold him down he'd have thrown them off like a dog shakes off water. And then what?

"But the thing that worried me most was that Tom would get so confused and panicky that he'd jump overboard. In my mind I had a completely clear picture of him doing it."

"Me too," Mitch said. "I have the same picture. He did, didn't he? He jumped in and you went after him and pulled him out."

Bliss said, "Ssshhh. Just listen, okay?"

"He didn't jump," Helen said. "He didn't go berserk either. Here we come to the point of the story—Helen's Finest Hour. How did I get started on this, anyway? It's disgusting."

The candle hissed and flared. The flame was burning in a pool of wax. Helen watched it flare up twice more, then it died and the room went gray.

Bliss began to rub Helen's back. "Go on," she said.

"I just talked him down," Helen said. "You know, I put my arm around his shoulder and said, 'Hey, Tom, isn't this something! Look at that big old whale! Wow! Here he comes again, Tom, hold on!' And then I'd laugh like crazy. I made like I was having the time of my life, and Tom fell for it. He calmed right down. Pretty soon after that the whale took off and we went back to shore. I don't know why I brought it up. It was just that even though I felt really afraid, I went ahead and acted as if I was flying high. I guess that's the thing I'm most proud of."

"Thank you, Helen," Mitch said. "Thank you for sharing that with us. I know it sounds phony, but I mean it."

"You don't talk about yourself enough," Bliss said. Then she called, "Okay, Ted—your turn."

Ted didn't answer.

Bliss called his name again.

"I think he's asleep," Mitch said. He moved closer to the sofa and looked at Ted. He nodded. "Dead to the world."

"Asleep," Helen said. "Oh, God."

Bliss hugged Helen from behind. "Mitch, come here," she said. "Love circle."

Helen pulled away. "No," she said.

"Why don't we wake him up?" Mitch suggested.

"Forget it," Helen told him. "Once Ted goes under he stays under. Nothing can bring him up. Watch." She went to the sofa, raised her hand, and slapped Ted across the face.

He groaned softly and turned over.

"See?" Helen said.

"What a slug," Bliss said.

"Don't you dare call him names," Helen told her. "Not in front of me, anyway. Ted is my husband. Forever and ever. I only did that to make a point."

Mitch said, "Helen, do you want to talk about this?"

"There's nothing to talk about," Helen answered. "I made my own bed." She hefted the bottle of wine. "Who needs a refill?"

Mitch and Bliss looked at each other. "My energy level isn't too high," Bliss said. Mitch nodded. "Mine's pretty low too."

"Then we'll just have to bring it up," Helen said. She left the room and came back with a candle and a mirror. She screwed the candle into the holder and held a match to the wick. It sputtered, then caught. Helen felt the heat of the flame on her cheek. "There," she said, "that's more like it." Mitch and Bliss drew closer as Helen took a glass vial from her pocket and spilled the contents onto the mirror. She looked up at them and grinned.

"I don't believe this," Bliss said. "Where did you get it?"

Helen shrugged.

"That's a lot of toot," Mitch said.

"We'll just have to do our best," Helen said. "We've got all day."

Bliss looked at the mirror. "I really should go to work."

"Me too," Mitch said.

He laughed, and Bliss laughed with him. They watched over Helen's shoulders as she bent down to sift the gleaming crystal. First she chopped it with a razor. Then she began to spread it out. Mitch and Bliss smiled up at her from the mirror, and Helen smiled back between them. Their faces were rosy with candlelight. They were the faces of three well-wishers, carolers, looking in at Helen through a window filling up with snow.

Desert Breakdown, 1968

Krystal was asleep when they crossed the Colorado. Mark had promised to stop for some pictures, but when the moment came he looked over at her and drove on. Krystal's face was puffy from the heat blowing into the car. Her hair, cut short for summer, hung damp against her forehead. Only a few strands lifted in the breeze. She had her hands folded over her belly, which made her look even more pregnant than she was.

The tires sang on the metal grillwork of the bridge. The river stretched away on both sides, blue as the empty sky. Mark saw the shadow of the bridge on the water with the car running through the girders, and the glint of water under the grillwork. Then the tires went silent. *California,* Mark thought, and for a time he felt almost as good as he'd expected to feel.

That soon passed. He'd broken his word, and he was going to hear about it when Krystal woke up. He almost turned the car around. But he didn't want to have to stop, and hoist Hans up on his shoulders, and watch Krystal point that camera at him again. By now Krystal had hundreds of pictures of Mark, and of Mark with Hans on his shoulders, standing in front of canyons and waterfalls and monumental trees and the three automobiles they'd owned since coming stateside.

Mark did not photograph well. For some reason he always looked discouraged. But those pictures gave the wrong idea. An old platoon sergeant of Mark's had an expression he liked to use—"free, white, and twenty-one." Well, that was an exact description of Mark. Everything was in front of him. All he needed was an opening.

Two hawks wheeled overhead, their shadows immense on the baking sand. A spinning funnel of dust moved across the road and disappeared behind a billboard. The billboard had a picture of Eugene McCarthy on it. McCarthy's hair was blowing around his head. He was grinning. The slogan below read A BREATH OF FRESH AIR. You could tell this was California because in Arizona a McCarthy billboard would last about five minutes. This one did have some bullet holes in it, but in Arizona someone would have burned it down or blown it up. The people there were just incredibly backward.

In the distance the mountains were bare and blue. Mark passed exit signs for a town called Blythe. He considered stopping for gas, but there was still half a tank and he didn't want to risk waking Krystal or Hans. He drove on into the desert.

They would make Los Angeles by dinnertime. Mark had an army buddy there who'd offered to put them up for as long as they wanted to stay. There was plenty of room, his buddy said. He was house-sitting for his parents while they made up their minds whether to get divorced or not.

Mark was sure he'd find something interesting in Los Angeles. Something in the entertainment field. He had been in plays all through high school and could sing pretty well. But his big talent was impersonation. He could mimic anybody. In Germany he'd mimicked a southern fellow in his company so accurately that after a couple of weeks of it the boy asked to be transferred to another unit. Mark knew he'd gone overboard. He laid off and in the end the boy withdrew his request for transfer.

His best impersonation was his father, Dutch. Sometimes, just for fun, Mark called his mother and talked to her in Dutch's slow, heavy voice, rolling every word along on treads, like a tank. She always fell for it. Mark would go on until he got bored, then say something like, "By the way, Dottie, we're bankrupt." Then she'd catch on and laugh. Unlike Dutch, she had a sense of humor.

A truck hurtled past. The sound of the engine woke Hans, but

Mark reached into the back and rubbed the satin edge of the baby blanket against his cheek. Hans put his thumb in his mouth. Then he stuck his rear end in the air and went back to sleep.

The road shimmered. It seemed to float above the desert floor. Mark sang along with the radio, which he'd been turning up as the signal grew weaker. Suddenly it blared. He turned it down, but too late. Hans woke up again and started fussing. Mark rubbed his cheek with the blanket. Hans pushed Mark's arm away and said, "No!" It was the only word he knew. Mark glanced back at him. He'd been sleeping on a toy car whose wheels had left four red dents on the side of his face. Mark stroked his cheek. "Pretty soon," he said, "pretty soon, Hansy," not meaning anything in particular but wanting to sound upbeat.

Krystal was awake now, too. For a moment she didn't move or say anything. Then she shook her head rapidly from side to side. "So hot," she said. She held up the locket-watch around her neck and looked at Mark. He kept his eyes on the road. "Back from the dead," he said. "Boy, you were really out."

"The pictures," she said. "Mark, the pictures."

"There wasn't any place to stop," he said.

"But you promised."

Mark looked at her, then back at the road. "I'm sorry," he said. "There'll be other rivers."

"I wanted that one," Krystal said, and turned away. Mark could tell that she was close to tears. It made him feel tired. "All right," he said. "Do you want me to go back?" He slowed the car to prove he meant it. "If that's what you want just say the word."

She shook her head.

Mark sped up.

Hans began to kick the back of the seat. Mark didn't say anything. At least it was keeping Hans busy and quiet. "Hey, gang," Mark said. "Listen up. I've got ten big ones that say we'll be diving into Rick's pool by six o'clock." Hans gave the seat a kick that he felt clear through to his ribs. "Ten big ones," he said. "Any takers?" He looked over at Krystal and saw that her lips were trembling. He patted the seat beside him. She hesitated, then slid over and leaned against him, as he knew she would. Krystal wasn't one to hold a grudge. He put his arm around her shoulder.

"So much desert," she said.

"It's something, all right."

"No trees," she said. "At home I could never imagine."

Hans stopped kicking. Then he grabbed Mark's ears. Krystal laughed and pulled him over the seat onto her lap. He immediately arched his back and slid down to the floor, where he began tugging at the gear shift.

"I have to stop," Krystal said. She patted her belly. "This one likes to sit just so, here, on my bladder."

Mark nodded. Krystal knew the English words for what Dottie had always been content to call her plumbing, and when she was pregnant she liked to describe in pretty close detail what went on in there. It made Mark queasy.

"Next chance we get," he said. "We're low on gas anyway."

Mark turned off at an exit with one sign that said GAS. There was no mention of a town. The road went north over bleached hardpan crazed with fissures. It seemed to be leading them toward a distant, solitary mountain that looked to Mark like a colossal sinking ship. Phantom water glistened in the desert. Rabbits darted back and forth across the road. Finally they came to the gas station, an unpainted cement-block building with some pickup trucks parked in front.

There were four men sitting on a bench in the shade of the building. They watched the car pull up.

"Cowboys," Krystal said. "Look, Hans, cowboys!"

Hans stood on Krystal's legs and looked out the window.

Krystal still thought everyone who wore a cowboy hat was a cowboy. Mark had tried to explain that it was a style, but she refused to understand. He stopped at a pump and turned off the engine.

The men stared at them, their faces dark under the wide brims of their hats. They looked as if they'd been there forever. One of them got up from the bench and walked over. He was tall and carried a paunch that seemed out of place on his bony frame. He bent down and looked inside the car. He had little black eyes with no eyebrows. His face was red, as if he were angry about something.

"Regular, please," Mark said. "All she'll take."

The man stared openly at Krystal's belly. He straightened up and walked away, past the men on the bench, up to the open door of the building. He stuck his head inside and yelled. Then he sat on the bench again. The man next to him looked down and mumbled something. The others laughed.

Somebody else in a cowboy hat came out of the building and went around to the back of the car.

"Mark," Krystal said.

"I know," Mark said. "The bathroom." When he got out of the car the heat took him by surprise; he could feel it coming down like rain.

The person pumping gas said, "You need oil or anything?" and that was when Mark realized it was a woman. She was looking down at the nozzle, so he couldn't see her face, only the top of her hat. Her hands were black with grease. "My wife would like to use your bathroom," he said.

She nodded. When the tank was full she thumped on the roof of the car. "Okay," she said, and walked back to the building.

Krystal opened the door and swung her legs out, then rocked forward and pushed herself up into the light. She stood for a moment, blinking. The four men looked at her. So did Mark. He made allowances for the fact that Krystal was pregnant, but she was still too heavy. Her bare arms were flushed from the heat. So was her face. She looked like one of those stein-slinging waitresses in the *Biergarten* where they used to drink. He wished these men could have seen how she looked wearing that black dress of hers, with her hair long, when they'd first started going out together.

Krystal shaded her eyes with one hand. With the other she pulled her blouse away from where it stuck to her skin. "More desert," she said. She lifted Hans out of the car and carried him toward the building, but he kicked free and ran over to the bench. He stood there in front of the men, naked except for his diaper.

"Come here," Krystal said. When he didn't obey she started after him, then looked at the men and stopped.

Mark went over. "Let's go, Hansy," he said, picking him up, feeling a sudden tenderness that vanished when the boy began to struggle.

The woman took Krystal and Hans inside the building, then came out and stood by the pile of scrap lumber beside the door. "Hans," she said. "That's a funny name for a little boy."

"It was her father's name," Mark said, and so it was. The original Hans had died shortly before the baby was born. Otherwise Mark never would have agreed. Even Germans didn't name their kids Hans anymore.

One of the men flicked a cigarette butt toward Mark's car. It fell just short and lay there, smoldering. Mark took it as a judgment on the car. It was a good one, a 1958 Bonneville he'd bought two weeks ago when the Ford started belching smoke, but a previous owner had put a lot of extra chrome on it and right now it was gleaming every which way. It looked foolish next to these dented pickups with their gun racks and dull, blistering paint. Mark wished he'd tanked up in Blythe.

Krystal came outside again, carrying Hans. She had brushed her hair and looked better.

Mark smiled at her. "All set?"

She nodded. "Thank you," she said to the woman.

Mark would have liked to use the bathroom too, but he wanted to get out of there. He started for the car, Krystal behind him. She laughed deep in her throat. "You should have seen," she said. "They have a motorcycle in their bedroom." Krystal probably thought she was whispering, but to Mark every word was like a shout. He didn't say anything. He adjusted the visor while Krystal settled Hans on the backseat. "Wait," she told Mark, and got out of the car again. She had the camera.

"Krystal," Mark said.

She aimed the camera at the four men. When she snapped the shutter their heads jerked up. Krystal advanced the film, then aimed the camera again.

"Krystal, get in!"

"Yes," Krystal said, but she was still aiming, braced on the open door of the car, her knees bent slightly. She snapped another picture and slid onto the seat. "Good," she said. "Cowboys for Reiner."

Reiner was Krystal's brother. He had once driven sixty miles to see *Shane.*

Mark didn't dare look over at the bench. He put the key in the ignition and glanced up and down the road. He turned the key. Nothing happened.

Mark waited for a moment. Then he tried again. Still nothing. The ignition went *tick tick tick tick,* and that was all. Mark turned it off and the three of them sat there. Even Hans was quiet. Mark felt the men watching him. That was why he didn't lower his head to the wheel. He stared straight ahead, furious at the tears stinging his eyes, blurring the line of the horizon, the shape of the building, the dark forms of the trucks, and the figure coming toward them over the white earth.

It was the woman. She bent down. "Okay," she said. "What's the trouble?" The smell of whiskey filled the car.

For almost half an hour the woman messed with the engine. She had Mark turn the key while she watched, then turn it some more while she did various things under the hood. At last she decided that the trouble was in the alternator. She couldn't fix it and had no parts on hand. Mark would have to get one in Indio or Blythe or maybe as far away as Palm Springs. It wasn't going to be easy, finding an alternator for a ten-year-old car. But she said she'd call around for him.

Mark waited in the car. He tried to act as if everything were all right, but when Krystal looked at him she made a sympathetic noise and squeezed his arm. Hans was asleep in her lap. "Everything will be fine," she said.

Mark nodded.

The woman came back toward the car, and Mark got out to meet her.

"Aren't you the lucky one," she said, handing him a piece of paper with an address written on it. "There wasn't anything in Indio," she said, "but this fellow in Blythe can fix you up. I'll need two dollars for the calls."

Mark opened his wallet and gave her the money. He had sixty-five dollars left, all that remained of his army severance pay. "How much will the alternator cost?" he asked.

She closed the hood of the car. "Fifty-six dollars, I think it was."

"Jesus," Mark said.

"You're lucky they had one."

"I suppose so," Mark said. "It just seems like a lot of money. Can you jump-start me?"

"If you've got cables. Mine are lent out."

"I don't have any," Mark said. He squinted against the sun. Though he hadn't looked directly at the men on the bench, he knew they'd been watching him and was sure they had heard everything. He was also sure they had jumper cables. People who drove trucks always carried stuff like that. But if they didn't want to help, he wasn't going to ask.

"I suppose I could walk up to the highway and hitch a ride," Mark said, more loudly than he meant to.

"I guess you could," the woman said.

Mark looked back at Krystal. "Is it okay if my wife stays here?"

"I guess she'll have to," the woman said. She took off her hat and wiped her brow with the back of her sleeve. Her hair was pure yellow, gathered in a loose bun that glowed in the light. Her eyes were a strangely pale blue. She put her hat back on and told Mark how to get to the parts store. She made him repeat the directions. Then he went back to the car.

Krystal looked straight ahead and bit her lip while Mark explained the situation. "Here?" she said. "You are going to leave us here?"

Hans was awake again. He had pulled the volume knob off the radio and was banging it on the dashboard.

"Just for a couple hours," Mark said, though he knew it would take longer.

Krystal wouldn't look at him.

"There's no choice," he said.

The woman had been standing next to Mark. She moved him aside and opened the door. "You come with me," she said. "You and the little one." She held out her arms. Hans went to her immediately and peered over her shoulder at the men on the bench. Krystal hesitated, then got out of the car, ignoring Mark's hand when he reached down to help her.

"It won't take long," he said. He smiled at Hans. "Pretty soon, Hansy," he said, and turned and began to walk toward the road.

The woman went inside with Hans. Krystal stood beside the car and watched Mark move farther and farther away, until the line of his body started to waver in the heat and then vanished altogether. It was like seeing someone slip below the surface of a lake.

The men stared at Krystal as she walked to the building. She felt heavy, and vaguely ashamed.

The woman had all the shades pulled down. It was like evening inside: dim, peaceful, cool. Krystal could make out the shapes of things but not their colors. There were two rooms. One had a bed and a motorcycle. The second, a bigger room, had a sofa and chairs on one side and on the other a refrigerator and stove and table.

Krystal sat at the table with Hans in her lap while the woman poured Pepsi from a large bottle into three tumblers full of ice. She had taken her hat off, and the weak light shining from the open door of the refrigerator made a halo around her face and hair. Usually Krystal measured herself against other women, but this one she watched with innocent, almost animal curiosity.

The woman took a smaller bottle off the top of the refrigerator. She wiggled it by the neck. "You wouldn't want any of this," she said. Krystal shook her head. The woman poured some of the liquor into her glass and pushed the other two glasses across the table. Hans took a drink, then started making motorboat noises.

"That boy," the woman said.

"His name is Hans."

"Not this one," the woman said. "The other one."

"Oh, Mark," Krystal said. "Mark is my husband."

The woman nodded and took a drink. She leaned back in her chair. "Where are you people headed?"

Krystal told her about Los Angeles, about Mark finding work in the entertainment field. The woman smiled, and Krystal wondered if she had expressed herself correctly. In school she had done well in English, and the American boys she talked to always complimented her, but during those two months with Mark's parents in Phoenix she had lost her confidence. Dutch and Dottie always looked bewildered when she spoke, and she herself understood almost nothing of what was said around her, though she pretended that she did.

The woman kept smiling, but there was a tightness to her mouth that made the smile look painful somehow. She took another drink.

"What does he do?" she asked.

Krystal tried to think how to explain what Mark did. When she first saw him, he had been sitting on the floor at a party and everyone around him was laughing. She had laughed too, though she didn't know why. It was a gift he had. But it was difficult to put into words. "Mark is a singer," she said.

"A singer," the woman said. She closed her eyes and leaned her head back and began to sing. Hans stopped fidgeting and watched her.

When the woman was through, Krystal said, "Good, good," and nodded, though she hadn't been able to follow the song and hated the style, which sounded to her like yodeling.

"My husband always liked to hear me sing," the woman said. "I suppose I could've been a singer if I'd wanted." She finished her drink and looked at the empty glass.

From outside Krystal heard the voices of the men on the bench, low and steady. One of them laughed.

"We had Del Ray to sing at our prom," the woman said.

The door banged. The man who'd stared at Krystal's belly stomped into the kitchen and stared at her again. He turned and started pulling bottles of Pepsi out of the refrigerator. "Webb, what do you think?" the woman said. "This girl's husband's a singer." She reached out and ran one hand up and down his back. "We'll need something for supper," she said, "unless you want rabbit again."

He kicked the refrigerator door shut with his foot and started out of the kitchen, bottles clinking. Hans slid to the floor and ran after him.

"Hans," Krystal said.

The man stopped and looked down at him. "That's right," he said. "You come with me."

It was the first time Krystal had heard him speak. His voice was thin and dry. He went back outside with Hans behind him.

The shoes Mark had on were old and loose, comfortable in the car, but his feet started to burn after a few minutes of walking in them. His eyes burned too, from sweat and the bright sun shining into his face.

For a while he sang songs, but after a couple of numbers his throat cracked with dryness and he gave it up. Anyway, it made him feel stupid singing about Camelot in this desert, stupid and a little afraid because his voice sounded so small. He walked on.

The road was sticky underfoot, and his shoes made little sucking noises at every step. He considered walking beside the road instead of on it but he was afraid a snake would bite him.

Though he wanted to stay cheerful, he kept thinking that now they'd never get to Los Angeles in time for dinner. They'd pull in late like they always did, stuff spilling out of the car, Mark humping the whole mess inside while Krystal stood by looking dazed in the glare of the headlights, Hans draped over her shoulder. Mark's buddy would be in his bathrobe. They'd try to joke but Mark would be too preoccupied. After they made up a bed for Krystal and put the crib together for Hans, which would take forever because half the screws were missing, Mark and his buddy would go down to the kitchen, drink a beer, and try to talk, but they'd end up yawning in each other's faces. Then they would go to bed.

Mark could see the whole thing. Whatever they did, it always turned out like this. Nothing ever worked.

A truck went past in the wrong direction. The two men inside were wearing cowboy hats. They glanced at Mark, then looked straight ahead again. He stopped and watched the truck disappear into the heat.

He turned and kept walking. Broken glass glittered along the roadside.

If Mark lived here and happened to be driving down this road and saw some person walking all by himself, he'd stop and ask if anything was wrong. He believed in helping people.

But he didn't need them. He could manage, just as he'd manage without Dutch and Dottie. He would do it alone, and someday they'd wish they had helped. He would be in some place like Las Vegas, performing at one of the big clubs. Then, at the end of his booking, he'd fly Dutch and Dottie out for his last big show—the finale. He'd fly them first class and put them up in the best hotel, the Sands or whatever, and get them front-row seats. And when the show was over, all the people going crazy, whistling and stamping on the floor and everything, he would call Dutch and Dottie up on the stage. He'd stand between them, holding their hands, and then, when all the clapping and yelling trailed off and everybody was quiet, smiling at him from the tables, he would raise Dutch and Dottie's hands above his head and say, "Folks, I just wanted you to meet my parents and tell you what they did for me." Here he'd stop for a second and get this really serious look on his face. "It's impossible to tell you what they did for me," he would say, pausing for effect, "because they didn't do *anything* for me! They didn't do *squat.*" Then he would drop their hands and jump off the stage, leaving them there.

Mark walked faster, leaning forward, eyes narrowed against the light. His hands flicked back and forth as he walked.

No, he wouldn't do that. People might take it wrong. A stunt like that could ruin his career. He'd do something even better. He'd stand up there and tell the whole world that without the encouragement and support the two of them had given him, the faith and love, et cetera, he would've thrown in the towel a long time ago.

And the great part was, *it wouldn't be true!* Because Dutch and Dottie wouldn't do a thing for him unless he stayed in Phoenix and got a "real job," like selling houses. But nobody would know that except Dutch and Dottie. They would stand up on the stage listening to all those lies, and the more he complimented them the more they'd see the kind of parents they could have been but weren't, and the more ashamed they would feel, and the more grateful to Mark for not exposing them.

He could hear a faint rushing sound in the hot air, a sound like applause. He walked faster still. He hardly felt the burning of his feet. The rushing sound grew louder, and Mark looked up. Ahead of him, no more than a hundred yards off, he saw the highway—not the road itself, but a long convoy of trucks moving across the desert, floating westward through a blue haze of exhaust.

The woman told Krystal that her name was Hope.

"Hope," Krystal said. "How lovely."

They were in the bedroom. Hope was working on the motorcycle. Krystal lay on the bed, propped up with pillows, watching Hope's long fingers move here and there over the machine, then back to the sweating glass at her side. Hans was outside with the men.

Hope took a drink. She swirled the ice around and said, "I don't know, Krystal."

Krystal felt the baby move inside her. She folded her hands across her belly and waited for the bump to come again.

All the lights were off except for a lamp on the floor beside Hope. There were engine parts scattered around her, and the air smelled of oil. She picked up a part and looked at it, then began to wipe it down with a cloth. "I told you we had Del Ray to our prom," she said. "I don't know if you ever heard of Del Ray where you came from, but us girls were flat crazy about him. I had a Del Ray pillow I slept on. Then he showed up and it turned out he was only about yay high." Hope held her hand a few inches above the floor. "Personally," she said, "I wouldn't look twice at a man that couldn't stand up for me if it came to the point. No offense," she added.

Krystal didn't understand what Hope had said, so she smiled.

"You take Webb," Hope said. "Webb would kill for me. He almost did, once. He beat a man that bad."

Krystal understood this. She felt sure it was true. She ran her tongue over her dry lips. "Who?" she asked. "Who did he beat?"

Hope looked up from the part she was cleaning. "My husband."

Krystal waited, uncertain whether she had heard this correctly.

"Webb and me were on a tear," Hope said. "When we weren't together, which was most of the time, we were always checking up on each other. Webb used to drive past my house at all hours and follow me everywhere. Sometimes he'd follow me places with his wife in the car next to him." She laughed. "It was a situation."

The baby was pressing against Krystal's spine. She shifted slightly.

Hope looked up at her. "It's a long story."

"Tell me."

Hope got up and went out to the kitchen. Krystal heard the crack of an ice tray. It was pleasant to lie here in this dark, cool room.

Hope came back and settled on the floor. "Don't get me going," she said. She took a drink. "It happened at the movie theater. We were coming out and Webb saw my husband put his arm around me and just completely lost his senses. I can tell you we did some fancy footwork after that. My husband had six brothers, and two of them in the police. We got out of there and I mean we *got*. Nothing but the clothes we had on. Never gone back since. Never will, either."

"Never," Krystal said. She admired the sound of the word. It was like Beethoven shaking his fist at the heavens.

Hope picked up the rag again. But she didn't do anything with it. She leaned against the wall, out of the little circle of light the lamp made.

"Did you have children?" Krystal asked.

Hope nodded. She held up two fingers.

"It must have been hard, not to see them."

"They'll do all right," Hope said. "They're both boys." She ran her fingers over the floor, found the part she'd been cleaning, and without looking at it began to wipe it down again.

"I couldn't leave Hans," Krystal said.

"Sure you could," Hope said. She sat there with her hands in her lap. Her breathing got deep and slow, and Krystal, peering through the gloom, saw that her eyes were closed. She was asleep, or just dreaming—maybe of that man out there.

The air conditioner went off abruptly. Krystal lay in the dark and listened to the sounds it had covered, the rasping of insects, the low voices of the men. The baby was quiet now. Krystal closed her eyes. She felt herself drifting, and as she drifted she remembered Hans. *Hans,* she thought. Then she slept.

Mark had assumed that when he reached the highway someone would immediately pick him up. But car after car went by, and the few drivers who looked at him scowled as if they were mad at him for needing a ride and putting them on the spot.

Mark's face burned, and his throat was so dry it hurt to swallow. Twice he had to leave the road to stand in the shade of a billboard. Cars passed him by for more than an hour, cars from Wisconsin and Utah and Georgia and just about everywhere. Mark felt like the whole country had turned its back on him. The thought came to him that he could die out here.

Finally a car stopped. It was a hearse. Mark hesitated, then ran toward it.

There were three people in the front seat, a man between two women. The space in the back was full of electrical equipment. Mark pushed some wires aside and sat cross-legged on the floor. The breeze from the air conditioner felt like a stream of cold water running over him.

The driver pulled back onto the road.

"Welcome to the stiffmobile," said the man in the middle. He turned around. His head was shaved except for one bristling stripe of hair down the center. It was the first Mohawk haircut Mark had ever seen on an actual person. The man's eyebrows were the same carroty color as his hair. Freckles covered his entire face and even the shaved parts of his skull.

"Stiffmobile, cliffmobile," said the woman driving. "Riffmobile."

"Bet you thought you'd be riding with a cold one," the man said.

Mark shrugged. "I'd rather ride with a cold one than a hot one."

The man laughed and pounded on the back of the seat.

The women also laughed. The one not driving turned around and smiled at Mark. She had a round, soft-looking face. Her lips were full. She wore a small gold ring in one side of her nose. "Hi," she said.

"Speaking of cold ones," the man said, "there's a case of 'em right behind you."

Mark fished a can of beer out of the cooler and took a long swallow, head back, eyes closed. When he opened his eyes again the man was watching him. They introduced themselves, all but the woman driving. She never looked at Mark or spoke, except to herself. The man with the Mohawk was Barney. The girl with the earring in her nose was Nance. They joked back and forth, and Mark discovered that Nance had a terrific sense of humor. She picked up on almost everything he said. After a while the ring stopped bothering him.

When Barney heard that Mark had been in the army he shook his head. "Pass on that," he said. "No bang-bang for Barney. I can't stand the sight of my own brains."

"Brains," the driver said. "Cranes, lanes, stains."

"Be cool," Barney told her. He turned back to Mark. "So what was it like over there?"

Mark realized that Barney meant Vietnam. Mark had not been to Vietnam. He'd had orders to go, but they got canceled just before he was supposed to ship out and were never reissued, he didn't know why. It was too complicated to explain, so he just said, "Pretty bad," and left it at that.

The mention of Vietnam broke the good feeling between them. They drank their beers and looked at the desert passing by. Then

Barney crumpled his can and threw it out the window. Hot air blew into Mark's face. He remembered what it was like out there, and felt glad to be right where he was.

"I could get behind another beer," Nance said.

"Right," Barney said. He turned around and told Mark to pop some more frosties. While Mark was getting the cans out of the cooler Barney watched him, playing his fingers over the top of the seat as if it were a keyboard. "So what's in Blythe?" he said.

"Smythe," the driver said. "Smythe's in Blythe."

"Smooth out," Nance said to her.

"I need a part," Mark said. He handed out the beers. "An alternator. My car's on the fritz."

"Where's your car?" Barney said.

Mark jerked his thumb over his shoulder. "Back there. I don't know the name of the place. It's just this gas station off the highway."

Nance was watching him intently. "Hey," she said. "What if you didn't stop smiling? What if you just kept smiling and never stopped?"

Barney looked at her, then back at Mark. "To me," he said, "there are places you go and places you don't go. You don't go to Rochester. You don't go to Blythe."

"You definitely don't go to Blythe," Nance said.

"Right," Barncy said. Then he listed some of the places where, in his opinion, you do go. They were going to one of them now, San Lucas, up in the mountains above Santa Fe. They were part of a film crew shooting a Western there. They'd shot another movie in the same place a year ago, and this was the sequel. Barney was a soundman. Nance did makeup. They didn't say anything about the driver.

"This place is unbelievable," Barney said. He paused and shook his head. Mark was waiting for him to describe San Lucas, but he just shook his head again and said, "It's just completely unbelievable."

"Really," Nance said.

It turned out that the star of the picture was Nita Damon. This was a real coincidence, because Mark had seen Nita Damon about six months ago in a show in Germany, a Bob Hope visit-with-the-troops kind of thing.

"That's amazing," Nance said. She and Barney looked at each other.

"You should scratch Blythe," Barney said.

Mark grinned.

Nance was staring at him. "*Marco,*" she said. "You're not a Mark, you're a Marco."

"You should sign on with us," Barney said. "Ride the stiffmobile express."

"You should," Nance said. "San Lucas is just incredible."

"Partyville," Barney said.

"Jesus," Mark said. "No. I couldn't."

"Sure you could," Barney said. "Lincoln freed the slaves, didn't he? Get your car later."

Mark was laughing. "Come on," he said. "What would I do up there?"

Barney said, "You mean like work?"

Mark nodded.

"No problem," Barney said. He told Mark that there was always something to do. People didn't show up, people quit, people got sick—there was always a call out for warm bodies. Once you found a tasty spot, you just settled in.

"You mean I'd be working on the movie? On the film crew?"

"Absitively," Barney said. "I guarantee."

"Jesus," Mark said. He looked at Barney, then at Nance. "I don't know," he said.

"That's all right," Barney said. "I know."

"Barney knows," Nance said.

"What have you got to lose?" Barney said.

Mark didn't say anything.

Barney watched him. "Marco," he said. "Don't tell me—you've got a little something else back there besides the car, right?" When Mark didn't answer, he laughed. "That was then," he said. "The old days. Gone with the wind."

"I have to think," Mark said.

"Okay, think," Barney said. "You've got till Blythe." He turned around. "Don't disappoint me."

Nance gave him a long, serious look. Then she turned around too. The top of her head was just visible over the high seat back.

The desert went past the window, always the same. The road had an oily look. Mark felt rushed, a little wild.

His first idea was to get the directions to San Lucas, then drive up with Krystal and Hans after the car was fixed. But then he wouldn't have enough money left for the gas, let alone food and motels and a place to live once they got there. He'd miss his chance.

Because that's what this was—a chance.

There was no point in fooling himself. He could go to Los Angeles and walk the streets for months, maybe years, without ever getting anywhere. He could stand outside closed doors and suck up to nobodies and sit in plastic chairs half his life without ever coming close to where he was right now, on his way to a guaranteed job in Partyville.

Los Angeles wasn't going to work. Mark could see that. He'd borrow money from his friend and start hustling and he wouldn't get the time of day from anyone, because he was hungry and nobody ever had time for hungry people. Hungry people got written off. It was like Dutch said—them that has, gets.

He'd run himself ragged and his money would disappear, the way all his other money had disappeared. Krystal would get worried and sad. After a couple of weeks Mark and his buddy wouldn't have anything to say to each other, and his buddy would grow tired of living with a guy he didn't really know that well and a yelling kid and a sad, pregnant woman. He'd tell Mark some lie to get rid of them—his girl was moving in, his parents had decided to stay together after all. By then Mark would be broke again. Krystal would have a fit and probably go into labor.

And when that happened? What then?

Mark knew what. Crawl home to Dutch and Dottie.

No. No sir. The only way he was going back to Phoenix was in a coffin.

The driver started talking to herself, and Barney rapped her on top of the head with his knuckles. "Do you want me to drive?" he said. It sounded like a threat. She quieted down. "All right," he said. Without looking back he said, "Five miles to Blythe."

Mark looked out the window. He couldn't get it out of his mind that here he had exactly what he needed. A chance to show what he was made of. He'd have fun, sure, but he'd also be at work on time in the morning. He would do what he was told and do it right. He would keep his eyes open and his mouth shut, and after a while people would notice him. He wouldn't push too hard, but now and then he might do a song at one of the parties, or impersonate some of the actors. He could just hear Nita Damon laughing and saying, *Stop it, Mark! Stop it!*

What he could do, Mark thought, was to call Krystal and arrange to meet up with her at his buddy's house in a month or two, after they'd shot the film. Mark would have something going then. He'd be on his way. But that wouldn't work either. He didn't know how to call her. She had no money. And she wouldn't agree.

Mark wasn't going to fool himself. If he left Krystal and Hans back there, she would never forgive him. If he left them, he'd be leaving them for good.

I can't do that, he thought. But he knew this wasn't true. He could leave them. People left each other, and got left, every day. It was a terrible thing. But it happened and people survived as they survived even worse things. Krystal and Hans would survive, too. When she understood what had happened she would call Dutch, who'd hit the roof, of course, and then, in the end, come through for them. He didn't have any choice. And in four or five years what happened today would be no more than a bad memory.

Krystal would do well for herself. Men liked her. Even Dutch liked her, though he'd been dead set against the marriage. Someday, sooner than later, she'd meet a good man who could take care of her. She and Hans and the new baby would be able to go to sleep at night without wondering what would happen to them when they woke up. They didn't need Mark. Without him they would have a better life than if he and Krystal had stayed together.

This was a new thought for Mark, and it made him feel a little aggrieved to see how unimportant he really was to Krystal. Before now he had always assumed that their coming together had been ordained, and that in marrying Krystal he had fulfilled some need of the universe. But if they could live without each other, and do even better without each other, then this wasn't true and had never been true.

They did not need each other. There was no particular reason for them to be together. So what was this all about? If he couldn't make her happy, what was the point? They were dragging each other down like two people who couldn't swim. If they were lucky, they might keep at it long enough to grow old in the same house.

It wasn't right. She deserved better, and so did he.

Mark felt that he had been deceived. Not by Krystal, she would never do that, but by everyone who had ever been married and knew the truth about it and never let on. The truth was, when you got married you had to give up one thing after another. It never ended. You had to give up your life—the special one you'd been meant to have—and stumble along where neither of you had ever thought of going or wanted to go. And you never knew what was really happening. You gave up your life and didn't even know it.

"Blythe," Barney said.

Mark looked at the town, what he could see of it from the road. Lines of heat quivered above the rooftops.

"Blythe," Barney said again. "Going, going, gone."

Krystal woke and bolted upright, blinking in the gloom. "Hans," she whispered.

"He's outside," Hope said. She was standing over the lamp, feeding shells into a shotgun. Her shadow swayed back and forth against the wall. "I'm going to get us some dinner," she said. "You just lie here and rest up. The boy will be fine." She finished loading the gun and pushed a few more shells into the pockets of her jeans.

Krystal lay on the bed, restless and thirsty but feeling too heavy to rise. The men had a radio on. A whiny song was playing, like the one Hope had sung in the kitchen. Krystal had not heard any good music for months now, since the day she left home. A warm day in early spring—sunlight flickering through the trees along the road. Trees. Streams swollen with snowmelt.

"Ah, God," Krystal said.

She pushed herself up and lifted the window shade and looked out at the desert, the mountains. And there was Hope, walking into the desert with her shotgun. The light was softer than before, still white but not so sharp. The tops of the mountains were touched with pink.

Krystal stared out the window. How could anyone live in such a place? There was nothing, nothing at all. Through all those days in Phoenix, Krystal had felt a great emptiness around her where she would count for no more than a rock or a spiny tree; now she was in the middle of it. She thought she might cry, but gave the idea up. It didn't interest her.

She closed her eyes and leaned her forehead against the glass.

I will say a poem, Krystal thought, *and when I am finished he will be here.* At first silently, because she had been trying to speak only English, then in a whisper, she recited a poem of Heine's the nuns had made her learn so long ago at school, the only poem she remembered. She repeated it, then opened her eyes. Mark was not there. As if she had really believed he would be there, Krystal kicked the wall with her bare foot. The pain made clear what she had been pretending not to know: that he had never really been there and never would be there in any way that mattered.

The window was warm against Krystal's forehead. She watched Hope move farther and farther away, then stop and raise her gun. A moment later Krystal heard the boom, and felt the glass shudder against her skin.

Mark was sore from sitting cross-legged on the bare floorboards. He stretched out his legs and listened to the driver talk to herself, straining to get the point of the things she said. There was sometimes rhyme but never any reason to her words. Every possibility of meaning trailed off into nonsense.

The hearse was moving at great speed, really racing. The driver passed every car they came upon. She changed lanes without purpose. Mark tried to find a break between her words to say something, just a note of caution, something about how tough the police were around here. The car was going faster and faster. He hoped that Barney would tell her to shut up and slow down, maybe even take over himself for a while, but he wasn't saying anything and neither was Nance. She had disappeared completely and all Mark could see of Barney were the bristles of his hair.

"Hey," Mark said. "What's the hurry?"

The driver seemed not to hear him. She passed another car and went on yakking to herself. She was gripping the steering wheel so tightly that her knuckles had turned white.

"Better slow down," Mark said.

"Butter sold owl," she said.

Mark leaned over the top of the seat to check out the speedometer, and Nance looked up from what she was doing to Barney down there. Her eyes met Mark's, and she held his gaze as she kept at it, languorously, luxuriously. Mark rocked back on his heels as if he'd been struck. "Stop the car," he said.

"Star the cop," the driver said. "Stop the war."

"Stop the car," Mark said again.

"Hey," Barney said. "What's the problem?" His voice was sleepy, remote.

"I want out," Mark said.

"No, you don't," Barney said. "You already decided, remember? Just be Marco." Mark heard Nance whispering. Then Barney said, "Hey—Marco. Come on up here. You're with us now."

"Stop the car," Mark said. He reached over the seat and began to rap on the driver's head, softly at first, then hard. He could hear the knocking of his knuckles against her skull. She came to a squealing stop right in the road. Mark looked back. There was a car bearing down on them. It swerved into the other lane and went past with its horn wailing.

"Okay, *Mark*," Barney said. "Ciao. You blew it."

Mark scrambled over equipment and cords and let himself out the back. When he closed the tailgate the driver pulled away, fast. Mark crossed the road and watched the hearse until it disappeared. The road was empty. He turned and walked back toward Blythe.

A few minutes later an old man stopped for him. He took a liking to Mark and drove him directly to the parts store. They were just closing up, but after Mark explained his situation the boss let him inside and found the alternator for him. With tax, the price came to seventy-one dollars.

"I thought it was fifty-six," Mark said.

"Seventy-one," the man said.

Mark stared at the alternator. "I've only got sixty-five."

"I'm sorry," the man said. He put his hands on the counter and waited.

"Look," Mark said, "I just got back from Vietnam. Me and my wife are on our way to Los Angeles. Once we get there I can send you the rest. I'll put it in the mail tomorrow morning, I swear."

The man looked at him.

Mark could see that he was hesitating. "I've got a job waiting."

"What kind of job?"

"I'm a soundman," Mark said.

"Soundman. I'm sorry," he said. "I know you think you'll send the money."

Mark argued for a while but without heat, because he knew that the man was right; he wouldn't send the money. He gave up and went back outside. The parts store adjoined a salvage yard filled with crumpled cars. Down the street was a gas station and a U-Haul depot. As Mark walked toward the gas station a black dog appeared on the other side of the salvage-yard fence and kept pace with him, silently baring his fangs whenever Mark glanced in his direction.

He was hot and tired. He could smell himself. He remembered the coolness of the hearse and thought, *I blew it.*

There was a pay phone outside the gas station. Mark got a handful of change and shut himself in. He wanted to call his buddy in Los

Angeles and figure something out, but he'd left the address book in the car and it turned out that the number was unlisted. He tried explaining things to the operator but she refused to listen. Finally she hung up on him.

He looked across the shimmering asphalt toward the salvage yard. The dog was still at the fence, watching him. The only thing he could do, Mark decided, was to keep calling Los Angeles information until he got a human being on the other end. There had to be somebody sympathetic out there.

But first he was going to call Phoenix and give Dutch and Dottie a little something to sleep on. He would put on his official voice and tell them that he was Sergeant Smith—no, *Smythe,* Sergeant Smythe of the highway patrol, calling to report an accident. A head-on collision just outside of Palm Springs. It was his duty, he was sorry to say— here his voice would crack—that there were no survivors. No, ma'am, not one. Yes, ma'am, he was sure. He'd been at the scene. The one good thing he could tell her was that nobody had suffered. It was over just like *that,* and here Mark would snap his fingers into the receiver.

He closed his eyes and listened to the phone ring through the cool, quiet house. He saw Dottie where she sat in her avocado kitchen, drinking coffee and making a list, saw her rise and gather her cigarettes and lighter and ashtray. He heard her shoes tapping on the tile floor as she came toward the phone.

But it was Dutch who answered. "Strick here," he said.

Mark took a breath.

"Hello," Dutch said.

"It's me," Mark said. "Dad, it's me—Mark."

Krystal was washing her face when she heard the gun go off again. She paused, water running through her fingers, then finished up and left the bedroom. She wanted to find Hans. He should have been changed long before now, and it was almost time for him to eat. She missed him.

Stepping carefully through the parts on the floor, she went into the main room. It was almost completely dark. Krystal turned the overhead light on and stood there with her hand against the wall.

Everything was red. The carpet was red. The chairs and the couch were red. The lamp shades were red and had little red tassels hanging down from them. The pillows on the couch were shaped like hearts and covered in a satiny material that looked wet under the light, so that for a moment they had the appearance of real organs.

Krystal stared at the room. In a novel she had once come upon the expression "love nest," and had thought of light-washed walls, tall pines reaching to the balcony outside. But this, she thought, looking at the room, this was a love nest. It was horrible, horrible.

Krystal moved over to the door and opened it a crack. Someone was lying on the front seat of the car, his bare feet sticking out the window, his boots on the ground below with yellow socks hanging from the tops. She could not see the men on the bench but one of them was saying something, the same word again and again. Krystal couldn't make it out. Then she heard Hans repeat the word, and the men laughed.

She opened the door wider. Still standing inside, she said, "Hans, come here." She waited. She heard someone whisper. "Hans," she said.

He came to the door. There was dirt all over his face but he looked happy.

"Come in," she said.

Hans looked over his shoulder, then back at Krystal.

"Come, Hans," she said.

He stood there. "Bitch," he said.

Krystal took a step backward. "No," she said. "No, no, no. Don't say that. Come, sweet boy." She held out her arms.

"Bitch," he said again.

"Oh!" Krystal said. She pushed the door open and walked up to Hans and slapped him across the face. She slapped him hard. He sat down and looked up at her. She had never done that before. Krystal took a flat board from the pile of scrap near the door. The three men on the bench were watching her from under their hats. "Who did that?" she said. "Who taught him that word?" When they didn't answer she started toward the bench, reviling them in German. They stood and backed away from her. Hans began to cry. Krystal turned on him. "Be quiet!" she said. He whimpered once and was still.

Krystal turned back to the men. "Who taught him that word?"

"It wasn't me," Webb said.

The other men just stood there.

"Shame," Krystal said. She looked at them, then walked over to the car. She kicked the boots aside. Holding the board with both hands, she swung it as hard as she could across the bare feet sticking out of the window. The man inside screamed.

"Get out," Krystal said. "Out, out, out!"

He scrambled out the other door and squinted at her over the top of the car. Without his big hat he looked like a grumpy baby, face all red and puffy. She hefted the board and he started dancing over the hot sand toward the building, his hair flapping up and down like a wing. He stopped in the shade and looked back, still shifting from foot to foot. He kept his eyes on Krystal. So did Hans, sitting by the door. So did the men near the bench. They were all watching to see what she would do next.

So, Krystal thought. She flung the board away, and one of the men flinched. Krystal almost laughed. *How angry I must look,* she thought, *how angry I am,* and then her anger left her. She tried to keep it, but it was gone the moment she knew it was there.

She shaded her eyes and looked around her. The distant mountains cast long shadows into the desert. The desert was empty and still. Nothing moved but Hope, walking toward them with the gun slung at her back, barrel poking over her shoulder. As she drew near, Krystal waved, and Hope raised her arms. A rabbit hung from each hand, swinging by its ears.

Say Yes

They were doing the dishes, his wife washing while he dried. He'd washed the night before. Unlike most men he knew, he really pitched in on the housework. A few months earlier he'd overheard a friend of his wife's congratulate her on having such a considerate husband, and he thought, *I try*. Helping out with the dishes was one way of showing how considerate he was.

They talked about different things and somehow got on the subject of whether white people should marry black people. He said that all things considered, he thought it was a bad idea.

"Why?" she asked.

Sometimes his wife got this look where she pinched her brows together and bit her lower lip and stared down at something. When he saw her like this he knew he should keep his mouth shut, but he never did. Actually it made him talk more. She had that look now.

"Why?" she asked again, and stood there with her hand inside a bowl, not washing it but just holding it above the water.

"Listen," he said, "I went to school with blacks and I've worked with blacks and lived on the same street with blacks and we've always gotten along just fine. I don't need you coming along now and implying that I'm a racist."

"I didn't imply anything," she said, and began washing the bowl again, turning it around in her hand as though she were shaping it. "I just don't see what's wrong with a white person marrying a black person, that's all."

"They don't come from the same culture as we do. Listen to them sometime—they even have their own language. That's okay with me, I *like* hearing them talk"—he did; for some reason it always lifted his mood—"but it's different. A person from their culture and a person from our culture could never really *know* each other."

"Like you know me?" his wife asked.

"Yes. Like I know you."

"But if they love each other," she said. She was washing faster now, not looking at him.

Oh boy, he thought. He said, "Don't take my word for it. Look at the statistics. Most of those marriages break up."

"Statistics." She was piling dishes on the drainboard at a terrific rate, just swiping at them with the cloth. Many of them were greasy, and he could see flecks of food between the tines of the forks. "All right," she said, "what about foreigners? I suppose you think the same thing about two foreigners getting married."

"Yes," he said, "as a matter of fact I do. How can you understand someone who comes from a completely different background?"

"Different," said his wife. "Not the same, like us."

"Yes, different," he snapped, angry with her for resorting to this trick of repeating his words so they sounded crass, or hypocritical. "These are dirty," he said, and dumped all the silverware back into the sink.

The water had gone flat and gray. She stared down at it, her lips pressed tight together, then plunged her hands under the surface. "Oh!" she cried, and jumped back. She took her right hand by the wrist and held it up. Her thumb was bleeding.

"Ann, don't move," he said. "Stay right there." He ran upstairs to the bathroom and rummaged in the medicine chest for alcohol, cotton, and a Band-Aid. When he came back down she was leaning against the refrigerator with her eyes closed, still holding her hand by the wrist. He took the hand and dabbed at her thumb with the cotton. The bleeding had stopped. He squeezed it to see how deep the wound was and a single drop of blood welled up, trembling and bright, and fell to the floor. Over the thumb she stared at him accusingly. "It's shallow," he said. "Tomorrow you won't even know it's there." He hoped that she appreciated how quickly he'd come to her aid. He had acted out of concern for her, with no thought of getting anything in return, but now the thought occurred to him that it would be a nice gesture on her part not to start up that conversation again, as he was tired of it. "I'll finish up here," he said. "You go and relax."

"That's okay," she said. "I'll dry."

He began to wash the silverware again, giving a lot of attention to the forks.

"So," she said, "you wouldn't have married me if I'd been black."

"For Christ's sake, Ann!"

"Well, that's what you said, didn't you?"

"No, I did not. The whole question is ridiculous. If you had been black we probably wouldn't even have met. You would've had your friends and I would've had mine. The only black girl I ever really knew was my partner in the debating club, and I was already going out with you by then."

"But if we had met, and I'd been black?"

"Then you probably would have been going out with a black guy." He picked up the rinsing nozzle and sprayed the silverware. The water was so hot that the metal darkened to pale blue, then turned silver again.

"Let's say I wasn't," she said. "Let's say I'm black and unattached and we meet and fall in love."

He glanced over at her. She was watching him, and her eyes were bright. "Look," he said, taking a reasonable tone, "this is stupid. If you were black you wouldn't be you." As he said this he realized it was absolutely true. There was no possible argument against the fact that she would not be herself if she were black. So he said it again: "If you were black you wouldn't be you."

"I know," she said, "but let's just say."

He took a deep breath. He had won the argument but still felt cornered. "Say what?" he asked.

"That I'm black, but still me, and we fall in love. Will you marry me?"

He thought about it.

"Well?" she said, and stepped close to him. Her eyes were even brighter. "Will you marry me?"

"I'm thinking," he said.

"You won't, I can tell. You're going to say no."

"Let's not move too fast on this," he said. "There are lots of things to consider. We don't want to do something we might regret for the rest of our lives."

"No more considering. Yes or no."

"Since you put it that way—"

"Yes or no."

"Jesus, Ann. All right—no."

"Thank you," she said, and walked from the kitchen into the living room. A moment later he heard her turning the pages of a magazine. He knew she was too angry to be actually reading it, but she wasn't snapping through the pages like he would've done; she turned them slowly, as if she were studying every word. She was demonstrating her indifference to him, and it had the effect he knew she'd intended. It hurt him.

He had no choice but to demonstrate his indifference to her. Quietly, thoroughly, he washed the rest of the dishes. Then he dried them and put them away. He wiped the counters and the stove and scoured the linoleum where the drop of blood had fallen. While he was at it, he decided, he might as well mop the whole floor. When he was done the kitchen looked new, just as it had when they were first shown the house, before they had ever lived here.

He picked up the garbage pail and went outside. The night was clear and he could see a few stars to the west, where the lights of the town didn't blur them out. On El Camino the traffic was steady and light, peaceful as a river. He felt ashamed that he'd let his wife get him into a fight. In another thirty years or so they both would be dead. What would all that stuff matter then? He thought of the years they had spent together and how close they were and how well they knew each other, and his throat tightened so that he could hardly breathe. His face and neck began to tingle. Warmth flooded his chest. He stood there for a while, enjoying these sensations, then picked up the pail and went out the back gate.

The two mutts from down the street had pulled over the garbage can again. One of them was rolling around on his back and the other had something in its mouth. When they saw him coming they trotted away with short, mincing steps. Normally he would've tossed a rock or two after them, but this time he let them go.

The house was dark when he came back inside. She was in the bathroom. He stood outside the door and called her name. He heard bottles clinking, but she didn't answer him. "Ann, I'm really sorry," he said. "I'll make it up to you, I promise."

"How?" she asked.

He wasn't expecting this. But from a sound in her voice, a level and definite note that was strange to him, he knew he had to come up with the right answer. He leaned against the door. "I'll marry you," he whispered.

"We'll see," she said. "Go on to bed. I'll be out in a minute."

He undressed and got under the covers. Finally he heard the bathroom door open and close.

"Turn off the light," she said from the hallway.

"What?"

"Turn off the light."

He reached over and pulled the chain on the bedside lamp. The room went dark. "All right," he said. He lay there, but nothing happened. "All right," he said again. Then he heard a movement across the room. He sat up but couldn't see a thing. The room was silent. His heart pounded as it had on their first night together, as it still did when he woke at a noise in the darkness and waited to hear it again— the sound of someone moving through the house, a stranger.

Mortals

The metro editor called my name across the newsroom and beckoned to me. When I got to his office he was behind the desk. A man and a woman were there with him, the man nervous on his feet, the woman in a chair, bony-faced and vigilant, holding the straps of her bag with both hands. Her suit was the same bluish gray as her hair. There was something soldierly about her. The man was short, doughy, rounded off. The burst vessels in his cheeks gave him a merry look until he smiled.

"I didn't want to make a scene," he said. "We just thought you should know." He looked at his wife.

"You bet I should know," the metro editor said. "This is Mr. Givens," he said to me, "Mr. Ronald Givens. Name ring a bell?"

"Vaguely."

"I'll give you a hint. He's not dead."

"Okay," I said. "I've got it."

"Another hint," the metro editor said. Then he read aloud, from that morning's paper, the obituary I had written announcing Mr. Givens's death. I'd done a whole slew of obits the day before, over twenty of them, and I didn't remember much of this one, but I did remember the part about him working for the IRS for thirty years. I'd recently had problems with the IRS, so that stuck in my mind.

As Givens listened to his obituary he looked from one to the other of us. He wasn't as short as I'd first thought. It was an impression he created by hunching his shoulders and thrusting his neck forward

135

like a turtle. His eyes were soft, restless. He used them like a peasant, in swift, measuring glances with his face averted.

He laughed when the metro editor was through. "Well, it's accurate," he said. "I'll give you that."

"Except for one thing." The woman was staring at me.

"I owe you an apology," I told Givens. "It looks like somebody pulled the wool over my eyes."

"Apology accepted!" Givens said. He rubbed his hands together as if we'd all just signed something. "You have to see the humor, Dolly. What was it Mark Twain said? 'The reports of my death—' "

"So what happened?" the metro editor said to me.

"I wish I knew."

"That's not good enough," the woman said.

"Dolly's pretty upset," Givens said.

"She has every right to be upset," the metro editor said. "Who called in the notice?" he asked me.

"To tell the truth, I don't remember. I suppose it was somebody from the funeral home."

"You call them back?"

"I don't believe I did, no."

"Check with the family?"

"He most certainly did not," Mrs. Givens said.

"No," I said.

The metro editor said, "What do we do before we run an obituary?"

"Check back with the funeral home and the family."

"But you didn't do that."

"No, sir. I guess I didn't."

"Why not?"

I made a helpless gesture with my hands and tried to appear properly stricken, but I had no answer. The truth was, I never followed those procedures. People were dying all the time. I hadn't seen the point in asking their families if they were really dead, or calling funeral parlors back to make sure the funeral parlors had just called me. All this procedural stuff was a waste of time, I'd decided; it didn't seem possible that anyone could amuse himself by concocting phony death notices and impersonating undertakers. Now I saw that this was foolish of me, and showed a radical failure of appreciation for the varieties of human pleasure.

There was more to it than that. Since I was still on the bottom rung in metro, I wrote a lot of obituaries. Some days they gave me a choice between that and marriage bulletins, but most of the time obits were all I did, one after another, morning to night. After four months of this duty I was full of the consciousness of death. It soured me. It puffed me up with morbid snobbery, the feeling that I knew a secret nobody else had even begun to suspect. It made me wearily philosophical about the value of faith and passion and hard work, at a time when my life required all of these. It got me down.

I should have quit, but I didn't want to go back to the kind of jobs I'd had before a friend's father fixed me up with this one—waiting on tables, mostly, pulling night security in apartment buildings, anything that would leave my days free for writing. I'd lived like this for three years, and what did I have to show for it? A few stories in literary journals that nobody read, including me. I began to lose my nerve. I'd given up a lot for my writing, and it wasn't giving anything back—not respectability, nor money, nor love. So when this job came up I took it. I hated it and did it badly, but I meant to keep it. Someday I'd move over to the police beat. Things would get better.

I was hoping that the metro editor would take his pound of flesh and let me go, but he kept after me with questions, probably showing off for Givens and his wife, letting them see a real newshound at work. In the end I was forced to admit that I hadn't called any other families or funeral homes that day, nor, in actual fact, for a good long time.

Now that he had his answer, the metro editor didn't seem to know what to do with it. It seemed to be more than he'd bargained for. At first he just sat there. Then he said, "Let me get this straight. Just how long has this paper been running unconfirmed obituaries?"

"About three months," I said. And as I made this admission I felt a smile on my lips, already there before I could fight it back or dissemble it. It was the rictus of panic, the same smile I'd given my mother when she told me my father had died. Of course the metro editor didn't know that.

He leaned forward in his chair and gave his head a little shake, the way a horse will, and said, "Clean out your desk." I don't think he'd meant to fire me; he looked surprised by his own words. But he didn't take them back.

Givens looked from one to the other of us. "Now hold on here," he said. "Let's not blow this all out of proportion. This is a live-and-learn situation. This isn't something a man should lose his job over."

"He wouldn't have," Mrs. Givens said, "if he'd done it right."

Which was a truth beyond argument.

I cleaned out my desk. As I left the building I saw Givens by the newsstand, watching the door. I didn't see his wife. He walked up to me, raised his hands, and said, "What can I say? I'm at a loss for words."

"Don't worry about it," I told him.

"I sure as heck didn't mean to get you fired. It wasn't even my idea to come in, if you want to know the truth."

"Forget it. It was my own fault." I was carrying a box full of notepads, files, and books. It was heavy. I shifted it under my other arm.

"Look," Givens said, "how about I treat you to lunch. What do you say? It's the least I can do."

I looked up and down the street.

"Dolly's gone on home," he said. "How about it?"

Though I didn't especially want to eat lunch with Givens, it seemed to mean a lot to him, and I didn't feel ready to go home yet. What would I do there? Sure, I said, lunch sounded fine. Givens asked me if I knew anyplace reasonable nearby. There was a Chinese joint a few doors down, but it was always full of reporters. I didn't want to watch them try to conjure up sympathy over my situation, which they'd laugh about anyway the minute I left, not that I blamed them. I suggested Tad's Steakhouse over by the cable-car turn-around. You could get a six-ounce sirloin, salad, and baked potato for a buck twenty-nine. This was 1974.

"I'm not that short," Givens said. But he didn't argue, and that's where we went.

Givens picked at his food, then pushed the plate away. When I asked if his steak was okay, he said he didn't have much appetite.

"So," I said, "who do you think called it in?"

His head was bent. He looked up at me from under his eyebrows. "Boy, you've got me there. It's a mystery."

"You must have some idea."

"Nope. Not a one."

"Think it could've been someone you worked with?"

"Nah." He shook a toothpick out of the dispenser. His hands were pale and sinewy.

"It had to be somebody who knows you. You have friends, right?"

"Sure."

"Maybe you had an argument, something like that. Somebody's mad at you."

He kept his mouth covered with one hand while he worked the toothpick with the other. "You think so? I had it figured for more of a joke."

"Well, it's a pretty serious joke, calling in a death notice on some-one. Pretty threatening. I'd sure feel threatened, if it was me."

Givens inspected the toothpick, then dropped it in the ashtray. "I hadn't thought of it like that," he said. "Maybe you're right."

I could see he didn't believe it for a second—had no idea what had happened. The words of death had been pronounced on him, and now his life would be lived in relation to those words, in failing opposition to them, until they overpowered him and became true. Or so it appeared to me.

"You're sure it isn't one of your friends," I said. "It could be a little thing. You played cards, landed some big ones, then folded early before he had a chance to recoup."

"I don't play cards," Givens said.

"How about your wife? Any problems in that department?"

"Nope."

"Everything smooth as silk, huh?"

He shrugged. "Same as ever."

"How come you call her Dolly? That wasn't the name in the obit."

"No reason. I've always called her that. Everybody does."

"I don't feature her as a Dolly," I said.

He didn't answer. He was watching me.

"Let's say Dolly gets mad at you, really mad . . . She wants to send you a message—something outside normal channels."

"Not a chance." Givens said this without bristling. He didn't try to convince me, so I figured he was probably right.

"You're survived by a daughter, right? What's her name again?"

"Tina," he said, with some tenderness.

"That's it, Tina. How are things with Tina?"

"We've had our problems. But I can guarantee you, it wasn't her."

"Well, hell's bells," I said. "Somebody did it."

I finished my steak, watching the show outside: winos, evangelists, outpatients, whores, fake hippies selling oregano to tourists in white shoes. Pure theater, even down to the smell of popcorn billowing out of Woolworth's. Richard Brautigan often came here. Tall and owlish, he stooped to his food and ate slowly, ruminating over every bite, his eyes on the street. Some funny things happened here, and some appalling things. Brautigan took it all in and never stopped eating.

I told Givens that we were sitting at the same table where Richard Brautigan sometimes sat.

"Sorry?"

"Richard Brautigan, the writer."

Givens shook his head.

I was ready to go home. "Okay," I said, "you tell me. Who wants you dead?"

"No one wants me dead."

"Somebody's imagining you dead. Thinking about it. The wish is father to the deed."

"Nobody wants me dead. Your problem is, you think everything has to mean something."

That was one of my problems, I couldn't deny it.

"Just out of curiosity," he said, "what did you think of it?"

"Think of what?"

"My obituary." He leaned forward and started fooling with the salt and pepper shakers, tapping them together and sliding them around like partners in a square dance. "I mean, did you get any feeling for who I was? The kind of person I am?"

I shook my head.

"Nothing stood out?"

I said no.

"I see. Maybe you wouldn't mind telling me, what exactly does it take for you to remember someone?"

"Look," I said, "you write obituaries all day, they sort of blur together."

"Yes, but you must remember some of them."

"Some of them, sure."

"Which ones?"

"Writers I like. Great baseball players. Movie stars I've been in love with."

"Celebrities, in other words."

"Some of them, yes. Not all."

"You can lead a good life without being a celebrity," he said. "People with big names aren't always big people."

"That's true," I said, "but it's sort of a little person's truth."

"Is that so? And what does that make you?"

I didn't answer.

"If the only thing that impresses you is having a big name, then you must be a regular midget. At least that's the way I see it." He gave me a hard look and gripped the salt and pepper shakers like a machine gunner about to let off a burst.

"That's not the only thing that impresses me."

"Oh yeah? What else, then?"

I let the question settle. "Moral distinction," I said.

He repeated the words. They sounded pompous.

"You know what I mean," I said.

"Correct me if I'm wrong," he said, "but I have a feeling that's not your department, moral distinction."

I didn't argue.

"And you're obviously not a celebrity."

"Obviously."

"So where does that leave you?" When I didn't answer, he said, "Think you'd remember your own obituary?"

"Probably not."

"No probably about it! You wouldn't even give it a second thought."

"Okay, definitely not."

"You wouldn't even give it a second thought. And you'd be wrong. Because you probably have other qualities that would stand out if you were looking closely. Good qualities. Everybody has something. What do you pride yourself on?"

"I'm a survivor," I said. But I didn't think that claim would carry much weight in an obituary.

Givens said, "With me it's loyalty. Loyalty is a very clear pattern in my life. You would've noticed that if you'd had your eyes open. When you read that a man has served his country in time of war, stayed married to the same woman forty-two years, worked at the same job, by God, that should tell you something. That should give you a certain picture."

He stopped to nod at his own words. "And it hasn't always been easy," he said.

I had to laugh, mostly at myself for being such a dim bulb. "It was you," I said. "You did it."

"Did what?"

"Called in the obit."

"Why would I do that?"

"You tell me."

"That would be saying I did it." Givens couldn't help smiling, proud of what a slyboots he was.

I said, "You're out of your ever-loving mind," but I didn't mean it. There was nothing in what Givens had done that I couldn't make sense of or even, in spite of myself, admire. He had dreamed up a way of going to his own funeral. He'd tried on his last suit, so to speak, seen himself rouged up and laid out, and listened to his own eulogy. And the best part was, he resurrected afterward. That was the real point, even if he thought he was doing it to throw a scare into Dolly or put his virtues on display. Resurrection was what it was all about, and this tax collector had gotten himself a taste of it. It was biblical.

"You're a caution, Mr. Givens. You're a definite caution."

"I didn't come here to be insulted."

"Relax," I told him. "I'm not mad."

He scraped his chair back and stood up. "I've got better things to do than sit here and listen to accusations."

I followed him outside. I wasn't ready to let him go. He had to give me something first. "Admit you did it," I said.

He turned away and started up Powell.

"Just admit it," I said. "I won't hold it against you."

He kept walking, head stuck forward in that turtlish way, navigating the crowd. He was slippery and quick. Finally I took his arm and pulled him into a doorway. His muscles bunched under my fingers. He almost jerked free, but I tightened my grip and we stood there frozen in contention.

"Admit it."

He shook his head.

"I'll break your neck if I have to," I told him.

"Let go," he said.

"If something happened to you right now, your obituary would be solid news. Then I could get my job back."

He tried to pull away again, but I held him fast.

"It'd make a hell of a story," I said.

His arm went slack. Then he said, almost inaudibly, "Yes." Just that one word.

This was the best I was going to get out of him. It had to be enough. When I let go of his arm he turned and ducked his head and took his place in the stream of people walking past. I started back to Tad's for my box. Just ahead of me a mime was following a young swell in a three-piece suit, catching to the life his leading-man's assurance, the supercilious tilt of his chin. A girl laughed raucously. The swell looked back and the mime froze. He was still holding his pose as I came by. I slipped him a quarter, hoping he'd let me pass.

Flyboys

My friend Clark and I decided to build a jet plane. We spent weeks perfecting our design at the draftsman's table in his bedroom. Sometimes Clark let me put on the green eyeshade and wield the compasses and calipers, but never for long. I drew like a lip-reader reads; watching me was torture for him. When he couldn't take it anymore he'd bump me aside, leaving me free to fool with his things—the samurai sword, the Webley pistol with the plugged barrel—and wander the house.

Clark's mom was usually out somewhere. I formed the habit of making myself a sandwich and settling back in the leather chair in the den, where I listened to old records and studied the family photo albums. They were lucky people, Clark's parents, lucky and unsurprised by their luck. You could see in the pictures that they took it all in stride, the big spreads behind them, the boats and cars, and their relaxed, handsome families who, it was clear, did not get laid off, or come down with migraines, or lock each other out of the house. I pondered each picture as if it were a door I might enter, until something turned in me and I grew irritable. Then I put the albums away and went back to Clark's room to inspect his work and demand revisions.

Sure and commanding in everything but this, Clark took most of my ideas to heart, which made a tyrant of me. The more attentive he was, the more I bullied him. His own proposals I laughed off as moronic jokes. Clark cared more for the perfection of the plane than for his own vanity; he thought nothing of crumpling a page he'd spent hours on and starting over because of some brainstorm I'd had. This wasn't humility, more an assurance that ran to imperturbable depths and rendered him deaf to any appeal when he rejected one of my inspirations. There were times—many times—when I contemplated that squarish head of his as I hefted the samurai sword, and imagined the stroke that would drop it to the floor like a ripe melon.

Clark was stubborn but there was no meanness in him. He wouldn't turn on you; he was the same one day as the next, earnest and practical. Though the family had money and spent it freely, he wasn't spoiled or interested in possessions except as instruments of his projects. In the eight or nine months we'd been friends we had shot two horror movies with his dad's 8-mm camera, built a catapult that worked so well his parents made us take it apart, and fashioned a monstrous, unsteerable sled out of a bed frame and five wooden skis we found in his neighbor's trash. We also wrote a radio mystery for a competition one of the local stations put on every year, Clark patiently retyping the script as I improvised more tortuous plot twists and highfalutin dialogue: "My dear Carstairs, it was really most astute of you to notice the mud on my smoking jacket. How unfortunate that you failed to decry the derringer in my pocket!" We were flabbergasted that we didn't win.

I supplied the genius, or so I believed. But I understood even then that Clark gave it form and did all the work. His drawings of our plane were crisp and minutely detailed, like real blueprints that a spy would cut somebody's throat for. As I pondered them at the end of the day (frontal and side views, views from above and behind and below), the separate designs locked together like a puzzle and lifted away from the flatness of the page. They became an airplane, a jet— my jet. And through all the long run home I was in the cockpit, skimming sawtooth peaks, weaving through steep valleys, buzzing fishermen in the sound and tearing over the city in such a storm of flash and thunder that football games stopped in midplay, cheerleaders gaping up at me, legs still flexed under their plaid skirts. A barrel roll, a waggle of the wings, and I was gone, racing up through the clouds. I could feel the g's in my arms, my chest, my face. The skin pulled back from my cheeks. Tears streaked from my eyes. The plane shook like crazy. When I couldn't go any higher, I went higher. Sweet Jesus, I did some flying!

Clark and I hadn't talked much about the actual construction of the jet. We let that question hang while we fine-tuned the plans. But the plans couldn't be worked on forever; we were getting bored and stale. And then Clark came up to me at recess one day and said he knew where we could get a canopy. When I asked him where, he looked over at the guy I'd been shooting baskets with and pushed his lips together. Clark had long ago decided that I was a security risk. "You'll see," he said, and walked off.

All afternoon I nagged him to tell me where the canopy was, who we were getting it from. He wouldn't say a thing. I wanted to tear him apart.

Instead of heading toward his place after school, Clark led me down the avenue past the post office and Safeway and the line of drive-ins and pinball joints where the high-school kids hung out. Clark had long legs and never looked right or left, he just flat-out marched, so I had to hustle to keep up. I resented being at his heels, sweaty and short of breath and ignorant of our destination, and most of all I resented his knowing that I'd follow him anyway.

We turned down the alley beside the Odd Fellows Hall and skirted a big lot full of school buses, then cut through a construction site that gave onto a park where I'd once been chased by some older boys. On the other side of the park we crossed the bridge over Flint Creek, swollen with a week's heavy rain. Beyond the bridge the road turned into a series of mudholes bordered by small, soggy-looking houses overhung by dripping trees. By then I'd stopped asking where we were going, because I knew. I had been this way before, many times.

"I don't remember Freddy having any airplane canopies around," I said.

"He's got a whole barnful of stuff."

"I know, I've seen it, but I didn't see any canopies."

"Maybe he just got it."

"That's a big fat maybe."

Clark picked up the pace.

I said, "So, Mr. Top Secret, how come you told Freddy about the plane?"

"I didn't. Sandra told him."

I let that ride, since I'd told Sandra.

Freddy lived at the dead end of the street. As Clark and I got closer I could hear the snarl of a chain saw from the woods behind the house. Freddy and I used to lose ourselves all day in there. I hung back while Clark went up to the house and knocked. Freddy's mother opened the door. She let Clark in and waited as I crossed the yard and mounted the steps. "Well, aren't you a sight for sore eyes," she said, not as a reproach, though it felt like one. She ruffled my hair as I went past. "You've grown a few inches."

"Yes, ma'am."

"Freddy's in the kitchen."

Freddy closed his book and stood up from the table. He smiled shyly. "Hi," he said, and I said hi back. It came hard. We hadn't spoken in almost a year, since he went into the hospital. Freddy's mother came in behind us and said, "Sit down, boys. Take off your coats. Freddy, put some of those cookies on a plate."

"I can't stay long," Clark said, but nobody answered him and he finally hung his jacket on a chair and pulled up to the table. It was a round table that took up most of the kitchen. Freddy's brother, Tanker, had carved pictures all over the tabletop, Field & Stream–type depictions of noble stags and leaping fish, eagles with rabbits in their talons, cougars crouched above mountain goats. He always kept his barlow knife busy while he drank Olympia and told his stories. Like the stories, the pictures all ran together. They would've covered the whole table by now if Tanker hadn't been killed.

The air smelled like laundry, and the windows were misted up. Freddy shook some Oreos onto a plate and handed it to me. I passed it on to Clark without taking any. The plate was dingy. Not encrusted, no major food groups in evidence—just dingy. Business as usual. I never ate at Freddy's unless I was starving. Clark didn't seem to notice. He grabbed a handful, and after a show of indecision Freddy's mother took one. She was a thin woman with shoulder blades that stuck out like wings when she hunched over, as she did now, nibbling at her Oreo. She turned to me, her eyes so sad I had to force myself not to look away. "I can't get over how you've grown," she said. "Freddy, hasn't he grown?"

"Like a weed," Freddy said.

"By leaps and bounds," I said, falling into our old game in spite of myself.

Clark looked back and forth between us.

Freddy's mother said, "I understand you boys are building an airplane."

"We're just getting started," Clark said.

"Well, that's just wonderful," Freddy's mother said. "An airplane. Think of that."

"Right now we're looking for a canopy," Clark said.

Nobody spoke for a while. Freddy's mother crossed her arms over her chest and bent down even farther. Then she said, "Freddy, you should tell your friends what you were telling me about that fellow in your book."

"That's okay," Freddy said. "Maybe later."

"About the mountains of skulls."

"Human skulls?" I said.

"Mountains of them," Freddy's mother said.

"Tamerlane," Freddy said. And without further delay he began to describe Tamerlane's revenge on the Persian cities that had resisted his progress. It was grisly stuff, and he didn't scrimp on details or try to hide his pleasure in them, or in the starchy phrases he'd picked up from whatever book he was reading. That was Freddy for you. Gentle as a lamb, but very big on the Vikings and Aztecs and Genghis Khan and the Crusaders, all the great old disembowelers and eyeball gougers. So was I. It was an interest we shared. Clark listened, looking a little stunned.

I never found out exactly how Tanker got killed; it was a motorcycle accident outside Spokane, that was all Freddy told me. You had to know Tanker to know what that meant. This was a very unlucky family. Bats took over their attic. Their cars laid transmissions like eggs. They got caught switching license plates and dumping garbage illegally and owing back taxes, or at least Ivan did. Ivan was Freddy's stepfather and a world of bad luck all by himself. He wasn't vicious or evil, just full of cute ideas that got him in trouble and made things even worse than they already were, like not paying property taxes on the basis of some veterans' exemption he'd heard about but didn't bother to read up on and that turned out not to apply to him. That brilliant stroke almost cost them the house, which Freddy's father had left free and clear when he died. Tanker was the only one in the family who could stand up to Ivan, and not just because he was bigger and more competent. Ivan had a soft spot for him. After the accident he took to his bed for almost a week, then vanished.

When Tanker was home everybody'd be in the kitchen, sitting around the table and cracking up at his stories. He told stories about himself that I would've locked away for good, like the time his bike broke down in the middle of nowhere and a car stopped but instead of giving him a lift the guys inside hit him over the head with a lunch bag full of fresh shit. Then a patrolman arrested him and made him ride to the station in his trunk—all in the middle of a snowstorm. Tanker told that story as if it were the most precious thing that ever happened to him, tears glistening in his eyes. He had lots of friends, wise guys in creaking leather jackets, and he filled the house with them. He could fix anything—plumbing, engines, leaky roofs, you name it. He took Freddy and me on fishing trips in his rattletrap truck, and gave us Indian names. I was Hard-to-Camp-With, because I complained and snored. Freddy was Cheap-to-Feed.

After Tanker got killed everything changed at Freddy's. The house had the frozen, echoey quiet of abandonment. Ivan finally came back from wherever he'd disappeared to, though he spent most of his time away on some new enterprise. When Freddy and I got to the house after school it was always dim and still. His mother kept to herself in the back bedroom. Sometimes she came out to offer us a sandwich and ask us questions about our day, but I wished she wouldn't. I had never seen such sorrow; it appalled me. And I was even more appalled by her attempts to overcome it, because they so plainly, pathetically failed, and in failing opened up the view of a world I had only begun to suspect, where wounds did not heal, and things did not work out for the best.

One day Freddy and I were shooting baskets in the driveway when his mother called him inside. We'd been playing horse, and I took advantage of his absence to practice my hook shot. My hook had Freddy jinxed; he couldn't even hit the backboard with it. I dribbled and shot, dribbled and shot, ten, twenty times, fifty times. Freddy still didn't come back. It was very quiet. The only sound was the ball hitting the backboard, the rim, the asphalt. I stopped shooting after a while and stood there waiting, bouncing the ball. The ball was over-inflated and rose fast to the hand, making a hollow whang shadowed by a high ringing note that lingered in the silence. It began to give me the creeps. But I kept bouncing the ball, somehow unable to break the rhythm I'd fallen into. My hand moved by itself, lightly palming the pebbled skin and pushing the ball down just hard enough to bring it back. The sound grew louder and larger and emptier, the sound of emptiness itself, emptiness throbbing like a headache. Spooked, I caught the ball and held it. I looked at the house. I thought of the woman closed up inside, and Freddy, closed up with her, swallowed by misery. The house seemed conscious in its stillness, expectant. It seemed to be waiting. I put the ball down and walked to the end of the driveway, then broke into a run. I was still running when I reached the park. That was the day the older boys chased me, their blood roused by the spectacle of my rabbity flight. They kept after me for a hundred yards or so and then fell back, though they could've caught me if they'd had their hearts in it. But they were running for sport; the seriousness of my panic confused them, put them off their stride.

Such panic . . . where did it come from? It couldn't have been just the situation at Freddy's. The shakiness of my own family was becoming more and more apparent. At the time I didn't admit to this knowledge, not for a moment, but it was always there, lingering in the gut: a sourness of foreboding, a cramp of alarm at any sign of misfortune or weakness in others, as if such things were catching.

Freddy had asthma. Not long after I ran away from his house he suffered a severe attack and went into the hospital. Our teacher told the class about it. She had everyone write get-well notes and handed out mimeographed sheets with the hospital's address and visiting hours. It was an easy walk. I knew I should go, and thought about it so much that whatever else I did that week seemed mainly to be *not going,* but I couldn't make myself do it. When Freddy came back to school I was unable to speak to him or even face him. I went straight home after the bell rang, using the main entrance instead of the side door where we used to meet. And then I saw that he was avoiding me too. He ate at the opposite end of the cafeteria; when we passed in the hallway he blushed and stared at the floor. He acted as if he'd done me some wrong, and the shame I felt at this made me even more skittish. I was very lonely for a time, then Clark and I became friends. This was my first visit to Freddy's since the day I bolted.

Clark polished off the Oreos as Freddy told his gruesome tale, and when he came to the end I started one of my own from a book my brother had given me about Quantrill's Raiders. It was a truly terrible story, a cruel, mortifying story—the star sociopath was a man named Bloody Bill. I was aware of Freddy watching me with something like rapture. Freddy's mother shook her head when the going got rough and made exclamations of shock and dismay—"No! He never!"—just like she used to do back when the three of us watched *Queen for a Day* every afternoon, drooling shamelessly over the weird, woeful narratives sobbed out by the competing wretches. Clark watched me without joy. He was impatient for business and too sane for all this ghoulish stuff. I knew that he was seeing me in a different way, a way he probably didn't like, but I kept piling it on. I couldn't let go of the old pleasure, almost forgotten, of having Freddy on my hook and feeling his own pleasure thrumming through the line.

Then the back door swung open and Ivan leaned his head into the kitchen. His face was even bigger and whiter than I remembered, and as if to confirm my memory he wore a red hunting cap that was too small and sat on his head like a party hat. Black mud encased his legs almost to his knees. He looked at me and said, "Hey, by gum! Long time no see!" One of the lenses of his spectacles had a daub of mud in the middle, like an eyeball on a pair of joke glasses. He looked at Clark, then at Freddy's mother. "Hon, you aren't gonna believe this— that darn truck got stuck again."

A damp wind was blowing. Freddy and Clark and I stood with shoulders hunched, hands in our pockets, and looked on as Ivan circled Tanker's old pickup and explained why it wasn't his fault the tires were mired almost to the axle. "The truth is, the old gal just can't pull her weight anymore." He gave the fender a rub. "Past her prime—has been for years."

"Yessir," Freddy said. "She's long in the tooth and that's a fact."

"There you go," Ivan said.

"Ready for the pasture," I said.

"Over the hill," Freddy said.

"That's it exactly," Ivan said. "I just can't bring myself to sell her." His jaw started quaking and I thought with horror that he was about to cry. But he didn't. He caught his lower lip under his teeth, sucked it musingly, and pushed it out again. His lips were full and expressive. I tended to watch them for signs of mood rather than his eyes, which he kept buried in a cunning squint.

"So," he said. "Gotta get the wood out. You fellows ready to use some of those muscles?"

Freddy and I looked at each other.

Clark was staring at the truck. "You want us to unload all of that?"

"Won't take an hour, strapping boys like you," Ivan said. "Maybe an hour by the time you load her up again," he added.

The truck bed was filled with logs, stacked as high as the sides and heaped to a peak in the middle. Ivan had been clearing out the woods behind the house. Most of it was gone by now, nearly an acre of trees turned into a stumpy bog crisscrossed by tire ruts filled with black water. Behind the bog stood the house of a family whose pale, stringy daughters quarreled incessantly with their mother, screaming as they ran out the door, screaming as they jumped into the souped-up cars of their boyfriends. The father and son also drove hot rods, maintaining them on parts cannibalized from the collection of wrecks in their backyard. They came out during the afternoons and weekends to crawl under the cars and shout at each other over the clanging of their wrenches. Freddy and I used to spy on the family from the trees, our faces darkened, twigs stuck in our hair. He wouldn't have to steal up on them now; they'd be in plain view all the time.

Ivan had been hard at work turning trees into firewood. But firewood was cheap, and whatever he got wouldn't be worth it—worth all the green and the birds and the scolding squirrels, the coolness in summer, the long shafts of afternoon light. This place had been Iroquois wilderness to me, English forest and African jungle. It had been Mars. Now gone, completely. I was a boy who didn't know he would never build a jet, but I knew that this lake of mud was the work of a fool.

"I'll bet you can drive it out without unloading," Clark said.

"Already tried." Ivan lowered himself onto a stump and looked around with a satisfied air. "Sooner you fellows get started, sooner you'll be done."

"A stitch in time saves nine," I said.

"No time like the present," Freddy said.

"There you go," Ivan said.

Clark had been standing on a web of roots. He stepped off and walked toward the truck. As he got closer the ground turned soupy and he went up on tiptoe, then began hopping from foot to foot, but there was no firm place to land and every time he jumped he went in deeper. When he sank past his ankles he gave up and mucked ahead, his sneakers slurping, picking up more goop with each step. By the time he reached the truck they looked like medicine balls. He crouched by one rear tire, then the other.

"We can put down corduroy tracks," he said.

Ivan winked in our direction. "Corduroy tracks, you say!"

"That's what they used to do when covered wagons got stuck," Clark said. "Put logs down."

"Son, does that look like a covered wagon to you?"

"Also artillery pieces. In the Civil War."

"Maybe we should just unload the truck," I said.

"Hold your horses." Ivan put his hands on his knees and studied Clark. "I like a boy with ideas," he said. "Go on, give it a stab."

"Never hurts to try," Freddy said.

"That's it exactly," Ivan said.

Freddy and I walked up to the barn for a couple of shovels. We cut wide of the ruts and puddles but the mud still sucked at our shoes. Once we were alone, I kept thinking how thin he'd gotten. I couldn't come up with anything to say. He didn't speak either.

I waited while Freddy went into the barn, and when he came back outside I said, "We're going to move." Though no one had told me any such thing, those words came to mind and it felt right to say them.

Freddy handed me a shovel. "Where to?"

"I don't know."

"When?"

"I'm not sure."

We started back.

"I hope you don't move," Freddy said.

"Maybe we won't," I said. "Maybe we'll end up staying."

"That would be great, if you stayed."

"There's no place like home."

"Home is where the heart is," Freddy said, but he was looking at the ground just ahead of him and didn't smile back at me.

We took turns digging out the wheels, one resting while the other two worked. Ivan laughed whenever we slipped into the mud, but otherwise watched in silence. It was impossible to dig and keep your feet, especially as we got deeper. Finally I gave up and knelt down to work—I got more leverage that way—and Clark and Freddy followed suit. I was sheathed in mud up to my waist and elbows. My condition was hopeless, so I stopped trying to spare myself and just let go. I surrendered to the spirit of the mud. It's fair to say I wallowed.

What we did, under Clark's direction, was cut a wide trench from the bottom of each tire forward about five feet, sloping up like a ramp. We jammed cordwood under the tires and then lined the ramps with more logs as we dug. We were about finished when the walls started to collapse. Clark took it personally. "Fudge!" he kept saying, and Ivan laughed and swayed back and forth on the stump. Clark yelled at Freddy and me to *dig! dig! dig!* and stretched flat on his stomach and scooped the sliding mud out with his hands. I could hear Freddy laboring for breath, but he didn't let up, and neither did I. We burrowed like moles and then came a moment when the tracks were clear and the walls holding, and Clark told Ivan to move the truck. Clark was excited and barked at him as he'd been barking at us. Ivan sat there blinking. Clark pitched some spare logs back into the truck. "Come on, guys," he said. "We'll push."

Ivan stood and brushed off his hands and walked over to the truck, still watching Clark. Before he climbed into the cab, he said, "Young fellow, if you ever need a job, call me."

Clark and Freddy and I braced ourselves against the tailgate as Ivan cranked the engine and put it in gear. The rear wheels started to spin, churning back geysers of mud. I was in the middle so I didn't catch much of it, but Freddy and Clark got plastered. Freddy turned away and then leaned forward again and started pushing with Clark and me. Ivan was rocking the truck to and fro, trying to get it onto the logs. It rose a little, hesitated, then slipped and spewed back another blast of mud. Clark and Freddy looked like they'd been stuccoed. They moved in closer beside me as Ivan got the truck rocking again. I held my breath against the heavy black exhaust. My eyes burned. The truck rocked and rose again, hanging on the lip. Clark grunted, again and again and again. I picked up his rhythm and pushed for all I was worth, and then my feet slid and I fell flat out as the truck jerked forward. The tires screamed on the wood. A log shot back and flipped past Clark's head. He didn't seem to notice. He was watching the truck. It gathered speed on the track we'd made and hit the mud again and somehow slithered on, languidly, noisily, rear end sashaying, two great plumes of mud arcing off the back wheels. The wheels spun wildly, the engine shrieked, logs tumbled off the sides. The truck slewed and swayed across the bog and rose abruptly, shedding skirts of mud, as it gained the broken asphalt in front of the barn. Ivan shifted gears, beeped merrily, and drove away.

"You all right?" Clark said.

Freddy was bent double, head almost between his knees. He held up a hand but went on panting. The truck had left behind an exaggerated silence in which I could hear the clutch and rasp of every breath he took. It sounded like hard work, hard and lonely. When I moved toward him he waved me off. Clark picked up a stick and began scraping his sneakers. This seemed an optimistic project, caked as he was to the eyeballs, and he went about it with method and gravity. Freddy straightened up. His face was pallid, his chest rose and fell like a bird's. He stood there awhile, watching Clark wield the stick. "We can get cleaned up at the house," he said.

"If it's okay with you," Clark said, "I'd like to take a look at that canopy."

I'd been hoping all afternoon that Clark would drop the subject of the canopy, because I knew as a matter of absolute fact that Freddy didn't have one. But he did. It was in the loft of the barn, where his father had stored items of special interest from the salvage yard he'd owned. In all the rainy afternoons we'd spent fooling around up there I must have seen it a hundred times, though having no use for it, not even recognizing what it was, I'd never taken note. The canopy was smaller than our plans specified, but the plans could be changed; this was the genuine article. Freddy played the flashlight slowly up and down the length of it. He must have prepared for this moment, because unlike everything else up there the canopy was free of dust—polished, even, by the look of it. The light picked up a few scratches. Otherwise it was perfect: clear, unbroken, complete with flashing. Simple, yet technical too. Real.

If I'd had any doubts, they left me. It was obvious that our jet was not only possible but as good as built. All we had to do was keep having days like this and soon the pieces would all come together, and we'd be flying.

Clark asked Freddy what he wanted for it.

"Nothing. It's just sitting here."

We poked around awhile and went back to the house, where Freddy's mother declared shock at our condition and ordered us to strip and hose off. Clark wouldn't do it, he just washed his face and hands, but I took a long shower and then Freddy's mother gave me some of Tanker's clothes to wear home and wrapped my own dismal duds in a butcher-paper parcel tied off with a string handle, like a mess of gizzards. Freddy walked us to the end of the street. The light was failing. I looked back and saw him still standing there. When I looked again he was gone.

We stopped on the bridge over Flint Creek and threw rocks at a bottle caught in some weeds. I was all pumped up from getting the truck out and seeing the canopy, plus Freddy's mother had lent me Tanker's motorcycle jacket, which, though it hung to my fingertips, filled me with a conviction of my own powers that verged on madness. I was half hoping we'd run into those older boys in the park so I could whip their asses for them.

I leaned over the railing, spat into the water.

"Freddy wants in," Clark said.

"He said that? He didn't tell me."

"You were in the shower."

"So what did he say?"

"Just that he wished he could come in with us on the plane."

"What, or he takes the canopy back?"

"No. He just asked."

"We'd have to redesign the whole cockpit. It would change everything."

Clark had a rock in his hand. He looked at it with some interest, then flipped it into the creek.

"What did you tell him?"

"I said we'd let him know."

"What do you think?"

"He seems okay. You know him better than I do."

"Freddy's great, it's just . . ."

Clark waited for me to finish. When it was clear that I wasn't going to, he said, "Whatever you want."

I told him that all things considered, I'd just as soon keep it to the two of us.

As we crossed the park he asked me to have dinner at his place so he wouldn't get skinned alive about his clothes. His dad was still in Portland, he said, as if that explained something. Clark took his time on the walk home, looking in shopwindows and inspecting cars in the lots we passed. When we finally got to the house it was all lit up and music was playing. Even with the windows closed we could hear strains of it from the bottom of the sidewalk.

Clark stopped. He stood there, listening. *"South Pacific,"* he said. "Good. She's happy."

Sanity

Getting from La Jolla to Alta Vista State Hospital isn't easy, unless you have a car or a breakdown. April's father had a breakdown and they got him out there in no time at all. The trip took longer for April and her stepmother; they had to catch two different buses, hike up a hot, winding road through the hospital grounds, then walk back down to the bus stop when the visit was over. There were few drivers on the road, and none stopped to offer a lift. April didn't blame them. They probably figured she and Claire were patients out for a stroll. That's what she would've thought, coming upon the two of them out here. One look and she'd have kept going.

Claire was tall and erect. She was wearing a smart gray suit and high heels and a wide-brimmed black hat. She carried herself a little stiffly because of the heels but kept up a purposeful, dignified pace. "Ship of State"—that was what April's father called Claire when she felt summoned to demonstrate her steadiness and resolve. April followed along in loose order. She stopped now and then to catch her breath and let some distance open up between them, then hurried to close it. April was a short muscular girl with a mannish stride. She was scowling in the hazy midsummer light. Her hands were red. She had on a sleeveless dress, yellow with black flowers, that she knew was ugly and wore anyway because it made people conscious of her.

Two cars went by, their tires moving over the tacky asphalt with the sound of tape being peeled. April's father had sold the Volkswagen for almost nothing a few days before he went into the hospital, and Claire wouldn't even look at anything else. She had some money in the bank but was saving it for a trip to Italy with her sister when April's father came home.

Claire had been quiet through most of the visit, quiet and on edge, and now that it was over she didn't try to hide her relief. She wanted to talk. She said the doctor they'd spoken with reminded her of Walt Darsh, her husband during the last ice age. That was how she located whatever had happened to her in the past—"during the last ice age." April knew she wanted to be told that she still looked good, and it wouldn't have been a lie to say so, but this time April said nothing.

She had heard about Walt Darsh before, his faithlessness and cruelty. Though the stories Claire told were interesting, they left April troubled, strange to herself. As soon as Claire got started, April said, "If he was so bad, how come you married him?"

Claire didn't answer right away. She walked more slowly, and inclined her long neck thoughtfully, and gave every sign of being occupied with a new and demanding question. She looked at April, then away. "Sex," she said.

April could see the glitter of windshields in the distance. There was a bench at the bus stop; when they got there she was going to lie down and close her eyes and pretend to sleep.

"It's hard to explain," Claire said cautiously, as if April had pressed her. "It wasn't his looks. Darsh isn't really what you'd call handsome. He has a sly, pointy kind of face . . . like a fox. You know what I mean? It isn't just the shape, it's the way he watches you, always grinning a little, like he's got the goods on you." Claire stopped in the shade of a tree. She took off her hat, smoothed back her hair, curled some loose strands behind her ears, then put her hat back on and set it just so across her forehead. She found a Kleenex in her purse and dabbed the corner of one eye where a thin line of mascara had run. Claire had the gift, mysterious to April, of knowing what she looked like even without a mirror. April's face was always a surprise to her, always somehow different than she'd imagined it.

"Of course that can be attractive too," Claire said, "being looked at like that. With most men it's annoying, but not always. With Darsh it was attractive. So I suppose you could say that it *was* his looks, in the literal sense. If you see the distinction."

April saw the distinction, also Claire's pleasure in having made it. She was unhappy with this line of talk but couldn't do anything about it, because it was her own fault that Claire believed she was ripe for unrestrained discussion of these matters. Over the last few months Claire had decided that April was sleeping with Stuart, the boy she went out with. This was not the case. Stuart dropped hints now and then in his polite, witty, hopeless way, but he wasn't really serious and neither was April. She hadn't told Claire the truth because in the beginning it was satisfying to be seen as a woman of experience. Claire was a snob about knowing the ways of the world; it pleased April to crowd her turf a little. Claire never asked, she simply assumed, and once that assumption took hold there was no straightening things out.

The brim of Claire's hat waved up and down. She seemed to be having an idea she agreed with. "Looks are part of it," she said, "definitely. But not the whole story. With sex, it never is just one thing, is it? Like technique, for instance." She turned and started down the road again, head still pensively bent. April could feel a lecture coming on. Claire taught sociology at the same junior college where April's father used to teach psych, and like him she was quick to mount the podium.

"People write about technique," she said, "as if it's the whole ball game, which is a complete joke. You know who's really getting off on technique? Publishers, that's who. Because they can turn it into a commodity. They can merchandise it as how-to, like traveling in Mexico or building a redwood deck. The only problem is, it doesn't work. You know why? Because it turns sex into a literary experience."

April couldn't stop herself from giggling. This made her sound foolish, as she knew.

"I'm serious," Claire said. "You can tell right away that it's coming out of some book. You start seeing yourself in one of those little squiggly drawings, with your zones all marked out and some earnest little cartoon guy working through them one by one, being really considerate."

Claire stopped again and gazed out over the fields that lined the road, resting one hand on top of a fence post. Back in the old days, according to April's father, the patients used to grow things in these fields. Now they were overgrown with scrubby trees and tall yellow grass. Insects shrilled loudly.

"That's another reason those books are worthless," Claire said. "They're all about sharing, being tender, anticipating your partner's needs, et cetera et cetera. It's like Sunday school in bed. I'm not kidding, April. That's what it's all about, this technique stuff. Judeo-Christian conscientiousness. The Golden Rule. You know what I mean?"

"I guess," April said.

"We're talking about a very basic transaction," Claire said. "A lot more basic than lending money to a friend. Think about it. Lending is a highly evolved activity. Other species don't do it, only us. Just look at all the things that go into lending money. Social stability, trust, generosity. Imagining yourself in the other person's place. It's incredibly advanced, incredibly civilized. I'm all for it. My point is, sex comes from another place. Sex isn't civilized. It isn't about being unselfish."

An ambulance went slowly past. April looked after it, then back at Claire, who was still staring out over the fields. April saw the line of her profile in the shadow of the hat, saw how dry and cool her skin was, the composure of her smile. April saw these things and felt her own sticky, worried, incomplete condition. "We ought to get going," she said.

"To tell the truth," Claire said, "that was one of the things that attracted me to Darsh. He was totally selfish, totally out to please himself. That gave him a certain heat. A certain power. The libbers would kill me for saying this, but it's true. Did I ever tell you about our honeymoon?"

"No." April made her voice flat and grudging, though she was curious.

"Or the maid thing? Did I ever tell you about Darsh's maid thing?"

"No," April said again. "What about the honeymoon?"

Claire said, "That's a long story. I'll tell you about the maid thing."

"You don't have to tell me anything," April said.

Claire went on smiling to herself. "Back when Darsh was a kid, his mother took him on a trip to Europe. The grand tour. He was too young for it, thirteen, fourteen—that age. By the time they got to Amsterdam he was sick of museums, he never wanted to see another painting in his life. That's the trouble with pushing culture at children, they end up hating it. It's better to let them come to it on their own, don't you think?"

April shrugged.

"Take Jane Austen, for example. They were shoving Jane Austen down my throat when I was in the eighth grade. *Pride and Prejudice.* Of course I absolutely loathed it, because I couldn't see what was really going on, the sexual play behind the manners, the social critique, the *economics.* I hadn't lived. You have to have some life under your belt before you can make any sense of a book like that.

"Anyway, Darsh dug in his heels when they got to Amsterdam. He wouldn't budge. He stayed in the hotel room all day long, reading mysteries and ordering stuff from room service, while his mother went out and looked at paintings. One afternoon a maid came up to the room to polish the chandelier. She had a stepladder, and from where Darsh was sitting he couldn't help seeing up her dress. All the way up, okay? And she knew it. He knew she knew, because after a while he didn't even try to hide it, he just stared. She didn't say a word. Not one. She took her sweet time up there too, polishing every pendant, cool as a cucumber. Darsh said it went on for a couple of hours, which means maybe half an hour—which is a pretty long time, if you think about it."

"Then what happened?"

"Nothing. Nothing happened. That's the whole point, April. If something had happened it would've broken the spell. It would have let out all that incredible energy. But it stayed locked in. It's always there, boiling away at this insane fourteen-year-old level, just waiting to explode. Maids are one of Darsh's real hot spots. He used to own the whole outfit, probably still does—you know, frilly white blouse, black skirt, black nylons with all the little snaps. It's a cliché, of course. Pornographers have been using it for a hundred years. But so what. It still works. Most of our desires are clichés, right? Ready to wear, one size fits all. I doubt if it's even possible to have an original desire anymore."

"He actually made you wear that stuff?"

April saw Claire freeze at her words, as if she'd said something hurtful and low. Claire straightened up and slowly started walking again. April hung back, then followed a few steps behind until Claire waited for her to catch up. After a time Claire said, "No, dear. He didn't make me do anything. It's exciting when somebody wants something that much. I loved the way he looked at me. Like he wanted to eat me alive, but innocent too.

"Maybe it sounds cheap. It's hard to describe."

Claire was quiet then, and so was April. She did not feel any need for description. She thought she could imagine the look Darsh had given Claire; in fact she could see it perfectly, though no one had ever given her such a look. Certainly not Stuart. She felt safe with him, safe and sleepy. Nobody like Stuart would ever make her as careless and willing as Darsh had made Claire in the stories she told about him. It seemed to April that she already knew Darsh, and that he knew her—as if he'd sensed her listening to these stories and was conscious of her interest.

They were almost at the road. April stopped to look back but the hospital buildings were out of sight now, behind the brow of the hill. She turned and walked on. She had one more of these trips to make. The week after that her father would be coming home. He'd been the-atrically calm all through their visit, sitting by the window in an easy chair, feet propped on the ottoman, a newspaper across his lap. He was wearing slippers and a cardigan sweater. All he needed was a pipe. He seemed fine, the very picture of health, but that was all it was: a picture. At home he never read the paper. He didn't sit down much either. The last time April saw him outside the hospital, a month ago, he was under restraint in their landlord's apartment, where he'd gone to complain about the shower. He'd been kicking and yelling. His glasses were hanging from one ear. He was shouting at her to call the cops, and one of the policemen holding him down was laughing helplessly.

He hadn't crashed yet. He was still flying. April had seen it in his eyes behind the lithium or whatever they were giving him, and she was sure that Claire had seen it too. Claire didn't say anything, but April had been through this with Ellen, her first stepmother, and she'd developed an instinct. She was afraid that Claire had already had enough, that she wasn't going to come back from Italy. Not back to them, anyway. It wouldn't happen according to some plan; it would just happen. April didn't want her to leave, not now. She needed another year. Not even a year—ten months, until she finished school and got herself into college somewhere. If she could cross that line she was sure she could handle whatever came later.

She didn't want Claire to go. Claire had her ways, but she had been good to her, especially in the beginning, when April was always finding fault. She'd put up with it. She'd been patient and let April come to her in her own time. One night April leaned against her when they were reading on the couch, and Claire leaned back, and neither of them drew away. It became their custom to sit like that, braced against each other, reading. Claire thought about things. She had always spoken honestly to April, though with a certain decorum. Now the decorum was gone. Ever since she got the idea that April was "intimate" with Stuart, Claire had withdrawn the protections of ceremony and tact, as she would soon withdraw the protections of her income and her care and her presence.

There was no hope of changing things back. And even if there were, even if by saying *I'm still a virgin* she could turn Claire into some kind of perfect mother, April wouldn't do it. It would sound ridiculous and untrue. It wasn't really true, except as a fact about her body, and April did not see virginity as residing in the body. To her it was a quality of the spirit, and something you could only surrender in spirit. She had done this; she didn't know exactly when or how, but she knew she had done this and she didn't regret it. She did not want to be a virgin and would not pretend to be one, not for anything. When she thought of a virgin she saw someone half naked, with dumb trusting eyes and flowers woven into her hair, bound at the wrists. She saw a clearing in the jungle, and in the clearing an altar.

Their bus had come and gone, and they had a long wait until the next one. Claire settled on the bench and started reading a book. April had forgotten hers. She sat with Claire for a while, then got up and paced the street when Claire's serenity became intolerable. She walked with her arms crossed and her head bent forward, frowning, scuffing her shoes. Cars rushed past blaring music; a big sailboat on a trailer; a convoy of military trucks, headlights on, soldiers swaying in back. The air was blue with exhaust. April looked in the window of a tire store and saw herself. She squared her shoulders, dropped her arms to her sides, and kept them there by an effort of will as she walked farther up the boulevard to where a line of plastic pennants fluttered over a Toyota lot. A man in a creamy suit was standing in the show-room window, watching the traffic. Even from where she stood April could see the rich drape of his suit. He had high cheekbones, black hair combed straight back from his forehead, and a big clean blade of a nose. He looked absolutely self-possessed and possibly dangerous, and April understood that he took some care to convey this. She knew he was aware of her, but he never bothered to turn in her direction. She wandered among the cars, then went back to the bus stop and slumped down on the bench.

"I'm bored," she said.

Claire didn't answer.

"Aren't you bored?"

"Not especially," Claire said. "The bus will be here before long."

"Sure, in about two weeks." April stuck her legs out and knocked the sides of her shoes together. "Let's take a walk," she said.

"I'm all walked out. But you go ahead. Just don't get too far away."

"Not *alone*, Claire. I didn't mean alone. Come on, this is boring."

April hated the sound of her voice and could tell Claire didn't like it either. Claire closed her book. She sat without moving, then said, "I guess I don't have any choice."

April rocked to her feet. She took a few steps and waited as Claire put the book in her purse, stood, ran her hands down the front of her skirt, and came slowly toward her.

"We'll just stretch our legs," April said. She led Claire up the street to the car lot, where she left the sidewalk and began circling a red Celica convertible.

"I thought you wanted to walk," Claire said.

"Right, just a minute," April said. Then the side door of the showroom swung open and the man in the suit came out. At first he seemed not to know they were there. He knelt beside a sedan and wrote something down on a clipboard. He got up and peered at the sticker on the windshield and wrote something else down. Only then did he permit himself to take notice of them. After he'd taken a long hard look at Claire, he told her to let him know if she needed anything. His voice had a studied, almost insolent neutrality.

"We're just waiting for a bus," Claire said.

"How does this car stack up against the RX-7?" April asked.

"You surely jest." He came toward them through the cars. "I could sell against Mazda any day of the week, if I were selling."

April said, "You're not a salesman?"

He stopped in front of the Celica. "We don't have salesmen here. We just collect money and try to keep the crowds friendly."

"You've got half of this crowd eating out of your hand," Claire said.

"That's a year old," he said. "Loaded to the gills. Came in last night on a repossession. It'll be gone this time tomorrow. Look at the odometer, sweet pea. What does the odometer say?"

April opened the door and leaned inside. "Four thousand and two," she said. She sat in the driver's seat and worked the gearshift.

"Exactly. Four K. Still on its first tank of gas."

"Little old lady owned it, right?" Claire said.

He gave her another long look before answering. "Little old

Marine. Went to the land of the great sand dune and didn't keep up his payments. I've got the keys right here."

"We can't. Sorry, maybe another day."

"I know, you're waiting for a bus. So kill some time."

April got out of the car but left the door open. "Claire, you have to try this seat," she said.

"We should go," Claire said.

"Claire, you just have to," April said. "Come on, Claire."

The man walked over to the open door and held out his hand. "Madame," he said. When Claire stayed where she was, he made a flourish and said, "Madame! *Entrez!*"

Claire walked up to the car. "We really should go," she said. She sat sideways on the seat and swung her legs inside, all in one motion. She nodded at the man, and he closed the door. "Yes," he said, "exactly as I thought. The designer was a friend of yours, a very special friend. This automobile was obviously built with you in mind."

"You look great," April said. It was true, and she could see that Claire was in complete possession of that truth. The knowledge was in the set of her mouth, the easy way her hands came to rest on the wheel.

"There's something missing," the man said. He studied her. "Sunglasses," he said. "A beautiful woman in a convertible has to be wearing sunglasses."

"Put on your sunglasses," April said.

"Please," the man said gently. He leaned against the car and stood over Claire, his back to April, and April understood that she was not to speak again. Her part in this was done; he would close the deal. He said something in a low voice, and Claire took her sunglasses from her purse and slipped them on. Then she handed him her hat. A gust of heat blew over the lot, rattling the pennants, as April walked toward the showroom. It looked cool in there behind the tinted glass. Quiet. They'd have coffee in the waiting area, old copies of *People*. She could give her feet a rest and catch up on the stars.

The Other Miller

For two days now Miller has been standing in the rain with the rest of Bravo Company, waiting for some men from another company to blunder down the logging road where Bravo waits in ambush. When this happens, if it happens, Miller will stick his head out of the hole he's hiding in and shoot off all his blank ammunition in the direction of the road. So will everyone else in Bravo Company. Then they'll climb out of their holes and get on some trucks and go home, back to the base.

This is the plan.

Miller has no faith in it. He has never yet seen a plan that worked, and this one won't either. His foxhole has about a foot of water in it. He has to stand on little shelves he's been digging out of the walls, but the soil is sandy and the shelves keep collapsing. That means his boots are wet. Plus his cigarettes are wet. Plus he broke the bridge on his molars the first night out while chewing up one of the lollipops he'd brought along for energy. It drives him crazy, how the bridge lifts and grates when he pushes it with his tongue, but last night he lost his willpower and can't keep his tongue away from it.

When he thinks of the other company, the one they're supposed to ambush, Miller sees a column of dry, well-fed men marching farther and farther away from the hole where he stands waiting for them. He sees them moving easily under light packs. He sees them stopping for a smoke break, stretching out under the trees on fragrant beds of pine needles, the murmur of their voices growing more and more faint as one by one they drift into sleep.

It's the truth, by God. Miller knows it like he knows he's going to catch a cold, because that's his luck. If he was in the other company they'd be the ones standing in holes.

Miller's tongue does something to the bridge and a thrill of pain shoots through him. He snaps up straight, eyes burning, teeth clenched against the yell in his throat. He fights it back and glares around him at the other men. The few he can see look stunned and ashen-faced. Of the rest he can make out only their poncho hoods, sticking out of the ground like bullet-shaped rocks.

At this moment, his mind swept clean by pain, Miller can hear the tapping of raindrops on his own poncho. Then he hears the pitchy whine of an engine. A jeep is splashing along the road, slipping from side to side and throwing up thick gouts of mud behind it. The jeep itself is caked with mud. It skids to a stop in front of Bravo Company's position, and the horn beeps twice.

Miller glances around to see what the others are doing. Nobody has moved. They're all just standing in their holes.

The horn beeps again.

A short figure in a poncho emerges from a clump of trees farther up the road. Miller can tell it's the first sergeant by how little he is, so little the poncho hangs almost to his ankles. The first sergeant walks slowly toward the jeep, big blobs of mud all around his boots. When he gets to the jeep he leans his head inside; a moment later he pulls it out. He looks down at the road. He kicks pensively at one of the tires, then looks up and shouts Miller's name.

Miller keeps watching him. Not until the first sergeant hollers his name again does Miller begin the hard work of hoisting himself out of the foxhole. The other men turn their blanched, weary faces up at him as he trudges past their holes.

"Come here, boy," the first sergeant says. He walks a little distance from the jeep and waves Miller over.

Miller follows him. Something is wrong. Miller can tell because the first sergeant called him boy instead of shit-bird. Already he feels a burning in his left side, where his ulcer is.

The first sergeant stares down the road. "Here's the thing," he begins. He stops and turns to Miller. "Goddamn it, anyway. Did you know your mother was sick?"

Miller doesn't say anything, just pushes his lips tight together.

"She must have been sick, right?" When Miller remains silent, the first sergeant says, "She passed away last night. I'm real sorry." He looks sadly up at Miller, and Miller watches his right arm beginning to rise under the poncho; then it falls to his side again. Miller can see that the first sergeant wants to give his shoulder a man-to-man kind of squeeze, but it just wouldn't work. You can only do that if you're taller than the other fellow or at least the same size.

"These boys here will drive you back to base," the first sergeant says, nodding toward the jeep. "You give the Red Cross a call and they'll take it from there. Get yourself some rest," he adds, then walks off toward the trees.

Miller retrieves his gear. One of the men he passes going back to the jeep says, "Hey, Miller, what's the story?"

Miller doesn't answer. He's afraid if he opens his mouth he'll start laughing and ruin everything. He keeps his head down and his lips tight as he climbs into the backseat of the jeep and doesn't look up until they've left the company a mile or so behind. The fat PFC sitting beside the driver is watching him. He says, "I'm sorry about your mother. That's a bummer."

"For sure," says the driver, another PFC. He shoots a look over his shoulder.

Miller sees his own face reflected for an instant in the driver's sunglasses. "Had to happen someday," he mumbles, and looks down again.

Miller's hands are shaking. He puts them between his knees and stares through the snapping plastic window at the trees. Raindrops rattle on the canvas overhead. He's inside, and everyone else is still outside. Miller can't stop thinking about the others standing around getting rained on, and the thought makes him want to laugh and slap his leg. This is the luckiest he has ever been.

"My grandmother died last year," the driver says. "But that's not the same thing as losing your mother. I feel for you, Miller."

"Don't worry about me," Miller tells him. "I'll get along."

The fat PFC beside the driver says, "Look, don't feel like you have to repress just because we're here. If you want to cry or anything, just go ahead. Right, Leb?"

The driver nods. "Just let it out."

"No problem," Miller says. He wishes he could set these fellows straight so they won't feel like they have to act mournful all the way to Fort Ord. But if he tells them what happened, they'll turn right around and drive him back to his foxhole.

Miller knows what happened. There's another Miller in the battalion with the same initials he's got, "W.P.," and this Miller is the one whose mother died. The army screws up their mail all the time, and now they've screwed this up. Miller got the whole picture as soon as the first sergeant started asking about his mother.

For once, everybody else is on the outside and Miller's on the inside. Inside, heading straight to a hot shower, dry clothes, a pizza, and a warm bunk. He didn't even have to do anything wrong to get here; he just did as he was told. It was their own mistake. Tomorrow he'll rest up like the first sergeant ordered him to, go on sick call about his bridge, maybe downtown to a movie after that. Then he'll call the Red Cross. By the time they get everything straightened out it will be too late to send him back to the field. And the best thing is, the other Miller won't know. The other Miller will have a whole other day of thinking his mother is still alive. You could even say that Miller is keeping her alive for him.

The man beside the driver turns around again and studies Miller. He has small dark eyes in a big white face covered with beads of sweat. His name tag reads KAISER. Showing little teeth square as a baby's, he says, "You're really coping, Miller. Most guys pretty much lose it when they get the word."

"I would too," the driver says. "Anybody would. It's *human*, Kaiser."

"For sure," Kaiser says. "I'm not saying I'm any different. That's going to be my worst day, the day my mom dies." He blinks rapidly, but not before Miller sees his little eyes mist up.

"Everybody has to go sometime," Miller says, "sooner or later. That's my philosophy."

"Heavy," the driver says. "Really deep."

Kaiser gives him a sharp look. "At ease, Lebowitz."

Miller leans forward. Lebowitz is a Jewish name. Miller wants to ask him why he's in the army, but he's afraid Lebowitz might take it wrong. Instead, conversationally, he says, "You don't see too many Jewish people in the army nowadays."

Lebowitz looks into the rearview, his thick eyebrows arching over his sunglasses. Then he shakes his head and says something Miller can't make out.

"At ease, Leb," Kaiser says again. He turns to Miller and asks him where the funeral will be held.

"What funeral?" Miller says.

Lebowitz laughs.

"Fuckhead," Kaiser says to him. "Haven't you ever heard of shock?"

Lebowitz is quiet for a moment, then he looks into the rearview again and says, "Sorry, Miller. I was out of line."

Miller shrugs. His probing tongue pushes the bridge too hard and he stiffens suddenly.

"Where did your mom live?" Kaiser asks.

"Redding," Miller says.

Kaiser nods. "Redding," he repeats. He keeps watching Miller. So does Lebowitz, glancing back and forth between the mirror and the road. Miller understands that they expected a different kind of performance than the one he's giving them, more emotional and all. They've seen other personnel whose mothers died and have certain standards he has failed to live up to. He looks out the window. They're driving along a ridgeline. Slices of blue flicker between the trees to the left of the road; then they hit a clear space and Miller can see the ocean below them, clear to the horizon under a bright, cloudless sky. Except for a few hazy wisps in the treetops they've left the clouds behind, back in the mountains, hanging over the soldiers there.

"Don't get me wrong," Miller says. "I'm sorry she's dead."

Kaiser says, "That's the way. Talk it out."

"It's just that I didn't know her all that well," Miller says, and after this monstrous lie a feeling of weightlessness comes over him. At first it makes him uncomfortable, but almost immediately he begins to enjoy it. From now on he can say anything.

He makes a sad face. "I guess I'd be more broken up and so on if she hadn't taken off on us the way she did. Right in the middle of harvest season. Just leaving us flat like that."

"I'm hearing a lot of anger," Kaiser tells him. "Face it down. Own it."

Miller got that stuff from a song, but he can't remember any more. He lowers his head and looks at his boots. "Killed my dad," he says after a time. "Died of a broken heart. Left me with five kids to raise, not to mention the farm." Miller closes his eyes. He sees a field all plowed up and the sun setting behind it, a bunch of kids coming in from the field with rakes and hoes on their shoulders. While the jeep winds down through the switchbacks he describes his hardships as the oldest child in this family. He's at the end of his story when they reach the coast highway and turn north. All at once the jeep stops rattling and swaying. They pick up speed. The tires hum on the smooth road, the rushing air whistles a single note around the radio antenna. "Anyway," Miller says, "it's been two years since I even had a letter from her."

"You should make a movie," Lebowitz says.

Miller isn't sure how to take this. He waits to hear what else Lebowitz has to say, but he's silent. So is Kaiser, who's had his back turned to Miller for several minutes now. Both men stare at the road ahead of them. Miller can see they've lost interest. He feels disappointed, because he was having a fine time pulling their leg.

One thing Miller told them was true: he hasn't had a letter from his mother in two years. She wrote him a lot when he first joined the army, at least once a week, sometimes twice, but Miller sent all her letters back unopened and after a year of this she finally gave up. She tried calling a few times but he wouldn't go to the telephone, so she gave that up too. Miller wants her to understand that her son is not a man to turn the other cheek. He is a serious man. Once you've crossed him, you've lost him.

Miller's mother crossed him by marrying a man she shouldn't have married. Phil Dove. Dove was a biology teacher at the high school. Miller was having trouble in the course, so his mother went to talk to Dove about it and ended up getting engaged to him. When Miller tried to reason with her, she wouldn't hear a word. She acted like she'd landed herself a real catch instead of someone who talked with a stammer and spent his life taking crayfish apart.

Miller did everything he could to stop the marriage, but his mother had blinded herself. She couldn't see what she already had, how good it was with just the two of them. How he was always there when she got home from work, with a pot of coffee all brewed up. The two of them drinking coffee together and talking about different things, or maybe not talking at all—just sitting in the kitchen while the room got dark around them, until the telephone rang or the dog started whining to get out. Walking the dog around the reservoir. Coming back and eating whatever they wanted for supper, sometimes nothing, sometimes the same dish three or four nights in a row, watching the programs they wanted to watch and going to bed when they wanted to and not because some other person wanted them to. Just being together in their own place.

Phil Dove got Miller's mother so mixed up that she forgot how good their life was. She refused to see what she was ruining. "You'll be leaving anyway," she told him. "You'll be moving on, next year or the year after," which showed how wrong she was about Miller, because he would never have left her, not ever, not for anything. But when he said this she laughed as if she knew better, as if he weren't serious. He was serious, though. He was serious when he promised he'd stay, and he was serious when he promised he'd never speak to her again if she married Phil Dove.

She married him. Miller stayed at a motel that night and two nights more, until he ran out of money. Then he joined the army. He knew that would get to her, because he was still a month shy of finishing high school, and because his father had been killed while serving in the army. Not in Vietnam but in Georgia, in an accident. He and another man were dipping mess kits in a garbage can full of boiling water and somehow the can fell over on him. Miller was six at the time. Miller's mother hated the army after that, not because her husband was dead—she knew about the war he was going to, she knew about ambushes and mines—but because of how it happened. She said the army couldn't even get a man killed in a decent fashion.

She was right too. The army was just as bad as she thought, and worse. You spent all your time waiting around. You lived a completely stupid existence. Miller hated every minute of it, but there was pleasure in his hatred because he believed that his mother must know how unhappy he was. That knowledge would be a grief to her. It wouldn't be as bad as the grief she'd given him, which was spreading from his heart into his stomach and teeth and everywhere else, but it was the worst grief he had power to cause, and it would serve to keep her in mind of him.

Kaiser and Lebowitz are describing hamburgers to each other. Their idea of the perfect burger. Miller tries not to listen but their voices go on, and after a while he can't think of anything but beefsteak tomatoes and Gulden's mustard and steaming, onion-stuffed meat crisscrossed with black marks from the grill. He's at the point of asking them to change the subject when Kaiser turns and says, "Think you can handle some chow?"

"I don't know," Miller says. "I guess I could get something down."

"We were talking about a pit stop. But if you want to keep going, just say the word. It's your ball game. I mean, technically we're supposed to take you straight back to base."

"I could eat," Miller says.

"That's the spirit. At a time like this you've got to keep your strength up."

"I could eat," Miller says again.

Lebowitz looks up into the rearview mirror, shakes his head, and looks away again.

They take the next turnoff and drive inland to a crossroads where two gas stations face two restaurants. One of the restaurants is boarded up, so Lebowitz pulls into the parking lot of the Dairy Queen across the road. He turns the engine off, and the three men sit motionless in the sudden silence. Then Miller hears the distant clang of metal on metal, the caw of a crow, the creak of Kaiser shifting in his seat. A dog barks in front of a rust-streaked trailer next door, a skinny white dog with yellow eyes. As it barks the dog rubs itself, one leg raised and twitching, against a sign that shows an outspread hand below the words KNOW YOUR FUTURE.

They get out of the jeep, and Miller follows Kaiser and Lebowitz across the parking lot. The air is warm and smells of oil. In the gas station across the road a pink-skinned man in a swimming suit is trying to put air in the tires of his bicycle, jerking at the hose and swearing loudly. Miller pushes his tongue against the broken bridge, lifting it gently. He wonders if he should try eating a hamburger and decides it can't hurt as long as he's careful to chew on the other side of his mouth.

But it does hurt. After a few bites Miller shoves his plate away. He rests his chin on one hand and listens to Lebowitz and Kaiser argue about whether people can actually tell the future. Lebowitz is talking about a girl he used to know who had ESP. "We'd be driving along," he says, "and out of the blue she'd tell me exactly what I was thinking about. It was unbelievable."

Kaiser finishes his hamburger and takes a drink of milk. "No big deal," he says. "I could do that." He pulls Miller's hamburger over to his side of the table and takes a bite out of it.

"Go ahead," Lebowitz says. "Try it. I'm not thinking about what you think I'm thinking about."

"Yes, you are."

"All right, now I am," Lebowitz says, "but I wasn't before."

"I wouldn't let a fortune-teller get near me," Miller says. "The way I see it, the less you know the better off you are."

"More vintage philosophy from the private stock of W. P. Miller," Lebowitz says. He looks at Kaiser, who's finishing Miller's hamburger. "Well, how about it? I'm up for it if you are."

Kaiser chews ruminatively. He swallows and licks his lips. "Sure," he says. "Why not? As long as Miller here doesn't mind."

"Mind what?" Miller asks.

Lebowitz stands and puts his sunglasses back on. "Don't worry about Miller. Miller's cool. Miller keeps his head when men all around him are losing theirs."

Kaiser and Miller get up from the table and follow Lebowitz outside. Lebowitz is bending down in the shade of a dumpster, wiping off his boots with a handkerchief. Shiny blue flies buzz around him.

"Mind what?" Miller repeats.

"We thought we'd check out the prophet," Kaiser tells him.

Lebowitz straightens up and the three of them start across the parking lot.

"I'd actually kind of like to get going," Miller says. When they reach the jeep he stops, but Lebowitz and Kaiser walk on. "Now listen," Miller says, and skips a little to catch up. "I have a lot to do," he says to their backs. "I have to get home."

"We know how broken up you are," Lebowitz tells him. He keeps walking.

"This won't take too long," Kaiser says.

The dog barks once and then, when it sees that they really intend to come within range of his teeth, runs around the trailer. Lebowitz knocks on the door. It swings open, and there stands a round-faced woman with dark, sunken eyes and heavy lips. One of her eyes has a cast; it seems to be watching something beside her while the other looks down at the three soldiers at her door. Her hands are covered with flour. She is a Gypsy, an actual Gypsy. Miller has never seen a Gypsy before, but he recognizes her as surely as he'd recognize a wolf if he saw one. Her presence makes his blood pound in his veins. If he lived in this place he would come back at night with other men, all of them yelling and waving torches, and drive her out.

"You on duty?" Lebowitz asks.

She nods, wiping her hands on her skirt. They leave chalky streaks on the bright patchwork. "All of you?" she asks.

"You bet," Kaiser says. His voice is unnaturally loud.

She nods again and turns her good eye from Lebowitz to Kaiser, then to Miller. Gazing at Miller, she smiles and rattles off a string of strange sounds, words from another language or maybe a spell, as if she expects him to understand. One of her front teeth is black.

"No," Miller says. "No, ma'am. Not me." He shakes his head.

"Come," she says, and stands aside.

Lebowitz and Kaiser mount the steps and disappear into the trailer. "Come," the woman repeats. She beckons with her white hands.

Miller backs away, still shaking his head. "Leave me alone," he tells her, and before she can answer he turns and walks away. He goes back to the jeep and sits in the driver's seat, leaving both doors open to catch the breeze. Miller feels the heat drawing the dampness out of his fatigues. He can smell the musty wet canvas overhead and the sourness of his own body. Through the windshield, covered with mud except for a pair of grimy half circles, he watches three boys solemnly urinating against the wall of the gas station across the road.

Miller bends down to loosen his boots. Blood rushes to his face as he fights the wet laces, and his breath comes faster and faster. "Goddamn laces," he says. "Goddamn rain." He gets the laces untied and sits up, panting. He stares at the trailer. Goddamn Gypsy.

He can't believe those two fools actually went inside there. Yukking it up. Playing around. That shows how stupid they are, because anybody knows that you don't play around with fortune-tellers. There's no predicting what a fortune-teller might say, and once it's said, no way of keeping it from happening. Once you hear what's out there it isn't out there anymore; it's here. You might as well open your door to a murderer as to the future.

The future. Didn't everybody know enough about the future already, without rooting around for the details? There's only one thing you have to know about the future: everything gets worse. Once you have that, you have it all. The specifics don't bear thinking about.

Miller certainly has no intention of thinking about the specifics. He peels off his damp socks and massages his crinkled white feet. Now and then he glances up toward the trailer, where the Gypsy is pronouncing fate on Kaiser and Lebowitz. Miller makes humming noises. He will not think about the future.

Because it's true—everything gets worse. One day you're sitting in front of your house poking sticks into an anthill, hearing the chink of silverware and the voices of your mother and father in the kitchen; then, at some moment you can't even remember, one of those voices is gone, and you never hear it again. When you go from today to tomorrow you're walking into an ambush.

What lies ahead doesn't bear thinking about. Already Miller has an ulcer, and his teeth are full of holes. His body's giving out on him. What will it be like when he's sixty? Or even five years from now? Miller was in a restaurant the other day and saw a fellow about his own age in a wheelchair, getting fed soup by a woman who was talking to some other people at the table. This boy's hands lay twisted in his lap like gloves somebody dropped there. His pants had crawled up halfway to his knees, showing pale, wasted legs no thicker than bones. He could barely move his head. The woman feeding him did a lousy job because she was too busy blabbing to her friends. Half the soup went onto the boy's shirt. Yet his eyes were bright and attentive. Miller thought: *That could happen to me.*

You could be going along just fine and then one day, through no fault of your own, something could get loose in your bloodstream and knock out part of your brain. Leave you like that. And if it didn't happen now, all at once, it was sure to happen slowly later on. That was the end you were bound for.

Someday Miller is going to die. He knows that and prides himself on knowing it when everyone else only pretends to, secretly believing they'll live forever. But this is not the reason the future is unthinkable to him. There is something else worse than that, something not to be considered, and he will not consider it.

He will not consider it. Miller leans back against the seat and closes his eyes, but his effort to trick himself into somnolence fails; behind his eyelids he is wide awake and fidgety with gloom, probing against his will for what he is afraid to find, until, with no surprise at all, he finds it. A simple truth. His mother is also going to die. Just like him. And there's no telling when. Miller cannot count on her to be there to come home to, and receive his pardon, when he finally decides she has suffered enough.

Miller opens his eyes and looks at the raw shapes of the buildings across the road, their outlines lost through the grime on the windshield. He closes his eyes again. He listens to himself breathe and feels the familiar, almost muscular ache of knowing that he is beyond his mother's reach. That he has put himself where she cannot see him or speak to him or touch him, resting her hands on his shoulders as she stops behind his chair to ask him a question or just stand for a moment, her mind somewhere else. This was supposed to be her punishment, but somehow it has become his own. He understands that it has to stop. It's killing him.

It has to stop now, and as if he'd been planning for this day all along Miller knows exactly what he will do. Instead of reporting to the Red Cross when he gets back to base, he'll pack his bag and catch the first bus home. No one will blame him for this. Even when they discover the mistake they've made they still won't blame him, because it would be the natural thing for a grieving son to do. Instead of punishing him they will probably apologize for giving him a scare.

He will take the first bus home, express or not. It will be full of Mexicans and soldiers. Miller will sit by a window and drowse. Now and then he'll come up from his dreams to stare out at the passing green hills and loamy plowland and the stations where the bus puts in, stations cloudy with exhaust and loud with engine roar, where the people he regards through his window will look groggily back at him as if they too have just come up from sleep. Salinas. Vacaville. Red

Bluff. When he gets to Redding Miller will hire a cab. He'll ask the driver to stop at Schwartz's for a few minutes while he buys some flowers, and then he will ride on home, down Sutter and over to Serra, past the ballpark, the grade school, the Mormon church. Right on Belmont. Left on Park. Leaning over the seat, saying, *Farther, farther, a little farther, that's it, that one there.*

The sound of voices behind the door as he rings the bell. Door swings open, voices hush. Who are these people? Men in suits, women wearing white gloves. Someone stammers his name, strange to him now, almost forgotten. *W-W-Wesley.* A man's voice. Miller stands just inside the door, breathing perfume. Then the flowers are taken from his hand and laid with other flowers on the coffee table. He hears his name again. It is Phil Dove, moving toward him from across the room. He walks slowly, with his arms raised, like a blind man.

Wesley, he says. *Thank God you're home.*

Two Boys and a Girl

Gilbert saw her first. This was in late June, at a party. She was sitting alone in the backyard, stretched out on a lawn chair, when he went to get a beer from the cooler. He tried to think of something to say to her, but she seemed complete in her solitude and he was afraid of sounding intrusive and obvious. Later he saw her again, inside—a pale, dark-haired girl with brown eyes and lipstick smears on her teeth. She was dancing with Gilbert's best friend, Rafe. The night after that she was with Rafe when he picked Gilbert up to go to another party, and again the night after that. Her name was Mary Ann.

Mary Ann, Rafe, and Gilbert. They went everywhere together that summer, to parties and movies and the lake, to the pools of friends, and on long aimless drives after Gilbert got off work at his father's bookstore. Gilbert didn't have a car, so Rafe did the driving; his grandfather had given him his immaculate old Buick convertible as a reward for getting into Yale. Mary Ann leaned against him with her bare fine-boned feet up on the dash, while Gilbert sprawled like a pasha in the back and handed out the beers and passed ironic comment on whatever attracted his notice.

Gilbert was deeply ironic. At the high school where he and Rafe had been classmates, the yearbook editors voted him Most Cynical. That pleased him. Gilbert believed disillusionment to be the natural consequence, even the duty, of a mind that could cut through the official version to the true nature of things. He made it his business to take nothing on trust, to respect no authority but that of his own judgment, and to be elegantly unsurprised at the grossest crimes and follies, especially those of the world's anointed.

Mary Ann listened to what he said, even when she seemed to be occupied with Rafe. Gilbert knew this, and he knew when he'd managed to shock her. She clenched her hands, blinked rapidly, and a red splotch, vivid as a birthmark, appeared on the milky skin of her neck. She wasn't hard to shock. Her father, a captain in the Coast Guard, was the squarest human being Gilbert had ever met. One night when he and Rafe were waiting for Mary Ann, Captain McCoy stared at Gilbert's sandals and asked what he thought about the beatniks. Mrs. McCoy had doilies all over the house, and pictures of kittens and the Holy Land and dogs playing poker, and in the toilets these chemical gizmos that turned the water blue. Gilbert felt sorry for Mary Ann whenever he took a leak at her house.

In early August Rafe went fishing in Canada with his father. He left Gilbert the keys to the Buick and told him to take care of Mary Ann. Gilbert recognized this as what the hero of a war movie says to his drab sidekick before leaving on the big mission.

Rafe delivered his instructions while he was in his room packing for the trip. Gilbert lounged on the bed watching him. He wanted to talk, but Rafe was playing his six-record set of *I Pagliacci*, which Gilbert didn't believe he really liked, though Rafe made occasional humming noises as if he knew the whole score by heart. Gilbert thought he was taking up opera the same way he'd taken up squash that winter, as an accessory. He lay back and was silent while Rafe went about his business; he was graceful and precise, assembling his gear without waste of motion or hesitation as to where things were. At one point he walked over to the mirror and studied himself as if he were alone, and Gilbert was surprised by the anger he felt. Then Rafe turned to him and tossed the keys on the bed and delivered his line about taking care of Mary Ann.

The next day Gilbert drove the Buick around town all by himself. He double-parked in front of Nordstrom's with the top down and smoked cigarettes and watched the women come out as if he were waiting for one of them. Now and then he examined his watch and frowned. He drove onto a pier at the wharf and waved at one of the passengers on the boat to Victoria. She was looking down at the water and didn't see him, not until she raised her eyes as the boat was backing out of the slip and caught him blowing her a kiss. She stepped away from the rail and vanished from sight. Later he went to La Luna, a bar near the university where he knew he wouldn't get carded, and sat where he could see the Buick. When the bar filled up he walked outside and raised the hood and checked the oil, right in front of La Luna's big picture window. To a couple walking past he said, "This damn thing drinks oil like it's going out of style." Then he drove off with the expression of a man with important and not entirely pleasant business to perform. He stopped and bought cigarettes in two different drugstores. He called home from the second store and told his mother he wouldn't be in for dinner and asked if he'd gotten any mail. "No," his mother said, "nothing." Gilbert ate at a drive-in and cruised for a while and then went up to the lookout above Alki Point and sat on the hood of the Buick and smoked in a moody, philosophical manner, deliberately ignoring the girls with their dates in the cars around him. A heavy mist stole in from the sound. Across the water the lights of the city blurred, and a foghorn began to call. Gilbert flipped his cigarette into the shadows and rubbed his bare arms. When he got home he called Mary Ann, and they agreed to go to a movie the following night.

After the movie Gilbert drove Mary Ann back to her house. Instead of going right inside she sat in the car and they went on talking. It was easy, easier than he'd imagined. When Rafe was with them, Gilbert could speak through him to Mary Ann and be witty or deep or outrageous. In the moments they'd been alone, waiting for Rafe to rejoin them, he always found himself tongue-tied, in a kind of panic. He'd cudgel his brains for something to say, and whatever he did come up with sounded tense and sharp. But that didn't happen, not that night.

It was raining. When Gilbert saw that Mary Ann wasn't in any hurry to get out, he cut the engine and they sat there in the faint marine light of the radio tuning band with liquid shadows playing over their faces from the rain streaming down the windows. The rain drummed in gusts on the canvas roof but inside it was warm and close, like in a tent during a storm. Mary Ann was talking about nursing school and her fear that she wouldn't measure up in the tough courses, especially Anatomy and Physiology. Gilbert thought she was being ritually humble and said, "Oh, come on, you'll do fine."

"I don't know," she said. "I just don't know." And then she told him how badly she'd done in science and math, and how two of her teachers had personally gone down to the nursing-school admissions office to help her get in. Gilbert saw that she really was afraid of failing, and for good reason. Now that she'd said so herself, it made sense to him that she struggled in school. She wasn't quick, wasn't clever. There was a simplicity about her.

She leaned back into the corner, watching the rain. She looked sad. Gilbert thought of touching her cheek with the back of his hand to reassure her. He waited a moment, then told her it wasn't exactly true that he was trying to make up his mind whether to go to the University of Washington or Amherst. He should have corrected that misunderstanding before. The actual truth was, he hadn't gotten into Amherst. He'd made it onto the waiting list, though with only three weeks left until school began he figured his odds were just about nil.

She turned and regarded him. He couldn't see her eyes. They were dark pools with only a glint of light at the bottom. She asked why he hadn't gotten in.

To this question Gilbert had no end of answers. He thought of new ones every day, and was sick of them all. "I stopped working," he said. "I just completely slacked off."

"But you should've gotten in wherever you wanted. You're smart enough."

"I talk a pretty good game, I guess." He took out a cigarette and tapped the end against the steering wheel. "I don't know why I smoke these damn things," he said.

"You like the way they make you look. Intellectual."

"I guess." He lit it.

She watched him closely as he took the first drag. "Let me," she said. "Just a puff."

Their fingers touched when he handed her the cigarette.

"You're going to be a great nurse," he said.

She took a puff of the cigarette and blew the smoke out slowly.

Neither of them spoke for a time.

"I'd better go in," she said.

Gilbert watched her go up the walkway to her house, face averted from the blowing rain. He waited until he saw her step inside, then turned the radio back up and drove away. He kept tasting her lipstick on the cigarette.

When he called from work the next day her mother answered and asked him to wait. Mary Ann was out of breath when she came to the phone. She said she'd been outside on a ladder, helping her dad paint the house. "What are you up to?" she asked.

"I was just wondering what you were doing," he said.

He took her to La Luna that night, and the next. Both times they got the same booth, right near the jukebox. "Don't Think Twice, It's All Right" had just come out and Mary Ann played it again and again while they talked. On the third night some guys in baseball uniforms were sitting there when they came in. Gilbert was annoyed and saw that she was too. They sat at the bar for a time but kept getting jostled by the drinkers behind them. They decided to go someplace else. Gilbert was paying his tab when the baseball players stood up to leave, and Mary Ann slipped into the booth just ahead of an older couple who'd been waiting nearby.

"We were here first," the woman said to Mary Ann as Gilbert sat down across from her.

"This is our booth," Mary Ann said, in a friendly, informative tone.

"How do you figure that?"

Mary Ann looked at the woman as if she'd asked a truly eccentric question. "Well, I don't know," she said. "It just is."

Afterward it kept coming back to Gilbert, the way Mary Ann had said "our booth." He collected such observations and pondered them when he was away from her: her breathlessness when she came to the phone, the habit she'd formed of taking puffs from his cigarettes and helping herself to his change to play the jukebox, how she listened to him with such open credulity that he found it impossible to brag or make excuses or say things merely for effect. He couldn't be facetious with Mary Ann. She always thought he meant exactly what he said, and then he had to stop and try to explain that he'd actually meant something else. His irony began to sound weak and somehow envious. It sounded thin and unmanly.

Mary Ann gave him no occasion for it. She took him seriously. She wrote down the names of the books he spoke of—*On the Road, The Stranger, The Fountainhead,* and some others he hadn't actually read but knew about and intended to read as soon as he found the time. She listened when he explained what was wrong with Barry Goldwater and *Reader's Digest* and the television shows she liked, and agreed that he was probably right. In the solemnity of her attention he heard himself saying things he had said to no one else, confessing hopes so implausible he had barely acknowledged them to himself. He was often surprised by his own honesty. But he stopped short of telling Mary Ann what was most on his mind, and what he believed she already knew, in case she didn't know or wasn't ready to admit she did. Once he said it, everything would change, for all of them, and he wasn't prepared to risk this.

They went out every night except two, once when Gilbert had to work overtime and once when Captain McCoy took Mary Ann and her mother to dinner. They saw a couple more movies and went to a party and to La Luna and drove around the city. The nights were warm and clear and Gilbert put the top down and poked along in the right lane. He used to wonder, with some impatience, why Rafe drove so slowly. Now he knew. To command the wheel of an open car with a girl on the seat beside you was to be established in a condition that only a fool would hasten to end. He drove slowly around the lake and downtown and up to the lookouts and then back to Mary Ann's house. The first few nights they sat in the car. After that, Mary Ann invited Gilbert inside.

He talked; she talked. She talked about her little sister, Colleen, who had died of cystic fibrosis two years before, and whose long, hard dying had brought her family close and given her the idea of becoming a nurse. She talked about friends from school and the nuns who'd taught her. She talked about her parents and grandparents and Rafe. All her talk was of her affections. Unconditional enthusiasm generally had a wearying effect on Gilbert, yet Mary Ann gave praise, it seemed to him, not to shine it back on herself or to dissemble some secret bitterness but because that was her nature. That was how she was, and he liked her for it, as he liked it that she didn't question everything but trusted freely, like a child.

She had been teaching herself the guitar, and sometimes she consented to play and sing for him, old ballads about mine disasters and nice lads getting hanged for poaching and noblewomen drowning their babies. He could see how the words moved her, so much that her voice would give out for moments at a time; then she would bite her lower lip and gaze down at the floor. She put folk songs on the record player and listened to them with her eyes closed. She also liked Roy Orbison and the Fleetwoods and Ray Charles. One night she was bringing some fudge from the kitchen just as "Born to Lose" came on. Gilbert stood and offered his hand with a dandified flourish that she could have laughed off if she'd chosen to. She put the plate down and took his hand and they began to dance, stiffly at first, from a distance, then easily and close. They fit perfectly. Perfectly. He felt the rub of her hips and thighs, the heat of her skin. Her warm hand tightened in his. He breathed in the scent of lavender water with the sunny smell of her hair and the faint salt smell of her body. He breathed it all in again and again. And then he felt himself grow hard and rise against her, so that she had to know, she just *had* to know, and he waited for her to move away. She didn't. She pressed close to him until the song ended, and for a moment or two after. Then she stepped back and let go of Gilbert's hand and in a hoarse voice asked him if he wanted some fudge. She was facing him but managing not to look at him.

"Maybe later," he said, and held out his hand again. "May I have the honor?"

She walked over to the couch and sat down. "I'm so clumsy."

"No, you're not. You're a great dancer."

She shook her head.

He sat down in the chair across from her. She still wouldn't look at him. She put her hands together and stared at them.

Then she said, "How come Rafe's dad picks on him all the time?"

"I don't know. There isn't any particular reason. Bad chemistry, I guess."

"It's like he can't do anything right. His dad won't let him alone, even when I'm there. I bet he's having a miserable time."

It was true that neither Rafe's father nor his mother took much pleasure in their son. Gilbert had no idea why this should be so. Still, it was a strange subject to have boiled up out of nowhere like this, and for her to be suddenly close to tears about. "Don't worry about Rafe," he said. "Rafe can take care of himself."

The grandfather clock chimed, then struck twelve times. The clock had been made to go with the living-room ensemble, and its tone, tinny and untrue, set Gilbert on edge. The whole house set him on edge: the pictures, the matching Colonial furniture, the single bookshelf full of condensed books. It was like a house Russian spies would practice being Americans in.

"It's just so unfair," Mary Ann said. "Rafe is so sweet."

"He's a good egg, Rafe," Gilbert said. "Most assuredly. One of the best."

"He is the best."

Gilbert got up to leave and Mary Ann did look at him then, with something like alarm. She stood and followed him outside onto the porch. When he looked back from the end of the walkway, she was watching him with her arms crossed over her chest. "Call me tomorrow," she said. "Okay?"

"I was thinking of doing some reading," he said. Then he said, "I'll see. I'll see how things go."

The next night they went bowling. This was Mary Ann's idea. She was a good bowler and frankly out to win. Whenever she got a strike she threw her head back and gave a shout of triumph. She questioned Gilbert's scorekeeping until he got rattled and told her to take over, which she did without even a show of protest. When she guttered her ball she claimed she'd slipped on a wet spot and insisted on bowling that frame again. He didn't let her, he understood that she'd despise him if he did, but her shamelessness somehow made him happier than he'd been all day.

As he pulled up to her house Mary Ann said, "Next time I'll give you some pointers. You'd be half decent if you knew what you were doing."

Hearing that "next time," he killed the engine and turned and looked at her. "Mary Ann," he said.

He had never said so much before.

She looked straight ahead and didn't answer. Then she said, "I'm thirsty. You want a glass of juice or something?" Before Gilbert could say anything, she added, "We'll have to sit outside, okay? I think we woke my dad up last night."

He waited on the steps while Mary Ann went into the house. Paint cans and brushes were arranged on top of the porch railing. Captain McCoy scraped and painted one side of the house every year. This year he was doing the front. That was just like him, to eke it out one side at a time. Gilbert had once helped the Captain make crushed ice for drinks. The way the Captain did it, he'd hold a single cube in his hand and clobber it with a hammer until it was pulverized. Then another cube. Then another. Et cetera. When Gilbert wrapped a whole tray's worth in a hand towel and started whacking it against the counter, the Captain grabbed the towel away from him. "That's not how you do it!" he said. He found Gilbert another hammer, and the two of them stood there hitting cube after cube.

Mary Ann came out with two glasses of orange juice. She sat beside Gilbert and they drank and looked out at the Buick gleaming under the streetlight.

"I'm off tomorrow," Gilbert said. "You want to go for a drive?"

"Gee, I wish I could. I promised my dad I'd paint the fence."

"We'll paint, then."

"That's all right. It's your day off. You should do something."

"Painting's something."

"Something you like, dummy."

"I like to paint. In fact I love painting."

"Gilbert."

"No kidding, I love to paint. Ask my folks. Every free minute, I'm out there with a brush."

"Like fun."

"So what time do we start? Look, it's only been three hours since I did my last fence, and already my hand's starting to shake."

"Stop it! I don't know. Whenever. After breakfast."

He finished his juice and rolled the glass between his hands. "Mary Ann." He felt her hesitate.

"Yes?"

He kept rolling the glass. "What do your folks think about us going out so much?"

"They don't mind. I think they're glad, actually."

"I'm not exactly their type."

"Hah. You can say that again."

"What're they so glad about, then?"

"You're not Rafe."

"What, they don't like Rafe?"

"Oh, they like him, a lot. A whole lot. They're always saying how if they had a son, and so on. But my dad thinks we're getting too serious."

"Ah, too serious. So I'm comic relief."

"Don't say that."

"I'm not comic relief?"

"No."

Gilbert put his elbows on the step behind him. He looked up at the sky and said carefully, "He'll be back in a couple of days."

"I know."

"Then what?"

She leaned forward and stared into the yard as if she'd heard a sound.

He waited for a time, aware of every breath he took. "Then what?" he said again.

"I don't know. Maybe . . . I don't know. I'm really kind of tired. You're coming tomorrow, right?"

"If that's what you want."

"You said you were."

"Only if you want me to."

"I want you to."

"Okay. Sure. Tomorrow, then."

Gilbert stopped at a diner on the way home. He ate a piece of apple pie, then drank coffee and watched the cars go past. To an ordinary person driving by he supposed he must look pretty tragic, sitting here alone over a coffee cup, cigarette smoke curling past his face. And the strange thing was, that person would be right. He was about to betray his best friend. To cut Rafe off from the two people he trusted most, and possibly, he understood, from trust itself. He would betray himself too—his belief, held deep under the stream of his flippancy, that he was steadfast and loyal. And he knew what he was doing. That was why this whole thing was tragic, because he knew what he was doing and could not do otherwise.

He had thought it all out. He could provide himself with reasons. Rafe and Mary Ann would have broken up anyway, sooner or later. Rafe was moving on. He didn't know it, but he was leaving them behind. He'd have roommates, guys from rich families who'd invite him home for vacation, take him skiing and sailing. He'd wear a tuxedo to debutante parties where he'd meet girls from Smith and Mount Holyoke, philosophy majors, English majors, girls with ideas who were reading the same books he was reading and other books too, who could say things he wouldn't have expected them to say. He'd get interested in one of these girls and go on road trips with his friends to her college. She'd come to New Haven. They'd rendezvous in Boston and New York. He'd meet her parents. And on the first day of his next trip home, honorable Rafe would enter Mary Ann's house and leave half an hour later with a sorrowful face and a heart leaping with joy. There wouldn't be many more trips home, not after that. What was here to draw him back from so far away? Not his parents, those crocodiles. Not Mary Ann. Himself? Good old Gilbert? Please.

And Mary Ann, what about Mary Ann? Once Rafe double-timed her and then dropped her cold, what would happen to that simple good-heartedness of hers? Would she begin to suspect it, stand guard over it? He was right to do anything to keep that from happening.

These were the reasons, and Gilbert thought they were good ones, but he could make no use of them. He knew he would do what he was going to do even if Rafe stayed at home and went to college with him, or if Mary Ann was somewhat more calculating. Reasons always came with a purpose, to give the appearance of a struggle between principle and desire. But there'd been no struggle. Principle had power only until you found what you had to have.

Captain McCoy was helping Mrs. McCoy into the car when Gilbert pulled up behind him. The Captain waited as his wife gathered her dress inside, then closed the door and walked back toward the Buick. Gilbert came around to meet him.

"Mary Ann tells me you're going to help with the fence."

"Yes, sir."

"There's not that much of it—shouldn't take too long."

They both looked at the fence, about sixty feet of white pickets that ran along the sidewalk. Mary Ann came out on the porch and mimed Hi.

Captain McCoy said, "Would you mind picking up the paint? It's that Glidden store down on California. Just give 'em my name." He opened his car door, then looked at the fence again. "Scrape her good. That's the secret. Give her a good scraping and the rest'll go easy. And try not to get any paint on the grass."

Mary Ann came through the gate and waved as her parents drove off. She said that they were going over to Bremerton to see her grandmother. "Well," she said. "You want some coffee or something?"

"I'm fine."

He followed her up the walk. She had on cutoffs, and he watched her smooth white legs flex as she climbed the porch steps. Captain McCoy had set out two scrapers and two brushes on the railing, all four of them exactly parallel. Mary Ann handed Gilbert a scraper and they went back to the fence. "What a day!" she said. "Isn't it the most beautiful day?" She knelt to the right of the gate and began to scrape. Then she looked back at Gilbert watching her and said, "Why don't you do that side over there? We'll see who gets done first."

There wasn't much to scrape, some blisters, a few peeling patches here and there. "This fence is in good shape," Gilbert said. "How come you're painting it?"

"It goes with the front. When we paint the front, we always paint the fence."

"It doesn't need it. All it needs is some retouching."

"I guess. Dad wanted us to paint it, though. He always paints it when he paints the front."

Gilbert looked at the gleaming white house, the bright weedless lawn trimmed to the nap of a crew cut.

"Guess who called this morning," Mary Ann said.

"Who?"

"Rafe! There was a big storm coming in so they left early. He'll be back tonight. He sounded really great. He said to say hi."

Gilbert ran the scraper up and down a picket.

"It was so good to hear his voice," Mary Ann said. "I wish you'd been here to talk to him."

A kid went by on a bicycle, cards snapping against the spokes.

"We should do something," Mary Ann said. "Surprise him. Maybe we could take the car over to the house, be waiting out front when he gets back. Wouldn't that be great?"

"I wouldn't have any way to get home."

"Rafe can give you a ride."

Gilbert sat back and watched Mary Ann. She was halfway down her section of the fence. He waited for her to turn and face him. Instead she bent over to work at a spot near the ground. Her hair fell forward, exposing the nape of her neck. "Maybe you could invite someone along," Mary Ann said.

"Invite someone. What do you mean, a girl?"

"Sure. It would be nice if you had a girl. It would be perfect."

Gilbert threw the scraper against the fence. He saw Mary Ann freeze. "It would *not* be perfect," he said. When she still didn't turn around, he stood and went up the walk and through the house to the kitchen. He paced back and forth. He went to the sink, drank a glass of water, and stood with his hands on the counter. He saw what Mary Ann was thinking of, the two of them sitting in the open car, herself jumping out as Rafe pulled up, the wild embrace. Rafe unshaven, reeking of smoke and nature, a little abashed at all this emotion in front of his father, but pleased, too, and amused. And all the while Gilbert looking coolly on, hands in his pockets, ready to say the sly mocking words that would tell Rafe that all was as before. That was how she saw it going. As if nothing had happened.

Mary Ann had just about finished her section when Gilbert came back outside. "I'll go get the paint," he told her. "I don't think there's much left to scrape on my side, but you can take a look."

She stood and tried to smile. "Thank you," she said.

He saw that she had been in tears, and this did not soften him but confirmed him in his purpose.

Mary Ann had already spread out the tarp, pulling one edge under the fence so the drips wouldn't fall on the grass. When Gilbert opened the can she laughed and said, "Look! They gave you the wrong color."

"No, that's exactly the right color."

"But it's *red*. We need white. Like it is now."

"You don't want to use white, Mary Ann. Believe me."

She frowned.

"Red's the perfect color for this. No offense, but white is the worst choice you could make."

"But the house is white."

"*Exactly*," Gilbert said. "So are the houses next door. You put a white fence here, what you end up with is complete boredom. It's like being in a hospital, know what I mean?"

"I don't know. I guess it is a lot of white."

"What the red will do, the red will give some contrast and pick up the bricks in the walk. It's just what you want here."

"Well, maybe. The thing is, I don't think I should. Not this time. Next time, maybe, if my dad wants to."

"Look, Mary Ann. What your dad wants is for you to use your own head."

Mary Ann squinted at the fence.

"You have to trust me on this, okay?"

She sucked in her lower lip, then nodded. "Okay. If you're sure."

Gilbert dipped his brush. "The world's bland enough already, right? Everyone's always talking about the banality of evil—what about the evil of banality?"

They painted through the morning and into the afternoon. Every now and then Mary Ann would back off a few steps and take in what they'd done. At first she kept her thoughts to herself. The more they painted, the more she had to say. Toward the end she went out into the street and stood there with her hands on her hips. "It's interesting, isn't it? Really different. I see what you mean about picking up the bricks. It's pretty red, though."

"It's perfect."

"Think my dad'll like it?"

"Your dad? He'll be crazy about it."

"Think so? Gilbert? Really?"

"Wait till you see his face."

The Chain

Brian Gold was at the top of the hill when the dog attacked. A big black wolflike animal attached to a chain, it came flying off a back porch and tore through its yard into the park, moving easily in spite of the deep snow, making for Gold's daughter. He waited for the chain to pull the dog up short; the dog kept coming. Gold plunged down the hill, shouting as he went. Snow and wind deadened his voice. Anna's sled was almost at the bottom of the slope. Gold had raised the hood of her parka against the needling gusts, and he knew she couldn't hear him or see the dog racing toward her. He was conscious of the dog's speed and of his own dreamy progress, the weight of his gum boots, the clinging trap of crust beneath the new snow. His overcoat flapped at his knees. He screamed one last time as the dog made its lunge, and at that moment Anna flinched away and the dog caught her shoulder instead of her face. Gold was barely halfway down the hill, arms pumping, feet sliding in the boots. He seemed to be running in place, held at a fixed, unbridgeable distance as the dog dragged Anna backward off the sled, shaking her like a doll. Gold threw himself down the hill helplessly, then the distance vanished and he was there.

The sled was overturned, the snow churned up; the dog had marked this ground as its own. It still had Anna by the shoulder. Gold heard the rage boiling in its gut. He saw the tensed hindquarters and the flattened ears and the red gleam of gum under the wrinkled snout. Anna was on her back, her face bleached and blank, staring at the sky. She had never looked so small. Gold seized the chain and yanked at it, but could get no purchase in the snow. The dog only snarled more fiercely and started shaking Anna again. She didn't make a sound. Her silence made Gold go hollow and cold. He flung himself onto the dog and hooked his arm under its neck and pulled back hard. Still the dog wouldn't let go. Gold felt its heat and the profound rumble of its will. With his other hand he tried to pry the jaw loose. His gloves were slippery with drool; he couldn't get a good grip. Gold's mouth was next to the dog's ear. He said, "Let go, damn you," and then he took the ear between his teeth and bit down with everything he had. He heard a yelp and something cracked against his nose, knocking him backward. When he pushed himself up the dog was running for home, jerking its head from side to side, scattering flecks of blood on the snow.

"The whole thing took maybe sixty seconds," Gold said. "Maybe less. But it went on forever." He'd told the story many times now and always mentioned this. He knew it was trite to marvel at how time could stretch and stall, but he was unable not to. Nor could he stop himself from repeating that it was a "miracle"—the radiologist's word—that Anna hadn't been crippled or disfigured or even killed; and that her doctor didn't understand how she'd escaped damage to her bones and nerves. Though badly bruised, her skin hadn't even been broken.

Gold loved his daughter's face. He loved her face as a thing in itself, to be wondered at, studied. Yet after the attack he couldn't look at Anna in the same way. He kept seeing the dog lunge at her, and himself stuck forever on that hill; then his heart began to kick, and he grew taut and restless and angry. He didn't want to think about the dog anymore—he wanted it out of the picture. It should be put down. It was crazy, a menace, and it was still there, waiting to tear into some other kid, because the police refused to do anything.

"They won't do a thing," he said. "Nothing."

He was going through the whole story again with his cousin Tom

Rourke on a Sunday afternoon, a week after the attack. Gold had called him the night it happened, but the part about the police was new, and Rourke got all worked up just as Gold expected. His cousin had an exacting, irritable sense of justice, and a ready store of loyal outrage that Gold had drawn on ever since they were boys. He had been alone in his anger for a week now and wanted some company. Though his wife claimed to be angry too, she hadn't seen what he had seen. The dog was an abstraction to her, and she wasn't one to brood anyway.

"What was their excuse?" Rourke wanted to know. "What reason did the cops give for their complete and utter worthlessness?"

"The chain," Gold said. "They said—this is the really beautiful part—they said that since the dog was chained up, no law was broken."

"But the dog *wasn't* chained up, right?"

"He was, but the chain reaches into the park. I mean *way* in—a good thirty, forty feet."

"By that logic, he could be on a chain ten miles long and legally chew up the whole fucking town."

"Exactly."

Rourke got up and went to the picture window. He stood close to the glass and glowered at the falling snow. "What is it with Nazis and dogs? They've got a real thing going, ever notice that?" Still looking out the window, he said, "Have you talked to a lawyer?"

"Day before yesterday."

"What'd he say?"

"She. Kate Stiller. Said the police were full of shit. Then she told me to forget it. According to her, the dog'll die of old age before we ever get near a courtroom."

"There's the legal system for you, Brian me boy. They'll give you all the justice you want, as long as it's up the ass."

There was a loud thump on the ceiling. Anna was playing upstairs with Rourke's boy, Michael. Both men raised their eyes and waited, and when no one screamed Gold said, "I don't know why I even bothered to call her. I don't have the money to pay for a lawyer."

"You know what happened?" Rourke said. "The cop who took the complaint fucked it up, and now the others are covering for him. So, you want to take him out?"

"The *cop*?"

"I was thinking of the dog."

"You mean kill the dog?"

Rourke just looked at Gold.

"Is that what you're saying? Kill the dog?"

Rourke grinned, but he still didn't say anything.

"How?"

"How do you want?"

"Christ, Tom, I can't believe I'm talking like this."

"But you are." Rourke shoved the Naugahyde ottoman with his foot until it was facing Gold, then sat on it and leaned forward, so close their knees were touching. "No poison or glass. That's chickenshit, I wouldn't do that to my worst enemy. Take him out clean."

"Christ, Tom." Gold tried to laugh.

"You can use my Remington, scope him in from the hill. Or if you want, get up close with the twelve-gauge or the forty-four Magnum. You ever fired a pistol?"

"No."

"Better forget the Magnum, then."

"I can't do this."

"Sure you can."

"They'll know it was me. I've been raising hell about that dog all week. Who do you think they're going to come after when it suddenly shows up with a hole in its head?"

Rourke sucked in his cheeks. "Point taken," he said. "Okay, you can't do it. But I sure as hell can."

"No. Forget it, Tom."

"You and Mary go out for the night. Have dinner at Chez Nicole or Pauly's, someplace small where they'll remember you. By the time you get home it's all over and you're clean as a whistle."

Gold finished his beer.

"We've got to take care of business, Brian. If we don't, nobody will."

"Maybe if *I* did it. *Maybe.* Having you do it—that just doesn't feel right."

"What about that dog still running wild after what it did to Anna? Does that feel right?" When Gold didn't answer, Rourke shook his knee. "Did you really bite the mutt's ear?"

"I didn't have any choice."

"You bite it off?"

"No."

"But you drew blood, right? You tasted blood."

"I got some in my mouth, yes. I couldn't help it."

"It tasted good, didn't it? Come on, Brian, don't bullshit me, it tasted good."

"There was a certain satisfaction," Gold said.

"You want to do what's right," Rourke said. "I appreciate that. I value that. It's your call, okay? But the offer stands."

Rourke produced the crack about Nazis and dogs not from deep reflection, Gold knew, but because to call people Nazis was his first response to any vexation or slight. Once he'd heard Rourke say it, though, Gold couldn't forget it. The picture that came to mind was one he'd pondered before: a line of frenzied dogs harrying Jews along a railway platform.

Gold was Jewish on his father's side, but his parents split up when he was young and he'd been raised Catholic by his mother. His name didn't suit him; to his ears it had an ironical ring. When you heard "Gold," what else could you think of but gold? With that name he should be a rich sharpie, not a mackerel-snapper with a dying business. The black kids who came into his video store were unmistakably of that opinion. They had a mock-formal way of saying "Mr. *Gold,*" drawing out the word as if it were the precious substance itself. Finding themselves a little short on the rental fee, some of them weren't above asking him to make up the difference out of his own deep pockets, and acting amazed if he refused. The rusty Toyota he kept parked out front was a puzzle to them, a conversation piece; they couldn't figure out why, with all his money, he didn't get himself a decent set of wheels. One night, standing at the counter with her friends, a girl suggested that Gold kept his Cadillac at home because he was afraid the brothers would steal it. They'd been goofing on him, just messing around, but when she said this everyone went silent as if a hard truth had been spoken.

Cadillac. What else?

After years of estrangement Gold had returned to the Catholic Church and went weekly to Mass to sustain his fragile faith, but he understood that in the eyes of the world he was a Jew. He had never known what to make of that. There were things he saw in himself that he thought of as Jewish, traits not conspicuous among the mostly Irish boys he'd grown up with, including his cousins. Bookishness, patience, a taste for classical music and complicated moralizing, aversion to alcohol and violence. All this he found acceptable. But he had certain other tendencies, less dear to him, that he also suspected of being Jewish. Corrosive self-mockery. Bouts of almost paralyzing skepticism. Physical awkwardness. A disposition toward passivity, even surrender, in the face of bullying people and oppressive circumstances. Gold knew that these ideas of Jewishness were held as well by anti-Semites, and he resisted their influence, though without much success.

In the already familiar picture that Rourke had conjured up, of Jews being herded by dogs, Gold sensed an instance of that resignation he so disliked in himself. He knew it was unfair to blame people for not fighting an evil that their very innocence made them incapable of imagining, yet, even while admitting that they were brutalized and starving and in shock, he couldn't help but wonder: *Why didn't one of them hit a guard—grab his gun—take some of the bastards with him?* Do *something?* Even in his awareness of the terrible injustice of this question, he'd never really laid it to rest.

And with that old image vivid in his thoughts, it seemed to Gold that the question had now been put to him. Why didn't *he* do something? His own daughter had been savaged by just such a dog, a flinch away from having her face torn off. He had seen its insanity, felt its furious will to hurt. And it was still out there, lying in wait, because no one, himself included, would do what needed to be done. He could not escape the consciousness of his own inaction. In the days following his conversation with Rourke, it became intolerable. No matter where he was, at home or in the store, he was also on that hill, unable to move or speak, watching the dog come at Anna with murder in its heart and the chain gliding behind like an infinite black snake.

He drove by the park late one day and stopped across the street from the house where the dog's owners lived. It was a Colonial with a line of dormer windows, a sprawling, expensive house like most of the others around the park. Gold thought he could guess why the police had been so docile. This wasn't a shooting gallery, a crib for perpetrators and scofflaws. The deep thunk of the brass knocker against the great green door, the glittering chandelier in the foyer, the Cinderella sweep of the staircase with its monumental newel post and gleaming rail—all this would tell you that the law was among friends here. Of course a dog needed room to roam. If people let their kids go tearing off every which way, they'd have to live with the consequences. Some folks were just natural-born whiners.

Though Gold despaired of the police, he believed he understood them. He did not understand the people who'd allowed this to happen. They had never called to apologize, or even to ask how Anna was. They seemed not to care that their dog was a killer. Gold had driven here with some notion of sitting down with them, helping them see what they ought to do—as if they'd even let him in the door. What a patsy!

He called Rourke that night and told him to go ahead.

Rourke was hot on the idea of Gold taking Mary out for dinner—his treat—on the big night. He had a theatrical conception of the event, which seemed to include the two of them toasting him with champagne while he did whatever he meant to do.

Gold refused the offer. Mary didn't know what they were up to, and he couldn't sit across a table from her for three hours, even as the deed was being done, without telling. She wouldn't like it, but she wouldn't be able to stop it; the knowledge would only be a burden to her. Gold employed a graduate student named Simms who covered the store at night, except for Tuesdays, when he had a seminar. Though Rourke was disappointed by Gold's humdrum dramaturgy, he assented: Tuesday night it was.

More snow fell that morning, followed by an ice storm. The streets and sidewalks were still glazed by nightfall and business was slow. Gold had a new release playing in the monitor above the counter, but he couldn't follow the plot through the frantic cutting and ugly music, so he stopped it halfway through and didn't bother to put in another. That left the store oddly quiet. Maybe for this reason his customers didn't hang around as usual, shooting the breeze with Gold and one another. They made their selections, paid, and left. He tried to read the paper. At eight-thirty Anna called to say she'd won a poster contest at school. After she hung up, Gold witnessed a fight in front of the Domino's across the street. Two men, drunk or drugged, had a shouting match, and one of them took a clumsy swing at the other. They grappled and fell down together on the ice. A deliveryman and one of the cooks came outside and helped them up, then walked them off in different directions. Gold microwaved the chili left over from Sunday dinner. He ate slowly, watching the sluggish procession of cars and the hunched, gingerly trudge of people past his window. Mary had laid on the cumin with a free hand, which was just how Gold liked it. His forehead grew damp with sweat, and he took off his sweater. The baseboard heaters ticked. The long fluorescent lights buzzed overhead.

Rourke called just before ten, when Gold was closing up. "Scooter has buried his last bone," he said.

"Scooter?"

"That was his name."

"I wish you hadn't told me."

"I got his collar for you—a little memento."

"For Christ's sake, Tom."

"Don't worry, you're clear."

"Just don't tell me any more," Gold said. "I'm afraid I'll say too much when the police come by."

"They're not gonna come by. The way I fixed things, they won't even know what happened." He coughed. "It had to be done, Brian."

"I guess."

"No guessing about it. But I've gotta say, it wasn't anything I'd want to do again."

"I'm sorry, Tom. I should've done it myself."

"It wasn't any fun, I'll tell you that." Rourke fell silent. Gold could hear him breathing. "I about froze my ass off. I thought they'd never let the damned beast out."

"I won't forget it," Gold said.

"*De nada*. It's over. Go in peace."

In late March, Rourke called Gold with a story of his own. He'd been gassing up on Erie Boulevard when a BMW backed away from the air hose and put a crease in his door. He yelled at the driver, a black man wearing sunglasses and a knit cap. The guy ignored him. He looked straight ahead and drove off across the lot into the road, but not before Rourke got a good look at his license plate. It was a vanity tag, easy to remember—SCUSE ME. Rourke called the police, who tracked the driver down and ticketed him for leaving the scene of an accident.

So far, so good. Then it turned out the driver didn't have insurance. Rourke's company agreed to cover most of the bill—eight hundred bucks for a lousy dent!—but that still left him with the three-hundred-dollar deductible. Rourke figured Mr. SCUSE ME should make up the difference. His insurance agent gave him the man's name and particulars, and Rourke started calling him. He called twice at reasonable hours, after dinner, but both times the woman who answered said he wasn't in and gave Rourke the number of a club on Townsend, where he got an answering machine. Though he left clear messages, he heard nothing back. Finally Rourke called the first number at seven in the morning and got the man himself, Mr. Vick Barnes.

"That's V-I-C-K," Rourke said. "Ever notice how they do that with their names? You shorten 'Victor,' you get 'Vic,' right? V-I-C. So where does the fucking k come from? Or take Sean, S-E-A-N. Been spelled like that for about five hundred years. But not them, they've gotta spell it S-H-A-W-N. Like they have a right to that name in the first place."

"What did he say?"

"Gave me a lot of mouth. First he gets indignant that I woke him up, then he says he's already been through all this shit with the police and doesn't believe he hit anybody anyway. Then he hangs up on me."

Rourke said he knew better than to call back; he wasn't going to get anywhere with this guy. Instead he went to the club, Jack's Shady Corner, where it turned out Mr. Vick Barnes worked as a deejay, and no doubt retailed dope on the side. All the deejays did. Where else would he get the dough for a new Beamer? But Rourke had to admit he was quite the pro, our Mr. Barnes, nice mellow voice, good line of patter. Rourke had a couple beers and watched the dancers, then went looking for the car.

It wasn't in the lot. Rourke poked around and found it off by itself in a little nook behind the club, where it wouldn't get run into by drunks. He was going back tonight to give Mr. Vick Barnes a taste of his own medicine, plus a little extra for the vigorish.

"You can't," Gold said. "They'll know it was you."

"Let 'em prove it."

Gold had understood from the start where this story was taking him, even if Rourke hadn't. When he said "I'll do it," he felt as if he were reading the words from a script.

"No need, Brian. I got it covered."

"Wait a minute. Just hang on." Gold put the receiver down and took care of an old woman who was renting *The Sound of Music*. Then he picked it up and said, "They'll bust you for sure."

"Look, I can't let this guy fuck me over and just walk away. Next thing, everybody in town'll be lining up to give me the wood."

"I told you, I'll handle it. Not tonight—there's a talent show at school. Thursday."

"You sure, Brian?"

"I said I'd do it. Didn't I just say I'd do it?"

"Only if you really want to. Okay? Don't feel like you have to."

Rourke stopped by the store Thursday afternoon with instructions and equipment: two gallons of Olympic redwood stain to pour over the BMW, a hunting knife to slash the tires and score the paint, and a crowbar to break the windshield. Gold was to exercise extreme caution. He should work fast. He should leave his car running and pointed in the direction of a clear exit. If for any reason things didn't look right he should leave immediately.

They loaded the stuff in the trunk of Gold's car.

"Where are you going to be?" Gold asked.

"Chez Nicole. Same place you'd have gone if you had any class."

"I had a good sole meunière last time I was there."

"Prime rib for this bad boy. Rare. Taste of blood, eh, Brian?"

Gold watched him drive off. It was a warm day, the third in a row. Last week's snow had turned gray and was offering up its holdings of beer cans and dog turds. The gutters overflowed with runoff, and the sun shone on the wet pavement and the broken glass in front of Domino's, which had abruptly closed three weeks earlier. Rourke's brake lights flashed. He stopped and backed up. Gold waited while the electric window descended, then leaned toward the car.

"Careful, Brian, okay?"

"You know me."

"Don't get caught. I have to say, that's something you definitely want to avoid."

Gold drove to the club at eleven-thirty, with the idea there wouldn't be much coming and going at that hour on a weeknight. The casual drinkers would already be home, the serious crowd settling in for the duration. A dozen or so cars were scattered across the lot. Gold backed into a space as close to the rear of the building as he could get.

He turned the engine off and looked around, then popped the trunk, took the crowbar, and moved into the shadows around back. The BMW was parked where Rourke said it would be, in the short driveway between the alley and the dumpster.

Gold had no intention of using the stain or the knife. Rourke had suffered a dent; that was no reason to destroy a man's car. One good dent in return would even things up, and settle his own debt in the bargain. If Rourke wanted more, he was strictly on his own.

Gold walked around the car—a beautiful machine, a gleaming black 328 with those special wheels that gang members were supposedly killing one another over. The dealership where Gold took his Toyota for repairs also had the local BMW boutique, and he always paid a visit to the showroom while he waited. He liked to open and close the doors, sit in the leather seats and work the gears, compare options and prices. Fully loaded, this model ran in the neighborhood of forty grand. Gold couldn't imagine Mr. Vick Barnes qualifying for that kind of a loan on a deejay's salary, so he must have paid in cash. Rourke was right. He was dealing.

Gold hefted the crowbar. He felt the driving pulse of the music through the club walls, heard the vocalist—he wouldn't call him a singer—shouting along with menace and complaint. It was a strange thing. You sold drugs to your own people, ruined their neighborhoods, turned their children into prostitutes and thugs, and you became a big shot. A man of property and respect. But try to run a modest business, bring something good into their community, and you were a bloodsucking parasite. Mr. *Gold*. He smacked the bar against his palm. He was thinking maybe he'd do a little something with that knife after all. The stain too. He could find uses for the stain.

A woman laughed in the parking lot and a man answered in a low voice. Gold crouched behind the dumpster and waited until their headlights raked the darkness and vanished. His hand was tight around the metal. He could feel his own rage, and distrusted it. Only a fool acted out of anger. No, he would do exactly what was fair, and nothing more.

Gold walked around to the driver's side of the BMW. He held the crowbar with both hands and touched the curved end against the door at bumper height, where Rourke's car would have been hit. He adjusted his feet. He touched the door again, then cocked the crowbar like a bat and swung it with everything he had, knowing just as the act passed beyond recall how absolutely he had betrayed himself. The shock of the blow raced up his arms. He dropped the crowbar and left it where it fell.

Victor Emmanuel Barnes found it there three hours later. He knelt and ran his hand along the jagged cleft in the car door, flecks of paint curling away under his fingertips. He knew exactly who had done this. He picked up the crowbar, tossed it on the passenger seat, and drove straight to the apartment building where Devereaux lived. As he sped through the empty streets he howled and pounded the dashboard. He stopped in a shriek of brakes and seized the crowbar and ran up the stairs to Devereaux's door. He pounded the door with his fist. "I told you next week, you motherfucker! I told you next week!" He heard voices, but when no one answered him he cursed them and began working at the door with the crowbar. It creaked and strained. Then it gave and Barnes staggered into the apartment, yelling for Devereaux.

But Devereaux wasn't home. His sixteen-year-old nephew Marcel was spending the night on the couch after helping Devereaux's little girl write an essay. He stood facing the door while Barnes jimmied it, his aunt and cousins and grandmother gathered behind him at the end of the hall, shaking and clinging to one another. When Barnes stumbled bellowing inside, Marcel tried to push him back out. They struggled. Barnes shoved him away and swung the crowbar, catching Marcel right across the temple. The boy's eyes went wide. His mouth opened. He sank to his knees and pitched facedown on the floor. Barnes looked at Marcel, then at the old woman coming toward him. "Oh God," he said, and dropped the crowbar and ran down the stairs and outside to his car. He drove to his grandmother's house and told her what had happened, and she held his head in her lap and rocked over him and wept and prayed. Then she called the police.

Marcel's death was on the morning news. Every half hour they ran the story, with pictures of both him and Barnes. Barnes was shown being hustled into a cruiser, Marcel standing before his exhibit at the All-County Science Fair. He had been an honors student at Morris Fields High, a volunteer in the school's Big Brother program, and a past president of the Christian Youth Association. There was no known motive for the attack.

Camera crews from the TV stations followed students from their buses to the school doors, asking about Marcel and getting close-ups of the most distraught. At the beginning of second period, the principal came on the PA system and said that crisis counselors were available for those who wished to speak to them. Any students who felt unable to continue with their classes that day were to be excused.

Garvey Banks looked over at his girlfriend, Tiffany. Neither of them had known Marcel, but it was nice out and there wasn't anything happening at school except people crying and carrying on. When he nodded toward the door, she gave him her special smile and gathered her books and collected a pass from the teacher. Garvey waited a few minutes, then followed her outside.

They walked up to Bickel Park and sat on a bench overlooking the pond. Two old white ladies were throwing bread to the ducks. The wet grass steamed in the sun. Tiffany put her head on Garvey's shoulder and hummed to herself. Garvey wanted to feel sad over that boy getting killed, but it was good being warm like this and close to Tiffany.

They sat on the bench in the sun. They didn't talk; they hardly ever talked. Tiffany liked to look at things and be quiet in herself. Pretty soon they'd rent a movie and go over to Garvey's. They'd kiss. Though they wouldn't take any chances, they'd make each other happy. All of that was going to happen, and Garvey was glad to wait for it.

After a while Tiffany stopped humming. "Ready, Gar?"

"Ready."

They stopped in at Gold's Video, and Garvey took *Breakfast at Tiffany's* off the shelf. They'd rented it the first time because of the title, then it became their favorite movie. Someday, they were going to live in New York City and know all kinds of people—that was for sure.

Mr. Gold was slow writing up the receipt. He looked sick. He counted out Garvey's change and said, "Why aren't you kids in school?"

Garvey felt cornered, and decided to blow a little smoke at the man. "Friend of mine got killed," he said.

"You knew him? You knew Marcel Foley?"

"Yes sir. From way back."

"What was he like?"

"Marcel? Hey, Marcel was the best. You got a problem, you took it to Marcel. You know, trouble with your girlfriend or whatever. Trouble at home. Trouble with a friend. Marcel had this thing—right, Tiff? He could bring people together. He just had this easy way and he talked to you like you were important, like everybody's important. He could get people to come together, know what I'm saying? Come together and get on with it. *Peacemaker.* Marcel was a peacemaker. And that's the best thing you can be."

"Yes," Mr. Gold said. "It is." He put his hands on the counter and lowered his head.

Then Garvey saw that he was grieving, and it came to him how unfair a thing it was that Marcel Foley had been struck down with his life still before him, all his sunny days stolen away. It was wrong, and Garvey knew it would not end there. He touched Mr. Gold's shoulder. "That man'll get his," he said. "He'll get what's coming to him. Count on it."

Smorgasbord

"A prep school in March is like a ship in the doldrums." Our history master said this, as if to himself, while we were waiting for the bell to ring after class. He stood by the window and tapped the glass with his ring in a dreamy, abstracted way meant to make us think he'd forgotten we were there. We were supposed to get the impression that when we weren't around he turned into someone interesting, someone witty and profound, who uttered impromptu bons mots and had a poetic vision of life.

The bell rang.

I went to lunch. The dining hall was almost empty, because it was a free weekend and most of the boys had gone to New York, or home, or to their friends' homes, as soon as their last class let out. About the only ones left were foreigners and scholarship students like me and a few other untouchables of various stripes. The school had laid on a nice lunch for us, cheese soufflé, but the portions were small and I went back to my room still hungry. I was always hungry.

Sleety rain fell past my window. The snow on the quad looked grimy; it had melted above the underground heating pipes, exposing long brown lines of mud.

I couldn't get to work. On the next floor down someone kept playing "Mack the Knife." That one song incessantly repeating itself made the dorm seem not just empty but abandoned, as if those who'd left were never coming back. I cleaned my room, then tried to read. I looked out the window. I sat down at my desk and studied the new picture my girlfriend had sent me, unable to imagine her from it; I had to close my eyes to do that, and then I could see her, her solemn eyes and the heavy white breasts she would gravely let me hold sometimes, but not kiss. Not yet, anyway. I had a promise, though. That summer, as soon as I got home, we were going to become lovers. "Become lovers." That was what she'd said, very deliberately, listening to the words as she spoke them. All year I had repeated them to myself to take the edge off my loneliness and the fits of lust that made me want to scream and drive my fists through walls. We were going to become lovers that summer, and we were going to be lovers all through college, true to each other even if we ended up thousands of miles apart again, and after college we were going to marry and join the Peace Corps and do something together that would help people. This was our plan. Back in September, the night before I left for school, we wrote it all down along with a lot of other specifics concerning our future: number of children (six), their names, the kinds of dogs we would own, a sketch of our perfect house. We sealed the paper in a bottle and buried it in her backyard. On our golden anniversary we'd dig it up and show it to our children and grandchildren to prove that dreams can come true.

I was writing her a letter when Crosley came to my room. Crosley was a science whiz. He won the science prize every year and spent his summers working as an intern in different laboratories. He was also a fanatical weight lifter. His arms were so knotty he had to hold them out from his sides as he walked, as if he were carrying buckets. Even his features seemed muscular. His face had a permanent flush. Crosley lived down the hall by himself in one of the only singles in the school. He was said to be a thief; that supposedly was the reason he'd ended up without a roommate. I didn't know if it was true and tried to avoid forming an opinion on the matter, but whenever we passed each other I felt embarrassed and looked away.

Crosley leaned in the door and asked me how things were.

I said okay.

He stepped inside and gazed around the room, tilting his head to read my roommate's pennants and the titles of our books. I was uneasy. I said, "So what can I do for you?" not meaning to sound as cold as I did but not exactly regretting it either.

He caught my tone and smiled. It was the kind of smile you put on when you pass a group of people you suspect are talking about you; his usual expression, in other words.

He said, "You know García, right?"

"García? Sure. I think so."

"You know him," Crosley said. "He runs around with Hidalgo and those guys. He's the tall one."

"Sure," I said. "I know who García is."

"Well, his stepmother's in New York for a fashion show or something, and tonight she's going to drive up and take him out to dinner. She told him to bring along some friends. You want to come?"

"What about Hidalgo and the rest of them?"

"They're at some kind of polo deal in Maryland. Buying horses. Or ponies, I guess it would be."

The notion of someone my age buying ponies to play a game was so unexpected that I couldn't quite take it in. "Jesus," I said.

"How about it?" Crosley said. "You want to come?"

I'd never even spoken to García. He was the nephew of a famous dictator, and all his friends were nephews and cousins of other dictators. They lived as they pleased here. Most of them kept cars a few blocks from the campus, though that was completely against the rules. They were cocky and prankish and charming. They moved everywhere in a body, sunglasses pushed up on their heads and jackets slung over their shoulders, twittering all at once like birds, *chinga* this and *chinga* that. The headmaster was completely buffaloed. After Christmas vacation a bunch of them came down with gonorrhea, and all he did was call them in and advise them that they should not be in too great a hurry to lose their innocence. It became a school joke. All you had to do was say "innocence" and everyone would crack up.

"I don't know," I said.

"Come on," Crosley said.

"But I don't even know the guy."

"So what? I don't either."

"Then why did he ask you?"

"I was sitting next to him at lunch."

"Terrific," I said. "That explains you. What about me? How come he asked me?"

"He didn't. He told me to bring someone else."

"What, just anybody? Just whoever happened to present himself to your attention?"

Crosley shrugged.

"Sounds great," I said. "Sounds like a recipe for a really memorable evening."

"You got something better to do?" Crosley asked.

"No," I said.

The limousine picked us up under the awning of the headmaster's house. The driver, an old man, got out slowly and then slowly adjusted his cap before opening the door for us. García slid in beside the woman in back. Crosley and I sat across from them on seats that pulled down. I caught her scent immediately. For some years afterward I bought perfume for women, and I was never able to find that one.

García erupted into Spanish as soon as the driver closed the door behind me. He sounded angry, spitting words at the woman and gesticulating violently. She rocked back a little, then let loose a burst of her own. I stared openly at her. Her skin was very white. She wore a black cape over a black dress cut just low enough to show her pale throat and the bones at the base of her throat. Her mouth was red. There was a spot of rouge high on each cheek, not rubbed in to look like real color but left there carelessly, or carefully, to make you think again how white her skin was. Her teeth were small and sharp looking, and she bared them in concert with certain gestures and inflections. As she talked her pointed little tongue flicked in and out.

She wasn't a lot older than we were.

She said something definitive and cut her hand through the air. García began to answer her but she said "No!" and chopped the air again. Then she turned and smiled at Crosley and me. It was a completely false smile. She said, "Where would you fellows like to eat?" Her voice sounded lower in English, even a little harsh. She called us "fallows."

"Anywhere is fine with me," I said.

"Anywhere," she repeated. She narrowed her big black eyes and pushed her lips together. I could see that my answer had disappointed her. She looked at Crosley.

"There's supposed to be a good French restaurant in Newbury," Crosley said. "Also an Italian place. It depends on what you want."

"No," she said. "It depends on what you want. I am not so hungry."

If García had a preference, he kept it to himself. He sulked in the corner, his round shoulders slumped and his hands between his knees. He seemed to be trying to make a point of some kind.

"There's also a smorgasbord," Crosley said. "If you like smorgasbords."

"Smorgasbord," she said. Obviously the word was new to her. She repeated it to García. He frowned, then answered her in a sullen monotone.

I couldn't believe Crosley had suggested the smorgasbord. It was an egregiously uncouth suggestion. The smorgasbord was where the local fatties went to binge. Football coaches brought whole teams in there to bulk up. The food was good enough, and God knows there was plenty of it, all you could eat, actually, but the atmosphere was brutally matter of fact. The food was good, though. Big platters of shrimp on crushed ice. Barons of beef. Smoked turkey. No end of food, really.

"You—do you like smorgasbords?" she asked Crosley.

"Yes," he said.

"And you?" she said to me.

I nodded. Then, not to seem wishy-washy, I said, "You bet."

"Smorgasbord," she said. She laughed and clapped her hands. "Smorgasbord!"

Crosley gave directions to the driver and we drove slowly away from the school. She said something to García. He nodded at both of us and gave our names, then looked away again, out the window, where the snowy fields were turning dark. His face was long, his eyes sorrowful as a hound's. He had barely said a word while we were waiting for the limousine. I didn't know why he was mad at his stepmother, or why he wouldn't talk to us, or why he'd even asked us along, but by now I didn't really care.

She studied us and repeated our names skeptically. "No," she said. She pointed at Crosley and said, "El Blanco." She pointed at me and said, "El Negro." Then she pointed at herself and said, "I am Linda."

"Leen-da," Crosley said. He really overdid it, but she showed her sharp little teeth and said, *"Exactamente."*

Then she settled back against the seat and pulled her cape close around her shoulders. It soon fell open again. She was restless. She sat forward and leaned back, crossed and recrossed her legs, swung her feet impatiently. She had on black high heels fastened by a thin strap; I could see almost her entire foot. I heard the silky rub of her stockings against each other, and breathed in a fresh breath of her perfume every time she moved. That perfume had a certain effect on me. It didn't reach me as just a smell. It was personal, it seemed to issue from her very privacy. It made the hair bristle on my arms and sent faint chills across my shoulders and the backs of my knees. Every time she moved I felt a little tug and followed her motion with some slight motion of my own.

When we arrived at the smorgasbord—Swenson's, or Hanson's, some such honest Swede of a name—García refused to get out of the limousine. Linda tried to persuade him, but he shrank back into his corner and would not answer or even look at her. She threw up her hands. "Ah!" she said, and turned away. Crosley and I followed her across the parking lot toward the big red barn. Her dress rustled as she walked. Her heels clicked on the cement.

You could say one thing for the smorgasbord; it wasn't pretentious. This was a real barn, not some quaint fantasy of a barn with butter-churn lamps and little brass ornaments nailed to the walls on strips of leather. The kitchen was at one end. The rest of it had been left open and filled with picnic tables. Blazing lightbulbs hung from the rafters. In the middle of the barn stood what my English master would have called "the groaning board"—a great table heaped with every kind of food you could think of, and then some. I'd been there many times and it always gave me a small, pleasant shock to see how much food there was.

Girls wearing dirndls hustled here and there, cleaning up messes, changing tablecloths, bringing fresh platters of food from the kitchen.

We stood blinking in the sudden light, then followed one of the waitresses across the floor. Linda walked slowly, gazing around like a tourist. Several men looked up from their food as she passed. I was right behind her, and I looked back at them forbiddingly so they'd think she was my wife.

We were lucky; we got a table to ourselves. Linda shrugged off her cape, then waved us toward the food. "Go on," she said. She sat down and opened her purse. When I looked back she was lighting a cigarette.

"You're pretty quiet tonight," Crosley said as we filled our plates. "You pissed off about something?"

"Maybe I'm just quiet, Crosley, you know?"

He speared a slice of meat and said, "When she called you El Negro, that didn't mean she thought you were a Negro. She just said that because your hair is dark. Mine is light, that's how come she called me El Blanco."

"I know that, Crosley. Jesus. You think I couldn't figure that out? Give me some credit, okay?" Then, as we moved around the table, I said, "You speak Spanish?"

"Un poco. Actually more like *un poquito."*

"What's García mad about?"

"Money. Something about money."

"Like what?"

"That's all I could get. But it's definitely about money."

I'd meant to start off slow, but by the time I reached the end of the table my plate was full. Potato salad, ham, jumbo shrimp, toast, barbecued beef, eggs Benny. Crosley's was full too. We walked back toward Linda, who was leaning forward on her elbows and looking around the barn. She took a long drag off her cigarette, lifted her chin, and blew a stream of smoke up toward the rafters. I sat across from her. "Scoot down," Crosley said, and bumped in beside me.

She watched us eat for a while.

"So," she said, "El Blanco. Are you from New York?"

Crosley looked up in surprise. "No, ma'am," he said. "I'm from Virginia."

Linda stabbed out her cigarette. Her long fingernails were painted the same deep red as the lipstick smears on her cigarette butt. She said, "I just came from New York and I can tell you that is one crazy place. Just incredible. Listen to this. I am in a taxicab, you know, and we are stopping in this traffic jam for a long time and there is a taxicab next to us with this fellow in it who stares at me. Like this, you know." She made her eyes go round. "Of course I ignore him. So guess what, my door opens and he gets into my cab. 'Excuse me,' he says, 'I want to marry you.' 'That's nice,' I say. 'Ask my husband.' 'I don't care about your husband,' he says. 'I don't care about my wife either.' Of course I had to laugh. 'Okay,' he says. 'You think that's funny? How about this?' Then he says—" Linda looked sharply at each of us. She sniffed and made a face. "He says things you would never believe. Never. He wants to do this and he wants to do that. Well, I act like I am about to scream. I open my mouth like this. 'Hey,' he says, 'okay, okay. Relax.' Then he gets out and goes back to his taxicab. We are still sitting there for a long time again, and you know what he is doing? He is reading the newspaper. With his hat on. Go ahead, eat," she said to us, and nodded toward the food.

A tall blonde girl was carving fresh slices of roast beef onto a platter. She was hale and bosomy—I could see the laces on her bodice straining. Her cheeks glowed. Her bare arms and shoulders were ruddy with exertion. Crosley raised his eyebrows at me. I raised mine back, though my heart wasn't in it. She was a Viking dream, pure gemütlichkeit, but I was drunk on García's stepmother and in that condition you don't want a glass of milk; you want more of what's making you stumble and fall.

Crosley and I filled our plates again and headed back.

"I'm always hungry," he said.

"I know what you mean," I told him.

Linda smoked another cigarette while we ate. She watched the other tables as if she were at a movie. I tried to eat with a little finesse and so did Crosley, dabbing his lips with a napkin between every bulging mouthful, but some of the people around us had completely slipped their moorings. They ducked their heads low to shovel up their food, and while they chewed it they looked around suspiciously and circled their plates with their forearms. A big family to our left was the worst. There was something competitive and desperate about them; they seemed determined to eat their way into a condition where they would never have to eat again. You'd have thought they were refugees from some great hunger, that outside these walls the land was afflicted with drought and barrenness. I felt a kind of desperation myself, as if I were growing emptier with every bite I took.

There was a din in the air, a steady roar like that of a waterfall.

Linda looked around with a pleased expression. Though she bore no likeness to anyone here, she seemed completely at home. She sent us back for another plate, then dessert and coffee, and while we were finishing up she asked El Blanco if he had a girlfriend.

"No, ma'am," Crosley said. "We broke up," he added, and his red face turned almost purple. It was clear that he was lying.

"You. How about you?"

I nodded.

"Ha!" she said. "El Negro is the one! So. What's her name?"

"Jane."

"Jaaane," Linda drawled. "Okay, let's hear about Jaaane."

"Jane," I said again.

Linda smiled.

I told her everything. I told her how my girlfriend and I had met and what she looked like and what our plans were—everything. I told her more than everything, because I gave certain coy though definite suggestions about the extremes to which our passion had already driven us. I meant to impress her with my potency, to enflame her, to wipe that smile off her face, but the more I told her the more wolfishly she smiled and the more her eyes laughed at me.

"Laughing eyes"—now there's a cliché my English master would've eaten me alive for. "How exactly did these eyes laugh?" he would have asked, looking up from my paper while my classmates snorted around me. "Did they titter, or did they merely chortle? Did they give a great guffaw? Did they, perhaps, *scream* with laughter?"

I am here to tell you that eyes can scream with laughter. Linda's did. As I played Big Hombre for her I could see exactly how complete my failure was. I could hear her saying, *Okay, El Negro, go on, talk about your little gorlfren, but we know what you want, don't we? You want to suck on my tongue and slobber on my titties and bury your face in me. That's what you want.*

Crosley interrupted me. "Ma'am . . ." he said, and nodded toward the door. García was leaning there with his arms crossed and an expression of fury on his face. When she looked at him he turned and walked out the door.

Her eyes went flat. She sat there for a moment. She began to take a cigarette from her case, then put it back and stood up. "We go," she said.

García was waiting in the car, rigid and silent. He said nothing on the drive back. Linda swung her foot and stared out the window at the passing houses and bright, moonlit fields. Just before we reached the school García leaned forward and began speaking to her in a low voice. She listened impassively and didn't answer. He was still talking when the limousine stopped in front of the headmaster's house. The driver opened the door. García fixed his eyes on her. Still impassive, she took her pocketbook out of her purse. She opened it and looked inside. She meditated over the contents, then withdrew a bill and offered it to García. It was a hundred-dollar bill. "Boolshit!" he said, and sat back. With no change of expression she turned and held the bill out to me. I didn't know what else to do but take it. She got another one from her pocketbook and presented it to Crosley, who hesitated even less than I had. Then she gave us the same false smile she'd greeted us with and said, "Good night, it was a pleasure to meet you. Good night, good night," she said to García.

The three of us got out of the limousine. I went a few steps, then slowed down and turned to look back.

"Keep walking!" Crosley hissed.

García yelled something in Spanish as the driver closed the door. I faced around again and walked with Crosley across the quad. As we approached our dorm he quickened his pace. "I don't believe it," he whispered. "A hundred bucks." When we were inside he stopped and shouted, "A hundred bucks! A hundred dollars!"

"Pipe down," someone called.

"All right, all right. Fuck you!" he added.

We went up the stairs to our floor, laughing and banging into each other. "Do you believe it?" he said.

I shook my head. We were standing outside my door.

"No, really now, listen." He put his hands on my shoulders and looked into my eyes. He said, "Do you fucking *believe* it?"

I told him I didn't.

"Well, neither do I. I don't fucking believe it."

There didn't seem to be much to say after that. I could have invited Crosley in, but to tell the truth I still thought of him as a thief. We laughed a few more times and said good night.

My room was cold. I took the bill out of my pocket and looked at it. It was new and stiff, the kind of bill you associate with kidnappings. The picture of Franklin was surprisingly lifelike. I looked at it for a while. A hundred dollars was a lot of money then. I'd never had a hundred dollars before, not in one chunk like this. To be on the safe side I taped it to a page in *Profiles in Courage*—page 100, so I wouldn't forget where it was.

I had trouble getting to sleep. The food I'd eaten sat like a stone in me, and I was miserable about the things I'd said. I understood that I had been a liar and a fool. I kept shifting under the covers, then sat up and turned on my reading lamp. I picked up the new picture my girlfriend had sent me, and closed my eyes, and when I had some peace of mind I renewed my promises to her.

We broke up a month after I got home. Her parents were away one night, and we seized the opportunity to make love in their canopied bed. This was the fifth time we'd made love. She got up immediately afterward and started putting her clothes on. When I asked her what the problem was, she wouldn't answer me. I thought, *Oh, Christ, what now.* "Come on," I said. "What's wrong?"

She was tying her shoes. She looked up and said, "You don't love me."

It surprised me to hear this, not so much that she said it but because it was true. Before this moment I hadn't known it was true, but it was—I didn't love her.

For a long time afterward I told myself that I'd never really loved her, though this wasn't true.

We're supposed to smile at the passions of the young, and at what we recall of our own passions, as if they were no more than a series of sweet frauds we'd fooled ourselves with and then wised up to. Not only the passion of boys and girls for each other but the others too—passion for justice, for doing right, for turning the world around. All these come in their time under our wintry smiles. Yet there was nothing foolish about what we felt. Nothing merely young. I just wasn't up to it. I let the light go out.

Sometime later I heard a soft knock at my door. I was still wide awake. "Yeah," I said.

Crosley stepped inside. He was wearing a blue dressing gown of some silky material that shimmered in the dim light of the hallway. He said, "Have you got any Tums or anything?"

"No. I wish I did."

"You too, huh?" He closed the door and sat on my roommate's bunk. "Do you feel as bad as I do?"

"How bad do you feel?"

"Like I'm dying. I think there was something wrong with the shrimp."

"Come on, Crosley. You ate everything but the barn."

"So did you."

"That's right. That's why I'm not complaining."

He moaned and rocked back and forth on the bed. I could hear real pain in his voice. I sat up. "You okay, Crosley?"

"I guess," he said.

"You want me to call the nurse?"

"God," he said. "No, that's all right." He kept rocking. Then, in a carefully offhand way, he said, "Look, is it okay if I just stay here for a while?"

I almost said no, then caught myself. "Sure," I told him. "Make yourself at home."

He must have heard my hesitation. "Forget it," he said. "Sorry I asked." But he made no move to go.

I felt confused, tender toward Crosley because he was in pain, repelled because of what I'd heard about him. Still, maybe what I'd heard about him wasn't true. I wanted to be fair, so I said, "Hey Crosley, do you mind if I ask you a question?"

"That depends." He was watching me, his arms crossed over his stomach. In the moonlight his dressing gown was iridescent as oil.

"Is it true that you got caught stealing?"

"You prick," he said. He looked down at the floor.

I waited.

"You want to hear about it," he said, "just ask someone. Everybody knows all about it, right?"

"I don't."

"That's right, you don't. You don't know shit about it and neither does anyone else." He raised his head. "The really hilarious part is, I didn't actually get caught stealing it, I got caught putting it back. Not to make excuses. I stole it all right."

"Stole what?"

"The coat," he said. "Robinson's overcoat. Don't tell me you didn't know that."

"Well, I didn't."

"Then you must've been living in a cave or something. You know Robinson, right? Robinson was my roommate. He had this camel's hair overcoat, this really beautiful overcoat. I kind of got obsessed with it. I thought about it all the time. Whenever he went somewhere without it, I'd put it on and stand in front of the mirror. Then one day I just took the fucker. I stuck it in my locker over at the gym. Robinson was really upset. He'd go to his closet ten, twenty times a day, like he thought the coat had just gone for a walk or something. So anyway, I brought it back. Robinson came into the room right when I was hanging it up." Crosley bent forward suddenly, then leaned back.

"You're lucky they didn't kick you out."

"I wish they had," he said. "The dean wanted to play Jesus. He got all choked up over the fact that I'd brought it back." Crosley rubbed his arms. "Man, did I want that coat. It was ridiculous how much I wanted it. You know?" He looked right at me. "Do you know what I'm talking about?"

I nodded.

"Really?"

"Yes."

"Good." Crosley lay back against the pillow, then lifted his feet onto the bed. "Say," he said, "I think I figured out how come García invited me."

"Yeah?"

"He was mad at his stepmother, right? He wanted to punish her."

"So?"

"So I'm the punishment. He probably heard I was the biggest douchebag in school, and figured whoever came with me would have to be a douchebag too. That's my theory, anyway."

I started laughing. It killed my stomach but I couldn't stop. Crosley said, "Come on, man, don't make me laugh," and he started too, laughing and moaning at the same time.

We lay without talking, then Crosley said, "El Negro."

"Yeah."

"What are you going to do with your C-note?"

"I don't know. What are you going to do?"

"Buy a woman."

"Buy a woman?"

"I haven't gotten laid in a really long time. In fact," he said, "I've never gotten laid."

"Me either."

I thought about his words. *Buy a woman.* He could actually do it. I could do it myself. I didn't have to wait, didn't have to burn like this for month after month until Jane decided she was ready to give me relief. Three months was a long time to wait. It was an unreasonable time to wait for anything if you had no good reason to, if you could just buy what you needed. And to think that you could buy this—buy a mouth for your mouth, and arms and legs to wrap you tight. I had never considered this before. I thought of the money in my book. I could almost feel it there. Pure possibility.

Jane would never know. It wouldn't hurt her at all, and in certain respects it might help, because it was going to be very awkward at first if neither of us had any experience. As a man, I should know what I was doing. Everything would be a lot better that way.

I told Crosley that I liked his idea. "The time has come to lose our innocence," I said.

"Exactamente," he said.

And so we sat up and took counsel, leaning toward each other from the beds, holding our swollen bellies, whispering back and forth about how this thing might be done, and where, and when.

Lady's Dream

Lady's suffocating. Robert can't stand to have the windows down because the air blowing into the car bothers his eyes. The fan is on but only at the lowest speed, as the sound annoys him. Lady's head is getting heavy, and when she blinks she has to raise her eyelids by an effort of will. The heat and dampness of her skin give her the sensation of a fever. She's beginning to see things in the lengthening moments when her eyes are closed, things more distinct and familiar than the dipping wires and blur of trees and the silent, staring man she sees when they're open.

"Lady?" Robert's voice calls her back, but she keeps her eyes closed.

That's him to the life. Can't stand her sleeping when he's not. He'd have some good reason to wake her, though. Never a mean motive. Never. When he's going to ask somebody for a favor he always calls first and just passes the time, then calls back the next day and says how great it was talking to them, he enjoyed it so much he forgot to ask if they'd mind doing something for him. Has no idea he does this. She's never heard him tell a lie, not even to make a story better. Tells the most boring stories. Just lethal. Considers every word. Considers everything. Early January he buys twelve vacuum-cleaner bags and writes a different month on each one so she'll remember to change them. Of course she goes as long as she can on every bag and throws away the extras at the end of the year, because otherwise he'd find and know. Not say anything—just know. Once she threw seven

229

away. Sneaked them outside through the snow and stuffed them in the garbage can.

Considerate. Everything a matter of principle. Justice for all; yellow, brown, black, or white, all are precious in his sight. Can't say no to any charity but always forgets to send the money. Asks her questions about his own self. *Who's that actress I like so much? What's my favorite fish?* Is calm in every circumstance. Polishes his glasses all the time. They gleam so you can hardly see his eyes. Has to sleep on the right side of the bed. The sheets have to be white. Any other color gives him nightmares, and forget about patterns. Patterns would kill him. Wears a hard hat when he works around the house. Says her name a hundred times a day. Always has. Any excuse.

He loves her name. Lady. Married her name. Shut her up in her name. Shut her up.

"Lady?"

Sorry, sir. Lady's gone.

She knows where she is. She's back home. Her father's away but her mother's home and her sister Jo. Lady hears their voices. She's in the kitchen running water into a glass, letting it overflow and pour down her fingers until it's good and cold. She lifts the glass and drinks her fill and sets the glass down, then walks slow as a cat across the kitchen and down the hall to the bright doorway that opens onto the porch where her mother and sister are sitting. Her mother straightens up and settles back again as Lady goes to the railing and leans on her elbows and looks down the street and then out to the fields beyond.

"Lordalmighty it's hot."

"Isn't it hot, though."

Jo is slouched in her chair, rolling a bottle of Coke on her forehead. "I could just die."

"Late again, Lady?"

"He'll be here."

"Must have missed his bus again."

"I suppose."

"I bet those stupid cornpones were messing with him like they do," Jo says. "I wouldn't be a soldier."

"He'll be here. Else he'd call."

"No sir, I wouldn't be a soldier."

"Nobody asked you."

"Now, girls."

"I'd like to see you a soldier anyway, sleeping all day and laying in bed eating candy. Mooning around. Oh, General, don't make me march, that just wears me out. Oh, do I have to wear that old green thing, green just makes me look sick, haven't you got one of those in red? Why, I can't eat lima beans, don't you know about me and lima beans?"

"Now, Lady . . ." But her mother's laughing and so is Jo, in spite of herself.

Oh, the goodness of that sound. And of her own voice. Just like singing. "General, honey, you know I can't shoot that nasty thing, how about you ask one of those old boys to shoot it for me, they just love to shoot off their guns for Jo Kay."

"Lady!"

The three of them on the porch, waiting but not waiting. Sufficient unto themselves. Nobody has to come.

But Robert is on his way. He's leaning his head against the window of the bus and trying to catch his breath. He missed the first bus and had to run to catch this one because his sergeant found fault with him during inspection and stuck him on a cleanup detail. The sergeant hates his guts. He's an ignorant cracker and Robert is an educated man from Vermont, an engineer just out of college, quit Shell Oil in Louisiana to enlist the day North Korea crossed the parallel. The only Yankee in his company. Robert says when they get overseas there won't be any more Yankees and Southerners, just Americans. Lady likes him for believing that, but she gives him the needle because she knows it isn't true.

He changed uniforms in a hurry and didn't check the mirror before he left the barracks. There's a smudge on his right cheek. Shoe polish. His face is flushed and sweaty, his shirt soaked through. He's watching out the window and reciting a poem to himself. He's a great one for poems, this Robert. He has poems for running and poems for drill, poems for going to sleep and poems for when the rednecks start getting him down.

> Out of the night that covers me,
> Black as the Pit from pole to pole,
> I thank whatever Gods may be
> For my unconquerable soul.

That's the poem he uses to fortify himself. He thinks it over and over even when they're yelling in his face. It keeps him strong. Lady laughs when he tells her things like this, and he always looks at her a little surprised and then he laughs too, to show he likes her sass, though he doesn't. He thinks it's just her being young and spoiled and that it'll go away if he can get her out of that house and away from her family and among sensible people who don't think everything's a joke. In time it'll wear off and leave her quiet and dignified and respectful of life's seriousness—leave her pure Lady.

That's what he thinks some days. Most days he sees no hope at all. He thinks of taking her home, into the house of his father, and when he imagines what she might say to his father he starts hearing his own excuses and apologies. Then he knows it's impossible. Robert has picked up some psychology here and there and believes he understands how he got himself into this mess. It's rebellion. Subconscious, of course. A subconscious rebellion against his father, falling in love with a girl like Lady. Because you don't fall in love. No. Life isn't a song. You choose to fall in love. And there are reasons for that choice, just as there's a reason for every choice, if you get to the bottom of it. Once you figure out your reasons, you master your choices. It's as simple as that.

Robert is looking out the window without really seeing anything.

It's impossible. Lady is just a kid, she doesn't know anything about life. There's a rawness to her that will take years to correct. She's spoiled and willful and half wild, except for her tongue, which is all wild. And she's Southern, not that there's anything wrong with that per se, but a particular kind of Southern. Not trash, as she would put it, but too proud of not being trash. Irrational. Superstitious. Clannish.

And what a clan it is, clan Cobb. Mr. Cobb a suspender-snapping paint salesman always on the road, full of drummer's banter and jokes about nigras and watermelon. Mrs. Cobb a morning-to-night gossip, weepily religious, content to live on her daughters' terms rather than raise them to woman's estate with discipline and right example. And the sister, Jo Kay. You can write that sad story before it happens.

All in all, Robert can't imagine a better family than the Cobbs to beat his father over the head with. That must be why he's chosen them, and why he has to undo that choice. He's made up his mind. He meant to tell her last time, but there was no chance. Today, no matter what. She won't understand. She'll cry. He will be gentle about it. He'll say she's a fine girl but too young. He'll say that it isn't fair to ask her to wait for him when who knows what might happen, and then to follow him to a place she's never been, far from family and friends.

He'll tell Lady anything except the truth, which is that he's ashamed to have picked her to use against his father. That's his own fight. He's been running from it for as long as he can remember, and he knows he has to stop. He has to face the man.

He will, too. Right after he gets home from Korea. His father will have to listen to him then. Robert will make him listen. He will tell him, he will face his father and tell him . . .

Robert's throat tightens and he sits up straight. He hears his breath coming so fast it sounds more like a gasp, and he wonders if anyone else has noticed. His heart is kicking. His mouth is dry. He closes his eyes and forces himself to breathe more slowly and deeply, imitating calm until it becomes almost real.

They pass the power company and the Greyhound station. Heat-flushed soldiers in shiny shoes stand around out front smoking. The bus stops on a street lined with bars, and the other men get off, hooting and pushing one another. There's just Robert and four women left on board. They turn off Jackson and bump across the railroad tracks and head east past the lumberyard. Black men are throwing planks into a truck, their shirts off, skin gleaming in the hazy light. Then they're gone behind a fence. Robert pulls the cord for his stop, waiting behind a wide woman in a flowered dress. The flesh swings like hammocks under her arms. She takes forever going down the steps.

The sun dazzles his eyes. He pulls down the visor of his cap and walks to the corner and turns right. This is Arsenal Street. Lady lives two blocks down where the street runs into fields. There was no plan to how it ends—it just gives out. From here on there's nothing but farms for miles. At night Lady and Jo Kay steal strawberries from the field behind their house, then dish them up with thick fresh cream and grated chocolate. The strawberries have been stewing in the heat all day and burst open at the first pressure of the teeth. Robert disapproves of reaping another man's harvest, though he eats his share and then some. The season's about over. He'll be lucky if he gets any tonight.

He's thinking about strawberries when he sees Lady on the porch, and in this moment the sweetness of that taste fills his mouth. He stops as if he's just remembered something, then comes toward her again. Her lips are moving but he can't hear her, he's aware only of the taste in his mouth, and the closer he comes the stronger it gets. His pace quickens; his hand goes out for the railing. He takes the steps as if he means to devour her.

No, she's saying, no. She's talking to him and to the girl whose life he seeks. She knows what will befall her if she lets him have it. Stay here on this porch with your mother and your sister, they will soon have need of you. Gladden your father's eye yet awhile. This man is not for you. He will patiently school you half to death. He will kindly take you among unbending strangers to watch him fail to be brave. To suffer his carefulness, and to see your children writhe under it and fight it off with every kind of self-hurting recklessness. To be changed. To hear yourself and not know who is speaking. Wait, young Lady. Bide your time.

"Lady?"

It's no good. The girl won't hear. Even now she's bending toward him as he comes up the steps. She reaches for his cheek, to brush away the smudge he doesn't know is there. He thinks it's something else that makes her do it, and his fine, lean face confesses everything, asks everything. There's no turning back from this touch. She can't be stopped. She has a mind of her own, and she knows something Lady doesn't. She knows how to love him.

Lady hears her name again.

Wait, sir.

She blesses the girl. Then she turns to the far-rolling fields she used to dream an ocean, this house the ship that ruled it. She takes a last good look, and opens her eyes.

Powder

Just before Christmas my father took me skiing at Mount Baker. He'd had to fight for the privilege of my company, because my mother was still angry with him for sneaking me into a nightclub during his last visit, to see Thelonious Monk.

He wouldn't give up. He promised, hand on heart, to take good care of me and have me home for dinner on Christmas Eve, and she relented. But as we were checking out of the lodge that morning it began to snow, and in this snow he observed some rare quality that made it necessary for us to get in one last run. We got in several last runs. He was indifferent to my fretting. Snow whirled around us in bitter, blinding squalls, hissing like sand, and still we skied. As the lift bore us to the peak yet again, my father looked at his watch and said, "Criminy. This'll have to be a fast one."

By now I couldn't see the trail. There was no point in trying. I stuck close behind him and did what he did and somehow made it to the bottom without sailing off a cliff. We returned our skis and my father put chains on the Austin-Healey while I swayed from foot to foot, clapping my mittens and wishing I was home. I could see everything. The green tablecloth, the plates with the holly pattern, the red candles waiting to be lit.

We passed a diner on our way out. "You want some soup?" my father asked. I shook my head. "Buck up," he said. "I'll get you there. Right, doctor?"

I was supposed to say, "Right, doctor," but I didn't say anything.

A state trooper waved us down outside the resort, where a pair of sawhorses blocked the road. He came up to our car and bent down to my father's window, his face bleached by the cold, snowflakes clinging to his eyebrows and to the fur trim of his jacket and cap.

"Don't tell me," my father said.

The trooper told him. The road was closed. It might get cleared, it might not. Storm took everyone by surprise. Hard to get people moving. Christmas Eve. What can you do.

My father said, "Look. We're talking about five, six inches. I've taken this car through worse than that."

The trooper straightened up. His face was out of sight but I could hear him. "The road is closed."

My father sat with both hands on the wheel, rubbing the wood with his thumbs. He looked at the barricade for a long time. He seemed to be trying to master the idea of it. Then he thanked the trooper and with a weird, old-maidy show of caution turned the car around. "Your mother will never forgive me for this," he said.

"We should've left this morning," I said. "Doctor."

He didn't speak to me again until we were in a booth at the diner, waiting for our burgers. "She won't forgive me," he said. "Do you understand? Never."

"I guess," I said, though no guesswork was required. She wouldn't forgive him.

"I can't let that happen." He bent toward me. "I'll tell you what I want. I want us all to be together again. Is that what you want?"

"Yes, sir."

He bumped my chin with his knuckles. "That's all I needed to hear."

When we finished eating he went to the pay phone in the back of the diner, then joined me in the booth again. I figured he'd called my mother, but he didn't give a report. He sipped at his coffee and stared out the window at the empty road. "Come on, come on," he said, though not to me. A little while later he said it again. When the trooper's car went past, lights flashing, he got up and dropped some money on the check. "Okay. *Vámonos*."

The wind had died. The snow was falling straight down, less of it now and lighter. We drove away from the resort, right up to the barricade. "Move it," my father told me. When I looked at him, he said, "What are you waiting for?" I got out and dragged one of the sawhorses aside, then put it back after he drove through. He pushed the door open for me. "Now you're an accomplice," he said. "We go down together." He put the car into gear and gave me a look. "Joke, son."

Down the first long stretch I watched the road behind us, to see if the trooper was on our tail. The barricade vanished. Then there was nothing but snow: snow on the road, snow kicking up from the chains, snow on the trees, snow in the sky, and our trail in the snow. Then I faced forward and had a shock. There were no tracks ahead of us. My father was breaking virgin snow between tall treelines. He was humming "Stars Fell on Alabama." I felt snow brush along the floorboards under my feet. To keep my hands from shaking I clamped them between my knees.

My father grunted thoughtfully and said, "Don't ever try this yourself."

"I won't."

"That's what you say now, but someday you'll get your license and then you'll think you can do anything. Only you won't be able to do this. You need, I don't know—a certain instinct."

"Maybe I have it."

"You don't. You have your strong points, sure, just not this. I only mention it because I don't want you to get the idea this is something anybody can do. I'm a great driver. That's not a virtue, okay? It's just a fact, and one you should be aware of. Of course you have to give the old heap some credit too. There aren't many cars I'd try this with. Listen!"

I did listen. I heard the slap of the chains, the stiff, jerky rasp of the wipers, the purr of the engine. It really did purr. The old heap was almost new. My father couldn't afford it, and kept promising to sell it, but here it was.

I said, "Where do you think that policeman went to?"

"Are you warm enough?" He reached over and cranked up the blower. Then he turned off the wipers. We didn't need them. The clouds had brightened. A few sparse, feathery flakes drifted into our slipstream and were swept away. We left the trees and entered a broad field of snow that ran level for a while and then tilted sharply downward. Orange stakes had been planted at intervals in two parallel lines and my father steered a course between them, though they were far enough apart to leave considerable doubt in my mind as to exactly where the road lay. He was humming again, doing little scat riffs around the melody.

"Okay, then. What are my strong points?"

"Don't get me started," he said. "It'd take all day."

"Oh, right. Name one."

"Easy. You always think ahead."

True. I always thought ahead. I was a boy who kept his clothes on numbered hangers to ensure proper rotation. I bothered my teachers for homework assignments far ahead of their due dates so I could draw up schedules. I thought ahead, and that was why I knew there would be other troopers waiting for us at the end of our ride, if we even got there. What I didn't know was that my father would wheedle and plead his way past them—he didn't sing "O Tannenbaum," but just about—and get me home for dinner, buying a little more time before my mother decided to make the split final. I knew we'd get caught; I was resigned to it. And maybe for this reason I stopped moping and began to enjoy myself.

Why not? This was one for the books. Like being in a speedboat, only better. You can't go downhill in a boat. And it was all ours. And it kept coming, the laden trees, the unbroken surface of snow, the sudden white vistas. Here and there I saw hints of the road, ditches, fences, stakes, though not so many that I could have found my own way. But then I didn't have to. My father was driving. My father in his forty-eighth year, rumpled, kind, bankrupt of honor, flushed with certainty. He was a great driver. All persuasion, no coercion. Such subtlety at the wheel, such tactful pedalwork. I actually trusted him. And the best was yet to come—switchbacks and hairpins impossible to describe. Except maybe to say this: if you haven't driven fresh powder, you haven't driven.

The Night in Question

Frances had come to her brother's apartment to hold his hand over a disappointment in love, but Frank polished off half the cherry pie she'd brought him and barely mentioned the woman. He was in an exalted state over a sermon he'd heard that afternoon. Dr. Violet had outdone himself, Frank told her; this was his best, the gold standard. Frank wanted to repeat it to Frances, as he used to act out movie scenes for her when they were young.

"Gotta run, Franky."

"It's not that long," Frank said. "Five minutes. Ten—at the outside."

Three years earlier he had driven her car into a highway abutment and almost died, then almost died again, in detox, of a grand mal seizure. Now he wanted to preach sermons at her. She supposed she was grateful. She said she'd give him ten minutes.

It was a muggy night, but as always Frank wore a long-sleeved shirt to hide the weird tattoos he woke up with one morning when he was stationed in Manila. The shirt was white, starched, and crisply ironed. The tie he'd worn to church was still cinched up hard under his prominent Adam's apple. A tall man in a small room, he paced in front of the couch while he gathered himself to speak. He favored his left leg, whose knee had been shattered in the crash; every time his right foot came down, the dishes clinked in the cupboards.

"Okay, here goes," he said. "I'll have to fill in here and there, but I've got most of it." He continued to walk, slowly, deliberately, hands behind his back, head bent at an angle that suggested meditation. "My dear friends," he said, "you may have read in the paper not long ago of a man of our state, a parent like many of yourselves here today . . . though a parent with a terrible choice to make. His name is Mike Bolling. He's a railroad man, Mike, a switchman, been with the railroad ever since he finished high school, same as his father and grandfather before him. He and Janice've been married ten years now. They were hoping for a whole houseful of kids, but the Lord decided to give them one instead, a very special one. That was nine years ago. Benny, they named him—after Janice's father. Though he died when she was just a youngster, she remembered his big lopsided grin and how he threw back his head when he laughed, and she was hoping some of her dad's spirit would rub off on his name. Well, it turned out she got all the spirit she could handle, and then some.

"Benny. He came out in high gear and never shifted down. Mike liked to say you could run a train off him, the energy he had. Good student, natural athlete, but his big thing was mechanics. One of those boys, you put him in the same room with a clock and he's got it in pieces before you can turn around. By the time he was in second grade he could put the clocks back together, not to mention the vacuum cleaner and the TV and the engine of Mike's old lawn mower."

This didn't sound like Frank. He was plain in his speech, neither formal nor folksy, so spare and sometimes harsh that his jokes sounded like challenges, or insults. Frances was about the only one who got them. This tone was putting her on edge. Something terrible was going to happen in the story, something Frances would regret having heard. She knew that. But she didn't stop him. Frank was her little brother, and she would deny him nothing.

When Frank was still a baby, not even walking yet, Frank Senior, their father, had set out to teach his son the meaning of the word "no." At dinner he'd dangle his wristwatch before Frank's eyes, then say *No!* and jerk it back just as the boy grabbed for it. When Frank persisted, Frank Senior would slap his hand until he was howling with fury and desire. This happened night after night. Frank would not take the lesson to heart; as soon as the watch was offered, he snatched at it. Frances followed her mother's example and said nothing. She was eight years old, and while she feared her father's attention she also missed it, and resented Frank's obstinacy and the disturbance it caused. Why couldn't he learn?

Then her father slapped Frank's face. This was on New Year's Eve. Frances still remembered the stupid tasseled hats they were all wearing when her father slapped her baby brother. In the void of time after the slap there was no sound but the long rush of air into Frank's lungs as, red-faced, twisting in his chair, he worked up a scream. Frank Senior lowered his head. Frances saw that he'd surprised himself and was afraid of what would follow. She looked at her mother, whose eyes were closed. In later years Frances tried to think of a moment when their lives might have turned by even a degree, turned and gone in some other direction, and she always came back to this instant when her father knew the wrong he'd done and was shaken, open to rebuke. What might have happened if her mother had come flying out of her chair and stood over him and told him to stop, now and forever? Or if she had only *looked* at him, confirming his shame? But her eyes were closed, and stayed closed until Frank blasted them with his despair and Frank Senior left the room. As Frances knew even then, her mother could not allow herself to see what she had no strength to oppose. Her heart was bad. Three years later she reached for a bottle of ammonia, said "Oh," sat down on the floor, and died.

Frances did oppose her father. In defiance of his orders, she brought food to Frank's room when he was banished, stood up for him, and told him he was right to stand up for himself. Frank Senior had decided that his son needed to be broken, and Frank would not break. He went after everything his father said no to, with Frances egging him on and mothering him when he got caught. In time their father ceased to give reasons for his displeasure. As his silence grew heavier, so did his hand. One night Frances grabbed her father's belt as he started after Frank, and when he flung her aside Frank head-rammed him in the stomach. Frances jumped on her father's back, and the three of them crashed around the room. When it was over Frances was flat on the floor with a split lip and a ringing sound in her ears, laughing like a madwoman.

Frank Senior said no to his son in everything, and Frances would say no to him in nothing. Frank was aware of her reluctance and learned to exploit it, most shamelessly in the months before his accident. He'd invaded her home, caused her trouble at work, nearly destroyed her marriage. To this day her husband had not forgiven Frances for what he called her complicity in that nightmare. But her husband had never been thrown across a room, or kicked, or slammed headfirst into a door. No one had ever spoken to him as her father had spoken to Frank. He had no idea what it was like to be helpless and alone. No one should be alone in this world. Everyone should have someone who kept faith, no matter what, all the way.

"On the night in question," Frank said, "Mike's foreman called up and asked him to take another fellow's shift at the drawbridge station where he'd been working. A Monday night it was, mid-January, bitter cold. Janice was at a PTA meeting when Mike got the call, so he had no choice but to bring Benny along with him. Though it was against the rules, strictly speaking, he needed the overtime and he'd done it before, more than once. Nobody ever said anything. Benny always behaved himself, and it was a good chance for him and Mike to buddy up, batch it a little. They'd talk and kid around, heat up some franks, then Mike would set Benny up with a sleeping bag and air mattress. A regular adventure.

"A bitter night, like I said. There was a furnace at the station, but it wasn't working. The guy Mike relieved had on his parka and a pair of mittens. Mike ribbed him about it, though pretty soon he and Benny put their own hats and gloves back on. Mike brewed up some hot chocolate, and they played gin rummy, or tried to—it's not that easy with gloves on. But they weren't thinking about winning or losing. It was good enough just being together, the two of them, with the cold wind blowing up against the windows. Father and son! What could be better than that? Then Mike had to raise the bridge for a couple of boats, and things got pretty tense because one of them steered too close to the bank and almost ran aground. The skipper had to reverse engines and go back downriver and take another turn at it. The whole business went on a lot longer than it should have, and by the time the second boat got clear Mike was running way behind schedule and under pressure to get the bridge down for the express train out of Portland. That was when he noticed Benny was missing."

Frank stopped by the window and looked out, unseeing, as if contemplating whether to go on. But then he turned away from the window and started in again, and Frances understood that this little moment of reflection was just another part of the sermon.

"Mike calls Benny's name. No answer. He calls him again, and he doesn't spare the volume. You have to understand the position Mike is in. He has to get the bridge down for that train, and he's got just about enough time to do it. He doesn't know where Benny is, but he has a pretty good idea. Just where he isn't supposed to be. Down below, in the engine room.

"The engine room. The mill, as Mike and the other operators call it. You can imagine the kind of power that's needed to raise and lower a drawbridge, aside from the engine itself—all the winches and levers, pulleys and axles and wheels and so on. Massive machinery. Gigantic screws turning everywhere, gears with teeth like file cabinets. They've got catwalks and little crawlways through the works for the mechanics, but nobody goes down there unless they know what they're doing. You have to know what you're doing. You have to know exactly where to put your feet, and you've got to keep your hands in close and wear all the right clothes. And even if you know what you're doing, you never go down there when the bridge is being moved. Never. There's just too much going on, too many ways of getting snagged and pulled into the works. Mike has told Benny a hundred times, 'Stay out of the mill.' That's the iron rule when Benny comes out to the station. But Mike made the mistake of taking him down for a quick look one day when the engine was being serviced, and he saw how Benny lit up at the sight of all that steel, all that machinery.

Benny was just dying to get his hands on those wheels and gears, to see how everything fit together. Mike could feel it pulling at Benny like a big magnet. He always kept a close eye on him after that, until this one night, when he got distracted. And now Benny's down in there. Mike knows it as sure as he knows his own name."

Frances said, "I don't want to hear this story."

Frank gave no sign that he'd heard her. She was going to say something else, then made a sour face and let him go on.

"To get to the engine room, Mike would have to go through the passageway to the back of the station and wait for the elevator, or else climb down the emergency ladder. He doesn't have time to do either. Doesn't have time for anything but lowering the bridge, and just barely enough time for that. He's got to get that bridge down now or the train is going into the river with everyone on board. This is the position he's in, this is the choice he has to make: his son, his Benjamin, or the people on that train.

"Now, let's take a minute to think about the people on that train. Mike's never met any of them, but he's lived long enough to know what they're like. They're like the rest of us. There are some who know the Lord, and love their neighbors, and live in the light. And there are the others. On this train are men who whisper over cunning papers and take from the widow even her mean portion. On this train is the man whose factories kill and maim his workers. There are thieves on this train, and liars, and hypocrites. There is the man whose wife is not enough for him, who cannot be happy until he possesses every woman who walks the earth. There is the false witness. There is the bribe taker. There is the woman who abandons her husband and children for her own pleasure. There is the seller of spoiled goods, the coward, and the usurer, and there is the man who lives for his drug, who will do anything for that false promise—steal from those who give him work, from his friends, his family, yes, even from his own family, scheming for their pity, borrowing in bad faith, breaking into their very homes. All these are on the train, awake and hungry as wolves, and also on the train are the sleepers, those who with open eyes sleepwalk through their days, neither doing evil nor resisting it, like soldiers who lie down as if dead and will not join the battle, not for their cities and homes, not even for their wives and children. For such people, how can Mike give up his son, his Benjamin, who is guilty of nothing?

"He can't. Of course he can't, not on his own. But Mike isn't on his own. He knows what we all know, even when we try to forget it: we are never alone, ever. We are in our Father's presence in the light of day and in the dark of night, even in that darkness where we run from Him, hiding our faces like fearful children. He will not leave us. No. He will never leave us alone. Though we lock every window and bar every door, still he will enter. Though we empty our hearts and turn them to stone, yet shall he make his home there.

"He will not leave us alone. He is with all of you here, as he is with me. He is with Mike, and also with the bribe taker on the train, and the woman who must have her friend's husband, and the man who needs a drink. He knows their needs better than they do. He knows that what they truly need is him, and though they flee his voice he never stops telling them that he is there. And at this moment, when Mike has nowhere to hide and nothing left to tell himself, then he can hear, and he knows that he is not alone, and he knows what it is that he must do. It has been done before, even by him who speaks, the Father of All, who gave his own Son, his beloved, that others might be saved."

"No!" Frances said.

Frank stopped and looked at Frances as if he couldn't remember who she was.

"That's it," she said. "That's my quota of holiness for the year."

"But there's more."

"I know, I can see it coming. The guy kills his kid, right? I have to tell you, Frank, that's a crummy story. What're we supposed to get from a story like that—we should kill our own kid to save some stranger?"

"There's more to it than that."

"Okay, then, make it a trainload of strangers, make it *ten* trainloads of strangers. I should do this because the so-called Father of All did it? Is that the point? How do people think up stuff like this, anyway? It's an awful story."

"It's true."

"*True?* Franky. Please, you're not a moron."

"Dr. Violet knows a man who was on that train."

"I'll just bet he does. Let me guess." Frances screwed her eyes shut, then popped them open. "The drug addict! Yes, and he reformed afterward and worked with street kids in Brazil and showed everybody that Mike's sacrifice wasn't in vain. Is that how it goes?"

"You're missing the point, Frances. It isn't about that. Let me finish."

"No. It's a terrible story, Frank. People don't act like that. I sure as hell wouldn't."

"You haven't been asked. He doesn't ask us to do what we can't do."

"I don't care what he asks. Where'd you learn to talk like that, anyway? You don't even sound like yourself."

"I had to change. I had to change the way I thought about things. Maybe I sound a little different too."

"Yeah, well you sounded better when you were drunk."

Frank seemed about to say something, but didn't. He backed up a step and lowered himself into a hideous plaid La-Z-Boy left behind by the previous tenant. It was stuck in the upright position.

"I don't care if the Almighty poked a gun in my ear, I would never do that," Frances said. "Not in a million years. Neither would you. Honest, now, little brother, if I was the one down in the mill, would you grind me up? Would you push the Francesburger button?"

"It isn't a choice I have to make."

"Yeah, yeah, I know. But say you did."

"I don't. He doesn't hold guns to our heads."

"Oh, really? What about hell, huh? What do you call that? But so what. Screw hell, I don't care about that. Do I get crunched or not?"

"Don't put me to the test, Frances. It's not your place."

"I'm down in the mill, Frank. I'm stuck in the gears and here comes the train with Mother Teresa and five hundred sinners on board, *whoo-whoo, whoo-whoo.* Who, Frank? Who's it going to be?"

248

Frances wanted to laugh. Glumly erect in the chair, hands gripping the armrests, Frank looked like he was about to take off into a hurricane. She kept that little reflection to herself. Frank was thinking, and she had to let him. She knew what his answer would be—in the end there could be no other answer—but he couldn't just say *she's my sister* and let it go at that. No, he'd have to noodle up some righteous, high-sounding reasons for choosing her. And maybe he wouldn't, at first, maybe he'd chicken out and come up with the Bible-school answer. Frances was ready for that; she could bring him around. Frances didn't mind a fight, and she especially didn't mind fighting for her brother. For her brother she'd fought neighborhood punks, snotty teachers and unappreciative coaches, loan sharks, landlords, bouncers. From the time she was a scabby-kneed girl she'd taken on her own father, and if push came to shove she'd take on the Father of All, that incomprehensible bully. She was ready. It would be like old times, the two of them waiting in her room upstairs while Frank Senior worked himself into a rage below, muttering, slamming doors, stinking up the house with the cigars he puffed when he was on a tear. She remembered it all—the tremor in her legs, the hammering pulse in her neck as the smell of smoke grew stronger. She could still taste that smoke and hear her father's steps on the stairs, Frank panting beside her, moving closer, his voice whispering her name and her own voice answering, as fear gave way to ferocity and unaccountable joy, *It's okay, Franky. I'm here.*

Firelight

My mother swore we'd never live in a boardinghouse again, but circumstances did not allow her to keep this promise. She decided to change cities; we had to sleep somewhere. This boardinghouse was worse than the last, unfriendly, funereal, heavy with the smells that disheartened people allow themselves to cultivate. On the floor below ours a retired merchant seaman was coughing his lungs out. He was a friendly old guy, always ready with a compliment for my mother as we climbed past the dim room where he sat smoking on the edge of his bed. During the day we felt sorry for him, but at night, as we lay in wait for the next racking seizure, feeling the silence swell with it, we hated him. I did, anyway.

My mother said this was only temporary. We were definitely getting out of there. To show me and maybe herself that she meant business, she went through the paper during breakfast every Saturday morning and circled the advertisements for furnished apartments that sounded, as she put it, "right for our needs." I liked that expression. It made me feel as if our needs had some weight in the world, and would have to be reckoned with. Then, putting on her shrewd face, my mother compared the rents and culled out the most expensive apartments and also the very cheapest. We knew the story on those, the dinky fridge and weeping walls, the tub sinking through the bathroom floor, the wife beater upstairs. We'd been that route. When my mother had five or six possibilities, she called to make sure they were still open, and then we spent the day going from one to another.

We couldn't actually take a place yet. The landlords wanted first and last months' rent, plus a cleaning deposit, and it was going to be a while before my mother could put all that together. I understood this, but every Saturday my mother repeated it again so I wouldn't get carried away. We were just looking. Getting a feel for the market.

There is pleasure to be found in the purchase of goods and services. I enjoy it myself now, playing the part of a man who knows what he wants and can take it home with him. But in those days I was mostly happy just to look at things. And that was lucky for me, because we did a power of looking and no buying.

My mother wasn't one of those comparison shoppers who head straight for the price tag, shaking their faces and beefing about the markup to everyone in sight. She had no great concern with price. She had no money either, but it went deeper than that. She liked to shop because she felt at home in stores and was interested in the merchandise. Salesclerks waited on her without impatience, seeing there was nothing mean or trivial in her curiosity, this curiosity that kept her so young and drove her so hard. She just had to see what was out there.

We'd always shopped, but that first fall in Seattle, when we were more broke than we'd ever been, we really hit our stride. We looked at leather luggage. We looked at televisions in large Mediterranean consoles. We looked at antiques and Oriental rugs. Looking at Oriental rugs isn't something you do lightly, because the men who sell them work like dogs, dragging them down from these tall piles and then humping them over to you, sweating and gasping, staggering under the weight, their faces woolly with lint. They tend to be small men. You can't be squeamish. You have to be free of shame, absolutely sure of your right to look at what you cannot buy. And so we were.

When the new fashions came in, my mother tried them on while I watched. She had once been a model and knew how to strike attitudes before the mirror, how to walk casually away and then stop, cocking one hip and glancing over her shoulder as if someone had just called her name. When she turned to me I expressed my judgments with a smile, a shrug, a sour little shake of the head. I thought she was beautiful in everything but I felt obliged to discriminate. She didn't like too much admiration. It suffocated her.

We looked at copper cookware. We looked at lawn furniture and pecan dining-room sets. We spent one whole day at a marina, studying the inventory of a bankrupt Chris-Craft dealership. The Big Giveaway, they called it. It was the only sale we ever made a point of going to.

My mother wore a smart gray suit when we went house hunting. I wore my little gentleman's outfit, a V-neck sweater with a bow tie. The sweater had the words FRATERNITY ROW woven across the front. We looked respectable, as, on the whole, we were. We also looked solvent.

On this particular day we were touring apartments in the university district. The first three we looked at were decent enough, but the fourth was a wreck—the last tenant, a woman, must have lived there like an animal in a cave. Someone had tried to clean it up, but even with the windows open and the cold air blowing through, the place smelled like rotten meat. The landlord said that the woman had been depressed over the breakup of her marriage. Though he talked about a paint job and new carpets, he seemed discouraged and soon fell silent. The three of us walked through the rooms, then back outside. The landlord could tell we weren't biting. He didn't even offer us a card.

We had one more apartment to look at, but my mother said she'd seen enough. She asked if I wanted to go down to the wharf, or home, or what. Her mouth was set, her face drawn. She tried to sound agreeable but she was in a black mood. I didn't like the idea of going back to the house, back to the room, so I asked if we could walk up to the university and take a look around.

She squinted up the street. I thought she was going to say no. "Sure," she said. "Why not? As long as we're here."

We started walking. There were big maples along the sidewalk. Fallen leaves scraped and eddied around our legs as the breeze gusted.

"You don't *ever* let yourself go like that," my mother said, hugging herself and looking down. "There's no excuse for it."

She sounded mortally offended. I knew I hadn't done anything, so I kept quiet. She said, "I don't care what happens, there is no excuse to give up like that. Do you hear what I'm saying?"

"Yes, ma'am."

A group of Chinese came up behind us, ten or twelve of them, all young men, talking excitedly. They parted around us, still talking, and rejoined like water flowing around a stone. We followed them up the street and across the road to the university, where we wandered among the buildings as the light began to fail and the wind turned raw. This was the first really cold day since we'd moved here and I wasn't dressed for it. But I said nothing, because I still didn't want to go home. I'd never set foot on a campus before and was greedily measuring it against my idea of what it should look like. It had everything. Old-looking buildings with stone archways and high, arched windows. Rich greenswards. Ivy. High on the west-facing walls, in what was left of the sunshine, the red leaves of the ivy glittered as the wind stirred them. Every so often a great roar went up from Husky Stadium, where a game was in progress. Each time I heard it I felt a thrill of complicity and belonging. I believed that I was in place here, and that the students we passed on the brick walkways would look at me and see one of themselves—*Fraternity Row*—if it weren't for the woman beside me, her hand on my shoulder. I began to feel the weight of that hand.

My mother didn't notice. She was in good spirits again, flushed with the cold and with memories of days like this at Yale and Trinity, when she used to get free tickets to football games from a girlfriend who dated a player. She had dated one of the players herself, an All-American quarterback from Yale named Dutch Diefenbacker. He'd wanted to marry her, she added carelessly.

"You mean he actually asked you?"

"He gave me a ring. My father sold it to him. He'd bought it for this woman he had a crush on, but she wouldn't accept it. What she actually said was, 'Why, I wouldn't marry an old man like you!'" My mother laughed.

"Wait a minute," I said. "You had a chance to marry an All-American from Yale?"

"Sure."

"So why didn't you?"

We stopped beside a fountain clotted with leaves. My mother stared into the water. "I don't know. I was pretty young then, and Dutch wasn't what you'd call a scintillating guy. He was nice . . . just dull. Very dull." She drew a deep breath and said, with some violence, "God, he was boring!"

"I would've married him," I said. I'd never heard about this before. That my mother, out of schoolgirl snobbery, had deprived me of an All-American father from Yale was outrageous. I would be rich now, and have a collie. Everything would be different.

We circled the fountain and headed back the way we'd come. When we reached the road my mother asked me if I wanted to look at the apartment we'd skipped. "Oh, what the heck," she said, seeing me hesitate. "It's around here somewhere. We might as well make a clean sweep."

I was cold, but because I hadn't said anything so far I thought it would sound false if I complained now, false and babyish. She stopped two girls wearing letter sweaters—*Coeds,* I thought, finding a cheap, keen excitement in the word—and while they gave her directions I studied the display in a bookstore window, as if I just happened to be standing beside this person who didn't know her way around.

The evening was clear and brief. At a certain moment the light flared weakly, and then it was gone. We walked several blocks, into a neighborhood of Victorian houses whose windows, seen from the empty street, glowed with rich, exclusive light. The wind blew at our backs. I was starting to shake. I still didn't tell my mother. I knew I should've said something earlier, that I'd been stupid not to, and now I fastened all my will on the effort to conceal this stupidity by maintaining it.

We stopped in front of a house with a turret. The upper story was dark. "We're late," I said.

"Not that late," my mother said. "Besides, the apartment's on the ground floor."

She walked up to the porch while I waited on the sidewalk. I heard the muted chime of bells and watched the windows for movement.

"Nuts . . . I should've called," my mother said. She'd just turned away when one of the two doors swung open and a man leaned out, a big man silhouetted in the bright doorway. "Yes?" he said. He sounded impatient, though when my mother turned to face him he added, more gently, "What can I do for you?" His voice was so deep I could almost feel it, like coal rumbling down a chute.

She told him we were here about the apartment. "I guess we're a little late," she said.

"An hour late," he said.

My mother exclaimed surprise, said we'd been walking around the university and completely lost track of the time. She was very apologetic but made no move to go, and it must have been clear to him that she had no intention of leaving until she'd seen the apartment. It was clear enough to me. I went down the walkway and up the porch steps.

He was big in every direction—tall and rotund with a massive head, a trophy head. He had the kind of size that provokes, almost inevitably, the nickname Tiny, though I'm sure nobody ever called him that. He was too grave, preoccupied, like a buffalo in the broadness and solemnity of his face. He looked down at us through black-framed glasses. "Well, you're here," he said, not unkindly, and we followed him inside.

The first thing I saw was the fire. I was aware of other things, the furniture, the churchlike expanse of the room, but my eyes went straight to the flames. They burned with a hissing sound in a fireplace I could have walked into without stooping, or just about. A girl lay on her stomach in front of the fire, one bare foot raised and slowly twisting, her chin propped in her hand. She was reading a book. She went on reading for a few moments after we came in, then sat up and said, very precisely, "Good evening." She had boobs. I could see them pushing at the front of her blouse. But she wasn't pretty. She was owlish and large and wore the same kind of glasses as the man, whom she closely and unfortunately resembled. She blinked constantly. I felt immediately at ease with her. I smiled and said hi, instead of assuming the indifference, even hostility, with which I treated pretty girls.

Something was in the oven, something chocolate. I went over to the fire and stood with my back to it, flexing my hands behind me.

"Oh yes, it's quite comfortable," the man said in answer to a comment of my mother's. He peered around curiously as if surprised to find himself here. The room was big, the biggest I'd ever seen in an apartment. We could never afford to live here, but I was already losing my grip on that fact.

"I'll go get my wife," the man said, then stayed where he was, watching my mother.

She turned, nodding pensively to herself. "All this room," she said. "It makes you feel so free. How can you bear to give it up?"

At first he didn't answer. The girl started picking at something on the rug. Then he said, "We're ready for a bit of a change. Aren't we, Sister?"

She nodded without looking up.

A woman came in from the next room, carrying a plate of brownies. She was tall and thin. Deep furrows ran down her cheeks, framing her mouth like parentheses. Her gray hair was pulled into a ponytail. She moved toward us with slow, measured steps, as if bearing gifts to an altar, and set the plate on the coffee table. "You're just in time to have some of Dr. Avery's brownies," she said.

I thought she was referring to a recipe. Then the man hurried over and scooped up a handful, and I understood. I understood not only that he was Dr. Avery, but also that the brownies belonged to him; his descent on the plate bore all the signs of jealous ownership. I was nervous about taking one, but Sister did it and survived, and even went back for another. I had a couple myself. As we ate, the woman slipped her arm behind Dr. Avery's back and leaned against him. The little I'd seen of marriage had disposed me to view public affection between husbands and wives as pure stagecraft—*Look, this is a home where people hug each other*—though she was so plainly happy to be where she was that I couldn't help feeling happy with her.

My mother prowled the room restlessly. "Do you mind if I look around?" she said.

Mrs. Avery asked Sister to show us the rest of the apartment.

More big rooms. Two of them had fireplaces. Above the mantel in the master bedroom hung a large photograph of a man with dark, thoughtful eyes. When I asked Sister who it was, she said, a shade importantly, "Gurdjieff."

I didn't mind her condescension. She was older, and bigger, and I suspected smarter than me. Condescension seemed perfectly in order.

"Gurdjieff," my mother said. "I've heard of him."

"*Gurdjieff*," Sister repeated, as though she'd said it wrong.

We went back to the living room and sat around the fire, Dr. and Mrs. Avery on the couch, my mother in a rocking chair across from them. Sister and I stretched out on the floor. She opened her book, and a moment later her foot rose into the air again and began its slow twisting motion. My mother and Mrs. Avery were talking about the apartment. I stared into the flames, the voices above me pleasant and meaningless until I heard my name mentioned. My mother was telling Mrs. Avery about our walk around the university. She said it was a beautiful campus.

"Beautiful?" Dr. Avery said. "What do you mean by beautiful?"

My mother looked at him. She didn't answer.

"I assume you're referring to the buildings."

"Sure. The buildings, the grounds. The general layout."

"Pseudo-Gothic humbug," Dr. Avery said. "A movie set."

"Dr. Avery believes that the university pays too much attention to appearances," Mrs. Avery said.

"That's all they pay attention to," Dr. Avery said.

"I wouldn't know about that," my mother said. "I'm not an expert on architecture. It looked nice enough to me."

"Yes, well that's the whole point, isn't it?" Dr. Avery said. "It *looks* like a university. The same with the so-called education they're selling. It's a counterfeit experience from top to bottom. Utterly hollow. All *materia,* no *anima.*"

He lost me there, and I went back to looking at the flames. Dr. Avery rumbled on. He had been quiet before, but once he got started he didn't stop, and I wouldn't have wanted him to. The sound of his voice made me drowsy with assurance, like the drone of a car engine when you're lying on the backseat, going home from a long trip. Now and then Mrs. Avery spoke up, expressing concord with something he had said, making her complete agreement known; then he resumed. Sister shifted beside me. She yawned, turned a page. The logs settled in the fireplace, very softly, like some old sleeping dog adjusting his bones.

Dr. Avery talked for quite a while. Then my mother spoke my name. Nothing more, only my name. Dr. Avery went on as if he hadn't heard. He was leaning forward, one finger wagging to the cadence of his words, glasses glinting as his great head shook. I looked at my mother. She sat stiffly in the rocker, her hands kneading the purse in her lap. Her face was bleak, frozen. It was the expression she wore when she got trapped by some diehard salesman or a pair of Mormons who wouldn't go away. She wanted to leave.

I did not want to leave. Nodding by the fire, torpid and content, I had forgotten that this wasn't my home. The heat and the firelight worked on me like Dr. Avery's voice, lulling me into a state of familial serenity such as these people seemed to enjoy. I even managed to forget they were not my family, and that they, too, would soon be moving on. I made them part of my story without any sense that they had their own to live out.

What that was, I don't know. We never saw them again. But now, so many years later, I can venture a guess. My guess is that Dr. Avery had been denied tenure by the university, and that this wasn't the first to prove itself unequal to him, nor the last. I see him carrying his fight against mere appearances from one unworthy institution to the next, each of them refusing, with increasing vehemence, his call to authenticity. Dr. Avery's colleagues, small minds joined to small hearts, ridicule him as a nuisance and a bore. His high-mindedness, they imply, is a cover for lack of distinction in his field, whatever that may be. Again and again they send him packing. Mrs. Avery consoles his wounded *anima* with unfailing loyalty, and ministers to his swelling *materia* with larger and larger batches of brownies. She believes in him. Her faith, whatever its foundation, is heroic. Not once does she imagine, as a lesser woman might, that her chances for common happiness—old friends, a place of her own, a life rooted in community—have been sacrificed not to some higher truth but to vanity and arrogance.

No, that part belongs to Sister. Sister will be the heretic. She has no choice, being their child. In time, not many years after this night, she will decide that the disappointments of her life can be traced to their failings. Who knows those failings better than Sister? There are scenes. Dr. Avery is accused of being himself, Mrs. Avery of being herself. The visits home from Barnard or Reed or wherever Sister's scholarship takes her, and then from the distant city where she works, become theatrical productions. Angry whispers in the kitchen, shouts at the dinner table, early departure. This goes on for years, though not forever. Sister makes peace with her parents. She even comes to cherish what she has resented, their refusal to talk and act as others do, their endless moving on, the bright splash of their oddity in the muddy flow. She finds she has no choice but to love them, and who can love them better than Sister?

It might have gone this way, or another way. I have made these people part of my story without knowing anything of theirs, just as I did that night, dreaming myself one of them. We were strangers. I'd spent maybe forty-five minutes in their apartment, just long enough to get warm and lose sight of the facts.

My mother spoke my name again. I stayed where I was. Usually I would have gotten to my feet without being prodded, not out of obedience but because it pleased me to anticipate her, to show off our teamwork. This time I just stared at her sullenly. She looked wrong in the rocking chair; she was too glamorous for it. I could see her glamour almost as a thing apart, another presence, a brassy impatient friend just dying to get her out of here, away from all this domesticity.

She said we ought to think about getting home. Sister raised her head and looked at me. I still didn't move. I could see my mother's surprise. She waited for me to do something, and when I didn't she rocked forward slowly and stood up. Everyone stood with her except me. I felt stupid and bratty sitting on the floor all by myself, but I stayed there anyway while she made the final pleasantries. When she moved toward the door, I got up and mumbled my good-byes, then followed her outside.

Dr. Avery held the door for us.

"I still think it's a pretty campus," my mother said.

He laughed—*ho ho ho.* "Well, so be it," he said. "To each his own." He waited until we reached the sidewalk, then turned the light off and closed the door. It made a solid bang behind us.

"What was all that about?" my mother said.

I didn't answer.

"Are you feeling okay?"

"Yes." Then I said, "I'm a little cold."

"Cold? Why didn't you say something?" She tried to look concerned, but I could tell she was glad to have a simple answer for what had happened back in the house.

She took off her suit jacket. "Here."

"That's okay."

"Put it on."

"Really, Mom. I'll be okay."

"Put it on, dimwit!"

I pulled the coat over my shoulders. We walked for a while. "I look ridiculous," I said.

"So . . . who cares?"

"I do."

"Okay, you do. *Sorry.* Boy, you're a regular barrel of laughs tonight."

"I'm not wearing this thing on the bus."

"Nobody said you had to wear it on the bus. You want to grab something to eat before we head back?"

I told her sure, fine, whatever she wanted.

"Maybe we can find a pizza place. Think you could eat some pizza?"

I said I thought I could.

A black dog with gleaming eyes crossed the street in our direction.

"Hello, sport," my mother said.

The dog trotted along beside us for a while, then took off.

I turned up the jacket collar and hunched my shoulders.

"Are you still cold?"

"A little." I was shivering like crazy. It seemed to me I'd never been so cold, and I blamed my mother for it, for taking me outside again, away from the fire. Though I knew it wasn't her fault, I blamed her anyway—for this and the wind in my face and for every nameless thing that was not as it should be.

"Come here." She pulled me over and began to rub her hand up and down my arm. When I leaned away she held on and kept rubbing. It felt good. I wasn't really warm, but I was as warm as I was going to get.

"Just out of curiosity," my mother said, "what did you think of the campus? Honestly."

"I liked it."

"I thought it was great," she said.

"So did I."

"That big blowhard," she said. "Where does he get off?"

I have my own fireplace now. Where we live the winters are long and cold. The wind blows the snow sideways, the house creaks, the windows glaze over with ferns of ice. After dinner I lay the fire, building four walls of logs like a roofless cabin. That's the best way. Only greenhorns use the teepee method. My children wait behind me, jockeying for position, furiously arguing their right to apply the match. I tell them to do it together. Their hands shake with eagerness as they strike the matches and hold them to the crumpled paper, torching as many spots as they can before the kindling starts to crackle. Then they sit back on their heels and watch the flame engulf the cabin walls. Their faces are reverent.

My wife comes in and praises the fire, knowing the pride it gives me. She lies on the couch with her book but doesn't read it. I don't read mine, either. I watch the fire, watch the changing light on the faces of my family. I try to feel at home, and I do, almost entirely. This is the moment I dream of when I am far away; this is my dream of home. But in the very heart of it I catch myself bracing a little, as if in fear of being tricked. As if to really believe in it will somehow make it vanish, like a voice waking me from sleep.

Bullet in the Brain

Anders couldn't get to the bank until just before it closed, so of course the line was endless and he got stuck behind two women whose loud, stupid conversation put him in a murderous temper. He was never in the best of tempers anyway, Anders—a book critic known for the weary, elegant savagery with which he dispatched almost everything he reviewed.

With the line still doubled around the rope, one of the tellers stuck a POSITION CLOSED sign in her window and walked to the back of the bank, where she leaned against a desk and began to pass the time with a man shuffling papers. The women in front of Anders broke off their conversation and watched the teller with hatred. "Oh, that's nice," one of them said. She turned to Anders and added, confident of his accord, "One of those little human touches that keep us coming back for more."

Anders had conceived his own towering hatred of the teller, but he immediately turned it on the presumptuous crybaby in front of him. "Damned unfair," he said. "Tragic, really. If they're not chopping off the wrong leg or bombing your ancestral village, they're closing their positions."

She stood her ground. "I didn't say it was tragic," she said. "I just think it's a pretty lousy way to treat your customers."

"Unforgivable," Anders said. "Heaven will take note."

She sucked in her cheeks but stared past him and said nothing. Anders saw that her friend was looking in the same direction. And then the tellers stopped what they were doing, the other customers slowly turned, and silence came over the bank. Two men wearing black ski masks and blue business suits were standing to the side of the door. One of them had a pistol pressed against the guard's neck. The guard's eyes were closed, and his lips were moving. The other man had a sawed-off shotgun. "Keep your big mouth shut!" the man with the pistol said, though no one had spoken a word. "One of you tellers hits the alarm, you're all dead meat."

"Oh, bravo," Anders said. " '*Dead meat.*' " He turned to the woman in front of him. "Great script, eh? The stern, brass-knuckled poetry of the dangerous classes."

She looked at him with drowning eyes.

The man with the shotgun pushed the guard to his knees. He handed the shotgun to his partner and yanked the guard's wrists up behind his back and locked them together with a pair of handcuffs. He toppled him onto the floor with a kick between the shoulder blades, then took his shotgun back and went over to the security gate at the end of the counter. He was short and heavy and moved with peculiar slowness. "Buzz him in," his partner said. The man with the shotgun opened the gate and sauntered along the line of tellers, handing each of them a plastic bag. When he came to the empty position he looked over at the man with the pistol, who said, "Whose slot is that?"

Anders watched the teller. She put her hand to her throat and turned to the man she'd been talking to. He nodded. "Mine," she said.

"Then get your ugly ass in gear and fill that bag."

"There you go," Anders said to the woman in front of him. "Justice is done."

"Hey! Bright boy! Did I tell you to talk?"

"No," Anders said.

"Then shut your trap."

"Did you hear that?" Anders said. " 'Bright boy.' Right out of *The Killers.*"

"Please, be quiet," the woman said.

"Hey, you deaf or what?" The man with the pistol walked over to

Anders and poked the weapon into his gut. "You think I'm playing games?"

"No," Anders said, but the barrel tickled like a stiff finger and he had to fight back the titters. He did this by making himself stare into the man's eyes, which were clearly visible behind the holes in the mask: pale blue and rawly red-rimmed. The man's left eyelid kept twitching. He breathed out a piercing, ammoniac smell that shocked Anders more than anything that had happened, and he was beginning to develop a sense of unease when the man prodded him again with the pistol.

"You like me, bright boy?" he said. "You want to suck my dick?"

"No," Anders said.

"Then stop looking at me."

Anders fixed his gaze on the man's shiny wing-tip shoes.

"Not down there. Up there." He stuck the pistol under Anders's chin and pushed it upward until he was looking at the ceiling.

Anders had never paid much attention to that part of the bank, a pompous old building with marble floors and counters and gilt scrollwork over the tellers' cages. The domed ceiling had been decorated with mythological figures whose fleshy, toga-draped ugliness Anders had taken in at a glance many years earlier and afterward declined to notice. Now he had no choice but to scrutinize the painter's work. It was even worse than he remembered, and all of it executed with the utmost gravity. The artist had a few tricks up his sleeve and used them again and again—a certain rosy blush on the underside of the clouds, a coy backward glance on the faces of the cupids and fauns. The ceiling was crowded with various dramas, but the one that caught Anders's eye was Zeus and Europa—portrayed, in this rendition, as a bull ogling a cow from behind a haystack. To make the cow sexy, the painter had canted her hips suggestively and given her long, droopy eyelashes through which she gazed back at the bull with sultry welcome. The bull wore a smirk and his eyebrows were arched. If there'd been a caption bubbling out of his mouth, it would have said HUBBA HUBBA.

"What's so funny, bright boy?"

"Nothing."

"You think I'm comical? You think I'm some kind of clown?"

"No."

"You think you can fuck with me?"

"No."

"Fuck with me again, you're history. *Capiche?*"

Anders burst out laughing. He covered his mouth with both hands and said, "I'm sorry, I'm sorry," then snorted helplessly through his fingers and said, *"Capiche*—oh, God, *capiche,"* and at that the man with the pistol raised the pistol and shot Anders right in the head.

The bullet smashed Anders's skull and plowed through his brain and exited behind his right ear, scattering shards of bone into the cerebral cortex, the corpus callosum, back toward the basal ganglia, and down into the thalamus. But before all this occurred, the first appearance of the bullet in the cerebrum set off a crackling chain of ion transports and neurotransmissions. Because of their peculiar origin these traced a peculiar pattern, flukishly calling to life a summer afternoon some forty years past, and long since lost to memory. After striking the cranium the bullet was moving at nine hundred feet per second, a pathetically sluggish, glacial pace compared with the synaptic lightning that flashed around it. Once in the brain, that is, the bullet came under the mediation of brain time, which gave Anders plenty of leisure to contemplate the scene that, in a phrase he would have abhorred, "passed before his eyes."

It is worth noting what Anders did not remember, given what he did recall. He did not remember his first lover, Sherry, or what he had most madly loved about her, before it came to irritate him—her unembarrassed carnality, and especially the cordial way she had with his unit, which she called Mr. Mole, as in *Uh-oh, looks like Mr. Mole wants to play.* Anders did not remember his wife, whom he had also loved before she exhausted him with her predictability, or his daughter, now a sullen professor of economics at Dartmouth. He did not remember standing just outside his daughter's door as she lectured

266

her bear about his naughtiness and described the appalling punishments Paws would receive unless he changed his ways. He did not remember a single line of the hundreds of poems he had committed to memory in his youth so he could give himself the shivers at will—not "Silent, upon a peak in Darien," or "My God, I heard this day," or "All my pretty ones? Did you say all? O hell-kite! All?" None of these did he remember; not one. Anders did not remember his dying mother saying of his father, "I should have stabbed him in his sleep."

He did not remember Professor Josephs telling his class how . Athenian prisoners in Sicily had been released if they could recite Aeschylus, and then reciting Aeschylus himself, right there, in the Greek. Anders did not remember how his eyes had burned at those sounds. He did not remember the surprise of seeing a college classmate's name on the dust jacket of a novel not long after they graduated, or the respect he had felt after reading the book. He did not remember the pleasure of giving respect.

Nor did Anders remember seeing a woman leap to her death from the building opposite his own just days after his daughter was born. He did not remember shouting, "Lord have mercy!" He did not remember deliberately crashing his father's car into a tree, or having his ribs kicked in by three policemen at an antiwar rally, or waking himself up with laughter. He did not remember when he began to regard the heap of books on his desk with boredom and dread, or when he grew angry at writers for writing them. He did not remember when everything began to remind him of something else.

This is what he remembered. Heat. A baseball field. Yellow grass, the whir of insects, himself leaning against a tree as the boys of the neighborhood gather for a pickup game. He looks on as the others argue the relative genius of Mantle and Mays. They have been worrying this subject all summer, and it has become tedious to Anders: an oppression, like the heat.

Then the last two boys arrive, Coyle and a cousin of his from Mississippi. Anders has never met Coyle's cousin before and will never see him again. He says hi with the rest but takes no further notice of him until they've chosen sides and someone asks the cousin what position he wants to play. "Shortstop," the boy says. "Short's the best position they is." Anders turns and looks at him. He wants to hear Coyle's cousin repeat what he's just said, though he knows better than to ask. The others will think he's being a jerk, ragging the kid for his grammar. But that isn't it, not at all—it's that Anders is strangely roused, elated, by those final two words, their pure unexpectedness and their music. He takes the field in a trance, repeating them to himself.

The bullet is already in the brain; it won't be outrun forever, or charmed to a halt. In the end it will do its work and leave the troubled skull behind, dragging its comet's tail of memory and hope and talent and love into the marble hall of commerce. That can't be helped. But for now Anders can still make time. Time for the shadows to lengthen on the grass, time for the tethered dog to bark at the flying ball, time for the boy in right field to smack his sweat-blackened mitt and softly chant, *They is, they is, they is.*

New Stories

That Room

The summer after my first year of high school, I got a case of independence and started hitchhiking to farms up and down the valley for daywork picking berries and mucking out stalls. Then I found a place where the farmer paid me ten cents an hour over minimum wage, and his plump, childless wife fed me lunch and fussed over me while I ate, so I stayed on there until school started.

While shoveling shit or hacking weeds out of a drainage ditch, I'd sometimes stop to gaze out toward the far fields, where the hands, as the farmer called them, were bucking bales of hay into a wagon, stacking them to teetering heights. Now and then a bark of laughter reached me, a tag end of conversation. The farmer hadn't let me work in the hay because I was too small, but I beefed up over the winter, and the following summer he let me join the crew.

So I was a hand. A hand! I went a little crazy with that word, with the pleasure of applying it to myself. Having a job like this changed everything. It delivered you from the reach of your parents, from the caustic scrutiny of your friends. It set you free among strangers in the eventful world, where you could practice being someone else until you *were* someone else. It put money in your pocket and allowed you to believe that your other life—your inessential, parenthetical life at home and school—was just a sop to those deluded enough to imagine you still needed them.

There were three others working the fields with me: the farmer's shy, muscle-bound nephew, Clemson, who was in my class at school but to whom I condescended because he was just an inexperienced kid, and two Mexican brothers, Miguel and Eduardo. Miguel, short and stolid and solitary, spoke very little English, but rakish Eduardo did the talking for both of them. While the rest of us did the heavy work, Eduardo provided advice about girls and told stories in which he featured as a trickster and deft, indefatigable swordsman. He played it for laughs, but in the very materials of his storytelling—the dance halls and bars, the bumbling border guards, the clod-brained farmers and their insatiable wives, the larcenous cops, the whores who loved him—I felt the actuality of a life I knew nothing about yet somehow contrived to want for myself: a real life in a real world.

While Eduardo talked, Miguel labored silently beside us, now and then grunting with the weight of a bale, his acne-scarred face flushed with heat, narrow eyes narrowed even tighter against the sun. Clemson and I sprinted and flagged, sprinted and flagged, laughing at Eduardo's stories, goading him with questions. Miguel never flagged, and never laughed. He sometimes watched his brother with what appeared to be mild curiosity; that was all.

The farmer, who owned a big spread with a lot of hay to bring in, should have hired more hands. He had only the four of us, and there was always the danger of rain. He was a relaxed, amiable man, but as the season wore on he grew anxious and began to push us harder and keep us longer. During the last week or so I spent the nights with Clemson's family, just down the road, so I could get to the farm with the others at sunup and work until dusk. The bales were heavy with dew when we started bringing them in. The air in the loft turned steamy from fermentation, and Eduardo warned the farmer that the hay might combust, but he held us to his schedule. Limping, sunburned, covered with scratches, I could hardly get out of bed in the morning. But although I griped with Clemson and Eduardo, I was secretly glad to take my place beside them, to work as if I had no choice.

Eduardo's car broke down toward the end of the week, and Clemson started driving him and Miguel to and from the decrepit motel where they lived with other seasonal workers. Sometimes, pulling up to their door, we'd all just sit there, saying nothing. We were that tired. Then one night Eduardo asked us in for a drink. Clemson, being a good boy, tried to beg off, but I got out with Miguel and Eduardo, knowing he wouldn't leave me. "Come on, Clem," I said, "don't be a homo." He looked at me, then turned the engine off.

That room. Jesus. The brothers had done their best, making their beds, keeping their clothes neatly folded in open suitcases, but you got swamped by the smell of mildew the moment you stepped inside. The floor was mushy underfoot and shedding squares of drab linoleum, the ceiling bowed and stained. The overhead light didn't quite reach the corners. Behind the mildew was another, unsettling smell. Clemson was a fastidious guy and writhed in distress as I made a show of being right at home.

We poured rye into our empty stomachs and listened to Eduardo, and before long we were all drunk. Someone came to the door and spoke to him in Spanish, and Eduardo went outside and didn't come back. Miguel and I kept drinking. Clemson was half asleep, his chin declining slowly toward his chest and snapping up again. Then Miguel looked at me. He slitted his eyes and looked at me hard, without blinking, and began to protest an injustice done him by our boss, or maybe another boss. I could barely understand his English, and he kept breaking into Spanish, which I didn't understand at all. But he was angry—I understood that much.

At some point he went across the room and came back and put a pistol on the table, right in front of him. A revolver, long barrel, most of the bluing worn off. Miguel stared at me over the pistol and resumed his complaint, entirely in Spanish. He was looking at me, but I knew he was seeing somcone else. I had rarely heard him speak before. Now the words poured out in an aggrieved singsong, and I saw that his own voice was lashing him on somehow, the very sound of his indignation proving that he had been wronged, feeding his rage, making him hate whoever he thought I was. I was too afraid to speak. All I could do was smile.

. . .

That room—once you enter it, you never really leave. You can forget you're there, you can go on as if you hold the reins, that the course of your life, yea even its *length,* will reflect the force of your character and the wisdom of your judgments. And then you hit an icy patch on a turn one sunny March day and the wheel in your hands becomes a joke and you no more than a spectator to your own dreamy slide toward the verge, and then you remember where you are.

Or you board a bus with thirty other young men. It's early, just before dawn. That's when the buses always leave, their lights dimmed, to avoid the attention of the Quakers outside the gate, but it doesn't work and they're waiting, silently holding up their signs, looking at you not with reproach but with sadness and sympathy as the bus drives past them and on toward the airport and the plane that will take you where you would not go—and at this moment you know exactly what your desires count for, and your plans, and all your strength of body and will. Then you know where you are, as you will know where you are when those you love die before their time—the time you had planned for them, for yourself with them—and when your daily allowance of words and dreams is withheld from you, and when your daughter drives the car straight into a tree. And if she walks away without a scratch you still feel that dark ceiling close overhead, and know where you are. And what can you do but what you did back in this awful room, with Miguel hating you for nothing and a pistol ready to hand? Smile and hope for a change of subject.

It came, this time. Clemson bolted up from his chair, bent forward, and puked all over the table. Miguel stopped talking. He stared at Clemson as if he'd never seen him before, and when Clemson began retching again Miguel jumped up and grabbed him by the shirt and pushed him toward the door. I took over and helped Clemson outside while Miguel looked on, shrieking his disgust. Disgust! Now *he* was the fastidious one. Revulsion had trumped rage, had trumped even hatred. Oh, how sweetly I tended Clemson that night! I thought he'd saved my life. And maybe he had.

The farmer's barn burned to the ground that winter. When I heard about it, I said, "Didn't I tell him? I did, I told that stupid sumbitch not to put up wet hay."

Awaiting Orders

Sergeant Morse was pulling night duty in the orderly room when a woman called, asking for Billy Hart. He told her that Specialist Hart had shipped out for Iraq a week earlier. She said, "Billy Hart? You sure? He never said a word about shipping out."

"I'm sure."

"Well. Sweet Jesus. That's some news."

"And you are? If you don't mind my asking."

"I'm his sister."

"I can give you his e-mail. Hang on, I'll find it for you."

"That's okay. There's people waiting for the phone. People who don't know any better than to breathe down other people's neck."

"It won't take a minute."

"That's okay. He's gone, right?"

"Feel free to call back. Maybe I can help."

"Hah," she said, and hung up.

Sergeant Morse returned to the paperwork he'd been doing, but the call had unsettled him. He got up and went to the water cooler and drew himself a glass and stood by the door. The night was sullenly hot and still: just past eleven, the barracks quiet, only a few windows glowing in the haze. A meaty gray moth kept thumping against the screen.

Morse didn't know Billy Hart well, but he'd had his eye on him. Hart was from the mountains near Asheville and liked to play the hick for the cover it gave him. He was forever running a hustle, Hart, engaged elsewhere when there was work to be done yet always on hand to fleece the new guys at poker or sell rides to town in his Mustang convertible. He was said to be dealing but hadn't got caught at it. Thought everyone else was dumb; you could see him thinking it, that tight little smile. He would trip himself up someday, but he'd do fine for now. Plenty of easy pickings over there for the likes of Billy Hart.

A good-looking troop, though. Some Indian there, those high cheekbones, deep-set black eyes; beautiful, really, and with that slow catlike way about him, cool, aloof, almost contemptuous in the languor and ease of his movements. Morse had felt the old pull despite himself, knowing Hart was trouble but always taut in his presence, fighting the stubborn drift of his gaze toward Hart's face, toward that look of secret knowledge playing on his lips. Hart was approachable, Morse felt sure of it, open to whatever might offer both interest and advantage. Still, Morse had kept his distance. He didn't give advantage, and couldn't take the risk of a foolish entanglement—not now, anyway.

He had spent twenty of his thirty-nine years in the army. He was not one of those who claimed to love it, but he belonged to it as to a tribe, bound to those around him by lines of unrefusable obligation, love being finally beside the point. He was a soldier, no longer able to imagine himself as a civilian—the formlessness of that life, the endless petty choices to be made.

Morse knew he belonged where he was, yet he'd often put himself in danger of scandal and discharge through chancy attachments. Just before his tour in Iraq there'd been the Cuban waiter, who turned out to be married, a compulsive liar—a liar for sport—and finally, when Morse broke it off, a blackmailer. Morse would not be blackmailed. He wrote down his commanding officer's name and telephone number. "Here," he said, "go on, call him"—and though he didn't think the man would actually do it, he spent the next few weeks hunched inwardly as if against a blow. Then he shipped out and soon came to life again, ready for the next excitement.

This turned out to be a young lieutenant who'd joined Morse's unit the same week he arrived. They went through orientation together, and Morse could tell that the lieutenant was drawn to him, though the lieutenant seemed unsure of his own disposition, even when he surrendered to it—with an urgency only heightened by the near impossibility of finding private time and space. In fact he was just discovering himself, and in the process he suffered fits of self-loathing so cruel and dark that Morse feared he would do himself harm or turn his rage outward, perhaps onto Morse himself, or bring them both to grief by bawling out a drunken confession to a fatherly colonel in some officers' bar.

It didn't come to that. The lieutenant had adopted a mangy one-eared cat while they were on patrol; the cat scratched his ankle and the scratch got infected, and instead of going for treatment he played the fool and tried to tough it out and damn near lost his foot. He was sent home on crutches five months into his tour. By then Morse was so wrung out that he felt not the slightest stirrings of pity—only relief.

He had no cause for relief. Not long after returning stateside, he was called to battalion headquarters for an interview with two smooth, friendly men in civilian clothes who claimed to be congressional aides from the lieutenant's home district. They said there was a sensitive matter before their congressman that required closer knowledge of the lieutenant's service in Iraq—his performance in the field, his dealings with other officers and with the troops who served under him. Their questions looped around conversationally, almost lazily, but returned again and again to his own relations with the lieutenant. Morse gave nothing away, even as he labored to appear open, unguarded. He figured these men for army narcs, whatever else they said. They let several weeks go by before calling him to another meeting, which they canceled without warning; Morse showed up, they didn't. He was still waiting for the next summons.

He had often wished that his desires served him better, but in this he supposed he wasn't unusual—that it was a lucky man indeed whose desires served him well. Yet he had hopes. Over the last few months he'd become involved with a master sergeant in division intelligence—a calm, scholarly man five years his senior. Though Morse could not yet think of himself as anyone's "partner," he had gradually forsaken his room in the NCO quarters to spend nights and weekends at Dixon's townhouse off post. The place was stuffed with ancient weapons and masks and chess sets Dixon had collected during his tours overseas, and at first Morse had felt a nervous sort of awe, as if he were in a museum, but that had passed. Now he liked having these things around him. He was at home there.

Dixon was due to rotate overseas before long, though, and Morse would soon receive new orders himself; then, he knew, it would get complicated. They would have to make certain judgments about each other and about themselves. They would have to decide how much to promise. Where this would leave them, Morse didn't know. But all that was still to come.

Billy Hart's sister called again at midnight, just as Morse was turning over the orderly room to another sergeant. When he picked up and heard her voice, he pointed at the door and the other man smiled and stepped outside.

"Would you like the address, then?" Morse asked.

"I guess. For all the good it'll do."

Morse had already looked it up. He read it to her.

"Thanks," she said. "I don't have a computer but Sal does."

"Sal?"

"Sally Cronin! My cousin."

"You could just go to an Internet café."

"Well, I suppose," she said skeptically. "Say—what'd you mean, maybe you could help?"

"I don't know, exactly," Morse said.

"You said it, though."

"Yes. And you laughed."

"That wasn't an actual laugh."

"Ah. Not a laugh."

"More like . . . I don't know."

Morse waited.

"Sorry," she said. "Look, I'm not asking for help, okay? But how come you said it? Just out of curiosity."

"No reason. I didn't think it out."

"Are you a friend of Billy's?"

"I like Billy."

"Well, it was nice. You know? A real nice thing to say."

After Morse signed out he drove to the pancake house she'd been calling from. As agreed, she was waiting by the cash register, and when he came through the door in his fatigues he saw her take him in with a sharp, measuring glance. She straightened up—a tall woman, nearly as tall as Morse himself, with lank brown hair and a long, tired-looking face, darkly freckled under the eyes. Her eyes were dark, but otherwise she looked nothing like Hart, and Morse was thrown by the sudden disappointment he felt and his impulse to flee.

She stepped toward him, head cocked to one side, as if making a guess about him. She wore a sleeveless red blouse and hugged her freckled arms against the chill of the air-conditioning. "So should I call you Sergeant?" she said.

"Randall."

"Sergeant Randall."

"Just Randall."

"Just Randall," she repeated, and offered him her hand. It was dry and rough. "Julianne. We're over in the corner."

She led him to a booth by the big window looking out on the parking lot. A fat-faced boy, maybe seven or eight, sat drawing a picture on the back of a place mat among the congealed remains of eggs and waffles and sausages. Holding the crayon like a spike, he raised his head as Morse slid onto the bench across from him. He had the same fierce brows as the woman and gave Morse a long unblinking look; then he sucked in his lower lip and returned to his work.

"Say hello, Charlie."

He went on coloring. Finally he said, "Howdy."

"Won't say 'hello,' this one. Says 'howdy' now. Don't know where he got it."

"That's all right. Howdy back at you, Charlie."

"You look like a frog," the boy said. He dropped the crayon and picked up another from the clutter on the table.

"Charlie!" she said. "Use your manners," she added mildly, beckoning to the waitress pouring coffee at a neighboring table.

"It's okay," Morse said. He figured he had it coming. Not because he looked like a frog—though he was all at once conscious of his wide mouth—but because he'd sucked up to the boy. *Howdy back at you!*

"What is wrong with that woman?" Julianne said, as the waitress gazed dully around the room. Then Julianne caught her eye, and she came slowly over to their table and refilled her cup. "That's some picture you're making," the waitress said. "What is it?" The boy ignored her. "You've got yourself quite the little artist there," she said to Morse, and moved dreamily away.

Julianne poured a long stream of sugar into her coffee.

"Charlie your son?"

She turned and looked speculatively at the boy. "No."

"You're not my mom," he murmured.

"Didn't I just say that?" She stroked his round cheek with the back of her hand. "Draw your picture, nosy. Kids?" she said to Morse.

"Not yet." He watched the boy smear blue lines across the place mat, wielding the crayon as if out of grim duty.

"You aren't missing anything."

"Oh, I think I probably am."

"Nothing but back talk and mess," she said. "Charlie's Billy's. Billy's and Dina's."

Morse would never have guessed it, to look at the boy. "I didn't know Hart had a son," he said, and hoped she hadn't heard the note of complaint that was all too clear and strange to him.

"Neither does he, the way he acts. Him and Dina both." Dina, she explained, was off doing her second round of rehab in Raleigh. Julianne and Belle—Julianne's mother, Morse gathered—had been looking after Charlie but didn't really get along, and after the last blowup Belle had taken off for Florida with a boyfriend, putting Julianne in a bind. She drove a school bus during the year and worked summers cooking at a Girl Scout camp, but with Charlie on her hands and no money for child care she'd had to give up the camp job. So she'd driven down here to try and shake some help out of Billy, enough to get her through until school started or Belle decided to come home and do her share, fat chance.

Morse nodded toward the boy. He didn't like his hearing all this, if anything could penetrate that concentration, but Julianne went on as if she hadn't noticed. Her voice was low, almost masculine, with a nasal catch in it like the whine of a saw blade binding. She didn't have the lazy music that Hart could play so well, and she seemed more truly of the hollows and farms of their home. She spoke of the people there as if Morse must know them too, as if she had no working conception of the reach of the world beyond.

At first Morse was expecting her to put the bite on him, but she never did. He didn't understand what she wanted from him, or why, unprompted, he'd offered to come here tonight.

"So he's gone," she said. "You're sure."

"Afraid so."

"Well. Good to know my luck's holding. Wouldn't want it to get worse." She leaned back and closed her eyes.

"Why didn't you call first?"

"What, let on I was coming? You don't know our Billy."

Julianne seemed to fall into a trance then, and Morse soon followed, lulled by the clink of crockery and the voices all around, the soft scratching of the crayon. He didn't know how long they sat like this. He was roused by the tapping of raindrops against the window, a few fat drops that left oily lines as they slid down the glass. The rain stopped. Then it came again in a rush, sizzling on the asphalt and glazing the cars in the parking lot, pleasant to watch after the long humid day.

"Rain," Morse said.

Julianne didn't bother to look. She might have been asleep but for the slight nod she gave him.

Morse recognized two men from his company at a table across the room. He watched them until they glanced over, then he nodded and they nodded back. Money in the bank—confirmed sighting of Sergeant Morse with woman and child. *Family.* He hated thinking so bitter and cheap a thought, and resented whatever led him to think it. Still, how else could they be seen, the three of them, in a pancake house at this hour? And it wasn't just their resemblance to a family. No, there was the atmosphere of family here, in the very silence of the table: Julianne with her eyes closed, the boy working away on his picture, Morse himself looking on like any husband and father.

"You're tired," he said.

The tenderness of his own voice surprised him, and her eyes blinked open as if she, too, was surprised. She looked at him with gratitude; and it came to Morse that she had called him back that night just for the reason she gave, because he'd spoken kindly to her.

"I am tired," she said. "I am that."

"Look, Julianne. What do you need to tide you over?"

"Nothing. Forget all that stuff—I was just blowing off steam."

"I'm not talking about charity, okay? Just a loan, that's all."

"We'll be fine."

"It's not like there's anyone waiting in line for it," he said, and this was true. Morse's father and older brother, finally catching on, had gone cold on him years ago. He'd remained close to his mother, but she died just after his return from Iraq. In his new will Morse named as sole beneficiary the hospice where she'd spent her last weeks. To name Dixon seemed too sudden and meaningful and might draw unwelcome attention, and anyway Dixon had made some sharp investments and was well fixed.

"I just can't," Julianne said. "But that is so sweet."

"My dad's a soldier," the boy said, head still bent over the place mat.

"I know," Morse said. "He's a good soldier. You should be proud."

Julianne smiled at him, really smiled, for the first time that night. She had been squinting and holding her mouth in a tight line; then she smiled and looked like someone else. Morse saw that she had beauty, and that her pleasure in him had allowed this beauty to show itself. He was embarrassed. He felt a sense of duplicity that he immediately, even indignantly, suppressed. "I can't force it on you," he said. "Suit yourself."

The smile vanished. "I will," she said, in the same tone he had used, harder than he'd intended. "But I thank you anyhow. Charlie," she said, "time to go. Get your stuff together."

"I'm not done."

"Finish it tomorrow."

Morse waited while she rolled up the place mat and helped the boy collect his crayons. He noticed the check pinned under the saltshaker and picked it up.

"I'll take that," she said, holding out her hand in a way that did not permit refusal.

Morse stood by awkwardly as Julianne paid at the register, then walked outside with her and the boy. They stood together under the awning and watched the storm lash the parking lot. Glittering lines of rain fell aslant through the glare of the lights overhead. The surrounding trees tossed wildly, and the wind sent gleaming ripples across the asphalt. Julianne brushed a lock of hair back from the boy's forehead. "I'm ready. How about you?"

"No."

"Well, it ain't about to quit raining for Charles Drew Hart." She yawned widely and gave her head a shake. "Nice talking to you," she said to Morse.

"Where will you stay?"

"Pickup."

"A pickup? You're going to sleep in a truck?"

"Can't drive like this." And in the look she gave him, expectant and mocking, he could see that she knew he would offer her a motel room, and that she was already tasting the satisfaction of turning it down. But that didn't stop him from trying.

"Country proud," Dixon said later that morning, when Morse told him the story. "You should have invited them to stay here. People like that, mountain people, will accept hospitality when they won't take money. They're like Arabs. Hospitality has a sacred claim. You don't refuse to give it, and you don't refuse to take it."

"Never occurred to me," Morse said, though in truth he'd had the same intuition, standing outside the restaurant with the two of them, wallet in hand. Even as he tried to talk Julianne into taking the money for a room, invoking the seriousness of the storm and the need to get the boy into a safe, dry place, he had the sense that if he simply invited her home with him she might indeed say yes. And then what? Dixon waking up and playing host, bearing fresh towels to the guest room, making coffee, teasing the boy—and looking at Morse in that way of his. Its meaning would be clear enough to Julianne. And what might she do with such knowledge? Out of shock and disgust, perhaps even feeling betrayed, she could ruin them.

Morse had thought of that but didn't really fear it. He liked her, and didn't think she would act meanly. What he feared, what he could not allow, was for her to see how Dixon looked at him, and then to see that he could not give back what he received. That things between them were unequal, and himself unloving.

So even while offering Julianne the gift of shelter he'd felt false, mealymouthed, as if he were trying to buy her off. And the unfairness of suffering guilt while pushing his money at her and having it refused proved too much for him. Finally he told her to sleep in the damned truck then if that's what she wanted.

"I don't want to sleep in the truck," the boy said.

"You'd be a sight happier if you did," Julianne said. "Now come on—ready or not."

"Just don't try to drive home," Morse said.

She put her hand on the boy's shoulder and led him out into the parking lot.

"You're too tired!" Morse called after her, but if she answered he couldn't hear it for the drumming of the rain on the metal awning. They walked on across the asphalt. The wind gusted, driving the rain so hard that Morse had to jump back a step. Julianne took it full in the face and never so much as turned her head. Nor did the boy. Charlie. He was getting something from her, ready or not, walking into the rain as if it weren't raining at all.

A White Bible

It was dark when Maureen left the Hundred Club. She stopped just outside the door, a little thrown by the sudden cold and the change from daylight to night. A gusting breeze chilled her face. Lights burned over the storefronts, gleaming on icy patches along the sidewalk. She reached in her pockets for her gloves, then hopelessly searched her purse. She'd left them in the club. If she went back for them she knew she'd end up staying—and sayonara to all her good intentions. Jane or one of the others would pick up the gloves and bring them to school on Monday. Still, she stood there. Someone came out the door behind her, and Maureen heard music and voices raised over the music. When the door swung shut she tightened her scarf and turned down the sidewalk toward the lot where she'd left her car.

Maureen had gone almost a block when she realized she was walking in the wrong direction. Easy mistake—the lot where they all usually parked had been full. She headed back, crossing the street to avoid the club. Her fingers had gone stiff. She put her hands in her coat pockets, then yanked them out when her right foot took a skid on the ice. After that she kept them poised at her sides.

Head bent, she shuffled in tender steps from one safe spot to the next—for all the world like her own worn-out, balding, arthritic mother. Maureen allowed herself this thought in self-mockery, to make herself feel young, but it didn't have that effect. The lot was farther than she'd been aware of as she strolled to the club with Molly and Jill and Evan, laughing at Evan's story about his domineering Swedish girlfriend. She'd had an awful day at school and was happy to let the week go, to lose herself in jokes and gossip and to feel the pale, late sunshine almost warm on her face. Now her face was numb and she was tense with the care of simply walking.

She passed a hunched, foot-stamping crowd waiting to get into Harrigan's, where she herself had once gone to hear the local bands. It had been called Far Horizon then. Or Lost Horizon. *Lost* Horizon, it was.

She scanned the faces as she walked by, helplessly on the watch for her daughter. She hadn't seen her in almost two years now, since Katie walked away from a full scholarship at Ithaca College to come back and live with one of Maureen's fellow English teachers from St. Ignatius. It turned out they'd been going at it since Katie's senior year at SI—and him a married man with a young daughter. Maureen had always tried to see Katie's willfulness as backbone, but this she could not accept. She had said some unforgivable things, according to Katie. Since when, Maureen wanted to know, had a few home truths become unforgivable?

She was still trying to bring Katie around when Father Crespi got wind of the whole business and fired the teacher. Maureen had not been Father Crespi's source, but Katie wouldn't believe it. She declared things at an end between them, and so far she had kept that vow, though she dumped the luckless fool within a few weeks of his leaving his wife.

Katie was still close to Maureen's mother. From her, Maureen had learned that Katie was doing temp work and keeping house with another man. Maureen couldn't get her to say more—she'd given her word! But the old bird clearly enjoyed not saying more, being in the know, being part of Maureen's punishment for driving Katie away, as she judged the matter.

Maureen crossed the street again and turned into the parking lot—an unpaved corner tract surrounded by a chain-link fence. The attendant's shack was dark. She picked her way over ridges of frozen mud toward her car. Last summer's special-offer paint job was already dull, bleached out by road salt. Through a scrim of dried slush on the window Maureen could see the stack of student blue books on the passenger seat—a weekend's worth of grading. She fished the keys from her purse, but her hand was dead with cold and she fumbled them when she tried to unlock the door. They hit the ground with a merry tinkle. She flexed her fingers and bent down. As she pushed herself back up a pain shot through her bad knee. "Goddammit!" she said.

"Don't curse!" The voice came from behind Maureen, a man's voice, but high, almost shrill.

She closed her eyes.

He said something she couldn't make out; he had some sort of accent. He said it again, then added, "Now!"

"What?"

"The *keys*. Give them to me."

Maureen held the keys out behind her, eyes pressed shut. She had just one thought: Do not see him. The keys were taken from her hand, and she heard the door being unlocked.

"Open it," the man said. "Open the door. Yes, now get in."

"Just take it," Maureen said. "Please."

"*Please,* you will get *in*. Please." He took her arm and half pushed, half lifted her into the car and slammed the door shut. She sat behind the steering wheel with her head bent, eyes closed, hands folded over her purse. The passenger door opened. "Compositions," the man muttered.

"Exams," she said, and cringed at her stupidity in correcting him.

Maureen heard the blue books thud onto the floorboards in back. Then he was on the seat beside her. He sat there a moment, his breath quick and shallow. "Open your eyes. Open! Yes, now drive." He jingled the keys.

Looking straight ahead over the wheel, she said, "I don't think I can." She sensed a movement toward her and flinched away.

He jingled the keys again beside her ear and dropped them in her lap. "Drive."

Maureen had once taken a class in self-defense. That was five years ago, after her marriage ended and left her alone with a teenage daughter—as if the dangers were outside somewhere and not already in the house, between them. She'd forgotten all the fancy moves but not her determination to fight, for Katie or for herself; to go on the attack, kick the bastard in the balls, scream and kick and hit and bite, fight to the very death. She hadn't forgotten any of this, even now, watching herself do nothing. She was aware of what she was failing to do—was unable to do—and the shock of understanding that she could not depend on herself produced a sense of resignation, an empty, echoing calm. With steady hands she started the car and pulled out of the lot and turned left as the man directed, away from the lights of the commercial zone, toward the river.

"Not so slow," he said.

She sped up.

"Slower!"

She slowed down.

"You are trying to be arrested," he said.

"No."

He made a mirthless laughing sound. "Do I look like a fool?"

"No . . . I don't know. I haven't seen you."

"I am not a fool. Turn right."

They were on Frontage Road now, heading upriver. The night was clear, and the almost full moon hung just above the old tanneries on the far bank. The moon made a broad silver path on the smooth water in the middle of the river, glimmering dully on the slabs of ice jammed up along the sides and turning Maureen's bare hands ghostly white on the steering wheel. They looked cold; they *were* cold. She felt chilled all through. She turned up the heater, and within moments the car was filled with the man's smell—ripe, musky, not unpleasant.

"You were using alcohol," he said.

She waited for him to say more. His knees were angled toward her, pressed together against the console. "A little," she said.

He was silent. His breathing slowed, deepened, and Maureen felt obscurely grateful for this. She could feel him watching her.

"There's over seventy dollars in my purse," she said. "Please just take it."

"Seventy dollars? That is your offer?" He laughed his unreal laugh.

"I can get more," she said. Her voice was small and flat—not her voice at all. She hesitated, then said, "We'll have to go to an ATM."

"This is not about money. Drive. Please."

And so she did. This was something she could do, drive a car on Frontage Road, as she'd done for almost thirty years now. She drove past the Toll House Inn, past the bankrupt development with its unfinished, skeletal houses open to the weather, past the road to the bridge that would take her home, past the burned-out house with the trailer beside it, on past the brickworks and the quarry and the farm her tannery-fleeing grandparents had worked as tenants, where, after several years of learning the hard way, the owner sold out and the new owner found more experienced hands and sent them packing, back across the river. When she was young Maureen and her sisters had picked strawberries with their mother on different farms, and she had marveled at how her mother could chat with a woman in the next row or just look dully into the distance while her fingers briskly ransacked the plants for ripe berries as if possessed of their own eyes and purpose. At the end of a day she'd look over Maureen's card—punched for a fraction of the flats she herself had picked—then hand it back and say, "At least that mouth of yours works."

Maureen drove on by the harshly lit 7-Eleven and the Christmas-tree farm and the old ferry pier where she and Francis, her ex-husband, then a sweet, shy boy, had parked after high-school dances to drink and make out; on through pale fields and brief stands of bare black trees that in summer made a green roof overhead. She knew every rise and turn, and the car took them easily, and she surrendered to the comfort of her own mastery of the road. The silent man beside her seemed to feel it too; it seemed to be holding him in a trance.

Then he shifted, leaned forward. "Turn right up there," he said in a low voice. "On that road, you see—that one up there, after the sign."

Maureen made the turn almost languidly. The side road was unplowed, covered with crusty snow that scraped against the under-carriage of the car. She hit a deep dip; the front end clanged, the wheels spun for a moment, then they caught and shot the car forward again, headlights jumping giddily. The road bent once and ended in a clearing surrounded by tall pines.

"You drive too fast," the man said.

She waited, engine running, hands still on the wheel, headlights ablaze on a Park Service sign picturing the local animals and plants. The peaked roof over the sign wore a hat of snow. Then it came to Maureen that she'd been here before—a trailhead, unfamiliar at first in its winter bleakness. She had come with Katie's scout troop to hike up to the palisades overlooking the river. The trail was historic, a route of attack for some battle in the Revolutionary War.

The man sniffed, sniffed again. "Beer," he said.

"I was having a drink with friends."

"*A drink?* You stink of it. The great lady teacher!"

That he knew she was a teacher, that he knew anything about her, snapped the almost serene numbness that had overtaken Maureen. She remembered his seeing the exam booklets. That could explain his knowledge of her work, but not his tone—the personal scorn and triumph in his discovery of her weakness, as he clearly saw it.

A small dull pain pulsed behind her eyes, all that was left of the drink she'd had. The heat blowing into the car was making her con-tacts dry and scratchy. She reached over to turn it down, but he seized her wrist and pulled it back. His fingers were thin and damp. He turned the heat up again. "Leave it like this—warm," he said, and dropped her hand.

She almost looked at him then, but stopped herself. "Please," she said. "What do you want?"

"This is not about sex," he said. "That is what you are thinking, of course. That is the American answer to everything."

Maureen looked ahead and said nothing. She could see the lights of cars on Frontage Road flickering between the tree trunks. Though she wasn't that far from the road, the idea of making a run for it struck her as a demeaning absurdity—herself flailing through the drifts like some weeping, dopey, sacrificial extra in a horror movie.

"You know nothing about our life," he said. "Who we are. What we have had to do in this country. I was a doctor! But okay, so they won't let me be a doctor here. I give that up. I give up the old life so my family will have this new life. My son will be a doctor, not me! Okay, I accept, that's how it is."

"Where are you from?" Maureen asked, and then said, "Never mind," hoping he wouldn't answer. It seemed to her that the musky smell was stronger, a little sour. She kept her eyes on the Park Service sign in the headlights but she was aware of the man's knees knocking rapidly and soundlessly together.

"'Never mind,'" he said. "Yes, that is exactly your way of thinking. That is exactly how the great lady teacher destroys a family. Without a thought. Never mind!"

"But I don't know your family." She waited. "I don't know what you're talking about."

"No, you don't know what I'm talking about. You have already forgotten. Never mind!"

"You have the wrong person," Maureen said.

"Have you told a lie, lady teacher?"

"Please. You must have the wrong person. What you're saying—none of it makes sense." And because this was certainly true, because nothing he'd said had anything to do with her, Maureen felt compelled—as prelude to a serious sorting out of this whole mess—to turn and look at him. He was leaning back against the door, hunched into a puffy coat of the vivid orange color worn by highway crews. In the reflected glare of the headlights his dark eyes had a blurred, liquid brightness. Above the straight line of his eyebrows the bald dome of his head gleamed dully. He wore a short beard, a few thin patches of it reaching high on his cheeks.

"I have the right person," he said. "Now you will please answer me."

She was confused; she shook her head as if to clear it.

"No?" he said. "The great lady teacher has never told a lie?"

"What are you talking about? What lie?"

A sudden glint of teeth behind the beard. "You tell me."

"Any lie? Ever?"

"Ever. Any lie or cheat."

"What do you think? Of course I have. Who hasn't, for God's sake?"

He rocked forward and jabbed his head at her. "Don't curse! No more cursing!"

Maureen could see his face clearly now, the full, finely molded, almost feminine lips, the long thin nose, the dark unexpected freckles across the bridge of his nose and under his eyes, vanishing into the beard. She turned away and leaned her throbbing head against the steering wheel.

"You can lie and cheat," he said. "That's okay, no problem. Who hasn't? Never mind! But for others—poof! No faults allowed!"

"This is crazy," she murmured.

"No, Mrs. Casey. What is crazy is to destroy a good boy's life for nothing."

Her breath caught; she raised her head and looked at him.

"Hassan makes one mistake—one mistake—and you destroy him. Understand this, most esteemed lady teacher: I will not allow it."

"Hassan? Hassan is your son?"

He leaned away again, lips pursed, cheeks working out and back, out and back, like a fish.

Hassan. She liked him, too much. He was tall and graceful and broodingly, soulfully handsome. Not very bright, Hassan, and bone idle, but with a sudden offhand charm that had amused her and distracted her from dealing firmly with him, as he well knew. He'd been getting away with murder all year, fudging on his homework, handing in essays he obviously hadn't written, and Maureen had done nothing except warn him. She hated calling people on their offenses: her own raised voice and shaking hands, her heart pumping out righteousness, all the rituals of grievance and reproach were distasteful to her, and had always held her back, up to a point. Beyond that point she didn't spare the lash. But she was slow to get there; her sisters had pushed her around, she'd spoiled her daughter, her husband's gambling had brought them to the brink of ruin before her own cowardice became too shameful to bear and she began to challenge his excuses and evasions, and finally faced him down—"ran him off," as Katie liked to say when she wanted to cut deep.

A similar self-disgust had caught up with Maureen this morning. After months of letting Hassan slide, she'd seen him blatantly cheating during an exam, and she'd blown—really blown, surprising even herself. She'd pulled him out of class and told him in some detail how little she thought of him, then sent him home with a promise—shouted at his back—to report his cheating to Father Crespi, who would certainly expel him. Hassan had turned then and said, evenly, "Stupid cow." And now, remembering that betrayal, the advantage he'd taken, his insulting confidence that he could cheat in front of her with impunity, she felt her fingers tighten on the steering wheel and she stared fixedly in front of her, seeing nothing.

"Hassan!" she said.

"I will not allow it," he repeated.

"Hassan has been cheating all year," she said. "I warned him. This was the last straw."

"*Warnings.* You should give him help, not warnings. It's hard for Hassan. He wasn't born here, his English is not good."

"Hassan's English is fine. He's lazy and dishonest, that's his problem. He'd rather cheat than do the work."

"Hassan is going to be a doctor."

"Sure."

"He will be a doctor! He will. And you won't stop him—you, a drunken woman."

"Oh," she said. "Of course. Of course. *Women.* All our fault, right? Bunch of stupid cows messing things up for the bulls."

"No! I bow before woman. Woman is the hand, the heart, the soul of her home, set there by God himself. All comes from her. All is owed to her."

"Now you're quoting," Maureen said. "Who's your source?"

"The home," he said. "Not the army. Not the surgery. Not the judge's chair, giving laws. Not the discotheque."

"Who's your source?" Maureen repeated. "God, is it?"

The man drew back. "Have some care," he said. "God is not mocked."

Maureen rubbed her scratchy eyes and one of her contacts drifted out of focus. She blinked furiously until it slipped back into place. "I'm turning the heat off," she said.

"No. Leave it warm."

But she turned it off anyway, and he made no move to stop her. He looked wary, watching her from his place against the door; he looked cornered, as if *she* had seized *him* and forced *him* to this lonely place. The car engine was doing something strange, surging, almost dying, then surging again. The noise of the blower had masked it. Piece of shit. Another paycheck down the drain.

"Okay, doctor," she said. "You've got your parent-teacher conference. What do you want?"

"You will not report Hassan to Mr. Crespi."

"Father Crespi, you mean."

"I call no man father but one."

"Wonderful. So you choose a school called St. Ignatius."

"I understand. This would not happen if Hassan were Catholic."

"Oh, *please.* Hassan can't speak English, Hassan needs help, Hassan isn't Catholic. Jesus! *I'm* not even Catholic."

He made his laughing sound. "So you choose a school called St. Ignatius. With your Jesus on the cross behind your desk—I have seen it myself at the open house. I was there! But no, she is not Catholic, not Mrs. Maureen Casey."

Even with the heat off, the air in the car was stale and acrid. Maureen opened her window halfway and leaned back, bathing her face in the cold draft. "That's right," she said. "I've had it with clueless men passing on orders from God."

"Without God, there is no foundation," he said. "Without God, we stand on nothing."

"Anyway, you're too late. I've already reported him."

"You have not. Mr. Crespi is out of town until Monday."

"Father Crespi. Well, I'm impressed. At least *you've* done your homework."

"Hassan is going to be a doctor," he said, rubbing his hands together, gazing down at them as if expecting some visible result.

"Look at me. *Look at me.* Now listen." She held the man's liquid eyes, held the moment, not at all displeased that what she was about to say, though true, would give him pain. "Hassan is not going to be a doctor," she said. "Wait—just listen. Honestly, now, can you picture Hassan in medical school? Even supposing he could get in? Even supposing he can get through college at all? Think about it—Hassan in medical school. What an idea! You could make a comedy—*Hassan Goes to Medical School.* No, Hassan will not be a doctor. And you know it. You have always known it." She gave that thought some room to breathe. Then she said, "So it doesn't really matter if I report him or not, does it?"

Still she held his eyes. His lips were working, he seemed about to say something, but no sound emerged.

She said, "So. Let's say I don't play along. Let's say I'm going to report him, which I am. What are you going to do about it? I mean, what were you thinking tonight?"

He looked away, back down at his hands.

"You followed me from school, right? You waited for me. You had this spot picked out. What were you going to do if I didn't play along?"

He shook his head.

"Well, what? Kill me?"

He didn't answer.

"You were going to kill me? Too much! Have you got a gun?"

"No! I own no guns."

"A knife?"

"No."

"What, then?"

Head bent, he resumed rubbing his hands together as if over a fire.

"Stop that. What, then?"

"Please," he said.

"Strangle me? With those? Stop that!" She reached over and seized his wrists. They were thin, bony. "Hey," she said, then again, "Hey!" When at last he raised his eyes to her, she lifted his hands and pressed the palms to her neck. They were cold, even colder than the air on her face. She dropped her own hands. "Go on," she said.

His fingers were icy against her neck. His eyes, dark and sad, searched hers.

"Go on," she said softly.

The engine surged, and he blinked as if startled and pulled his hands away. He rested them in his lap, looked at them unhappily, then put them between his knees.

"No?" she said.

"Mrs. Casey . . ."

She waited, but that was all he said. "Tell me something," she said. "What did your wife think of this brainstorm? Did you tell her?"

"My wife is dead."

"I didn't know that."

He shrugged.

"I'm sorry."

"Mrs. Casey . . ."

Again she waited, then said, "What?"

"The window? It is very cold."

Maureen had a mind to say no, watch him freeze, but she was getting pretty numb herself. She rolled the window up.

"And please? The heater?"

Maureen drove back down Frontage Road. He kept his face to the other window, his back to her. Now and then she saw his shoulders moving but he didn't make a sound. Though she'd planned to put him out by the turnoff for her bridge, let him find his own way home from there, as she approached the intersection she couldn't help asking where he'd left his car. He said it was in the same lot where she'd parked hers. Ah, yes. That made sense. She drove on.

They didn't speak again until she stopped just up from the parking lot, under a streetlight, in plain view of the drunks walking past. Even here, cocooned in the car, engine surging, Maureen could feel the heavy bass thump of the music coming from Harrigan's.

"Hassan will be dismissed from school?" he asked.

"Probably. He's spoiled, it'll do him good in the long run. You're the one I haven't made up my mind about. You're the one on the hot seat. Do you understand?"

He bowed his head.

"I don't think you do. Forget the prison time you're looking at—you haven't even said you're sorry. I said it, about your wife, which makes me the only one who's used that word tonight. Which strikes me as pretty damned ridiculous, given the circumstances."

"But I am. I am sorry."

"Yeah—we'll see. One thing, though. Suppose I'd promised not to report Hassan. Whatever made you think I'd keep my word?"

He reached into the breast pocket of his coat and took out a white book and laid it on the dashboard. Maureen picked it up. It was a Bible, a girl's Bible bound in imitation leather with gilt lettering on the cover. "You would swear," he said. "Like in court, to the judge."

Maureen opened it, riffled the thin, filmy pages. "Where did you get this?"

"Goodwill."

"Oh, dear," she said. "You really thought you could save him."

He pushed the door open. "I am sorry, Mrs. Casey."

"Here." Maureen held out the Bible, but he put up the palms of his hands and backed out of the car. She watched him make his way down the street, a short man, hatless, his bright puffy coat billowing in the gusts. She saw him turn into the parking lot, then forgot to make sure he actually pulled out, as she'd intended, because she got caught up leafing through the Bible. Her father had given her one just like it after her confirmation. She still kept it on her bedside table.

This Bible had belonged to Clara Gutierrez. Below her name someone had written an inscription in Spanish. Maureen couldn't make it out in the dim light, only the day, large and underlined— *Pascua 1980*. Where was she now, this Clara? What had become of her, this ardent, hopeful girl in her white dress, surrounded by family, godparents, and friends, that her Bible should end up in a Goodwill bin? Even if she no longer read it, or believed it, she wouldn't have thrown it away, would she? Had something happened? Ah, girl, where were you?

Her Dog

When Grace first got Victor, she and John walked him on the beach most Sundays. Then a Chow-Chow bit some kid and the parks department restricted dogs to the slough behind the dunes. Grace took Victor there for years, and after she died John stepped in and maintained the custom, though he hated it back there. The mushy trail hedged with poison oak. Baking flats of cracked mud broken by patches of scrub. The dunes stifled the sea breeze, leaving the air still and rank and seething with insects.

But Victor came alive here in spite of himself. At home he slept and grieved, yet grief could not deaden the scent of fallow deer and porcupine, of rabbits and rats and the little gray foxes that ate them. Dogs were supposed to be kept on the leash for the sake of the wildlife, but Grace had always left Victor free to follow his nose, and John couldn't bring himself to rein him in now. Anyway, Victor was too creaky and cloudy-eyed to chase anything; if he did catch some movement in the brush he'd lean forward and maybe, just to keep his dignity, raise a paw—*Eh? That's right, run along there!*—and then go back to smelling things. John didn't hurry him. He lingered, waving away the mosquitoes and flies that swarmed around his head, until the hint of some new fragrance pulled Victor farther along the trail.

Victor was drawn to the obvious delights—putrefying carcasses, the regurgitations of hawks and owls—but he could just as easily get worked up over a clump of shrubbery that seemed no different than the one beside it. He had his nose stuck deep in swamp grass one damp morning when John saw a dog emerge from the low-hanging mist farther up the trail. It was a barrel-chested dog with a short brindled coat and a blunt pink snout, twice Victor's size, as big as a lab but of no breed familiar to John. When it caught sight of Victor it stopped for a moment, then advanced on stiffened legs.

"Scram!" John said, and clapped his hands.

Victor looked up from the grass. As the dog drew near he took a step in its direction, head craned forward, blinking like a mole. *Huh? Huh? Who's there? Somebody there?*

John took him by the collar. "Beat it!" he said. "Go away."

The dog kept coming.

"Go!" John shouted again. But the dog came on, slowly now, almost mincing, with an unblinking intentness. It kept its yellow eyes on Victor and ignored John altogether. John stepped in front of Victor, to break the dog's gaze and force himself on its attention, but instead it left the trail and began to circle around him, eyes still fixed on Victor. John moved to stay between them. He put his free hand out, palm facing the dog. Victor gave a grumble and strained forward against his collar. The dog came closer. Too close, too intent, it seemed to be gathering itself. John reached down and scooped Victor up and turned his back on the dog. He rarely had occasion to lift Victor and was always surprised at his lightness. Victor lay still for a moment, then began struggling as the dog moved around to face them. "Go away, damn you," John said.

"Bella! Whoa, Bella." A man's voice: sharp, nasal. John looked up the trail and saw him coming, shaved head, wraparound sunglasses, bare arms sticking out of a leather vest. He was taking his sweet time. The dog kept circling John. Victor complained and squirmed impatiently. *Put me down, put me down.*

"Get that dog away from us," John said.

"Bella? He won't hurt you."

"If he touches my dog I'll kill him."

"Whoa, Bella." The man sauntered up behind the dog and took a leash from his back pocket. He reached for the dog but it dodged him and cut back in front of John, keeping Victor in view. "Shame, Bella!

Shame on you. Come back here—right now!" The man put his hands on his hips and stared at the dog. His arms were thick and covered with tattoos, and more tattoos rose up his neck like vines. His chest was bare and pale under the open vest. Beads of sweat glistened on the top of his head.

"Get control of that dog," John said. He turned again, Victor still fidgeting in his arms, the dog following.

"He just wants to make friends," the man said. He waited until the dog's orbit brought him closer, then made a lunge and caught him by the collar. "Bad Bella!" he said, snapping on the leash. "You just have to be everybody's friend, don't you?"

John set Victor down and leashed him and walked him farther up the trail. His hands were shaking. "That dog is a menace," he said. "*Bella*. Jesus."

"It means 'handsome.' "

"No, actually, it means 'pretty.' Like a girl."

The man looked at John through his bubbly black shades. How did he see anything? It was irritating, like the display of his uselessly muscled, illustrated arms. "I thought it meant 'handsome,' " he said.

"Well it doesn't. The ending is feminine."

"What are you, a teacher or something?"

The dog suddenly lunged against its leash.

"We're going," John said. "Keep your dog away from us."

"So, are you a teacher?"

"No," John lied. "I'm a lawyer."

"You shouldn't have said that about killing Bella. I could sue you, right?"

"Not really, no."

"Okay, but still, you didn't have to get all belligerent. Do you have a card? This friend of mine had his film script totally ripped off by Steven Spielberg."

"I don't do that kind of law."

"You should talk to him. Like, D-day? You know, all those guys on the beach? Exactly the way my friend described it. *Exactly.* "

"D-day happened," John said. "Your friend didn't make it up."

"Okay, sure. But still."

"Anyway, that movie was years ago."

"So you're saying statute of limitations?"

The opening notes of "Ode to Joy" shrilled out. "Hang on," the man told him. He took a cell phone from his pocket and said, "Hey, lemme call you back, I'm in kind of a legal conference here."

"No!" John said. "No, you can talk. Just please keep Bella on the leash, okay?"

The man gave the thumbs-up and John led Victor away, up into the mist the other two had come out of. Right away his skin felt clammy. The bugs were loud around his ears. He was still shaking.

Victor stopped to squeeze out a few turds, then looked up at John. *My savior. I guess I should be panting with gratitude. Licking your hand.*

No need.

How'd you put it? I'll kill him if he touches my dog. What devotion! Almost canine. Victor finished and made a show of kicking back some dirt. He raised his head and tested the air like a connoisseur before starting up the trail, feathery tail aloft. *I could've handled him.*

Maybe so.

He wasn't going to do anything. Anyway, since when do you care? It's not like you even wanted me. If it hadn't been for Grace, those guys at the pound would've killed me.

It wasn't you I didn't want—you in particular. I just wasn't ready for a dog.

I guess not. The way you carried on when Grace brought me home. What a brat.

I know.

All your little conditions for keeping me. I was her dog. All the feeding, all the walking, picking up poop, baths, trips to the vet, arrangements with the kennel when you went out of town—her responsibility.

I know.

Her dog, her job to keep me out of the living room, out of the study, off the couch, off the bed, off the Persian rug. No barking, even when someone came right past the house—right up to the door!

I know, I know.

And when they kicked me off the beach, remember that? No way you were going to get stuck back here. No, Grace had to walk me in the swamp while you walked along the ocean. I hope you enjoyed it.

I didn't. I felt mean and foolish.

But you made your point! Her dog, her responsibility. You let her walk me in the rain once when she had a cold.

She insisted.

Then you should've insisted more.

Yes. That's what I think, too, now.

I miss her! I miss her! I miss my Grace!

So do I.

Not like me. Did I ever bark at her?

No.

You did.

And she barked back. We disagreed sometimes. All couples do.

Not Grace and Victor. Grace and Victor never disagreed. Did I ignore her?

No.

You ignored her. She would call your name and you would go on reading your paper, or watching TV, and pretend you hadn't heard. Did she ever have to call my name twice? No! Once and I'd be there, looking up at her, ready for anything. Did I ever want another mistress?

No.

You did. You looked at them in the park, on the beach, in other cars as we drove around.

Men do that. It didn't mean I wanted anyone but Grace.

Yes, you did.

Maybe for an hour. For a night. No longer.

Then I loved her more than you. I loved her with all my heart.

You had no choice. You can't be selfish. But we men—it's a wonder we forget ourselves long enough to buy a birthday card. As for love . . . we *can* love, but we're always forgetting.

I didn't forget, not once.

That's true. But then you missed out on being forgiven. You never knew how it feels to be welcomed home after you've wandered off.

Without forgiveness we're lost. Can't do it for ourselves. Can't take ourselves back in.

I never wandered off.

No. You're a good dog. You always were.

Victor left the trail to inspect a heap of dirt thrown up by some tunneling creature. He yanked at the leash in his excitement. John unclipped him and waited as Victor circled the mound, sniffing busily, then stuck his nose in the burrow and began to dig around it. To watch him in his forgetfulness of everything else was John's pleasure, and this is where he found it, Sundays in the bog with Victor. He looked up through a haze of insects. A buzzard was making lazy circles high overhead, riding the sea breeze John could not feel down here, though he could faintly make out the sounds it carried from beyond the dunes, of crying gulls and crashing waves and the shrieking children who fled before them. Victor panted madly, hearing none of this. He worked fast for an old fellow, legs a blur, pawing back clumps of black earth. He lifted his dirty face from the hole to give a hunter's yelp, then plunged back in.

A Mature Student

Theresa left the library for a cigarette and came upon Professor Landsman in the smokers' corner under the overhang. Professor Landsman taught the Art History survey course Theresa was taking. She was alone, leaning back in one of the two plastic chairs they'd set out for incorrigibles, eyes half closed against the afternoon sun. It was late March and the day was warm; snow had fallen a few nights earlier, and patches still remained here and there in deep shade, but the rest had melted. A glaring sheet of water covered the courtyard below. Theresa slid her book bag under the other chair and lit up.

Professor Landsman didn't appear to notice her. She had her long legs stretched straight out, high-heeled boots crossed at the ankle. She was a tall woman with unruly red hair and a harsh accent of some kind. She didn't wear glasses but was obviously nearsighted; whenever she bent over her notes during lectures her hair swung forward into her eyes, and she pushed it back with an exasperated gesture that dramatized the unveiling of her face—the sharp cheekbones and wide, heavily lipsticked mouth. Today she wore a black coat draped over her shoulders and another of her long, beautiful scarves; in class she restlessly tugged and rearranged them as she spoke. Though not beautiful she had a certain glamour, vivid on this large urban campus where the women faculty dressed as sensibly as the men—as Theresa herself.

They had never spoken. Between Professor Landsman's lectures Theresa attended a discussion section led by a boyish graduate student from New Zealand who also graded her papers. In class Professor Landsman asked questions rarely, grudgingly. A good answer earned a curt nod; anything less and she responded with impatience, mockery, or despair. Only the boldest took the bait, Theresa not among them.

She had almost finished her cigarette when Professor Landsman said, "You're in my class."

"Yes, ma'am."

Professor Landsman turned and looked her up and down. "So. You are auditing, I suppose?"

Theresa understood the question. She had a good twenty years on the other students in the lecture hall, and knew that she looked it. "No," she said, "I'm a regular student. Hotel management."

"Hotel management! And this is a degree? Extraordinary. Such a country. One is found criminal for smoking, but one may become a scholar of bed-and-breakfast."

"Yeah, well, I'm taking your class just for interest. I've always loved art, not that I know jack about it." Theresa flicked the ember off her cigarette and fieldstripped the butt and scattered the grains of tobacco with her toe. When she looked up Professor Landsman was watching her intently.

"How very odd," she said.

"Old habit," Theresa said. "I really like your class, by the way."

"Do you? Why?"

"Probably for the same reasons you liked the first art history class you ever took."

"And what do you suppose those were?"

"Jesus. Okay, you want to know why I like your class. Well, big surprise, the art. Especially the paintings. Caravaggio! I really love Caravaggio. And quite the character, eh? So, yeah, learning about the paintings and the painters, all the history. You seem to know your stuff. And I get a kick out of how bitchy you are. Professor." This was true. Theresa didn't care for the chummy, ingratiating atmosphere she'd found in other of her courses.

"Ah. And you are from . . ."

"California. Mostly. You?"

Professor Landsman examined her without answering. Theresa knew what she was seeing: the sun-weathered face, one eyelid drooping a little from a childhood case of Bell's palsy. Finally Professor Landsman said, "How did you form such a habit?"

"Excuse me?"

"The cigarette. This business with the cigarette."

"Oh, it's something you pick up in the service."

"You were a *soldier*?"

"A Marine. Twenty-two years."

Theresa was ready for the next question. No, she answered, she hadn't been to Iraq. She didn't say that she had served two tours in Saudi Arabia helping manage an R&R center; that during the second tour her Marine husband, who'd rotated home from Iraq just before she left, had fallen in love with a friend's widow; that her son had graduated from high school without Theresa there to see it, then broken his promise to go on to college and enlisted in the Marines himself.

At forty-one Theresa was living alone for the first time in her life. It suited her. She went out to dinner now and then with the manager of the local Sheraton, whom she'd met after a presentation he'd given to one of her classes, but for now—to his evident impatience—she wasn't interested in anything more than some appreciative company and a chance to dress up a little. She woke early without an alarm and made coffee and turned on the classical music station and slipped back under the covers with a book. On weekdays she sampled lunch specials at the cheap foreign restaurants around the university. Every other night, sometimes more, she swam at the university pool; she hadn't taken a run since getting her discharge and intended never to run again. She was glad for her new life here in Illinois, most of a continent away from Camp Pendleton—a gladness that still surprised her, as she was surprised by her own freedom from regret. The sudden, breathless fear she sometimes felt was only for her son. He was out of boot camp now and in desert training at Twentynine Palms.

"So you love *art*," Professor Landsman said. "Let me guess. You paint in your free time, scenes from western life. The bleached skulls of cows on the pioneer trail. Pacific seascapes—the lonely lighthouse, storm-tossed waves breaking on the rocks below."

"You must be kidding. I can't even draw a circle."

"Nor can I. Few can, actually. So—this is correct?" She tore her cigarette open and spilled the tobacco out at her feet.

"Close enough."

"Now the enemy will never know I was here."

"Except for the filter you dropped."

"What did you do with yours?"

"I don't smoke filters. I should. But I'm quitting—this summer for sure."

"Such cowardice! You, a Marine, deserting the field."

"I wouldn't put it like that." Theresa heard the coldness in her own voice and only mildly regretted it.

"Oh, I have made a gaffe," Professor Landsman said. "It was a joke."

"I know."

"A stupid joke." She tugged on the ends of her scarf. "The way one uses words here, among one's clever colleagues, like a game, one grows careless. Of course such words have meaning." She took a pack of cigarettes from her coat pocket, shook one out and lit it.

"You don't talk carelessly in class," Theresa said.

"No, that's true. I am serious. Perhaps too serious?" Professor Landsman leaned her head back and closed her eyes and blew out a stream of smoke, exposing a splotchy purple birthmark on her neck. In almost the same moment, eyes still closed, she twitched the scarf and the birthmark vanished.

"Sure you're serious," Theresa said. "You should be, you're the professor."

"The word 'cowardice,' for you, must be the worst of insults."

"I don't know. I can think of a few others."

"But certainly you would hold courage at a premium, and despise cowardice. Such would be the very fundamentals of your existence."

"I'm just a student, remember? Bed-and-breakfast."

"Please don't condescend. You understand me."

"Look, Professor Landsman." Theresa meant to say that all this was behind her and that in any case she knew no more about courage than the next person, but at her name Professor Landsman shifted and looked at her so seriously, so gravely, that Theresa found herself unable to speak. Instead she turned away and pretended to take an interest in the students crossing the courtyard. Two laughing boys sped by on bicycles, snowmelt hissing under their tires, tails of spray arcing up behind. Theresa watched them pass out of sight. A long cigar-shaped cloud drifted in front of the sun, and just like that the courtyard was in twilight. She crossed her arms against the sudden coolness.

"For some of us," Professor Landsman said, "courage does not come so easily."

"I think maybe you have the wrong idea," Theresa said. "I've never been in combat. I'm not sure what I'd do. Nobody is."

"Oh, I am," Professor Landsman said. "I wither under fire. I leave my comrades to their fate."

"Maybe. People surprise themselves. You just don't know until you've been there."

"But I have been there."

"In Iraq?"

"No, not in Iraq! Not combat with a gun—I've never so much as *touched* a gun—but combat nevertheless."

"Well, then . . . you don't need my opinion." Theresa picked up her book bag from under the chair and prepared to take her leave.

"I was nineteen, like one of these." Professor Landsman nodded at the students walking by. "At university, a happy fugitive from a boring little town known for its sausage. I had friends and I was in love. With art, with the city, with a man, a *married* man, so sophisticated I was—in love even with myself! Imagine! I had many friends and many daring ideas that must be shared. Talk talk talk, and of course they followed this river of brave words right to my door. An old story, to be sure. But I think you will find it interesting."

This sounded strangely like a warning. Certainly Theresa was left feeling more awkward than curious. She was getting cold and wanted to leave but didn't see how she could, not now, and of course she was flattered that her attention seemed important to this forceful, accomplished woman, her professor. But she kept her bag in her lap, holding the straps with both hands.

"So, the approach. Just one of them, the first time. A young man, quite handsome and well spoken, you might take him for a student or a young lecturer. But he knew about me. That is, he knew about my friends, and my lover, and my interest in politics—my interest in *change,* as he put it. He, too, was interested in change, he said. So were others whom I might imagine to be unfriendly. They could offer us certain protections. Some clarifications would be necessary from time to time, only to help them understand our ideas for the future, so that they might better protect us from less sympathetic elements. He was very smooth—too smooth for his own purpose. Simple cluck that I was, I could hardly understand what he was proposing. Then I was shocked. Indeed, I made a fine show of my indignation and nobly sent him on his way.

"More fool me. I should have made my pact with this devil. My God, the two who finally got their hooks in me! The man a licensed paranoiac, an accountant of meaningless facts all rendered sinister by the infinite connections he saw between them. Everything had meaning. A student goes home for a visit with her sick mama, meat-packers in the same town protest unsanitary conditions—hah! Clandestine meetings! Agitation! Case closed! And he smelled like a closet. You know—what's the word?—naphtha.

"But the woman, the woman was worse. He at least aspired to rationality. She was free of such bourgeois affectations. She required no theory and no evidence. She knew who the enemy was and what was to be done. Yes, and to do it, to frighten and compel, to put you on your knees where you belonged—that was her vocation and her pleasure."

"Where was this?"

"What?" Professor Landsman looked at her as if the question were stupid or, worse, a breach of trust.

"Where did all this happen?" Theresa was caught up now, lost in what Professor Landsman was telling her. Partly it was a habit formed in the lecture hall, where she was used to surrendering to Professor Landsman's voice. But in her lectures Professor Landsman was lively, even passionate, and highly particular. Her manner now was different, and this cool formality of expression, the absence of names, the featureless ground on which the story proceeded, had all somehow delivered Theresa into a fog of abstraction. She was feeling the cold as an emanation of her uncertainty. She needed to know where she was.

"What difference does it make?" Professor Landsman said. She pursed her lips. "Prague," she said in a low voice.

Prague. Okay. Theresa read history; she knew about Prague. Wenceslas Square. The Russian tanks coming in, security police beating on kids, hauling them off to prison. The president of the country kidnapped and taken to Russia. "Prague," she said. "This was 1968, right?"

"No," Professor Landsman said. "Later. It doesn't matter, it was happening all the time, and not only in Prague. This is an old story, as I say. One believes the enemy is at one's back, somewhere—perhaps closing in. Therefore one must find the enemy at any cost, and hurt him. So. The man. At first I thought I could match him at his game, using facts of my own as counters to his. But always, always, he surprised me. No sane person could have imagined what was perfectly obvious to him. His theories, expounded over hours in that horrid little room, dumbfounded me—quite literally. He rendered me speechless. But he didn't break me. It was the woman who broke me."

"What was her name?"

"Her name? Do you think they offered their names? Even a false name would have given me some way of imagining them, addressing them. Some admission of likeness."

"You were what, nineteen?" Theresa said. "Just a kid."

"Save your pity for my friends," Professor Landsman said. "I sold them all out in the end. My friends, my lover, two of my professors."

At that moment the sun broke clear, and thick, low slants of light flooded the wet courtyard and caught both women full in the face. Professor Landsman shielded her eyes. The timing of this sunburst struck Theresa as absurdly dissonant, even mischievous. It made her a little giddy, and then contrite to have had these feelings as Professor Landsman was telling such a sad story.

"What did she do to you, this woman?" Theresa asked, carefully shading her voice.

"Nothing. She did nothing to me." Professor Landsman sounded cross, as if conscious herself of some disrespect in this last bright flourish of the day.

"But you said that she was the one who, you know . . ."

"Yes. She was the one. But really, she did nothing to me but recognize me, and reveal myself to me as I was. Do you understand? I could see it in how she looked at me, always that look of recognition, of knowing that I was a coward and would soon become her creature, and that everything leading up to that point—the endless meetings, the harangues and accusations, the threats to my family, the promises—how can I describe it? As if these were rites that must be observed, honored to the full for all the pleasure and pain they could afford, but that the end was inevitable and already known to us both by the plain fact of my cowardice. That was her power, and how it reduced me! How it made me squirm! I needed only to look at her, that smile always in her eyes. She knew me. She simply made me know myself. So you see, here is one soldier you do not want in the trench with you."

"Come on," Theresa said. "It was just a technique, the way she treated you, how she made you feel—like a coward. They trained her to do that."

"No, you give them too much credit. But what if they had? It was still true."

"What happened to your friends?"

"I don't know. Doubtless they were watched. Perhaps some of them were turned. But nothing obvious—nothing I could see before I left. They like to let these things ripen." She pushed her hair back roughly with both hands and smiled. "You are thinking: *Irksome woman! Why must I hear all this?*"

"Don't say that." Theresa leaned toward her. The books in her bag pressed up against her belly. "Listen, Professor Landsman."

She held up her palm in warning. "Please, I am allergic to commiseration."

"Just listen. People can be trained to build you up, make you feel brave so you act brave. It's a regular science. Don't you think it can work in reverse?"

"No matter. What happened, happened." She pushed her chair back and stood, squinting in the light. "How I've gone on! You are too patient."

Theresa stood with her. "You were nineteen. Now you're in your fifties, right? Do you think a person your age, with all your education, all the places you've been and the people you've known—wait, now, hear me out—do you think you should pass sentence on some kid who's scared half to death, and all alone, and getting pushed around by creeps who really know how to do it? Would you judge your own child that way?"

"I have no child. More cowardice."

"I'm sorry. But you know what I mean."

"Americans!" Professor Landsman was fumbling with the buttons of her coat. "Such faith in the future, where all shall be reconciled. Such compassion toward the past, where all may be forgiven, once understood. Really, you have no comprehension of history. Of how *done* it is, how historical. One may not redeem a day of it, not a moment of it, with all these empathies and tender discernments. One may visit it only as one visits a graveyard, hat in hand. One may read the inscriptions on the stones. One may not rewrite them."

Theresa shouldered her bag. "Got it. Thanks for straightening me out."

"Oh, now I've abused your kindness. I had no right to burden you with my useless old stories. You must forgive me."

"Am I allowed to?"

"Ha!" she said, and looked down, and nodded. "I would ask," she began.

"Sure," Theresa said. "Naturally. Not a word."

"Thank you."

That was when Theresa knew she would have to drop the course.

When she got home from her swim that night she made herself a tuna salad and studied her notes for an econ exam. Then, wistfully, she leafed through her art history textbook, *Gardner's Art Through the Ages*, lingering over Fra Angelico's *Annunciation*. At first her eyes were drawn to the angel, that radiance, that almost wild look of joy and promise, but it was Mary's expression that held her—accepting, yes, but sorrowful too, as if she already knew what was to befall her child in this world.

Theresa's son was good about writing, but tonight there'd been nothing. She went back to the computer—still nothing. She opened his last two e-mails and reread them. Here, running through the joking, witty accounts of his days and tasks, of challenges overcome, were the names of his new friends, fondly repeated, and the modest pride he took in their respect. A bookish, reticent boy in high school, he was discovering that he could be tough and competent. A man others could rely on—even look up to. Theresa was glad for all that, though she knew none of it would necessarily save him in the end. The big thing was to be lucky. Most were, after all; most came home alive—almost everyone. The odds were on his side, and so on hers. She kept this thought close by. She often had need of it.

But tonight she felt another fear, worse in its way, because there were no odds to set against it. Not what might happen to him, but what he might become. Soon enough he would be among strange people who would hate him on sight. Any of them might be meaning to kill him. In the face of so much hatred and danger, how could he escape feeling hatred himself? For all of them? Theresa had seen how the young men looked after a few months in that place; she knew how they talked, and the silences that opened up between them.

Her son was already learning the pleasure of being strong, and the special pleasure of being stronger than others. He'd been skinny and shy when young, and from sixth grade into seventh the bullying had gotten so nasty she'd had to go to the principal of his school. She hadn't thought of it for some time, but tonight Theresa remembered the look on his face after one of the bad days—the blackness of his bitterness and shame. When he came into power now over those who hated him and frightened him, how would he resist putting them on their knees, making them squirm? And then what? What would happen in some little room where hatred and power and fear came together, and there was nobody to say no? Her boy had a good heart. He had a soul. For the first time, she feared he might lose it.

Theresa wanted to warn him, but the light, merry tone of their correspondence had become a sort of rule between them. She would have to break it, to trespass. Though she didn't have the words now, she would find them. He wouldn't like it. He'd be insulted. Good— then he might remember, when that day came.

She looked again at the Fra Angelico before getting up from her desk. No, by God, she would not drop the class. She would sit toward the front of the lecture hall as she always did, and if it bothered Professor Landsman to have Theresa watching her, listening to her pronouncements, all the while knowing what she knew, whose fault was that? Professor Landsman had a job to do. If she was uneasy she would just have to find a way through her unease, or get used to it, like everyone else.

The Deposition

The witness was playing hard to get. Statements he had made earlier to his girlfriend, another nurse, statements crucial to Burke's case, the witness now declined to repeat under oath. He claimed not to remember just what he'd said, or even to recall clearly the episode in question: an instance of surgical haste and sloppiness amounting to malpractice. As the result of a routine procedure—removal of a ganglion cyst—outrageously, indefensibly botched, Burke's client had lost the fine motor skills of her left hand. She'd worked the reservations desk at a car-rental office; what was to become of a fifty-eight-year-old booking agent who could no longer use a keyboard?

Burke decided to ask for a breather. He'd flown out from San Francisco only the day before to take this deposition in person. He was still ragged from the unpleasant journey: delayed departure from SFO, a run through Dulles to make his puddle jumper to Albany, then the poky drive upriver to New Delft. Long trip, sleepless night. He'd shown some temper at the witness's forgetfulness, and the witness had in turn become sullen and grudging, the last thing Burke wanted. He hoped that a little time off would cool things down and allow the man's conscience to help out his memory, if he was still open to such influences. Burke suspected that he was.

Witness's counsel agreed to the break: forty-five minutes. Burke turned down the offer of cake and coffee in favor of a brisk walk. He left the building, a Federalist mansion converted to law offices, and started down the hill toward the river. It was a fine October afternoon, warm and golden, trees ablaze, air dense with the must of fallen leaves. That smell, the honeyed light . . . Burke faltered in his march, subdued by the memory of days like this in the Ohio town where he'd grown up. There was that one Indian summer, his junior year in high school, when day after day, flooded with desire, shaking with it, he'd hurried to an older girl's house to glory in her boldness for a mad hour before her mother got home from work. Julie Rose. The hourglass birthmark on her throat . . . he could still see it, and the filmy curtains fluttering at her bedroom window, the brilliance of the leaves stirring in the warm breeze.

But what crap! Wallowing in nostalgia for a place he'd come to despise and dreamed only of escaping.

The river was farther than Burke had thought. He was a big bull-shouldered man who struggled to trim his bulk with diets and exercise, but he'd been putting in long hours lately, eating on the fly and missing his workouts; even this easy jaunt was making him sweat. He loosened his tie. When he reached the bottom of the hill he took off his suit jacket and flung it over his shoulder.

Burke had hoped to find a path beside the river, but the way was barred by a pair of factory buildings that loomed along the bank behind padlocked chain-link fences. The factories were derelict, bricks fallen from the walls, all but the highest windows broken; these glittered gaily in the late sunshine. Splintered pallets lay here and there across the weed-cracked asphalt of the factory yards. He examined this scene with sour recognition before turning away.

Burke followed the fence a few hundred yards and then circled back uphill on what appeared to be a commercial street. A cloying, briny smell poured from the open door of a Chinese takeout, a half-eaten plate of noodles surrounded by soy-sauce packets on the single table inside. The bespectacled woman at the counter looked up from her newspaper to meet his gaze. He looked away and walked on, past an old movie theater with empty poster casings and a blank marquee; a dog-grooming salon, its windows filled with faded snapshots of a man with orange hair grinning over various pooches made ridiculous by his labors; past a five-and-dime converted to a Goodwill, and a tailor shop with a CLOSED sign in the window. On the corner stood an abandoned Mobil station, windows boarded over, the pumps long gone.

Burke stopped and looked up at the winged red horse still rearing over the lot, then took in the block he'd just traveled. A stooped woman in an overcoat was hobbling down the opposite sidewalk—the only person in sight. It might have been a street in his hometown, with its own bankrupt industries and air of stagnation. Burke's widowed mother still lived in the old house. He visited dutifully with his wife, who claimed to find the town charming and soothingly tranquil, but Burke couldn't imagine living there and wasn't sure why anyone else did.

In fact, it seemed to him that for all the talk of family and faith and neighborliness—the heartland virtues held up in rebuke of competitive, materialistic Gomorrahs like San Francisco—there was something not quite wholesome in this placidity, something lazy and sensual. Burke felt it when he wandered the streets of his hometown, and he felt it now.

He crossed against the light, quickening his pace; he would have to move smartly to make it back in time. All signs of commerce ended at the gas station. He passed several blocks of small houses squeezed together on puny lots—no doubt the homes of those who'd spent their lives in the factories. Most of them were in bad repair: roofs sagging, paint scaling, screens rusting out. No disposable income around here.

Burke knew the story—he'd bet the farm on it. Unions broken or bought off. Salaries and benefits steadily cut under threat of layoffs that happened anyway as the jobs went to foreign wage slaves, the owners meanwhile conjuring up jolly visions of the corporate "family" and better days to come, before selling out just in time to duck the fines for a century of fouling the river; then the new owners, vultures with MBAs, gliding in to sack the pension fund before declaring bankruptcy. Burke knew the whole story, and it disgusted him— especially the workers who'd let the owners screw them like this while patting them on the head, congratulating them for being the backbone of the country, salt of the earth, the true Americans. Jesus! And still they ate it up, and voted like robbers instead of the robbed. Served them right.

Burke's pounding heart sent a rush of heat to his face and left him strangely light-headed, as if he were floating above the sidewalk. He took the hill in long, thrusting strides. A boy with blond dreadlocks was raking leaves into a garbage bag. As Burke went past, the boy leaned on the rake and gaped at him, a jarring, surflike percussion leaking from his earphones.

The whole country was being hollowed out like this, devoured from the inside, with nobody fighting back. It was embarrassing, and vaguely shameful, to watch people get pushed around without a fight. That's why he'd taken on his little pop-eyed pug of a client with the fucked-up hand—she was a battler. Stonewalled at every turn, bombarded with demands for documents, secretly videotaped, insulted with dinky settlement offers, even threatened with a countersuit, she just lowered her head and kept coming. She'd spent all her savings going after the surgeon who'd messed her up, to the point where she'd had to move to San Francisco to live with her son, a paralegal in Burke's firm. Her lawyer back here in New Delft had suffered a stroke and bowed out. The case was a long shot but Burke had taken it on contingency because he knew she wouldn't back off, that she'd keep pushing right to the end.

And now it seemed she might have a chance after all. They'd gotten a break the past month, hearing about this nurse's complaints to his now-embittered ex-girlfriend. The account Burke had of these conversations was hearsay, not enough in itself to take to court or even to compel a fair settlement, but it told him that the witness harbored feelings of guilt and anger. That he had some pride and resented being made party to a maiming. He was no doubt under great pressure to stand by the surgeon, but the witness hadn't actually denied seeing what he'd seen or saying what he'd said. He simply claimed not to recall it clearly.

What a man forgets he can remember. It was a question of will. And even in the witness's evasions Burke could detect his reluctance to lie and, beyond that, his desire—not yet decisive but persistent and troubling—to tell the truth.

Burke believed that he had a gift for sensing not only a person's truthfulness on a given question, but also, and more important, his natural inclination toward the truth. It was like a homing instinct in those who had it. No matter what the risk, no matter how carefully they might defend themselves with equivocation and convenient lapses of memory, it was still there, fidgeting to be recognized. Over the years he had brought considerable skill to the work of helping people overcome their earlier shufflings and suppressions, even their self-interest, to say what they really wanted to say. The nurse needed to tell his story; Burke was sure of that, and sure of his own ability to coax the story forth. He would master this coy witness.

And as he considered how he would do this he felt himself moving with ease for the first time that day. He had his rhythm and his wind, a pleasant sense of strength. But for his flimsy, very expensive Italian loafers, he might have broken into a run.

The houses were growing larger as he climbed, the lawns deeper and darker. Great maples arched high above the street. Burke slowed to watch a sudden fall of leaves, how they rocked and dipped and stalled in their descent, eddying in gusts so light and warm he hardly felt them on the back of his neck, like teasing breaths. Then a bus roared past and pulled to the curb just ahead, and the doors hissed open, and the girl stepped out.

Burke held back—though barely aware of holding back, or of the catch in his throat. She was tall, to his eyes magnificently tall. He caught just a glance of lips painted black before her long dark hair swung forward and veiled her face as she looked down to find her footing on the curb. She stopped on the sidewalk and watched the bus pull away in a belch of black smoke. Then she set her bag down and stretched luxuriously, going up on her toes, hands raised high above her head. Still on tiptoe, she joined her fingers together and moved her hips from side to side. She was no more than twenty feet away, but it was clear to Burke that she hadn't noticed him, that she thought she was alone out here. He felt himself smile. He waited. She dropped her arms, did a few neck rolls, then hiked her bag back onto her shoulder and started up the street. He followed, matching his pace to hers.

She walked slowly, with the deliberate, almost flat-footed tread of a dancer, toes turned slightly outward. She was humming a song. Her knee-length plaid skirt swayed a little as she walked, but she held her back straight and still. The white blouse she wore had two sweat-spots below her shoulder blades. Burke could picture her leaning back against the plastic seat on the bus, drowsing in the swampy air as men stole looks at her over their folded papers.

The tone of her humming changed, grew more rhythmic, less tuneful. Her hips rolled under the skirt, her shoulders shifting in subtle counterpoint. On the back of her right calf there was a dark spot the size of a penny—maybe a mole, or a daub of mud.

She fell silent and reached into her bag. It was a large canvas bag, full to bulging, but she found what she was after without looking down and brought it out and slipped it over her wrist, a furry red band. She reached both hands behind her neck and gathered her hair and lifted it and gave her head a shake and let her hair fall back. She was moving even more slowly now, languorously, dreamily. Again she reached back and lifted her hair and began twisting it into a single strand. In one motion she gave it a last twist and slid the red band off her wrist and up the thick rope of hair, pulled it forward over her shoulder, and commenced picking at the ends.

Burke stared at the curve of her neck, so white, so bare. It looked damp and tender. She went on in her slow glide and he followed. He had been walking in time with her but such was his absorption that he lost the beat, and at the sound of his footsteps she wheeled around and looked into his face. Burke was right behind her—he had closed the distance without realizing it. Her eyes went wide. He was held by them, fixed. They were a deep, bruised blue, almost violet, and darkly rimmed with liner. He heard her suck in a long ragged breath.

Burke tried to speak, to reassure her, but his throat was tight and dry and not a sound came. He swallowed. He couldn't think what to say.

He stood looking into her face. Blotchy white skin, the pathetic hipness of the black lips. But those eyes, the high and lovely brow—beautiful; more beautiful even than he had imagined. The girl took a step back, her eyes still holding his, then turned and began angling across a lawn toward a large white house. Halfway there she broke into a run.

This somehow released Burke. He continued on his way, deliberately holding himself to a dignified pace, even stopping for a moment to put on his suit jacket—shoot the cuffs, shrug into the shoulders, give a tug at the lapels. He did not allow himself to look back. As the tightness in his throat eased he found himself hungry for air, almost panting, and realized that he'd taken hardly a breath while walking behind the girl. How frightened she seemed! What was *that* all about, anyway? He put this question to himself with a wonderment he didn't actually feel. He knew; he knew what had been in his face. He let it go.

Burke walked on. He had just reached the top of the hill, some nine or ten long blocks from where he'd left the girl, and was about to turn right toward the law office, already in view at the end of the cross street, when a siren yelped behind him. Only one sharp, imperative cry, nothing more—but he recognized the sound, and stopped and closed his eyes for a moment before turning to watch the cruiser nosing toward the curb.

He waited. A gray-haired woman glared at him from the rear window. The girl was beside her, leaning forward to look at him, nodding to the cop in front. He opened a notebook on the steering wheel, wrote something, then laid the notebook on the seat beside him, set his patrolman's cap on his head, adjusted its angle, and got out of the cruiser. He walked around to the back door and held it open as the woman and the girl slid out. Each of these actions was executed with plodding deliberation, *performed,* Burke understood, as an unnerving show of method and assurance.

He nodded as the cop came toward him. "Officer. What can I do for you?"

"Identification, please."

Burke could have objected to this, but instead he shrugged, fetched his wallet from his jacket pocket, and handed over his driver's license.

The cop examined it, looked up at Burke, lowered his eyes to the license again. He was young, his face bland as a baby's in spite of his wispy blond mustache. "You're not from here," he finally said.

Burke had a business card ready. He held it out, and after eyeing it warily the cop took it. "I'm a lawyer," Burke said. "Here to take a deposition, in, let's see . . ." He held up his watch. "Three minutes ago. Four-thirty. Right down there on Clinton Street." He gestured vaguely. "So what's the problem?"

The gray-haired woman had come up close to Burke and was staring fiercely into his face. The girl lingered by the cruiser, pallid, hands dangling awkwardly at her sides.

"We have a complaint," the officer said. "Stalking," he added uncertainly.

"*Stalking?* Stalking *who?*"

"You know who," the woman said in a gravelly voice, never taking her eyes off him. She was handsome in a square-jawed way and deeply tanned. Ropy brown arms sticking out of her polo shirt, grass stains on the knees of her khakis. Burke could see her on the deck of a boat, coolly reefing sails in a blow.

"The young lady there?" Burke asked.

"Don't play cute with me," the woman said. "I've never seen anyone so terrified. The poor thing could hardly speak when she came to my door."

"Something sure scared her," the cop said.

"And what was my part in this?" Burke looked directly at the girl. She was hugging herself, sucking on her lower lip. She was younger than he'd thought; she was just a kid. He said, gently, "Did I do something to you?"

She glanced at him, then averted her face.

In the same voice, he said, "Did I *say* anything to you?"

She stared at the ground by her feet.

"Well?" the cop said sharply. "What'd he do?"

The girl didn't answer.

"Aren't you the smooth one," the woman said.

"I do remember passing her a while back," Burke said, addressing himself to the cop. "Maybe I surprised her—I guess I must have. I was in kind of a hurry." Then, speaking with absolute calm, Burke explained his business in New Delft, and the forty-five-minute break, and the route he'd taken and the necessity of moving right along to get back on time, even if that meant overtaking other people on the sidewalk. All this could be confirmed at the law office—where they'd be already waiting for him—and Burke invited the cop to come along and settle the matter forthwith. "I'm sorry if I surprised you," he said in the girl's direction. "I certainly didn't mean to."

The cop looked at him, then at the girl. "Well?" he repeated.

She turned her back to them, rested her elbows on the roof of the cruiser, and buried her face in her hands.

The cop watched her for a moment. "Ah, jeez," he said. He gave the driver's license another once-over, handed it back with the card, and walked over to the girl. He murmured something, then took her by the elbow and began to help her into the backseat.

The woman didn't move. Burke felt her eyes on him as he replaced the license and card in his wallet. Finally he looked up and met her stare, so green and cold. He held it and did not blink. Then came a flash of bursting pain and his head snapped sideways so hard he felt a crack at the base of his neck. The shock scorched his eyes with hot, blinding tears. His face burned. His tongue felt jammed back in his throat.

"Liar," she said.

Until Burke heard her voice he didn't understand that she'd struck him—he was that stunned. It gave him a kind of relief, as if without knowing it he'd been gripped by fear of something worse.

He heard the doors of the cruiser slam shut, one-two! He bent down with his hands on his knees, steadying himself, then straightened up and rubbed at his eyes. The cruiser was gone. The left side of his face still burned, hot even to the touch. A bearded man in a black suit walked past him down the hill, shooting Burke a glance and then locking his gaze straight ahead. Burke checked his watch. He was seven minutes late.

He took a step, and another, and went on, amazed at how surely he walked, and how lightly. Down the street a squirrel jabbered right into his ear, or so it seemed, but when he glanced up he found it chattering on a limb high above him. Still, its voice was startling—raw, close. The light in the crowns of the trees had the quality of mist.

Burke stopped outside the law office and gave his shoes a quick buff on the back of his pant legs. He mounted the steps and paused at the door. The blow was still warm on his cheek. Did it show? Would they ask about it? No matter—he'd think of something. But he couldn't help touching it again, tenderly, as if to cherish it, as he went inside to nail this witness down.

Down to Bone

He had an appointment at a funeral home and was itching to leave. His mother was dying, here in her own bed, as she had wished, with him in attendance. He'd been feeding her ice chips. It was the only thing he could do for her anymore. She seemed to be sleeping again, but he forced himself to wait a little longer before he left.

He eased himself onto the couch he'd been camping on and resumed leafing through one of her photo albums. It had been his favorite when he was a boy, because it showed his mother when she was a girl, in a sepia world of flapper dresses and frilly-legged bathing suits and Franklin touring cars. Here she was at her first communion, the very image of his own young daughter. The resemblance made him homesick; it was that close. His mother stared heavenward in an unctuously reverent pose surely dictated by her father, for neither unction nor reverence formed any part of her nature. She'd always treated his own bouts of religious faith with plain puzzlement.

And here, a little older on the fantail of a ship, flanked by her frail sweet-faced mother and her father, a short man in Navy uniform, arms crossed over his chest. A right prick, that one. A tireless pedant, a cheapskate, a bully. When her mother died he made her leave school and turned her into a house slave. She ran away at seventeen, after he fired his pistol at a boy hiding in their backyard, waiting for her to sneak out. She rarely spoke of him, and then with tight lips. At his funeral she had worn an expression of rare, adamant coldness, almost of triumph. Why had she gone at all? Just to make sure?

Ah, and this one, the best one, his mother standing before a long surfboard stuck in the sands of Waikiki Beach, where she'd been taught to ride the waves by Duke Kahanamoku himself. She was lean and lovely and faced the camera with a bravado that made him stare. This was his mother, the great friend of his youth.

He was going to be late for his appointment. It was Friday afternoon, and if he didn't go now he'd have to wait till Monday. The thought of not getting out touched him with a kind of panic. He stood over his mother and looked down at her thin white hair, a mist above her scalp. Her shoulders rose and fell with the shallow rasp of her breathing. He whispered to her. Waited, whispered again. Nothing.

On his way out he stopped in the staff room and asked Feliz, the young woman on duty, to look in now and then and feed his mother some ice chips if she woke up before he returned. She agreed, but he could feel her resentment. She was new on the staff and afraid of his mother's wasted body, as he was; he'd seen her timidity that morning when the two of them sponged his mother down, and he supposed she'd seen his.

"Please," he said. "I won't be gone long."

"Yes, okay," she said, but she would not meet his eyes.

Christ, it was good busting out of there—firing up the lollipop-red Miata he'd rented and gunning it out of the parking lot, the sun on his face. The travel agent who'd booked his flight to Miami had gotten him a bargain rate on a midsize Buick sedan, but once he stepped out of the terminal and into the warm twilight he was overcome by the idea of a convertible; and when he went back inside and the beautiful Latina at the counter mentioned she had a Miata available, he took it without hesitation, though it was ridiculously overpriced and, given the occasion, maybe a little festive.

He'd never driven a sports car before. He liked being close to the road and open to the sky, feeling the velvety sea air wash over him.

During his hours in the darkened, lavender-scented apartment he was aware of the car outside and the thought of it pleased him.

He hadn't found much to be pleased with, least of all the long hours of useless witness to his mother's dying—not being able to reach her, not knowing what to do or say. None of this was as he'd hoped—the two of them recalling old times as the shadows lengthened, reclaiming their partnership, abolishing the wariness that had somehow grown up between them. He tried; he talked brightly of his wife and children, all the while knowing she was beyond curiosity, if she could understand him at all. He did it, he knew, to drown out the hard work of her breathing, to fill his own head with the sound of ordinary talk and distract himself from his impatience for the end— for her sake, he tried to believe: for her *release*.

He felt he'd been cast in a low part, as when he ransacked the apartment for her jewelry. He had done this after a funeral-home director told him that others with acccss—caregivers, building staff— might help themselves if he didn't get there first. "It happens all the time," the man said sadly. It was a ghoulish business, rifling through every drawer and cupboard while his mother lay curled on her bed. Now and then she stirred and he froze like a thief, hand in a coat pocket, under a pile of sweaters, holding his breath. It was all there, everything he remembered, anyway, and none of it worth stealing; maybe his daughter could use this stuff for playing dress-up. And he'd given himself yet another reason for feeling morally dwarfed by the underpaid women who'd looked after his mother and liked her and now simply and helplessly grieved for her.

The funeral home was just a few blocks away. This was the fourth one he'd arranged to visit. He was after the most basic plan: cremation, placement of ashes in a generic container, filing of death certificates. His mother wanted cremation and would certainly approve of his comparison shopping. She herself had a flinty incapacity for the pieties of mourning. Two weeks after her last husband's death she was on a cruise ship in the Aegean. When her cocker spaniel—Mugsy, dearer to her than any husband—got run over by a truck, she bought a life-size statue to mark his resting place in her backyard, yet the statue was of an Airedale; she'd picked it up for a song after the guy who'd commissioned it reneged on the deal.

Grolier and Sons Colonial Memorial Chapel had a Spanish-mission look that immediately put him on alert. Who but the bereaved would pay for the fancy tile roof, the faux bell tower? The prices he'd already been quoted ranged from eleven hundred to a ballsy eighteen hundred bucks for the same minimal service. What kind of nerve did Grolier and Sons have?

He was met at the door by a tall woman in a black suit. She had close-cut black hair with a streak of white across one temple, and her lips were painted a deep maroon. She regarded him so fixedly as he introduced himself that he stammered his own name and lost hers altogether. "Come," she said, and he followed her down the hallway in a trail of perfume spiced faintly with sweat. The building was cool and silent, hushed. The woman told him that everyone else was out on duty. They had two burials that afternoon, and she'd left one of them early to meet with him. If she seemed—"how does one say?—*out of sorts,* yes, out of sorts," it was because she'd been caught in traffic and reached the home only a few minutes earlier, late for their appointment. She thought she might have missed him. Most unprofessional! But it seemed he had been late too, no? So they were even. "Even-steven."

The woman showed him to a small office and listened while he described his mother's situation and what he had in mind. She kept her eyes straight on him as he spoke. He was again made awkward by the directness of her gaze.

"This is the hardest part," she said. "My old papa died last year and I know this is no picnic. You were close to your mother, yes?"

"We were close."

"I can tell," she said.

He asked her what Grolier and Sons would charge for what he wanted.

"So," she said. "Down to business." With a few practiced tugs she pulled off the black gloves she was wearing, then shrugged off her jacket and took a printed sheet from the tray on her desk and began to mark various lines with a highlighter. Her fingers were plump and bare of rings. Of course—the gloves. As he waited, her name came back from wherever it had gone. Elfie. It didn't fit. There was nothing elfin about her, nothing light or elusive. In this little room he could smell her plainly through her perfume, more salt than sour. Her breasts swelled the fabric of her sleeveless blouse, and her arms were heavy and rounded, not fat but with the fullness of forty-five, fifty years. She had a large, almost coarse mouth. She pursed her lips as she toted up her figures, then pushed the paper across the desk and sat back.

"You can do better," she said. "I can recommend other homes better for you."

His eyes went straight to the bottom of the page. Twenty-three hundred. He was careful to show no reaction to this almost comical sum. "I'll think about it," he said.

"Grolier and Sons Colonial Memorial Chapel is a full-service home," she said. "Everything top drawer. You want Grandpa buried in a Viking longboat, you come to Grolier and Sons Colonial Memorial Chapel. Don't laugh. I could tell you stories. Now—shame on me! You will forgive me for leaving you high and dry all this time. Orange juice? Evian?"

He was about to refuse, but the juice sounded good, and he said so.

"Or beer? I have beer."

He hesitated.

"Good," she said. "I shall join you." She rolled her chair to a small refrigerator in the corner. "Water," she said, rummaging. "Water, water, water."

"Water will be fine."

"No. Too late for that. Come."

She led him farther down the hall to a large office paneled in dark wood and furnished like a gentleman's club. Oriental rugs, red leather sofa and chairs, bookshelves filled with leather-bound books. Elfie waved him to a chair. She took a bottle and two tall glasses from a refrigerator built into the wainscoting. She poured the beer with some care, handed him a glass, and settled herself behind a massive desk covered with photographs in silver frames. *"Salut,"* she said.

"Salut."

She took a long drink and ran her tongue over her lips. Then she bent forward abruptly and turned one of the photographs facedown on the desktop.

"This is good," he said.

"Czech pilsner. The best."

"Are you Czech?"

"Would you think me Japanese had I given you Asahi? No. I am from Wien. Have you been?"

"Twice. Beautiful city." He was pleased at knowing that Wien was Vienna.

"I suppose you went for the opera."

Tempted to lie, he decided against it. "No," he said. "I don't like opera."

"Nor do I. I find it preposterous." She reached out and turned another photograph over.

"So," he said, "how did you end up here?"

"Miami, USA? Or Grolier and Sons Colonial Memorial Chapel?"

"Either. Both."

"That's a long story."

"Ah, the old Foreign Legion dodge."

She cocked her head and waited.

"When you ask a legionnaire about himself, he always says, 'That's a long story.' They tend to have histories that don't bear much scrutiny."

"As do we all."

"As do we all," he said, not unhappy to be thought the owner of such a history.

"Were you a legionnaire?"

"Me? No."

"But you were a soldier. I can tell."

"A long time ago."

"Oh, a long time ago! You are so old."

"Thirty years ago."

"It leaves a mark," she said. "I can always tell."

"Really?"

"Always."

They talked on, and all the while it seemed to him that they were having another conversation. In this parallel conversation he was saying, *I do like the way you talk,* and she was saying, *I know you do, and what else do you like?* He was saying, *I like your mouth and how you look at me over the glass when you drink your beer,* and she was saying, *I have my momentary weaknesses, and I think you may be one of them, and so?*

He'd sensed this kind of communion before. Now and then, when he was younger, it proved to be not entirely one-sided. He felt it less often these days, and when he did he tended to discount it as wishful thinking. Soon enough he would ridicule himself for imagining that he was an object of desire to this woman, who after all was simply winding down after a long hot day and enjoying—playfully, to be sure—the interest he couldn't conceal.

That's how he'd see it later on, leaving *some* room to wonder, naturally. But in the instant he had no doubt that he was indeed her momentary weakness, that if he stood and took his glasses off she'd smile up at him and say, *Yes, and so?* He had no doubt that if he came around that desk she would stand and meet him with that loose-looking mouth of hers, then sink with him to the floor, onto that nice Bokhara, her hand at his belt, her breath in his ear, *Ah, my legionnaire!*

And why not! They were both realists, they hated opera, they knew what was waiting for them in another twenty, thirty years, if not tomorrow. Why shouldn't they kick off their clothes and come at each other and make love—no, not make love: fuck! Fuck like champions in the sight of heaven and earth, just because they wanted to, without a thought in their heads but *yes yes yes!*

All he had to do was take off his glasses and stand up.

Why didn't he, then? All sorts of reasons, no doubt: a long habit of fidelity, if not the actual virtue; the absolute trust of his children;

perhaps even a childish sense of being watched by the God he lazily believed in. Any of these might have been at work below the horizon of his awareness. What he *was* aware of, all at once, was the irritation of finding himself in a play he disliked—Freud's play. Freud! Why did he have to go and think of *him*? He could just see the Viennese smarty-pants stroking his beard in smug recognition of the part he was playing, abandoning himself to Eros to obliterate his fear of death. The Great Explainer would have a field day with his mortuary lust, his deep pleasure in a drink by the beach, in sunlight and the sound of breaking waves, in fleeing his mother's apartment late at night to cruise down Collins Avenue in a red sports car, watching the girls in their slinky dresses and towering heels shimmy and sway as they moved from club to club.

He had, that is to say, a picture of himself enacting the most exhausted and demeaning of clichés. It offended him. It chilled him. He finished his beer, thanked the woman for her time, and shook her soft hand at the office door. He insisted on seeing himself out so he wouldn't have her at his back, watching him cross the empty parking lot toward that gleaming, ridiculous Miata.

As he approached his mother's apartment he heard raised voices speaking Spanish. Her door was open. *No,* he thought, *no, not while I was gone.* But he found her still alive; she didn't die until later that night, while he was down the street eating a plate of fried plantains. At this moment she was thrashing weakly back and forth between Feliz, who looked coldly at him, and an older woman named Rosa. His mother was shouting, the same word: "Daddy! Daddy!" Her eyes were open but unseeing. Rosa crooned to her in foreign singsong while Feliz tried to hold her hands.

"Daddy!"

"He's here," Rosa said. "Your daddy's here."

"Daddy!"

Rosa raised her eyes to him, pleading.

"I'm here," he said, and she fell back and looked up at him. He took Feliz's place beside her on the bed and stroked her hand. It was down to bone.

"Daddy?"

"It's all right. I'm here."

"Where were you?"

"At work."

The room was dim. The two women moved like shadows behind him. He heard the door click shut.

"I was alone."

"I know. It's all right now."

Her fingers tightened on his.

He no longer knew how to be a son, but he still knew how to be a father. He held her hand in both of his. "Everything's fine, sweetheart. Everything's going to be fine. You're my own darling, my sweet pea, my good girl."

"Daddy," she whispered. "You're here."

Nightingale

Dr. Booth took several wrong turns during the drive upstate. It vexed him to get lost like this in front of his son, especially since the fault lay with the lousy map the Academy had sent him, but Owen was in one of his trances and didn't seem to notice. His eyes were fixed on the far distance and his lips formed whispery sounds in a cadence that suggested poetry or music. Dr. Booth knew better than to try and make sense of it, but he couldn't stop himself. He thought he recognized one word—*nightingale*—and that awoke a memory of three children, himself and his older sisters, sitting in a garden at dusk while somewhere above them a bird sang. It was, he knew, a trick memory, a mirage; there had been no such garden and no such evening. Still, the thought of his sisters, one drowned in a boating accident courtesy of her dimwit husband, the other far away and silent for years, made him even gloomier than he already was.

Owen did not want to go to the Academy. He'd made this plain when the idea first came up, but as Dr. Booth and his wife continued to discuss it, doubtfully to begin with, then slowly surrendering to its tidal pull, the boy had less and less to say. He receded farther into the very remoteness Dr. Booth had been trying to lure him out of, and now, having failed, proposed to damn well *force* him out of with the school's help.

Dr. Booth had never heard of Fort Steele Academy until the brochure arrived in his mailbox. The cover showed a pair of uniformed boys standing guard on either side of a gate. It was snowing, and they appeared to have been there for some time; a good two inches had gathered on their epaulets and caps. The last page of the brochure carried a statement by the commandant, Colonel Karl: "It is no kindness to the young to pretend that life is not a struggle. The world belongs to men of unbending will, and the sooner that lesson is learned, the better. We at Fort Steele are dedicated to teaching it by every means at our disposal."

Dr. Booth could well understand why Owen didn't want to go to the Academy. He was comfortable at home. He had his foolish dog, his lazy friends, the big house with all its sunny corners for reading, or for staring at nothing and making funny noises, or whatever he did all day. When Dr. Booth went into the kitchen, there was Owen. In the living room, Owen again. The front yard, Owen; the backyard, the basement, the hammock—Owen! As a boy, Dr. Booth had delivered a hundred and eighty newspapers before school and hustled subscriptions at night. He played football. He ran for president of his class. Those memories of his own youth had figured heavily in the decision to send Owen away, but now, reviewing the list yet again, he thought he must be leaving something out, something conclusive. There was more; surely there was more.

"It won't be so bad," he said.

Owen was silent.

"Give it a chance, son. You might even like it." When Owen still didn't answer, Dr. Booth said—almost cried out—"It's for your own good."

"I know," Owen said.

"You do?"

"Yes."

"How do you know?"

"Because it's what you want."

This was the very answer Dr. Booth would have hoped for, and he knew he should be satisfied with it, but he wasn't. It troubled him. Just then the road came to a fork not indicated on his map, so he had to do some guesswork. He decided to take the right branch, then at the last moment swerved onto the left, which led through a dense stand of maples that hung darkly overhead and opened up to reveal, across from a field golden with hay, the gates of Fort Steele Academy. Dr. Booth slowed down. He wasn't ready, he wanted a moment to probe the doubt he felt, but when his car came into view the two cadets at the gate snapped to attention and held their salutes until he'd driven between them onto the grounds of the school. Owen braced his hands against the dashboard, and Dr. Booth heard him say something under his breath. They bumped over the cobbled lane toward a courtyard bordered on three sides by gray stone buildings. Two flags hung from the pole in the yard: Old Glory on top, the school crest flapping below—twin sabers crossed above a castle. A line of cadets waited in the circular drive at the end of the lane, legs slightly apart, arms behind their backs. Like the guards at the gate, they wore black uniforms with white belts. Their eyes were shadowed by the gleaming bills of their caps.

"Son," Dr. Booth said, "what did you mean, it's what I want?"

Owen stared at him without comprehension, then looked back at the line of cadets.

Dr. Booth stopped the car. "Well? Owen? What do I want?"

"For me to grow up," Owen said, watching one of the cadets march toward them. He was tall and his chin was long and sharp and his belt buckle flashed like a beacon. Carrying a clipboard in a crisp, pre-scribed-looking way, he stopped in front of the car and waited as Dr. Booth and Owen got out.

"Name, sir?"

"Booth."

The cadet ran a finger down the clipboard. "Booth, Owen G., blood type A."

"That's my boy." Dr. Booth smiled at Owen, who stared dead ahead. He'd attempted to square his thin shoulders and was holding his arms straight at his sides. He had never looked so young. Dr. Booth made up his mind to have a talk with Colonel Karl before he left. He wasn't going to leave his son here without some definite assurances.

"Private Booth is late, sir. Roll call for new men was thirteen hundred hours."

"I'm aware of that. We had some trouble getting here. A lot of trouble, in fact. That map is practically worthless."

"I'm sure you have excellent reasons, sir. The fact remains, Private Booth is late. Private Booth will report immediately to the quartermaster. When Private Booth has drawn his gear, he will move smartly to D Barrack and await orders. Corporal Costello will escort him. You can leave his bags here." He snapped his fingers, and another cadet stepped forward from the line.

Owen turned quickly and held out his hand. Dr. Booth understood that he did this to prevent the embrace he'd known was coming, which his wounded father was tempted to impose on him anyway. But he took his son's hand in his own.

"Good-bye, sir," Owen said. Then he fell in behind Corporal Costello and followed him across the courtyard, trying to match the cadet's precise stride and rigid carriage. He didn't even come close, and Dr. Booth knew he never would. The distracted saunter he kept breaking into wasn't an accident of age, something to be outgrown or overcome; it was, in truth, nothing less than Owen himself.

"I need to speak with Colonel Karl," Dr. Booth said.

"Colonel Karl is busy, sir," the cadet said.

Dr. Booth insisted, and finally the cadet had another boy take him to a windowless lounge in the basement of the far building. He was alone there. An aerial photograph of the school took up most of one wall; otherwise the room was bare of ornament. Four overstuffed chairs faced a coffee table on which lay an Academy brochure identical to the one Dr. Booth had received. He picked it up and slowly turned the pages, then put it down and paced the room. A silent grandfather clock, hands frozen at 6:18, stood in one corner, an empty umbrella stand in another. Time passed. When Dr. Booth went upstairs to the door he'd entered though, the courtyard was empty. The flags drooped on their pole. He stepped outside and, seeing no one, followed a brick walkway around back in the direction Owen had gone. The path skirted a deserted football field with bleachers on one side, then led past a pond covered with lily pads. On the opposite bank, black against the hazy sky, rose the stone walls and battlemented tower of what Dr. Booth recognized from the brochure as Memorial Chapel. He stepped off the path and pushed through clumps of sumac and elder to the other side of the pond.

One half of the arched door was locked, the other slightly ajar. Dr. Booth listened, heard nothing, and entered the chapel. Weak light fell aslant through long, narrow windows that looked like gun slits. It seemed to dim rather than brighten the oak pews and stone floors. There was no organ. The altar was bare. On the platform in front of it, facing the pews, someone had placed a high-backed wooden chair. Dr. Booth could not make out its purpose. Anyone wishing to address the congregation would surely use the carved pulpit, with its superior elevation and authority. One would stand, not sit. He studied the chair from the rear of the chapel, then started down the aisle. In obedience to an impulse he was hardly aware of but could not resist, Dr. Booth held his upper body stiff and paused for a beat after each step, one foot trailing, heel raised. Though he'd never marched before, in this fashion he covered the length of the aisle and climbed to the altar, where he executed a perfect about-face and then, as if on command, lowered himself onto the chair, back straight, hands in his lap.

How quiet it was. Dr. Booth looked out at the somber pews where the cadets would file in and stand waiting before taking their seats in a single motion—one great creak, then silence. Whoever sat in this chair could see the face of every cadet. Dr. Booth could almost see the faces himself, row after row of them, faintly luminous in the shadows. He could feel them watching him behind their unblinking eyes, weighing him on the scales, and finally it came to him that this was the place of judgment. This was where you sat to have your faults revealed and to receive your sentence. Dr. Booth looked away, at the heavy beams overhead, the roof slanting up into darkness. He closed his eyes. Still he saw the faces of the cadets, taut and pale above their black uniforms. He strained to find among them some glint of fellow feeling, some intimation of mercy; he found none. Mercy there was none.

The door swung open at the rear of the chapel and a cadet stood silhouetted in the doorway. "Sir," he said.

Dr. Booth stood clumsily, knocking over the chair. He set it right and hurried up the aisle. "Coming," he called out.

The cadet held the door for him and followed him outside, where another cadet—the tall one who'd scolded him for being late—passed on Colonel Karl's deepest regrets that, due to prior obligations, he was unable to speak with him this afternoon. Dr. Booth could return the next morning, if he wished, or call for an appointment at some later date.

Dr. Booth supposed he could raise a fuss and make it impossible for Colonel Karl not to see him, but he was worried about the trouble this might cause Owen, and anyway he had to get back on the road if he was to reach home before dark. He was ready to leave Fort Steele Academy—ready, in fact, almost to the point of panic—so he accepted Colonel Karl's message without protest and allowed the two cadets to take him back to his car. They led him like a prisoner, the tall one in front, the other at his heels, but saluted sharply when he started the engine and drove back down the lane. The guards at the gate also saluted. In the field across the road a green tractor moved slowly along the fence, pulling a mower. The smell of fresh-cut hay filled the car and lingered until Dr. Booth was several miles away, and lost again.

He parked on the shoulder, engine ticking, and choked back his rage just enough to hold the goddamn-son-of-a-bitch map without tearing it to pieces. With a trembling finger he tried to retrace his route: he'd taken this road through the maple grove beyond the school, yes, then it must've been this one, here, that had carried him over an unmarked bridge and thence to a triple fork, also unmarked, where he'd been forced to make the first of a long series of choices without any guidance whatsoever, before finally coming to rest in this vast flatland whose very existence went completely unremarked on the map.

A water tower gleamed in the distance. The reek of manure lay heavy on the air. Three white-faced cows watched from the fence to his left as Dr. Booth continued to study the map, this time in reverse, trying to find the various roads he and Owen had followed from home to the Academy. Only the first couple of turns off the interstate were correctly indicated. It was a pure miracle he'd ever found the school, given that he had been forced to navigate by hunches. The map simply did not correspond to the land.

He crumpled it and threw it out the window. One of the cows took a step backward, then continued to ruminate and stare. Dr. Booth was thinking about the aerial photograph in the lounge. He remembered it in detail, and something about it had begun to bother him. There was no pond in the picture, and the chapel stood a good distance from its actual location, forming part of a quadrangle. That quadrangle did not exist. Like the map, the aerial photograph was a fiction.

Once Dr. Booth recognized this, he had to entertain a number of questions he'd been trying to ignore. During his time at the Academy, he had seen only a few cadets—the guards, and the ones who'd taken charge of Owen. Where were all the other boys in this school of five hundred? Why hadn't he run across any of them out marching around, or at least heard their voices? How had *their* parents found the school? Why wouldn't Colonel Karl see him, or have the grace to send a deputy?

Dr. Booth turned the car around and started back the way he'd come. He was determined not to leave Owen in that place. He saw a crossroad approaching and knew without doubt that he should turn right. This certainty felt surprising and tonic, like the first deep breath when he left the hospital at day's end. He finally knew where he was going.

How had this happened? The brochure had arrived—but why? And why had he considered it at all—surrendering his boy to unknown disciplines and judgments, to powers he knew nothing about except that they were without patience, humor, or mercy? Of all mysteries, this was the most perplexing.

His wife had resisted, but in spite of his own doubts he'd bullied her along until she, like Owen, saw the futility of argument. They had no choice in the matter; nor, it then seemed to him, did he. From the moment he saw the name of the school he had known, unhappily, in fact miserably, that Owen would go there. His attempts to talk himself out of it left him even more helplessly snarled in reasons for sending the boy away, reasons that now seemed trivial, unjust, puzzling.

He had compared Owen with himself—his boyhood of newspaper hustling, athletics, and school politics. But he'd never actually been elected to any office; offering himself up year after year, he received nothing for his pains but more humiliation. And his father had made him take on the paper route because they needed the money; he'd hated every minute of it, the waking in darkness, the cold and rain, how his customers cried poor and hid from him. He'd played varsity football, yes, but only in his senior year, when his little brother took over the route. Owen was younger, much younger, than he had been then. How had he forgotten?

And what about all the reasons he'd given himself? Time for the boy to wake up and get out of the house, show some pluck, some drive, some willpower—that was always the closing argument, the clincher. But why? Owen did well in school. He was quiet and liked to read and wasn't much of an athlete, but he wasn't lazy or lacking in courage; he and his friends routinely rode their bikes up and down hills that verged on the perpendicular. And those sounds Owen made—what was the harm there? Why shouldn't he dream up poems, or songs, or whatever they were? Why shouldn't he *dream*? He was a child.

Dr. Booth turned left at a fork and navigated a run of sharp turns as if he'd spent his life on this road. The haze was gone, the late-afternoon light almost painfully clear. Pumpkins gleamed in a passing field.

He had wanted Owen out of the house. That was the truth, and it made no sense to him now. The impatience he'd felt when coming upon his son reading or playing with his dog, doing nothing, or dreaming—why? What was the crime? As a boy, he himself had wanted nothing more than the chance to dream. It came seldom in that crowded, industrious house, and never lasted long. Why should he begrudge his son what he had most desired? Why begrudge him his very childhood?

Neat files of tall corn flicked past. Dr. Booth drove faster, as fast as he dared, through corkscrew turns, down straightaways, over gravel fire roads and glistening blacktop, past marsh and field, up hilltops awash in light and deep into valleys abysmal. As he drove he pondered his son's face as if it were a map, as if he were learning where to turn from the curve of Owen's neck, the slant of his eyebrow. And then it began to fade. At first he barely noticed. The long fine line of the nose blurred subtly. The cheeks paled, the smile grew faint, the light dulled and died from the eyes. He fiercely studied every feature even as it ebbed away, trying to hold the ghostly image, keep it in mind long enough to find his way back to the true face. Then it vanished, and he was lost again. He passed through a dark wood. The trees closed above him almost protectively, and when he left their embrace he slowed and pulled to the side of the road. The sun was going down over the field to his right, where a tractor moved slowly in the distance, cutting the last rows of hay.

Dr. Booth got out of the car. He crossed the road and gazed up the hill. Another field, also full of new-mown hay. The smell went to his head. He stood there a moment, then ducked through the fence and walked resolutely forward, staring up the hill as he climbed. When he reached the crest he stopped. All around him the fields rolled empty away. He felt a stone under his shoe, nudged it aside, then bent to pick it up. Not a stone, in fact. A button—a metal button caked with mud. He picked at it until the brass was revealed, then examined it in the last light of day. Under the verdigris he could make out a pair of crossed swords. A military button, then. An old one. Something must have happened here, long ago—surely that was why he'd been drawn to this place. A battle had been fought, no quarter given; boys became men, and were lost. Wasn't that the way of it? He slipped the button in his pocket and started down the hill.

The Benefit of the Doubt

The number 64 bus stops at St. Peter's, so it's always crammed with pilgrims or suckers, depending on your point of view—a happy hunting ground for pickpockets. Mallon was not a pilgrim, or by his own reckoning a sucker. His estranged wife was Swiss-Italian; he spoke the language fluently and came often to Rome on agency business and was on the 64 that day, a thief's hand in his pocket, only because he had an appointment near the Vatican and got caught in a flash summer downpour with no cabs in sight.

The bus was packed with wet, steamy people. They swayed into one another at the stops and turns, and it was during one of these mash-ups that Mallon felt the hand casing his rear pockets, both empty: his billfold, passport tucked inside, was buttoned into the breast pocket of his suit jacket. The touch was heavy, crude. Before he could turn and give the thief a warning look, the hand slid into his right front pocket. The blatancy of the move was astonishing—executed with no more finesse than if Mallon himself had done it, diving for some change.

The hand went in, and damn if it didn't stay in. This pocket was empty too, but the hand seemed unwilling to accept the fact. Mallon became curious as to just how long this could go on. There was a lulling detachment in observing such ineptitude at work, a safe, dreamy amusement. The air was warm, swampy. The bus stopped to take on still more passengers, and the thief was pressed up against Mallon's back. His hand continued to burrow around like a mouse nosing for crumbs. Just then the bus lurched forward and the thief clawed at Mallon's leg as he stumbled back. This shocked Mallon out of his trance. He braced himself, gathered his strength, and drove his right elbow back into a surprising pillowy softness. A hot blast of breath sprayed his neck and the hand vanished. Mallon turned to gloat and saw a man bent double, arms across his belly. He was making little mewing noises. The passengers around him, mostly Filipinos by the look of them, watched him anxiously—a short round man all in black, black leather jacket creased across his back, baggy black pants, pointy black shoes as small as a child's. His scalp showed through his thin dark hair, long strands dangling toward the floor. Nobody looked at Mallon, and already the bus was slowing down for his stop. But the pickpocket still held himself and made these appalling sounds.

Mallon leaned down and took his arm. He tried to raise him up but the pickpocket wouldn't budge. "Let's go," Mallon said in Italian. "Let's go, you're all right. Come on." The pickpocket pulled away and kept fighting for breath in strangled gasps. Mallon rested a hand on his back as the door of the bus hissed shut—he'd missed his stop. "Okay," he said. "Let's go. Come. Come." He took the man's arm again and coaxed him toward the door, steadying him through the jerky weavings of the bus and then the abrupt shuddering stop. The door opened and he helped him down the steps, still bent and gasping, people making room as if for a leper.

The rain had stopped but the sky was dark and menacing. Mallon led the pickpocket under the awning of a shop and watched him retch dramatically, though without result. Mallon patted his shoulder. He could see the passersby keeping their eyes dead ahead, as he would have done, and saw how their faces stiffened with obscure shame. A poster of the *Pietà* loomed over Mallon in the shopwindow, above a display of pious plaster statuettes and gaudy rosaries.

You don't want to be seen looking at your watch at such a moment—a man apparently dying at your knees—but the big clock on the sidewalk was completely out of whack, like all the public clocks in Rome, so Mallon really had no choice. It was ten past four. He was ten

minutes late and had at least a five-minute walk back to Dottore Silvestri's office. An important meeting. Yesterday's discussion had
gone badly, with Mallon pouncing on several misrepresentations in
Il Dottore's proposal. The development agency Mallon worked for
could make all the difference to Silvestri's program, which envi-
sioned several water-purification projects in East Africa. The distor-
tions in the grant application were only to be expected of such a
document, and in fact the board of Mallon's agency had already
decided to back the program. He was here to walk Dottore Silvestri
through the terms of the award, not show off his talent for smelling
horse shit. He'd given Il Dottore a taste of the lash yesterday, and
probably left him thinking that the whole thing was headed down the
drain. Mallon needed to correct that impression before it got back to
his superiors in Geneva.

He leaned down to the pickpocket. The heaving and gasping had
stopped, but he was still making a show of breathlessness. "That's
better," Mallon said. "Can you stand up? Try to stand up. Here," he
said, and gripped the pickpocket's arm and forced him upright until
he saw his face for the first time. It was a round dark face with a small
round mouth, lips as full and tender-looking as a girl's. Despite the
sheen of sweat on the puffy cheeks, the vanity of the pencil-line mustache, the sparse streaks of hair plastered across the damp forehead,
Mallon had an impression of dignity, and of dignity offended. As the
pickpocket labored for breath, he gazed up at Mallon with his dark
eyes. *How could you?* they seemed to ask.

Mallon might have said, *Because you tried to steal from me.* But he
was still conscious of the flush of joy he'd felt when his blow struck
home—when he knew he'd hurt the man. It lingered in the faint tin-
gling of his skin, an edgy sense of buoyancy, vitality. Where that joy
came from he couldn't say, though he knew that its roots were deeper
than some clumsy failed larceny.

Fat drops of rain begin to patter on the awning.

"How are you?" Mallon said. "Can you walk?"

The pickpocket turned away as if insulted by the hypocrisy of Mallon's concern. He leaned against the store window with both hands,

and his head sank lower as his shoulders rose and fell. A gray-haired woman inside the store rapped on the glass and made a shooing motion. When the pickpocket ignored her she rapped harder and kept rapping. He really was a little man; she glared down at him like a schoolmarm scolding a guilty child.

"I have to go," Mallon said. "I'm sorry." He looked up at the sky. He'd have liked to call Silvestri, tell him he was on his way, but his cell phone was back at the hotel and there was no public telephone in sight. "I'm sorry," he said again, and stepped into the rain and walked quickly up the street.

One of the ubiquitous Bangladeshi umbrella hustlers was working the corner, and Mallon had just shelled out seven euros when he heard a woman shouting. He didn't want to look back but did. It was the signora from the shop, pushing and batting the pickpocket away from the window while he hunched and covered his head like a boxer trying to get through the last seconds of a round. Mallon slipped his billfold back into his jacket pocket and took the umbrella the Bangladeshi had opened for him. He hesitated, then turned back.

The pickpocket was out on the sidewalk now, in the rain. The woman stood just under the awning with her arms crossed over her chest.

"Excuse me, signora," Mallon said, coming up to them. "This man isn't well. He needs to rest a moment."

"I know these people," she said. "We don't want them here."

The rain fell in sheets, running down the pickpocket's shiny scalp and face. Strings of water hung like a fringe from the hem of his leather jacket, dripping onto the sagging pants and dainty shoes.

"Here," Mallon said, and offered him the umbrella, but in response he only gave Mallon a hurt look and lowered his head again, as if refusing to conspire in the pretense that there was any mercy to be found in nature or man. Mallon bumped him in the shoulder with the handle of the umbrella. "Go on—take it!" he said. And finally, with a beaten, unwilling look, the pickpocket did. He stood between Mallon and the signora, panting softly, holding the umbrella at a careless angle. Oblivious to the water sliding down it onto his back, he seemed unable to move. So too the signora, steadfast in her icy pose. Mallon stepped under the awning, not so much to get out of the rain as to break free of this tableau.

And that was when he saw a taxi round the corner with a light glowing on its roof. It was absurd to hope for an empty cab in rain like this, most likely the driver had simply forgotten to turn the light off, but Mallon ran out waving his arm and the cab veered sharply to the curb, sending a comber of water over his shoes. He opened the door but couldn't help looking back. The pickpocket had lowered the umbrella to the ground upside down and was leaning on the shaft, head hung low, neck bared to the sky. The signora remained on guard.

"Wait," Mallon told the driver, then went back and grabbed the pickpocket's sleeve and pushed him into the cab. He closed the umbrella and tossed it onto the floor at his feet. "Okay," he said, "where do you live?"

"No Gypsies!" the driver snapped. He was twisted around, glowering at the man.

"Gypsy? Look, he's not well. I'll pay," Mallon added.

The driver shook his head. "No Gypsies." He was a thick-shouldered guy with a long jaw, a hawkish beak, and heavy black eyebrows. His shaved head was blue with stubble. "Get him out," he said. Mallon was thrown by his anger and the dissonant paleness of his eyes, and before he could reply the driver seized the pickpocket's jacket and gave him a shake. "Out, you!"

"No." Mallon slid onto the seat next to the pickpocket. "He needs to get home," he said. "I'll come along."

The driver stabbed a finger at Mallon. "Out."

Mallon looked at the driver's nameplate: Michele Kadare. "It's the law," he said, bluffing. "If you don't take us, Signor Kadare, I'll report you and you'll lose your license. Believe me—I am quite serious."

The driver fastened those pale eyes on him, the windshield wipers scraping jerkily across the glass, then turned and put his hands on the steering wheel. His meaty fingers were as white and hairless as chalk. He raised his eyes to the rearview mirror and exchanged stares with Mallon. "Okay, Mr. American," he said. "You pay."

The driver proceeded in silence across the river and on through snarls of traffic. The pickpocket had given no address; in halting Italian he said to follow Via Tiburtina toward Tivoli, that he would direct him from there. Then he leaned back into his corner with his eyes half closed, wheezing raggedly. He might've been hamming it up a bit, but Mallon was much bigger and had hit him very hard. He saw no choice but to give him the benefit of the doubt.

The rain slackened to drizzle, and a sulfurous yellow light suffused the air. Mallon could feel his wet socks turning warm. Now and then the driver looked at him in the mirror. Kadare. Not an Italian name. Mallon had once read a book by an Albanian writer named Kadare, so maybe he was from Albania. That would make sense, somehow, just as it had made sense when the driver called the pickpocket a Gypsy, which explained the signora's saying "these people," and also Mallon's jittery apprehension about the man—an inkling of some mysterious difference that both put him on edge and intrigued him. But how did the driver and the signora *know* the man was a Gypsy? It wasn't as if he had a violin in his hand and a ring in his ear. Mallon could spot Gypsy women, with their kerchiefs and long bright skirts and their bold, flatfooted way of moving down a sidewalk, but the men eluded him. To his eye the pickpocket could have been Portuguese or Indian or even one of those swart little Neapolitans. But the signora and the driver had known instantly, jolted by some ancient Old World instinct, an alarm in the blood, only a tingle of which reached Mallon from what his forebears must have brought from Ireland and Poland and Russia.

Generally he felt himself well rid of all that peasant malarkey—salt over the shoulder, garlic hanging from the lintel, the terror of black birds and spilled wine and a stranger's gaze—though he sometimes wondered whether, in passing through the American filter, his blood had grown not clear but watery, as if some essential agent of character, of self, was bound up in these old instincts and had been leached out along with them.

The pickpocket's wet leather jacket gave off a faint pissy smell. Mallon rolled the window down a few inches and was overcome by the freshness of the air. He closed his eyes, savoring the play of the breeze over his face. When he opened them again he caught the driver watching him in the mirror.

"Are you from Albania?" Mallon asked.

The driver tapped the meter. It was already up to eighteen euros, and they still hadn't reached Via Tiburtina. "Cash only, Mr. American. No magic American credit cards."

"How much farther?" Mallon asked the pickpocket, who was holding both hands to his chest and rocking back and forth. He stared straight ahead and didn't answer.

Kadare. Could be Albanian. The book Mallon had read concerned a boy waiting to be killed by a rival clan after shooting one of their sons in revenge for the murder of his brother. The blood feud went back so far that no one could even remember its cause, but men continued to die for it and, more, to live for it. It gave them clear paths of duty and honor, as well as the power of martyrdom over their women; it imbued mean lives and deaths with tragic purpose. But what Mallon remembered best was the boy's blooming alertness as the knowledge that he would soon be killed settled ever deeper. He quickened to the sun in his face and the smell of lamb's fat dripping on coals, the glow of white boulders on the crags that loomed all around him. He wandered deserted roads and was never alone: Death beside him filled him with life until his cup ran over and he gave up his place to another murdering boy.

Mallon had liked the book, though guiltily. He'd resisted his fascination with this violent backward culture, and disapproved of the idea that having death at your elbow gave meaning and beauty to life. He felt quite sure that most people would prefer safety from assault, not to mention decent shelter and food on the table, to exquisite intimations of mortality—if such sensations even existed. They were a fiction of religious and romantic pathology, that's what Mallon had thought, until he started having them himself.

His daughter began complaining of headaches not long after her eleventh birthday and was found to have a brain tumor. She'd survived it, and her tests had been negative for the three years since, but there had been times during Lucy's long course of radiation and chemotherapy when both Mallon and his wife had been sure they were going to lose her. Chiara grew bitter. She moved through the days in a cold rage, saying nothing, eating almost nothing, withdrawing into the guest room, where she'd slept since the month after Lucy's diagnosis. She often said that she wished she'd never been born.

Not Mallon. During his daughter's sickness he had become intensely conscious of life as something good in itself, his own as well as hers. This took the form of patience rather than cheer or even hope, and he'd known better than to offer it in answer to Chiara's despair, but he could see that she somehow sensed it anyway and resented it, as she'd come to resent so much about him since Lucy got sick—his composure, his ability to keep working, his voice and touch, even his newfound pleasure in food, which he would not be frowned out of and indulged to the point that for the first time he got a little paunchy.

One leaden January afternoon, walking a lakeside path after leaving the hospital, Mallon had looked up and watched the dark waves race toward shore and understood that his wife no longer loved him. Would she ever love him again? He didn't think so, and time had proved him right. Though Chiara tried to include him in her happiness when Lucy came home for good, she just didn't like having him around. Mallon thought that shame was at the root of her unease, for she had treated him badly, yet he knew Chiara wouldn't recognize that; she was smart and highly educated, a curator of rare manuscripts at the University of Geneva, but personal analysis bored her, especially the analysis of her own emotions. She trusted in their essential validity and accepted their rule without question. Though Mallon had prized this quality when she defied her family by throwing over an approved fiancé to marry him, it now made his case hopeless.

They had been separated for over a year. She kept the apartment. He'd rented a studio nearby, so he and Lucy could visit back and forth as the spirit moved them. That was the idea. In practice Chiara's coldness to him became so painful that he rarely went there and had to wait for Lucy to come to him, which she did less often than he wished. He couldn't blame her. She was busy with school and friends and boys and her choir—with everything he'd prayed she would live to enjoy.

As a project evaluator for his agency, Mallon had always had to fight for time at home. Lately he'd been less resolute. In the last two months he'd spent just nine days in Geneva between stints in Zimbabwe and Uganda, where he'd lived in expensive hotels with broken air-conditioning and empty swimming pools, sandbagged machine-gun positions near the entrance, and an obvious tap on the phone. The local project managers wore him out with PowerPoint presentations and meetings with regional government officials. In their new Land Cruisers they drove him to sites where great things were just about to happen, afterward laying on long speechy dinners and sometimes a tribal spectacle of some kind.

And nothing was going to change—not really. Those struggling, malnourished people he glimpsed through the tinted windows of speeding cars would be in the same fix when the next evaluator came through, already under pressure to sign off on failing or bogus projects so as not to mortify those who'd approved them in the first place.

The people would be in the same fix, there'd just be more of them; but at least they weren't ridiculous. That condition was reserved for the managers, with their Benson & Hedges cigarettes and Cartier lighters and gold Rolex watches and Armani cologne and the smooth European liquor they forced on Mallon with watchful, uncertain pride. And in his opinion they were ridiculous precisely because he and others like him, visitors from the greater ridiculousness, had made them so—creating an entire class of anxious, alienated charlatans out of fat checks and aspirations so stupidly good, so uncomfortable with reality, that only deceit could satisfy them. And for this Mallon had left a good job at Nestlé, embarrassed by his success in a world where the pursuit of money and its blessings now seemed almost virtuously straightforward.

They were on Via Tiburtina. The driver tapped the meter—forty-one euros—and gave Mallon a pale stare in the mirror. The traffic moved at a crawl except for the motorinos whining up the shoulder and daring the narrow gaps between lanes. The road was lined with gas stations and strip malls, discount furniture stores and car dealerships strung with fluttering pennants. Plastic bags scudded along the road, snagged on cyclone fences. If not for the passing glimpse of a Roman wall or remnant arches of an aqueduct in a distant field, Mallon could have thought himself back in Illinois.

The pickpocket leaned forward and croaked something.

"Where?" the driver said.

The pickpocket pointed to a supermarket on the other side of the road.

The driver jerked the cab into the turn lane and waited for a break in the traffic. None came. He didn't swear, didn't say a word, though Mallon could see the muscles working in his jaw and felt sure that he was nerving himself to take a chance. "Wait," he said, but just then an oncoming truck slowed down for them and the driver shot across the road and into the parking lot. The pickpocket directed him around to the rear of the store, where an unpaved road led out of the lot and past a long line of metal storage sheds and then a fenced compound filled with rusting machinery and great wooden spools of cable. The driver was going too fast for the road; the cab floated queasily between deep, jarring potholes.

"Farther," the pickpocket said. "A little farther."

And then the road gave out onto a field of mud. At the far end, several small trailers and campers had been drawn up beside an unfinished apartment block, windows empty of glass, balconies unrailed, water stains streaking the cement walls. Indifferent to the rain, two boys were bouncing on a mattress in the middle of the field, watched by a bunch of other kids sitting on the shells of two wrecked cars. They jumped down and ran shouting toward the cab as it followed a crunching path through a waste of metal drums and tires and sodden newspapers and weirdly bright plastic bottles. A shaggy, swaybacked pony had his muzzle buried in a cardboard box. He shied away as the parade went past, throwing a kick to cover his retreat. One of the boys jumped onto the hood of the cab and grinned at the driver: strong white teeth in a muddy face. The driver stared dead ahead.

The pickpocket ignored them too. He had the aloof, preoccupied air of a man in the back of a chauffeured limousine. "Over there," he said, and gestured languidly toward the apartment block. The cab slowed to a stop and the boy on the hood slid down and raised his fists like a champion and his friends laughed and bumped him with their hips.

The pickpocket got out of the cab. One of the boys called out to him, "Miri!"—and others joined in, "Miri! Miri!"—but he gave no sign of hearing. When Mallon got out with him to say a last word of some kind, the pickpocket turned away and took a few steps, then stopped and bent his head like a mourner. Mallon went over to him. "Wait a moment," he said to the driver, taking the pickpocket's elbow.

"No. Pay now. Forty-eight euros."

"Just wait. Keep your meter on, you'll get paid."

The entranceway was covered with plastic sheeting. The pickpocket pushed it aside and Mallon followed closely, helping him into the lobby—a raw cement cave littered with broken tiles that gleamed in the light of a kerosene lamp hanging from the ceiling. An old Gypsy woman was bent over a steaming metal tub set above a camp stove, rubbing a cloth against a washboard. She straightened up and looked at Mallon. Her dark face was webbed with deep wrinkles and folds from which her little eyes gleamed as from a hiding place. Her head was pulled low, her shoulders raised almost to her ears, frozen in a shrug. In a croaky voice she said something Mallon didn't understand. The pickpocket drooped and murmured pathetically. The old woman tossed the cloth into the tub and wiped her hands on the front of her dress and led them across the lobby and down a dark hall to a doorway over which a blanket had been hung. She held back the blanket, and Mallon let go of the pickpocket's elbow. "Okay, you're home," he said, and the pickpocket ducked inside without a word.

The old woman, still holding the blanket, jerked her head toward the doorway.

"No, I can't," Mallon said.

"Avanti," she said impatiently, her teeth flashing gold.

Mallon went in.

Mallon went in amazed at his own docility and bilious with dread. Why? What did he expect, his gut knotting up as he passed the threshold? Certainly not this room—the muted light, the neatly made bed in the corner, the glossy yellow sofa and matching chair, the artificial palm tree. Not this room, and not the two beautiful children gaping up at him. One was a girl of eight or nine, the other a boy a little older, both of them thin and dark and large-eyed. They stood on either side of the pickpocket, the girl hugging his arm and leaning against him. The children moved back as the old woman brushed past Mallon and took the pickpocket by the shoulders of his leather jacket and stripped it off with a series of rough jerks that made him stagger. Without the jacket he looked even smaller, smaller and rounder. Growling, she nudged him toward the bed and said something to the girl, who helped him lie down and then knelt to slip off his little shoes.

The old woman looked on, one hand at her hip. Then she turned to Mallon. "Sit!" she said. Before he could answer she pointed at the yellow chair and waited until he obeyed. Then she said, "Stay!" and left the room.

The pickpocket lay on his back, sighing deeply. The girl studied Mallon from the foot of the bed, the boy from beside the large window at the end of the room. The window had been covered with plastic that diffused a pearly gray light. The girl had long thin arms with big bony elbows and wore a T-shirt with a panda on it. Mallon smiled at her. "Your papa?" he asked, nodding at the pickpocket.

No answer, but she took a step toward Mallon.

"Uncle?"

The boy and girl looked at each other, and she laughed an outright adult sort of laugh and then pulled the collar of her T-shirt up over her mouth like a veil.

The old woman called out from somewhere. The girl dropped her eyes demurely and joined her hands across her waist and crossed the room in short mincing steps as if imitating a woman with bound feet. The boy continued to stare. Mallon thought of stealing away, but the chair was deep and soft, and before he could collect the will to push himself out of it the girl returned and stood right in front of him with a bowl of unwrapped chocolates and a plastic bottle of Coca-Cola. Though Mallon shook his head no, she kept offering these gifts, holding his eyes with hers and nodding all the while, so that to refuse seemed impossible. He took the Coke. It was warm and filled his mouth with foam but he made a show of appreciation, tipping his head back and closing his eyes before setting the bottle down on the floor.

The pickpocket groaned and rolled toward the wall, mumbling to himself. The girl turned to look at him and then at the boy, who drifted over to the other side of Mallon's chair. The girl leaned back against Mallon's knee, bouncing off him rhythmically, impersonally, as a child will do when caught by some distant thought or object of interest. Out of pure instinct he put his arm around her waist and pulled her onto his lap, then looked at the boy standing there alone and gathered him up too. This felt entirely natural, apparently to them as well; light and noodly, they settled against him, heads on his chest. From above they looked identical. A pleasant, loamy smell rose up from their hair. The pickpocket rolled onto his back again and started to snore. "Miri," the boy whispered, then began to imitate him with wickedly accurate smacks and snorts. The girl was shaking. She put her hands over her mouth but laughter exploded through her fingers.

Mallon let his head fall back. He was tired and the chair was comfortable and the boy and girl were warm and familiar against him. He closed his eyes. The boy didn't keep up the funny stuff for long. He grew still and so did the girl. Mallon could feel them breathe, young, shallow breaths, oddly synchronous. The idea came to him that maybe they were twins. Dully considering the mystery of twins, he remembered for the first time in years a pair of boys he'd grown up with—Jerry and Terry, or was it Jerry and Larry?—but lost his thread and was content to let it go and be afloat, carried along by the pickpocket's snores until he could almost hear them as his own. Later, he wondered how long this lasted. Not long, he guessed, though when he felt the children leave him and grudgingly opened his eyes he was as fresh as if he'd slept for hours.

The old woman was standing in front of the chair. "That man out there wants you," she said.

They were back on Via Tiburtina, still a good distance from central Rome and his hotel, the fare up to one hundred sixteen euros, when Mallon clapped his hand to his chest. The driver caught the motion and raised his eyes to the mirror. Mallon, looking out the rain-glazed window, let nothing show. The moment passed. He yawned ostentatiously, then under the pretense of shifting and stretching he patted himself down and confirmed that his billfold was gone.

They drove on into lashing rain and the glare of headlights. It was only just past six but the sky was black and flickered with lightning. Mallon's mouth was dry. He took a breath so deep that the driver glanced up again when he let it out.

"I have a problem."

The driver's eyes snapped back and forth between the road and the mirror.

"I've lost my wallet."

"What?"

"My wallet is gone."

"You are saying you have no money?"

"Not with me, no. I can get some at the hotel. The manager will advance it against my bill."

The driver leaned forward, peering into the slant of rain, and flicked on the turn signal.

"I may not be able to get it tonight, but I can get it tomorrow, for sure. It depends on whether the manager is in. Signor Marinelli. He knows me." Mallon sounded to himself like a prattling fraud, but he added, "I will pay you."

"You knew," the driver said.

"What? What did you say?"

No answer. The driver eased the cab onto the shoulder of the road and brought it to a stop. There was something terrible in his deliberateness, his silence, the rigid set of his neck. He sat there, hands on the wheel, looking straight ahead. "Mr. American," he said, and made a noise between his teeth. Cars went by. The rain drummed on the roof. Mallon wanted to say something but was afraid to—as if the driver's hatred were a gas that would blow at a word. He felt he'd somehow lost the right to speak.

"Get out," the driver said.

By the time Mallon unfolded himself from the cab and closed the door his pant legs were already wet and clinging. Only as the driver pulled away did he remember the umbrella. Rain streamed down his face. He took his suit jacket off and draped it over his head, holding the collar forward like a bill, and trudged along the shoulder for a while, then walked backward when the wind gusted into his face. Something caught his foot and almost pitched him over. A half-buried block of cement had torn the heel off his shoe. He picked up the heel, looked it over, then tossed it aside and kept walking.

What was the driver getting at? *You knew?* Knew what? And why at those words had he felt caught out, laid bare? The driver couldn't have known what Mallon knew, but Mallon knew what Mallon knew. He'd come awake to it only at this accusation, but he knew, all right, and had known at the very moment back in that room, at rest yet not asleep, the hand slipping across his chest, between jacket and shirt, then the discreet caress of the billfold sliding free and the lightness that followed, as if it had been a weight of lead. That lightness—the strangest thing!

Thunder rumbled somewhere. The blown rain plastered Mallon's shirt to his back and glittered in the headlights of the cars rushing toward him. On a whim he stuck out his thumb. He hadn't hitchhiked since college, and not much then. Maybe the tie would help. Or maybe it would seem wrong, too calculated or cunning—a danger sign. And of course he was soaking wet, as anyone could see. Would he offer himself a ride? He soon gave it up and turned around and saw the taillights of a car not far ahead, a man hurrying toward him with an open umbrella.

It was the driver. He walked with a dipping limp on short legs. He came up to Mallon and held out the umbrella, which billowed and heaved in the wind.

"Too late for that," Mallon said.

"No, please." He held it uselessly over Mallon's head. "Come, please. Come." He escorted him back to the cab and opened the door. "Please," the driver said again when Mallon hesitated.

He got in. "I will pay you," he said.

"No. No fare. Look!" He touched the meter. It was off.

"Nonsense. Of course I'll pay you."

"No—a gift. But please no report, okay?"

Mallon saw the man's eyes in the mirror. "Ah," he said.

"No report?"

"No report. But I'm still going to pay you."

"My gift to you. American, right? California?"

Mallon took the easy way out and said yes. Illinois just confused people; he hadn't been there in years anyway.

"What car do you have? Chevrolet? This taxi, it belongs to my wife's father. Michele. He's sick. No money, you know?"

The driver chattered on: his father-in-law's sickness, his sister's sickness, a problem with the taxi license. As he talked he checked the mirror for Mallon's response. He sounded like a project director making excuses, wheedling for a passing grade. Mallon was bored and disappointed. So much for the fierce mountain clansman, the implacable avenger he'd imagined and feared.

Mallon's wet clothes had turned clammy. His feet were swimming in the ruined shoes. No matter—he had another pair in his room, and another suit, and still more at home. Of course the hotel manager would greet him with cries of sympathy and give him whatever he needed until Geneva wired him money in the morning. He was minutes away from a hot shower. He would step out of it into his air-conditioned room and stand by the window. The terry bathrobe was thick and soft, and he would settle into it, hands deep in the pockets, as he watched the people on the street below. He could already see himself doing this. By tomorrow afternoon he'd have a new passport, new lines of credit, the works. He knew that many men, even most men, losing what he had lost today—their money, the very proof of their identity—would find themselves helpless in the world. He was not one of them. He would not be allowed such a fall. And for all his brooding over the alienations inflicted by comfort and privilege, would he have it any other way? No, he supposed not. He was certainly ready for this little adventure to come to an end.

By the time they pulled up in front of the hotel the storm had passed and the doorman was shielding his eyes against a flare of evening light from the top of the street. The driver beat him to Mallon's door and held it open, offering his hand as if to a woman. Mallon ignored it, emerged damp and blinking.

"Okay?" the driver said. "The umbrella, where is your umbrella?" He leaned past Mallon into the cab. "There! Friends, okay?"

"No report," Mallon said.

"Mr. California!" the driver said. "Hollywood, right?"

"Of course," Mallon said. "Hollywood."

Deep Kiss

When Joe Reed was a boy of fifteen, his craziness over a girl became such a burden to his family, and such a curiosity to the small town where they lived, that his mother threatened to pack him off to his married sister in San Diego. But before this could happen Joe's father died and his mother collected a large sum from Northwestern Mutual, sold the family pharmacy, and moved both Joe and herself to California.

Thirty years passed. In that time he heard nothing from the girl, Mary Claude Moore, but now and then word of her reached him through people back in Dunston. She dropped out of high school in her senior year, had a baby, got married, divorced, then remarried a few years later. That second marriage was the last thing Joe knew about Mary Claude until he learned of her death.

He'd dropped by his mother's house one Sunday afternoon. She couldn't keep the house up anymore, alone as she was, and failing, and she'd finally agreed to buy into an assisted-living "community"— oh how she hated that word, how icily she served it up. Joe had come by to make sure everything was in order for the realtor's walk-through later that week. They had coffee together and that was when she told him about Mary Claude and gave him the letter. He didn't want to be thinking about what his reaction looked like, or ought to look like, so he excused himself and took the letter outside, to the backyard.

According to the newspaper clipping his mother's friend had

enclosed, Mary Claude appeared to have fallen asleep at the wheel and drifted into the oncoming lane of traffic. She'd been killed outright and so had the driver of the car she hit, a dentist from Bellingham heading home from a weekend of fishing. That was the newspaper account. The unofficial version, which his mother's friend disparaged but passed along anyway, was that Mary Claude had been having a fling with a real estate agent named Chip Ryan. He drove the same unusual car as the dentist, a red Mercedes station wagon, and Mary Claude had an equally distinctive old Mustang convertible, powder blue. Both of them lived outside town and frequently passed each other coming and going. The story was, whenever they met on an empty stretch of road they played a game where they switched lanes at the last moment. A sort of lovers' game. Mary Claude had mistaken the dentist's car for Chip's, and that was that.

Joe could hardly make sense of the story. His mother's friend doubted it was true, but conceded it certainly was a puzzle how Mary Claude could have fallen asleep just a hundred feet past a series of tight curves. Still, she wrote, there were probably other explanations that wouldn't insult her memory and give needless pain to her family.

The newspaper article said that Mary Claude and her husband owned a tavern. They must have done well; not long before all this, the chamber of commerce had named them Businesspersons of the Year. She was survived by her husband, three children, two grandchildren. For some reason the paper hadn't run a picture of her with the piece. Joe was glad of this omission.

Joe had lived another, submerged life, parallel to the one known by those around him. In this other life he hadn't left for California but had stayed on in Dunston with Mary Claude. He fell into this dream during the first months after the move, in the immensity of summer on a sunstruck street where old people peered anxiously from behind their parted blinds and sprinklers ran at night on lawns visited only by the Mexicans who mowed them. When his mother left her darkened bedroom long enough to chase him outside, Joe took the *Saturday Evening Post* to a pool in a nearby park and watched the girls oil each other and shriek when loitering bravos splashed water on them. He lay on his stomach and stared at the *Post* and lived his ghost life with Mary Claude.

After Joe started school, his mother took an accounting job at an office-furniture store. A few months later she and another woman formed a partnership and bought the owner out. Joe's mother began to dress smartly. She wore her hair straight instead of piled up on her head, and let a gray streak show through. One night at dinner she said "Joe!" so insistently that he realized she'd been speaking to him without his knowing it, and when he looked at her she said, "You can't bring him back, son. You have to let him go." Joe was embarrassed at the depth of her misunderstanding, but he played along and let her think she'd read his mind.

The high school was new and bright and vast. In the echoing hallways the voices of the students mingled in a roar that Joe came to hear as an aspect of the silence in which he passed his days. He sometimes went home without having spoken a word to anyone. It seemed to him that he might go through the whole year that way, and the next year too, until he graduated, but before long he became friends with his biology lab partner, who took him to parties and introduced him to girls. When Joe got his driver's license that spring he began dating Carla. He aced his courses and played Officer Krupke in *West Side Story.* In the fall of his senior year he and Carla left a dance early and went to a motel. It was the first time for both of them, and a failure. They tried again a few days later in Carla's bedroom and had better luck, and by Christmas Joe was starting to see Courtney on the sly. He didn't really prefer her, but it seemed inevitable that sooner or later either he or Carla would be unfaithful, and he wanted to be the one. This became far more complicated than he'd expected. Joe was soon exposed and denounced by both girls as a heartless cheat, which did not, it turned out, entirely discourage other girls from going out with him.

And through all this he continued his phantom life with Mary

Claude. He was with her on a blanket in a moonlit clearing or in a car parked above the river with Ray Charles on the radio, her fingertips grazing the back of his neck, her mouth open to his, her caramel taste on his lips and tongue and deep in his throat. Only the kiss was a memory; only the kiss was real. He'd hardly been anywhere with Mary Claude except when they could sneak off at school, and a few times in town. But from the kiss he made everything else, or everything else made itself, for that was how it happened—without any effort of imagination or sense of unreality, he watched his life with Mary Claude go on as he had once believed it would. The scenes grew more particular as time passed, each new one framed by those that had gone before, and always with a kiss at the heart of it.

At Berkeley Joe went out with Lauren, and when she left for a year at the Sorbonne there was Toni, then Candace. He and Candace shared a house with two other couples until they graduated and afterward rented an apartment of their own through Joe's first year of medical school. Then Candace went to New York to visit her family and never came back. She sent Joe a letter in which she asked his forgiveness for the problems she'd caused through her alcoholism, which she was now in the process of confronting. She said she couldn't return to the life she'd led in Berkeley, as he surely understood.

No, Joe didn't understand. They'd had their troubles, the two of them; he'd been going all out and so had Candace, waitressing nights as she worked toward a degree in dance therapy. Of course there were problems, but nothing all that serious, and he certainly didn't begrudge her a little relaxation. Yet when Joe's mother heard about Candace leaving, the first thing she said was that she hoped she'd get some help for her drinking. Joe hadn't mentioned the letter.

Until he finished his training and met the woman he would marry, Joe had no more love affairs, just occasional sessions with women working too hard themselves to want much more of him. The practicality of these arrangements gave the whole enterprise a starkly biological cast, which made Joe nervously conscious of his masculine duty and thus left him unmanned with oppressive frequency. By the time he started his residency, in Seattle, he'd entered a state of near quarantine that made his shadow life more moony and detailed than ever.

Dunston was just three hours north of Seattle. Joe sometimes thought of driving up on a free afternoon, but never did. By then he'd heard that Mary Claude was married again. There was no purpose in making the trip except to see her, and he was afraid she wouldn't want to see him, and also afraid that she would. It was too late for that. She had a daughter and a husband and a house to run, she had work to do. So did he—useful, exacting work. It depended on a clarity Joe knew he couldn't rely on, that he had to improvise day by day. He'd lost it before and could not risk losing it again.

When Mary Claude was killed, Joe had been married for seventeen years. His wife, Liz, was a pediatrician in the same clinic where he practiced as an internist. They had a son in his junior year of high school, a daughter a year younger. The boy was a gifted cellist, unworldly, an aesthete. Their daughter was more calculating but fiercer in her attachments once she'd made them. Joe began taking her rock climbing when she was still in grade school and found her to be the most fearless and inventive partner he'd ever had.

Then came a time when his daughter ceased to confide. Both daughter and son developed private sources of amusement, and Joe began to detect a certain condescension in their handling of him. His children were slipping away into the deep forest; he tried not to hurry them with the panic he felt at the gathering signs of their departure.

Liz, too, kept changing on him. When they first met she was girlish and unsure of herself in spite of being three years older than Joe, but since then she'd grown calm and regal, which both unsettled and excited him. In their lovemaking he approached her almost wistfully and sometimes concluded with a bark of triumph, as if he'd brought a notorious virgin to ground. Away from her for more than a day or two, Joe hardly knew who he was.

And still through all these years he had thoughts of Mary Claude. He thought of her sitting across from him at a kitchen table, barely awake, drinking coffee. The kitchen was small and untidy, and Mary Claude's robe gaped open as she bent to drink. She saw him looking and looked back at him. He stood. She put her cup down and waited. He thought of them standing on a porch and waving as friends drove off. And when they were alone Mary Claude turned to him and slipped an arm around his waist, and they went slowly inside and up the stairs, stopping to kiss on the landing. Sometimes he thought of what was to follow, but this was the moment he lingered on, the kiss. Joe remembered very well what it was like to kiss Mary Claude; he'd done it as much as anyone could for as long as they were together, which came to just over three months.

Her father owned a dairy farm several miles out of town. Her mother had moved away when Mary Claude was eleven, taking her along. She married again, but things did not go well between her daughter and this new husband, and she sent Mary Claude back to her father when she was fifteen. Joe had gone through grade school barely noticing her, drab little hick that she was, but she came back a different girl, flaunting and witchy. She mouthed off to the teachers and walked around in a pout with her back arched like a bow. She had no friends except for an equally friendless cousin. During volleyball games in her gym class she baited the other girls by deliberately hitting the ball out-of-bounds or into the net. She cut classes and smoked and made out with other girls' boyfriends, or so it was said, and Joe, curious to test the rumor, found it to be true: Mary Claude went behind the school with him during a dance to which he'd brought another girl, and kept him out there for over an hour. He knew she was doing it to shame his date—at first anyway, until she warmed to him—but once he started he couldn't stop kissing her.

Joe had by then kissed several girls and thought he had a pretty fair idea of the possibilities. Kissing was good, but he tended to think of it as a beachhead from which to launch more serious operations, or as a safe harbor when, inevitably, he was forced to retreat. But he didn't remember to try anything else that night, leaning against the gymnasium wall with this girl who tasted so good and pressed so fully against him, humming in his ear when they stopped to breathe and swaying to the music that rattled the high windows above them. There were other couples along the wall, and Joe knew his date would hear about this, but when he started to lean away Mary Claude laid her fingers along his cheeks and guided his mouth back to hers, and after that he forgot about leaving. He would have stayed there all night, with no sense of time passing, but finally a girl came out and told Mary Claude that her ride was waiting to take her home. She turned to go, then stopped and kissed Joe again. He walked around the school twice before going back inside. The gym was almost empty. His date had left with friends.

When he saw Mary Claude in the hallway on Monday morning he didn't pretend that nothing had happened. Nor did she. She let him take her books and walk her to class. At the lunch period they went to the cafeteria and sat across from each other. He understood what would happen—the hush around them, how they'd be looked at, even by his friends. Joe knew the rules. He'd been a shit and hurt a nice girl, and for Mary Claude, of all people. You could make out with Mary Claude, but you had to laugh about it later and cut her dead. They ate without talking. Her color was high, otherwise she gave nothing away. She helped herself to his carrots, and that was that. They were a pair.

There was a fern-choked gully behind the school. There were the stands by the football field. Empty classrooms. They met before school started and at lunch and for a few minutes after school, until her bus left. Joe didn't say much. When he heard the things he said, he felt hopeless. Mary Claude was either stone silent or gabby. She often got on a jag between kisses when they were making out, a steady murmur, vague, domestic, whatever came to mind. Joe liked feeling her low voice against his chest but paid little attention to what she said and afterward remembered almost none of it.

She tasted of lipstick and cigarettes and candy. When she opened her mouth to his the first sensation was a shock of relief as the tightness melted in a rush from his neck and shoulders. And then he was swaying with her, drinking that smoky sweetness, drinking forgetfulness of the schoolwork he hadn't done, the stammer he was developing, his mother dazed and pale, the room at the end of the hallway where his father lay gasping for the next breath like a trout dropped on the riverbank. He forgot to plan what to try next, where to touch, how hard to press. He stopped thinking ahead; there was no ahead, no before and no after. He was itchy with thirst and deeply satisfied all at once.

And Mary Claude was thirsty for him. He'd never had this happen before, a girl impatient for the taste of him, greedy for it. She didn't like to break off; when he leaned away for a breath she would close her fingers in his hair and pull him back to her. She sometimes said his name in a low, almost mocking way as they were about to return to class, and the sound of it whipped him back around as if she'd yanked on a leash.

Mary Claude soon grew careless with their privacy. She didn't care who saw them, or when. She'd command a kiss—a profound kiss—as she boarded her bus, or in the hallway, even on the street in town when her father let her go in for some shopping after school. Joe knew this was beyond carelessness, that she was making a display of their appetite, perhaps especially of his appetite for her. He could see she was proud of her claim on him, and this made him proud and brazen too. He didn't mind if people thought they were ridiculous, even a sort of joke, the two of them "stitched together at the mouth," as his mother put it. She'd heard about them, of course; she heard everything in the pharmacy.

At first she came at him aslant about it, then she lost patience. Was this the time to be carrying on with some girl? This was not the time, couldn't he see that? Now, of all times? Couldn't he sit with his father awhile instead of mooning in his room and tying up the telephone? Would that be too much to ask? Joe knew he should care that he was giving his mother trouble, but nothing she said touched him. It wasn't out of concern for her that he ruined everything.

. . .

He and Mary Claude were in the stands during a basketball game. She was bored and wanted to leave, go outside. Joe kept putting her off; the game was close. She started to play with the hair at the nape of his neck. He liked the feeling and almost surrendered to it, then something came over him and he shrugged her hand off. He felt Mary Claude go still beside him. He knew she was looking at him, but he kept his eyes on the players and even shouted when one of them muffed a pass. Mary Claude slid her fingers back into his hair, tightened them, and began to turn his head toward hers. Without taking his eyes from the game he gave a rough shake and pulled away. Mary Claude stood up and waited there a moment; though Joe knew he could still turn to her, even then he did not. She made her way to the aisle. He watched her descend the steps and cross in front of the stands and leave the gym. The game had become meaningless to him, but he sat through the rest of it. His mouth was dry, his heart thudding as if he were hollow.

Joe phoned Mary Claude when he got home. No answer. He called again just before he went to bed, and someone picked up but didn't say anything. "Mary Claude," he said. "Mary Claude, please."

She wouldn't answer. He knew she was waiting for him to give an account, to justify himself, and he couldn't think what to say. In the end, all he could say was her name. "Mary Claude."

Then she hung up.

She hung up whenever he called. He pushed notes into her locker and got no answer. He met her bus every morning, and she walked right past him. He waited outside her classrooms and followed her down the hall and out to the bus stop after school. He knew he was making a fool of himself, but he had no choice; there was no other way to be close to her. When his mother demanded that he leave the girl alone, it made no difference. He kept trailing her. And still Mary Claude did not relent.

They had one class together, Washington State history. She sat two seats ahead of him in the next row to the left. He could watch Mary Claude without her seeing him watch her, though of course she knew. Back when they were together, before he ruined it all, she turned her head every little while to look at him and always found his eyes on her. She didn't turn now, but had to know—yawning, lifting her hair away from her neck with both hands and letting it fall again—*had* to know that he was watching her. And the way she slipped one foot out of its loafer and slowly scratched the other ankle with it—all this was to sharpen the ache he felt. The curve of her neck as she inspected her fingernails. Her lips, pursed with impatience as the class wore on.

He was alert to any movement that allowed him a view of Mary Claude's mouth. She often turned to look at the clock over the door, and Joe never failed to seize that glint of her face in profile. When he saw her mouth he leaned forward, narrowing the distance by at least that much. It was wrong that he couldn't put his mouth to hers, it was an impossible mistake that kept him confused and on edge.

She must be feeling what he was feeling; Joe was sure of that. If he was cut off from her, she was cut off from him. Once it was over everything would be the same between them, maybe better, because they would value more what they'd lost and had to find again, but it went on and on, and Joe came to understand that Mary Claude didn't know how to end it—that she was waiting for him to do it. But what could he do when she wouldn't speak to him? When she wouldn't even look at him?

Then she began keeping company with Al Dodge, a senior, a quiet and well-liked boy who struggled in school and had a limp from polio. He lived just up the road from Mary Claude and drove to school, and she started riding with him instead of taking the bus. They sometimes ate lunch together. Joe was thrown, at first; then he saw that this was his signal. He waited for Al outside the wood shop and began to tell him about Mary Claude and himself, how they were meant to be together. Al tried to brush past, but Joe wasn't through talking and blocked his way. Al pushed at him, and his bad leg gave out and he went down, his metal brace clattering on the cement.

When Joe bent to help him up two boys ran over and shouldered him aside. One of them gave Joe a look as he struggled to lift Al to his feet. Joe wanted to explain everything, and the impossibility of ever doing this left him no choice but to smile at the boy and tell him to go fuck himself.

He could see when he got home that his mother already knew about it. She set him to work in the pharmacy and spoke to him only when she had to. While he was doing the dishes that night she came to the kitchen and told him that his sister and her husband were willing to have Joe come live with them until things got sorted out—until his father died, he took her to mean. Her face was flushed, her eyes brilliant, she stood erect in the doorway and forced him to look at her. She was magnificent, and he resented it. Did he want to go to San Diego? Did he want to do that? No? Was he sure? All right, she said. She needed him here. But one more thing like this, he'd be on the first bus out of town. Did he understand? Good. Now she wanted Joe to go to his father and make the same promise to him.

Joe did no such thing. He listened to the weird submarine clankings emanating from his father's oxygen tank and studied the pattern in the rug and answered a few wheezy questions about his schoolwork and then he got the hell out of there, but not before his father put his dry yellow hand on Joe's wrist and pulled him down into an embrace that left him sick with horror.

He stopped following Mary Claude to her classes. She rode to school with Al Dodge and sometimes walked with him between classes, but Joe could see there was nothing between them. She was alone, as before. So was he, more than ever—the guy who picked on cripples. Though Joe didn't follow Mary Claude he still watched her, from nearby when he could but mostly from a distance, cocking her hip to hold her locker door open, sitting at the end of a cafeteria table and tearing at the peel of an orange with her strong fingers. It was late May. In a couple of weeks school would be over and he'd have no hope of breaking this spell he'd brought on them.

He decided he would kiss her. She was like him. After the first taste she always wanted another, and then another, until she lost herself. That was what they needed—to lose themselves again.

Mary Claude's gym teacher took the girls outside on warm days for softball and track. Joe's French class met that period, though he sometimes cut out early to stand in the shade of the trees at the near end of the field and watch Mary Claude. She suited up with the other girls but usually drifted into the stands to smoke and chew the fat with her cousin Ruth, who was half Indian and never talked to anyone except her relatives. Mary Claude was pale anyway, and beside Ruth she gleamed like a white stone in a streambed. When the teacher led the class back inside, Mary Claude always made a point of lagging, as if the force that compelled the others had no hold on her. Even Ruth couldn't endure this exquisite dawdling and left her behind.

Mary Claude had her eyes on the ground, arms crossed, as she started in from the field. Joe didn't know if she'd seen him or not. He stood under a horse-chestnut tree beside the path that led to the locker rooms; the tree was in bloom, and his eyes had gone weepy from the pollen. When she drew near, he spoke her name and she looked up without surprise. He'd had something all planned out to say, but now that he was close to her he forgot what it was.

She waited, arms still crossed. Then she said, "You been *crying*?"

Joe wasn't sure what happened next. Even right after it happened he had no confidence in any account, even in his own memory, and accepted the blame that fell on him without protest and without belief.

But he knew that it started with Mary Claude's crack about his eyes. He heard her mockery as forgiveness; forgiveness and summons. It sent a rush of heat to his face. He could still feel it, thinking back. Then he lost the thread. He remembered holding one of her hands in both of his, and Mary Claude leaning away and looking at him, but struggling? Perhaps. Then he remembered being with her under the tree, his arms around her, though how they got there he couldn't say. Maybe he just led her there, maybe he really did force her. The one thing he was sure of was that her mouth was opening to

his when the gym teacher grabbed his collar. Even as she wrenched
him back, shirtfront bunched at his throat, he was straining forward
to seal the kiss. Then Mary Claude turned aside and started crying,
and he knew he'd have to start all over again.

He didn't argue with anything anyone said. His mother surprised
him by trying to make the principal feel sorry for her, something he'd
never seen her do, but it didn't pay off; he refused to let Joe finish out
the year. As he was clearing out his locker a couple of seniors walked
past and made smooching sounds, and other students took it up as
Joe carried his stuff down the hallway.

His mother talked about sending him to San Diego that weekend.
Though he'd made up his mind to refuse, it never came to a test. Late
Wednesday afternoon his father went into a coma; until he died that
evening Joe kept the watch with his mother, prowling the room while
she held her husband's hand. Now and then Joe looked at the figure
in the bed, then turned away, to the window with its darkening view
of the neighbor's yard, to the bookcase, to the photographs on the
bureau and nightstand. Joe in his Little League uniform. Joe looking
over the edge of his crib. Joe and his father beside the Skagit River,
holding up a pair of big steelhead.

He helped his mother make the calls and settle the funeral
arrangements. He gave his father's best friend all his fishing gear and
boxed up his clothes for the Goodwill. He was steady at his mother's
side, gallant and grave. On the night after the funeral he slipped
downstairs and felt for the car keys on the hook where they were kept.
Not there. Not there the next night either. So—his mother had sec-
ond-guessed him. Joe was surprised that she'd calculated so coolly in
her grief. It made him think differently of her. Better, and worse.

Both house and business were sold within the week to a couple
from Vancouver. It had all been arranged months back, pending his
father's death. Joe was doing an inventory for the new owner, kneel-
ing on the floor with a clipboard, when he heard someone walk up the
aisle and stop behind him. He glanced back, and there was Mary
Claude's father.

Joe had seen Mr. Moore from a distance a few times but never really considered him, didn't think of him except as a vague shadow cast by Mary Claude; he was unprepared for the man's actual presence. Mr. Moore loomed over Joe, catching a dusty beam of light square in the face. Wetness gleamed in the slack right corner of his mouth, and his right shoulder sagged as if he were holding a bucket. He wore new overalls and fresh-scraped boots, the marks of the stick still showing through a film of dried mud across the toe caps. He smelled strongly of camphor. His eyes were a pale, watery blue. He didn't narrow them against the light but looked down at Joe studiously. Joe was sure he knew everything, not only what he'd done with his daughter, and tried to do, but everything he'd dreamed of doing, even his plan to somehow get her in the car and run away to Canada.

Mr. Moore seemed about to say something, but instead he bent down and gave Joe's shoulder a squeeze. Then he turned and walked back down the aisle.

Joe took the letter into his mother's yard and studied it. Hunched in a lawn chair, elbows on his knees, he waited to be struck; down the street someone was blasting a Strauss waltz through an open window, and he couldn't stop himself from following it, even conducting it with minute twitches of his head, though he'd lost his taste for old Vienna after Candace went on a Strauss binge the year before she left. The chair had looked dry when he sat down, but the morning's dew still lingered between the straps of webbing and seeped into his pants, warm, clinging. The grass needed a trim. Joe knew that if he looked up he'd see his mother watching him from the kitchen window, pulling a long face for what she imagined he was feeling. What he did feel was embarrassment at this hambone attempt to create sorrow by imitating it.

He rocked to his feet, looked sourly around, then started toward the shed where the mower was kept. It would come later, if it came at all. Sometimes it didn't. He lost patients and hardly ever thought of them again, and then with a regret that he recognized as mostly formal.

No, if it came it would come from behind and push him into a hole so deep he'd forget what it was like to be out of it. That was what happened with his beautiful niece Angela, his sister's only child. Joe had warned her—she had diabetes and was drinking heavily—but somehow he'd failed to expect it himself. He got clobbered a few weeks after her death, laid low. And something like that happened to him after his son was born. One night, holding the baby, he remembered with suspicious clarity his own father holding him, looking down at him, and smiling; there was that roguish gap between his teeth, the crazy upcurved eyebrow. It was a look of unguarded benevolence. Joe knew it well, he'd grown up in the light of his father's pleasure in him, and now he figured that by some trick of the mind he had imposed it on a scene too distant for recall.

False or not, he couldn't shake the memory. And others followed that he knew to be true, though he hadn't thought of them for years: his father's amused, bottomless patience in teaching him to drive or tie flies or work the cash register; the stories he told about growing up wild in rural Georgia, and about his older brother Chet. Chet had been killed on Peleliu, his body unfound, and Joe's father was never able to hide the grief that still overcame him because of that death.

Joe's parents had been close to forty when he was born. He guessed he'd been something of an accident, but a welcome one, especially to his father. They'd been friends. And yet Joe had somehow come to resent his father's sickness as a betrayal, a desertion. He didn't think it out in those terms, didn't think it out at all, but it felt like that, then, as if his father had willfully—perversely—surrendered to the weak, wheezing, yellow-faced sufferer who'd taken his place. Joe's knowledge of his own real desertion, the depth of its injustice and cruelty, came slowly. He'd managed it well enough until the birth of his son, then hardly at all. For weeks it seemed that every new joy came with a shadow of remembrance and shame. His wife grew impatient with his moods, then disgusted. But what was he to do?

Others might forgive you—he knew his father would—but how do you forgive yourself? You don't, really. Yet one day the weight is lighter, and the next lighter still, and then you barely know it's there, if it's there at all. So it is with the best of men and the worst of men, and so it was with Joe.

The lawn mower had a bent blade and shook convulsively as he maneuvered it around the yard. It was folly to use it in this condition, but the pushing felt good and he kept muscling it on. He spun through a corner and saw his mother in the kitchen window, her face overlaid with leaves reflected from the orange tree. She looked worried. Joe raised a hand and she gave a little wave back, the same regretful gesture she used to make from the departing car when they left him at scout camp in the summer—except that she was strong and handsome then, and now she was old and had to wear a diaper. He turned his attention to the rock border where he'd pranged the blade last time, and when he looked up again she was gone.

He squared the yard and kept moving toward the middle. The shaking of the mower no longer held his interest. It was part of the cadence of the work, like the crisp turns he made and the extra push he gave when he hit a thick clump of grass. His hands tingled; his brow dripped; his shirt was soaked through. As he worked he ceased to think, or to feel himself think, and then it came to him. Chip Ryan, the real estate agent Mary Claude had been fooling around with . . . little Chip! He hadn't placed him at first because the boy was so young, just seven or eight, when Joe left Dunston. Chip's older brother had been a friend of his. Chip used to hang around while they played records and talked, but he didn't butt in or act bratty. Joe had been struck by that—what a nice kid he was, little Chip, sitting there with his pet rabbit, stroking its ears while he looked up at the big boys.

Little Chip and Mary Claude.

The letter didn't say whether Chip was married or single. Either way he was on the prowl, or they wouldn't be telling that story. And of all the women in that long green valley, he had to pick Mary Claude. If it was true. But of course it was. Leave it to Mary Claude to come up with a game like that, all or nothing, no room for error.

He bullied the mower through the last couple of turns and cut the engine. A pall of exhaust hung above the yard. He heard the music again. Violins. Strauss, still. He nodded helplessly along as he toweled himself off with his shirt. He'd heard the piece fifty times, a hundred times, Candace dancing naked through their apartment to the rise and fall of it, gleaming with sweat, eyes half closed—but when he reached for the name he felt it slip away. It baffled him that he couldn't hold on to something he'd known so well, and he stood fixed in his puzzlement as the song swelled to a finish and died, and a dog barked somewhere, and another waltz began.

These stories originally appeared the following publications: "In the Garden of the North American Martyrs," "Next Door," and "Two Boys and a Girl" in *Antaeus;* "The Liar," "The Other Miller," "Sanity," and "A White Bible" in *The Atlantic;* "Flyboys" in *Doubletake;* "The Chain," "Smorgasbord," and "Soldier's Joy" in *Esquire;* "Lady's Dream" in *Harper's;* "Say Yes" (as "Washing Up") in *The Missouri Review;* "Powder" in *The New York Times Magazine;* "Awaiting Orders," "The Benefit of the Doubt," "Bullet in the Brain," "Deep Kiss" (as "Kiss"), "The Deposition," "Down to Bone" (as "The Most Basic Plan"), "The Night in Question," "Nightingale," and "That Room" (as "In the Hay") in *The New Yorker;* "A Mature Student" in *Playboy;* "Firelight" in *Story;* "Hunters in the Snow" and "Leviathan" in *Triquarterly;* "Desert Breakdown, 1968" and "The Rich Brother" in *Vanity Fair;* and "Her Dog" in *Walrus.* "Mortals" was originally published in *Listening to Ourselves: More Stories from "The Sound of Writing"* edited by Alan Cheuse and Caroline Marshall (Doubleday & Company, Inc., New York, 1994).

"In the Garden of the North American Martyrs," "Next Door," "Hunters in the Snow," and "The Liar" were published in *In the Garden of the North American Martyrs* by Tobias Wolff (Ecco, 1981); "Soldier's Joy," "The Rich Brother," "Leviathan," "Desert Breakdown, 1968," and "Say Yes" were published in *Back in the World* (Houghton Mifflin, 1985); "Mortals," "Flyboys," "Sanity," "The Other Miller," "Two Boys and a Girl," "The Chain," "Smorgasbord," "Lady's Dream," "Powder," "The Night in Question," "Firelight," and "Bullet in the Brain" were published in *The Night in Question* by Tobias Wolff (Alfred A. Knopf, 1996).

A NOTE ON THE TYPE

The text of this book was set in Filosofia, a typeface designed by Zuzana Licko in 1996 as a revival of the typefaces of Giambattista Bodoni (1740–1813). Basing her design on the letterpress practice of altering the cut of the letters to match the size for which they were to be used, Licko designed Filosofia Regular as a rugged face with reduced contrast to withstand the reduction to text sizes, and Filosofia Grand as a more delicate and refined version for use in larger display sizes.

Licko, born in Bratislava, Czechoslovakia, in 1961, is the co-founder of Emigre, a digital type foundry and publisher of *Emigre* magazine, based in Northern California. Founded in 1984, coinciding with the birth of the Macintosh, Emigre was one of the first independent type foundries to establish itself by focusing on personal computer technology.

BLOOMSBURY

Also available by Tobias Wolff

Old School

At one prestigious American public school, the boys like to emphasise their democratic ideals – the only acknowledged snobbery is literary snobbery. Once a term, a big name from the literary world visits and a contest takes place. The boys have to submit a piece of writing and the winner receives a private audience with the visitor.

But then it is announced that Hemingway, the boys' hero, is coming to the school. The competition intensifies, and the morals the school and the boys pride themselves on — honour, loyalty and friendship — are crumbling under the strain. Only time will tell who will win and what it will cost them.

'A beautifully crafted all-American coming-of-age tale'
Esquire

'This is the kind of novel that endures – wise, clever and written with immense heart'
Observer

'Exceptionally good ... comparable to the work of Philip Roth. This reviewer was tempted to send Wolff a fan letter'
Blake Morrison, *Sunday Telegraph*

ISBN: 978 0 7475 7465 1 / Paperback / £7.99

BLOOMSBURY

This Boy's Life

At just ten years old, Tobias Wolff is reluctantly on the road.
His restless, spirited mother is desperate to build a better life for
them both, but Tobias is struggling with this ever-changing routine.
When they finally reach Utah, he decides to change his name to
Jack, after his hero Jack London, because he longs for adventure
and to start afresh. *This Boy's Life* traces Jack's experiences
growing up against the background of a violent and wildly
optimistic America.

'Wolff has revived the dignity of the memoir with *This Boy's Life*,
which is bursting with energetic delight in recollection and written
with an addictive, economical style that also manages to be richly
evocative and lyrical'
Time Out

'I loved *This Boy's Life* ... A painful, wry and beautifully written
autobiographical account of growing up in a shifting and shiftless family'
Richard Eyre

'Wolff's years as Jack are recreated in this superb book with an
honesty and detachment that are frequently unsparing to his past self'
Sunday Times

ISBN: 978 0 7475 4601 6 / Paperback / £7.99

Order your copy:
By phone: 01256 302 699
By email: direct@macmillan.co.uk
Online: www.bloomsbury.com/bookshop
Prices and availability subject to change without notice.

www.bloomsbury.com/tobiaswolff